INDIA'S STORY

Kathlyn S. Starbuck is the author of *Time in Mind*. She lives in San Diego with her husband, fantasy writer Raymond E. Feist, and their daughter, Jessica-Michele, three horses and the requisite two cats.

By the same author

TIME IN MIND

Acknowledgements

There are people who read for me, to help me catch the patently stupid things I do at two in the morning, all by myself when what just came out of the keyboard *seems* pretty amusing . . .

Diane Clark, Raymond Feist, Lori Jean Pelentay, Deborah Smith, and Marcia Tremblay, thank you for doing work for me and considering it fun. Thank you for accepting as payment a few lines in the front of a book for all the hours spent tracking down the inconsistencies and mangled grammar. I appreciate your help.

Thank you also to David Gerrold, since it's his fault I finished this book to begin with!

SCIENCE
FICTION
FANTASY

KATHLYN S. STARBUCK

India's Story

HarperCollins*Publishers*

For *my father, who never,*
ever *betrayed my trust in him.*

HarperCollins Science Fiction & Fantasy
An Imprint of HarperCollins*Publishers*
77–85 Fulham Palace Road,
Hammersmith, London W6 8JB

A Paperback Original 1993

1 3 5 7 9 8 6 4 2

A catalogue record for this book
is available from the British Library

ISBN 0 586 21768 1

Set in Linotron Sabon by
Rowland Phototypesetting Ltd
Bury St Edmunds, Suffolk

Printed in Great Britain by
HarperCollinsManufacturing Glasgow

Prologue

You're certain she has the power?

If you don't trust me, you should have thought about that before we started this.

You're right. The brash young man looked at the still form of the girl lying on the floor. *She just doesn't look strong enough to survive what we're about to do.* He looked up at the man who stood next to him, also looking at the girl on the floor. *It's very important she survive,* the young man said. *Very important she remain intact, as well. She's no good to me as a vegetable.*

Your concern is touching, said the older man dryly.

No, the younger man disagreed. *It really isn't. She's not a useful tool if she can't be manipulated. She can't be manipulated if she can't function. You understand the difference?*

The older man nodded. *So you trust we can do the job? I guess we'll find out.*

She has the power. We're just tapping into it much sooner than she would have on her own. Are you ready? The older man held out his hands, palms open and down, running them over the still form on the floor, several feet above her.

The younger man opened his mind and linked his power to the other man's. Together, they lowered their combined conscious level and sought out the Collective Unconscious, the societal id. Their bodies still stood in the small, dark room, but their minds had reached the plane of the Disembodied, the lost souls whose energy the men would use to accomplish their task. Around them was darkness so complete that motion was undetectable, but the Disembodied were all around them, pressing in to touch their minds and free them from corporeal existence.

The men pushed the Disembodied away from them, keeping them at bay while they sought to contact the girl's mind. She had been heavily drugged in an effort to keep her subconscious from wandering too far away from her body, so they had little trouble locating her and bringing her into the circle they had created in the midst of the chaos of the Collective Unconscious.

Do you feel this? asked the portion of the joined minds that was the older man. He directed the younger man toward the encapsulation in the girl's mind.

The younger man grasped it, surprised by the size and density of the cyst. *This is it?* he asked in awe. He already knew the answer, but it gave him time to come to grips with what they were about to do.

Come on, we don't have much time. Together, they reached out toward the energy of the souls pressing around them, tapping it and drawing it into themselves, using it to amplify their own power. They had done this before, but only a couple of times. Neither was comfortable with the swelling sense of wild power, but it was necessary to the task, so they drew it into themselves, hoping they would be able to control it and avoid being sucked in by the siren cry of the lost souls, the souls who had given up, had been given up.

They focused the incredible energy to a point as fine and sharp as a needle and brought it to the shell of the cyst.

Carefully, now, came the thought, though neither could have said whose it was. The needle was pressed slowly, gently into the resisting surface. *You see how thick it is? It would have taken many decades for her to wear it away on her own.*

With a surgeon's delicacy the needle was introduced to the cyst, slowly penetrating each protective layer, careful not to disturb the energies beginning to radiate from it.

Now we begin to draw on these energies as well, came the mutual thought. *We can use her own power to help wake it up. It will also help her with the Opening Sickness, making it much less incapacitating and of briefer duration.* They drew the energy into themselves, combining it with the power drawn from the Disembodied, and honed the needle even finer.

My head will burst, came an unbidden thought. It was part of the linked minds, but didn't belong to either of the men. A lash of energy reached out for the source and silenced it.

The needle penetrated the last layer of the encapsulated power suddenly and the men had to draw it back quickly to prevent it from puncturing the other side. *We remove it very slowly now.*

It won't rupture?

No. This way, it will leak out slowly and be easier to contain. We don't know how much power she has and we don't want to find out the hard way that we can't contain her. It will be easier to establish blocks around the cyst and maintain them if there is only a slow introduction of power to her conscious mind. It's more important to keep her from discovering what she can do than it is for us to find out.

The needle was almost out, so both men set up the barriers necessary to keep the girl's power in check and carefully withdrew from the cyst.

She will be fine.

A scream split the darkness far away, loud and angry for all the distance, and accompanied by rattling and hissing.

It comes.

The Disembodied stirred, hissing among themselves, imitating the sound of the approaching creature.

Are we done here?

Taking the mind of the girl, the men fled the Collective

Unconscious, fleeing from the screaming, hissing, angry creature.

It was much closer this time, said the younger man, disentangling his mind from the older man's and the girl's. Once again they stood in the small, dark room. Side by side, they stood over the body of the girl. *What do we do with her now?*

You have a good psi-mechanic? asked the older man.

The younger man nodded.

Have him take the first shift. I have to get back to the school. Keep an eye on her and call me if there are any problems. Otherwise, the two of you should be able to control the Opening Sickness.

He doesn't know I possess any psi-powers, the younger man objected. *It suits my purposes for now that he not find out.*

Then I suggest you hire another, said the older man impatiently. *Don't call me if you can possibly help it.* He left the room, shutting the door softly behind him.

With a shrug, the younger man crossed the room and tapped numbers into a receiver. 'Yeah, come down here now,' he said into it a few moments later. He thumbed the disconnect and turned to look at the girl lying still on the floor. They'd have to get a cot in here.

Shannon woke slowly with a feeling in her bones that something wasn't right. She stretched cautiously, checking herself first. Physically, she felt fine. Nothing wrong in her mind except a feeling that something wasn't right.

Eyes closed, she lay in bed and scanned the environment telepathically, but nothing seemed amiss. With a sigh, she got up and dressed.

India was late for class, but that was nothing new. Shannon used the time to clean and balance her energies thoroughly, by grounding and centering.

She finished her task, but India still had not shown up.

The small fear Shannon had awakened with niggled at the back of her mind, but she wasn't really thinking about it. She straightened up the classroom. By the time she had finished, India was over an hour late. The small fear had grown into a big worry.

Shannon left the classroom to look for India. The most obvious place was her bedroom, so she started there. The bed had been slept in, but was now empty. Shannon shut the door and started asking everyone she passed if they had seen India.

'Last night,' was the only answer she got. She scanned the area again, hoping to find something she had missed earlier, but there was no sign of India's presence. Shannon widened her scope, but still her search came up empty.

Extremely concerned, Shannon went to Ashraf's study. The hallways had never seemed quite so long and forbidding before. She found herself wondering why the buildings were so huge when the total population they housed was so small. There were no lifts, and no beltways down the longer halls. Whole floors of buildings were not in use and the various departments had put as much space between themselves as possible. Administration had separated themselves from the school buildings entirely, and occupied the top floor of an otherwise empty building across the courtyard. Shannon found the walk to Ashraf's office almost as disconcerting as the man himself.

'She wouldn't have taken off on her own, would she?' Shannon demanded of him. 'Not before she had to, anyway.'

'Are you asking me, or telling me?' Ashraf asked mildly. 'You worked most closely with her; what do you think she'd do?'

'Isn't there any way to trace her?' asked Shannon.

'Not if she doesn't want to be found,' said Ashraf pointedly. 'If she's gone on to the Inn, we'll have to let Anara know she's coming.'

'Shall I do that, then?' Shannon volunteered.

'I think we both should,' he said.

Shannon studied Ashraf closely. 'You don't think she left to go to the Inn, do you?' she asked finally.

Ashraf shook his head. 'I don't know what to think.'

Shannon suppressed a shudder and opened her mind to Ashraf's telepathic contact. She had never liked anyone else in her mind that way, but Ashraf in particular was such a strong presence that Shannon always felt her own personality becoming subsumed.

It will be over soon, Ashraf whispered in her mind. More strongly, he sent a call to Anara.

Ashraf? came the astonished reply. Anara was always caught off guard by Level One's infrequent contact.

And Shannon, he said. *I consulted with you a while ago about a young girl we have here.*

Anara said, *Have you had any luck?*

Shannon thought Anara sounded like she knew what the answer to that was.

We were going to be sending her along to you tomorrow, Ashraf continued, ignoring Anara's tone. *During the night, India left. We don't know if it was voluntary and we don't know where she's gone. Shannon has searched for India to the extent of her range, but she can't be found.*

Or doesn't want to be found, Anara said. *I'll keep an eye out for her, then. Do you think she'll show up here?*

I'd already given her instructions, Shannon put in. *But we hadn't gone over them in any great detail. It's possible she could show up on your doorstep.*

Let's keep our fingers crossed, said Anara before she broke the contact.

Shannon hastily withdrew her mind from contact with Ashraf's. 'I guess now all we can do is wait,' she said.

Ashraf nodded absently, but his attention was focused on the window opposite him.

Shannon let herself out of his study quietly and went back to her classroom to finish the day's teaching.

Bob strode into the office and slammed the door shut behind him.

The man behind the large, cluttered desk looked up, unimpressed. 'Did you get her?' he asked, stubbing out a cigarette in an already-full ashtray.

'You ought to quit that,' said Bob, sweeping the ashtray off the desk and into the waste basket that stood beside it. 'It stinks and it's bad for your health,' he finished as he dropped into the chair in front of the desk. 'Yeah, I got her. That stinks, too.'

The man behind the desk templed his fingers and studied Bob: medium age, medium height, medium weight, medium coloring. Completely medium. Perfect camouflage. No one noticed him wherever he went. An ideal agent.

Bob stared around the office. It galled him to be working for a younger man who had so little experience in the field. He was uncomfortable making eye contact, so he looked instead at the stark, white walls and the glossy centerfold pictures that adorned them. The furniture was cheap, heavy wood and the chairs were covered with even cheaper Naugahyde. There were no windows and only one door. The smell of stale smoke permeated everything and the air was still striated with the smoke of the most recent incineration. 'She's down the hall,' he added uncomfortably.

'Any suggestions?'

Bob turned to glare at his boss. 'You could let her go!' he snapped. 'You could find another way to do it, or let your first major coup be a little less spectacular. You're playing with fire. She's a kid!'

'I could also let you go,' the younger man said quietly.

'But you aren't going to do that, because you need what I can do for you, and as long as I have a job to do, I'm going to do it. Right?' Bob leaned back in his chair and put his feet up on the desk. 'Even if I don't want to.'

'We understand each other,' said the younger man, smiling. He stood up. 'Go do your job,' he said, dismissing Bob.

Bob got to his feet and shoved his hands into his pockets. 'Yes, sir.'

Down the hall, Bob came to a guarded door.

'Has she had the hypo yet?' he asked the man who stood on the right.

'Yes, sir!' he said, snapping to attention. 'At 6.15, sir, per your orders.'

'Fine,' Bob murmured, thumbing the door-lock and entering the room.

In the dim interior, he could see the cot against the far wall. There was a chair beside it. Otherwise, the room was bare; no windows, no pictures, nothing. There was no blanket on the cot. The tiny figure lying on it shivered slightly in spite of the drugs and the temperature-controlled environment.

Bob stuck his head back outside the door and told the guard, 'Get a blanket in here, at least.' Then he shut the door and went to the chair. 'India, we have some talking to do,' he said, picking up her hand.

India shifted slightly on the cot, but didn't awaken. The door opened again and a guard handed a blanket in to Bob.

'Do you want the lights up at all?' he asked.

Bob shook his head. 'Just make sure we aren't interrupted. Hypnosis is a tricky thing when drugs are involved.'

'Yeah, sure,' the guard said with a knowing snort. He shut the door before Bob could object.

He turned back to India and spread the blanket over her. He sat down in the chair and scooted it closer to the cot. Picking up her hand again, he leaned forward and smoothed the tangled curls from her face. 'I hate this,' he said aloud.

He didn't really expect India to hear him or understand, but he felt better telling her anyway. Sitting back in the chair, Bob closed his eyes and established a light telepathic contact with India.

Bob?

Her mind was groggy, but the drugs hadn't sent her as far away as he had hoped they would by now.

You ask too many rude questions, he said. The hypo would only take care of her body. He needed control of her mind. He could feel the shift in her thoughts as the post-hypnotic suggestion began to work. *Do you know why you've been brought back here?*

He was staggered by the blast of derision, but India didn't say a word.

I hate this, Bob thought to himself.

That doesn't seem to be stopping you, came the reply.

I don't have any choice, he objected.

Oh, have some backbone! India sneered. *You have a choice. You could refuse. You could quit.*

It's not like that, Bob protested.

It's not like that! India mocked. *Jesus, Bob. Take some responsibility for your decisions. I'm not going to feel sorry for you or tell you it's okay, what you're doing to me. You know it isn't. So you do a lousy job and they keep having to bring me in to redo the stuff you botch and you keep feeling guilty about it and doing lousy work ... Where does it end, Bob?*

You don't understand my situation, he began.

And I'm not likely to as long as they block off that information in your own mind while you work with me. Who owns you? What is it they have on you?

Enough about me, Bob said pleasantly, changing the subject. *We have quite a bit to do here, and the sooner we get done, the sooner we can get on about our business.*

He withstood another blast of derision.

India lay still on the cot and said nothing.

Bob sighed. He dropped her hand and sat back in his chair.

Your blocks have been slipping gradually over the last few months, he said, rubbing his forehead and the bridge of his nose with two fingers. He could still feel the electricity of her touch. He was certain they didn't know what they were playing with.

India stared silently at her eyelids.

Bob's chair tipped sideways and dumped him on the floor.

Did that make you feel better? he asked as he regained his seat.

You don't really expect me to cooperate with you, she said.

Bob went to the door. 'Please bring me another hypo,' he told the guard.

I won't let you take my mind from me, India whispered in the periphery of Bob's mind.

He shivered. *Not take. Just hide. Just temporarily.*

It amounts to the same thing, she whispered. *This isn't exactly ethical. Who are you people? What do you want from me? Why can't you just ask outright?*

Bob came back to the cot holding the hypo. He bent to administer the drug, but the syringe spun out of his hand and shattered on the floor. *You can't stop me,* he told her.

India heard the tenseness in his voice. *I'll keep trying.*

You'll only be postponing the inevitable, he said, backing toward the door.

As it opened, India shoved him through using everything Shannon had taught her, and slammed the door shut. Through the telepathic link, she heard Bob tell the guard to flood the chamber with a sedative gas.

Then she heard a hiss in the ventilation ducts.

Chapter One

The candle hovered in front of India as she clung to the face of the cliff. The flame sputtered as her concentration shifted. She was clinging by her fingers, jammed into handholds on the bare rock. One foot hung free; there was no place nearby to step.

The candle was her only source of light and also the only thing that seemed to be keeping the large arachnid-like creature at bay. It wasn't doing a very good job. India had been pinned this way for several minutes evaluating her situation and taking stock of her options. At present, they seemed bleak.

A hairy, chitinous leg reached over the edge, probing with a stiff claw for its victim. India pressed closer to the cold rock, trying to stay out of reach and not lose her grip.

Frustrated, the creature screamed in rage and scuttled back and forth on the ledge above, sending a shower of loose rock into the chasm below.

India's fingers were scraped and bleeding. Her muscles ached and she didn't know how much longer she would be able to hold on. The more she worried about it, the more the candle guttered, casting jumpy shadows against the rock. Encouraged by the apparent movement, the creature on the ledge above resumed its agitated probing.

'Where am I?' she cried.

She strained her eyes against the darkness, but beyond the candle flame nothing was visible.

'Gods,' she moaned. She pressed her cheek against the cold stone and sent a thought to whatever deity might be listening. 'Get me out of here, please.'

The situation wasn't going to change on its own. India took a deep breath, and held it a moment while she got the candle under control. As the light steadied, her surroundings became much clearer. She let her breath go in a long sigh. There were hand and footholds to the left if she could get to them before the creature got to her. Her fingers flexed painfully as she loosened her grip and reached for the next outcropping of stone.

A claw flicked down at her, grazing her face and fanning an incredible stench into her nostrils. India reeled, missed her grab for the rock, and found herself hanging over the abyss. With a strangled cry, India lunged for the handhold and dragged herself across to the next foothold. The creature continued to scream and snap its claws at India, but didn't leave its ledge.

Slowly and painfully, India made her way across the face and out of the huge arachnid's reach. By now, her candle had burned quite low, but she couldn't reach into her pack to pull out another one. She would have to get to where she could take off her pack soon, or climb the last of the cliff in the dark.

She could no longer see or hear the creature, but she couldn't see another ledge that would be broad enough to walk on, either.

'Oh, gods, gods, please get me out of here,' she cried again. She reached for the next handhold and risked squinting at the candle. The flame flickered lower.

Then something in her mind wobbled and she saw herself in a place she was certain she had never been.

India sat cross-legged in mid-air. A chair floated nearby and a small constellation of books circled above her. Her head ached slightly with her efforts and she wanted very much to quit.

It was a bright, sunny day outside, and India would rather have been lying in the meadow behind the Level

One Academy, reading a good book or taking a nap. Town was only a few miles away and the walk there was very pleasant on a day like this. She couldn't remember the last time she had done any shopping. India could feel her concentration shifting even though there was no window in the classroom to distract her.

Catch this, her teacher commanded, tossing a lit candle into the fray. The flame guttered as the candle flew through the air.

India closed her eyes and tried to focus her attention on strengthening the flame while adding the candle to the other objects she was levitating.

Good! Now, rotate until you are upside down.

India grimaced and squeezed her eyes more tightly shut. As her orientation shifted, so did her perception of where the objects were around her. She could feel her grasp on them changing, and several of the books moved out of their assigned places. India halted her rotation and moved the books back into their original positions. The chair and candle were doing fine. She resumed her own movement.

It had taken her months to do this exercise without dropping everything she was levitating except herself. She was still unable to do it without losing her spatial perception.

That's better! Shannon exclaimed.

'Oh, please,' India pleaded as she fought to retain her hold on herself and the objects around her. 'Not telepathy while I'm upside down! You shift my concentration when you do that.'

I know, Shannon giggled. *You need to learn how to focus your attention and energy. Distractions are a part of almost everything.*

India hung upside down and concentrated on her small flotilla. Her copper curls hung down below her and her green eyes were fixed on Shannon's upside-down face. The wide blue eyes and pale blonde hair looked like they belonged on a doll, not a person. Even upside down, Shannon was pretty.

India could feel the blood rushing to her head but she maintained her cross-legged position, her hands resting palm up on her knees.

Remember to breathe, Shannon admonished.

My head feels like it's going to explode, India thought grimly, figuring if she used telepathy, she might get a bit more sympathy. She took a deep breath and exhaled slowly.

Raise yourself toward the ceiling, keeping everything else exactly as it is, said Shannon.

Still upside down, India floated up toward the ceiling until she was sitting on it. She managed to maintain her tiny cosmos, ignoring the pounding in her temples.

'I think that's enough for this afternoon,' said Shannon. 'Put the candle down first.'

India obeyed.

'Now the chair, then stack the books on the seat from largest to smallest.'

Still sitting on the ceiling, India lowered the chair and began sorting and stacking books. A door opened and someone walked into the room.

'When you finish that, you may bring yourself down,' said Shannon magnanimously.

When her feet were back on the floor, India inhaled and exhaled deeply several times and studied the newcomer.

He was tall, with fierce, dark eyes and a hard, angular face. His skin and hair were dark also. He wore cotton trousers and a loose tunic. His feet were bare. India noticed idly that he had the most improbably long toes she had ever seen. She glanced back up at his face.

He studied her silently for so long that India became uncomfortable and looked away. India was surprised to notice that Shannon stood a bit apart from them, watching warily with her arms crossed over her chest and her head cocked sideways. She frowned, pulling pale blonde eyebrows down over pale blue eyes. It was impossible for Shannon to look stern or angry. She always took things in her stride. What would she have to be worried about?

India looked back at the stranger.

'You can't stay here,' he said.

India stared at him uncomprehendingly. She heard Shannon suck in a breath sharply, but her vision seemed to be closing in. She couldn't see anything beyond the dark, cold stranger.

'W . . .' India swallowed and tried again. 'Where will I go?' she asked.

Ignoring her question, he turned to Shannon. 'You were supposed to have told her,' he said with a jerk of his head toward India. 'It can't be put off any longer.'

'But I'm getting through!' Shannon protested. 'I'm teaching . . .'

'There has been no progress,' he cut Shannon off. 'You aren't doing her any favors by delaying her departure.'

India's universe had been reduced to the man who was talking about her as though she weren't there. He had managed to pull the rug out from underneath her and she didn't even know who he was. 'Shannon?' she croaked. She cleared her throat. 'Shannon?'

The spell was broken. The man looked at India again, then he strode from the room as abruptly as he had entered it.

'Where will I go?' India asked again.

'Another place. Another teacher,' Shannon said.

'I don't want another teacher,' India objected.

'It isn't up to us.' Shannon sighed and sat down on the floor. She pulled her legs up into the lotus.

India sat down opposite her. 'Who was he?' she asked.

Shannon glanced reflexively at the door. 'I guess you could call him the headmaster.' She shrugged. 'It's up to him. He made his decision several weeks ago. I was supposed to have told you by now, prepared you for the journey you have ahead of you, but I thought I was getting through your barriers. I thought we were making progress. He came in here to tell me I was deluding myself.'

'But . . .' India began.

Shannon shook her head. 'If he says you must go, then that's it.'

'So what I feel and what I want are of no importance?' India demanded indignantly.

'That's right,' Shannon nodded. Her short, blonde hair bounced with the movement of her head.

'That's not fair!' India exclaimed.

'Life's not fair,' said Shannon with exaggerated patience. 'There are barriers in your mind that we can't break down, and twenty-some-odd years of memories you don't seem to have any more. Without the information they've concealed, we won't discover why you're here. Ashraf thinks there's a woman who can help you.'

'Why can't you help me?' India pleaded.

'I've tried,' said Shannon. 'I don't like to admit failure, but there doesn't seem to be anything I can do for you. There may not be anything she can do for you either, but we owe it to you to try.'

'Why?' India asked, incredulous.

'Because everyone is entitled to live their own life; make their own mistakes in it and have their own successes. No one has the right to take that away from anyone else,' Shannon said simply.

'But why is that your responsibility?' India persisted.

'Because you showed up on our doorstep. It became our responsibility.' Shannon shrugged. 'I've tried, but Ashraf thinks Anara can help you better. She's a special teacher, and a good one. You'll like her, actually. Everyone does.'

'What is she like?' India asked doubtfully.

Shannon thought a moment and then rocked forward on her thighs conspiratorially. 'She's like fresh-baked bread and Christmas morning and hand-knit shawls and grand-mothers, except that she's much younger than the average grandmother. She's round and small and brown and moves constantly, like a bird. She laughs a lot and makes people feel good about themselves.'

India chuckled uncomfortably and shifted on her seat. 'And how do I get to her?'

Shannon frowned and looked past India's shoulder for a moment. 'It's a long and dangerous journey,' she said at last, looking India in the eye. 'And you have to go by yourself.'

'I haven't been alone since I got here!' India objected.

'No one else can go with you,' she repeated gently. 'This you have to do alone. You will cross time as well as space. You will have to get yourself to another dimension.'

'What?' India asked in disbelief. 'Oh, come on. Crossing dimensions?'

'Well, I guess more accurately, you have to find the Inn between dimensions. That's where Anara works.'

'She holds classes at an Inn that doesn't exist?' India snorted. 'Give me a break. You've been here too long. Ashraf has done something to your head, too!'

'Actually, she's a cook,' said Shannon. 'She cooks and cleans rooms at a hostel.' She held up a hand to forestall any further comments from India. 'She's also an extremely good teacher. She used to work here.'

'She got expelled, too?' asked India.

Shannon shifted uncomfortably. 'Uh, yeah, sort of,' she said.

'What was she kicked out for?' India asked, probing for the dirt.

'She disobeyed Ashraf,' Shannon said shortly.

India took the hint. 'Well, then how do I get there from here?'

'You leave at sunset,' Shannon began.

'Tonight?' India interrupted with a gasp.

'Tomorrow,' Shannon corrected. 'You leave at sunset. The path outside the door will start you off. Go north. You will levitate a lit candle, concentrating on its flame, not on where you are going. Your intuition will guide your feet along the correct path. You will cross the dimensions in this way. If you deviate from these instructions, you won't arrive at the hostel.'

'Why?' asked India. She was trying to remember which direction north was from the front door of this place.

'Because in the middle of the night you will cross Shark's Tooth Pass. If you don't concentrate on the flame of your candle, you'll probably fall off a cliff somewhere along the way and die.'

'*Wo*nderful,' said India. 'Terrific! I don't subscribe to the cure-me-or-kill-me school of thought. How 'bout I just go home and we forget the whole thing?'

'India,' Shannon looked concerned. 'You owe it to yourself to make your mind whole again. We aren't doing this to be mean.'

'I know,' India sighed. 'I've just been so scared for so long.' She drew her knees up to her chest and clasped her arms around them, resting her chin between them.

Shannon reached out and touched India's freckled cheek with a pale, white finger. 'I wish there had been more I could have done,' she said regretfully.

That night, India lay awake for a long time before sleep closed over her.

With a sigh, India began buildering again. Her muscles burned and knotted, but she reached for the next handhold and pulled herself forward. There had to be a path up here somewhere. She was expected at Level Two, after all. There had to be a way to get there from here.

If only she knew where here was . . .

Craning her neck, India looked above her to see if a ledge existed higher up, but the rock stretched upward unbroken. She started to look down, and decided that might not be such a good idea.

The candle flickered and died.

India clung to the rock trying to ease the cramps in her fingers without losing her precarious grip. She pressed her cheek against the cool rock as though drawing strength from it, and reached out into the darkness.

Inch by inch, she worked along the rock until finally her foot struck an outcropping that turned into a ledge of sizable proportions. Gratefully, India threw herself down onto it and stripped out of her pack. Shaking, she struggled with bloody fingers at the knots that held her pack closed, then spent time rummaging through her clothing to find another candle.

Finally getting it lit, she was able to take a long look at her surroundings. The ledge narrowed slightly on its far side, turning into a path, but beyond the candle's illumination India couldn't tell if it would continue.

India fumbled through her pack for her chronometer and ran across some trail rations she had stashed. She wolfed down a portion of them as she continued to search for the timepiece. It was not as late as she had expected. 'Fear and pursuit are great motivators,' she murmured wryly.

Now, if she could only find out where she was, and where she was going, she'd be all set.

Something strange had happened on the path and India couldn't figure out what it was. Her mind had been absent until the claw reached out from the darkness and struck her.

In a blinding flash, India had returned to consciousness and realized that she was not where she had expected to be. Her mind told her she was on her way to Level Two, but something about it felt wrong.

Searching her mind now, she couldn't find anything to suggest there had been conflict. Then she felt the strange

9

wobbling sensation, as if something in her mind had slipped, and suddenly, she was no longer on the ledge.

India crouched on the floor of a dark closet in one of the many spare rooms on the third floor of her father's home. Her breath sobbed in and out of her lungs. She struggled to be quiet and remain hidden.

Downstairs, she could hear angry shouting and the crash and shatter of breakables being thrown.

Someone rushed past the door of the bedroom India hid in. Probably one of the maids, she thought. Going downstairs to start cleaning up the wreckage of this temper, she guessed as she tried to get further into the corner of the closet.

The shouting downstairs grew louder and more coherent. India could hear footsteps now also. He was coming closer. She could also hear other, more agitated voices and could picture a small entourage following her father around the house as he bellowed and threw whatever came to hand.

India hoped his heart would attack him.

The footsteps reached the stairs.

India fought to control the sound of her breathing.

'Damn it! I said get out of my way!' her father shouted.

India could hear his feet on the steps. He was coming up to find her.

She whimpered and tried to push further into the corner. The sound of her heart blotted out the noise of her father coming up the stairs.

The closet door swept open and a large hand reached inside, grabbing her arm.

India was jerked out of the closet and onto her feet. Blinking against the sudden light, India noticed that the people who had been following her father and talking to him had disappeared.

Her arm throbbed against the bruising grip of her

father's fingers. India didn't look at him, but she knew the expression on his face.

Grim. Controlled and utterly devoid of contortion. His eyes would be squinted slightly at the outer corners and his mouth would be pressed together in a hard line. It was difficult to reconcile that face to the bellowing voice and shattering glass, but he managed to keep control of his appearance throughout any tirade.

The grip tightened. India sucked air through her teeth, but managed not to make any noise. Crying only made him angrier.

'I got a call from your teacher today,' he said quietly. His voice was as grim and expressionless as his face, but India could hear the control. The longer he held himself in check, the worse it would be in the long run.

India said nothing, continuing to stare very carefully at the wall just past his elbow.

'Do you know why she bothered me at home?' he asked, still controlling his voice.

India shook her head slightly. She knew why her teacher had called, but saying so would only make the punishment worse. He would say she was smart-mouthing him. It would give him an excuse to punish her for two offenses instead of just the one.

The fingers closed even more tightly around India's arm. It burned more than it hurt now, but it still hurt badly. India gritted her teeth against a whimper.

'She says you're a discipline problem.' The grip tightened. 'She says you disrupt the class.' He shook her. 'She says her efforts at maintaining order in the class are thwarted by you at every turn.' He shook her harder. 'She asked me to discuss this with you.' His voice was escaping his control.

Tears slipped down India's cheeks, but she didn't make a sound. Her head felt like it might just fall off and roll away, the way he was shaking her.

Then India saw his other arm raise up in her periphery. She flinched in spite of herself. His open hand looked like a bear's paw as it descended. She could almost see the claws, just like in the wildlife videos, heavy and powerful. He caught her across the side of the head and dislocated her jaw again.

'Talking doesn't seem to get through to you, though, does it?' he asked rhetorically, again raising his hand.

India stood straighter in his grasp, took a deep breath and looked up to meet the next blow.

His hand landed heavily in the same place. Pain shot from her jaw up into her temples and down into her neck, but she didn't flinch.

Unblinking, India met her father's eyes, daring him to hit her again, driving him further into unreasoning rage.

Grabbing her other arm, he picked her up and shook her until her teeth cracked together. 'I do not want to hear any more of this!' he shouted and threw her to the floor. 'From her or you,' he warned.

India lay still until her father left the room. As his footsteps faded downstairs, India sat up and gingerly tested herself. Her fingers tingled as the blood flow was restored. She flexed them, testing the muscles in her upper arms. Nothing seemed broken.

Steeling herself, India popped her jaw back into place and worked it a few times to make sure everything was okay.

She stood up and brushed her skirt to straighten it, pushed her hair out of her face, and moved over to the mirror above the dresser. The red marks his fingers had left on her cheek would fade soon, leaving no bruise or welt. She would be able to go out in public without anyone knowing what had happened.

She decided to go pack. This time she really would run away.

*   *   *

The sun finally set.

India was given dinner by one of the maids. She wasn't particularly hungry, but forced herself to eat everything on her plate. She didn't know when her next meal might be.

Her bag was packed and hidden under the bed. She had no particular destination in mind, just away from this house and her father.

'Are you finished?' the maid asked from the doorway.

India jumped.

'I'm sorry,' the maid apologized. 'I didn't mean to startle you. May I take your plate?'

India nodded. 'Thanks.'

'Would you like the VidCon on?' asked the maid as she collected India's plate and glass.

'Thanks,' India said again. She would program it to shut itself off at her regular bedtime. No one would check on her as long as the VidCon and the lights were turned off by ten.

The maid said: 'VidCon on, please', and left India on her own for the evening as usual.

The console against the far wall came to life. Everything that India used had been keyed to respond only when the word 'please' was used in the request. If she didn't then say 'thank you', the equipment would immediately shut itself off. This was her father's idea of teaching India manners.

'Thank you,' she said automatically. 'Please set automatic shut-off for ten o'clock, p.m.'

The console obliged her.

'Thank you,' she said again.

India pulled her suitcase out from under the bed and placed it by the window. She got her coat out of the closet and threw it, and her bag, out the window. She shut the window quietly and set the lights to go off a couple of minutes after the VidCon. Then she slipped out of her room and crept down the stairs.

The only tricky place would be the hallway outside her father's office.

He was always there until very late at night, but sometimes he went down to the kitchen or the bar. If he did that tonight, he might catch her. He didn't like it when she left her room at night.

As she padded down the hall, she could hear voices coming from behind her father's door.

'. . . shipment's due in this week. Are you sure you can trust the new Customs Officer?'

'Who do you think planted him there?' her father answered with an assured chuckle.

'I also don't like the questions I've been getting about your girl lately.'

Her father snorted derisively. 'She's a kid, for Christ's sake. What does an eight-year-old know?'

'Yeah,' the other man said uncomfortably. 'I guess she pretty much stays out of the way. I just don't like the questions I've been hearing. Maybe you should have someone keeping an eye on her, just in case.'

'I'll handle my kid my own way,' her father said tightly.

India continued through the hall and down the other stairs to the ground floor of the huge house. She wondered what the shipment was this time. Smack? Thionite? Whores? She might be only eight, but she was no dummy.

There were lights on down the servants' corridor, but no one was moving around on the first floor. The back door squealed loudly as India pulled it open. She froze, straining her ears in the silence, waiting to see if anyone had heard the noise and was coming to check. No one came, and at last India walked outside and pulled the door shut behind her.

The bag and coat had fallen close together. India had no trouble locating them in the dark. She pulled the coat on, slung her bag over her shoulder, and walked as quickly as she could away from her father and his house.

Two days later, she was found and returned by some of her father's men.

With a shudder, India stuffed the chronometer into her pack. Gathering the rest of her belongings, she slung the pack over her shoulders and started off down the mountain holding the new candle.

The hostel came into sight just after sunrise. It was a small cottage near a thicket of trees, set back from the path quite a ways. She would have missed it, but the smells of breakfast cooking over a wood fire caught her attention.

India's stomach rumbled. She had fallen into the rhythm of walking and a state of self-hypnosis, forgetting even that she was still moving. The smell of porridge, bacon and eggs, and coffee brought her back to the trail and the forest. Slowly, she approached the hostel.

The door swung open at her touch and revealed a long room dominated by an enormous oak-plank table and many chairs. There were no windows or pictures, and only one other door to her right. The far wall was a fireplace larger than any India had ever seen. Various cooking surfaces had been built into the interior in a haphazard fashion and the hearth level changed according to the whim of its designer.

A small, round woman with brown hair and a very red face knelt in front of a black kettle hanging over the flame. She stirred the steaming contents of the pot slowly as she tossed things into it and muttered to herself. Eggs fried in a huge pan near her elbow, catching the drippings of an animal, dressed and spitted, which turned above the fire. Coffee brewed in a pot on the hearth.

Her mouth watering, India came into the room and put her pack on the table.

'Get that thing off of there! It's filthy and I just washed the table up for breakfast.' The woman stood brandishing her wooden spoon. India scooped up her pack and brushed at the place it had rested on. Looking at her bloody, dirty fingers, she realized suddenly what a sight she must be. Backing away, she clutched her pack to her small chest with one hand, and made a pass at her scraggly auburn curls with the other.

'I'm sorry . . .' she began.

'Sorry, nothing. You're a mess!' the woman exclaimed. 'Go wash up in there and then come help me with this,' she said, pointing toward a door India hadn't noticed before. 'You'll find the ewer in there. And also a clean towel.'

Without a word, India walked to the door and opened it. Inside was a table with a pitcher and bowl. A small stack of clean towels and a bar of soap sat next to them; a brackish mirror hung on the wall above it. An old-fashioned commode stood against the other wall. There were no windows, and no light fixtures, but the room was brightly lit anyway.

Suppressing a shudder, India entered the room and pulled the door closed behind her. She dropped her pack on the floor, poured water from the ewer into the bowl, and picked up the soap. Her fingers stung unbearably and made her cry, but India scrubbed her hands and face until they were clean. Then she got a comb from her pack and set about unsnarling her hair.

Hoping enough time had passed to get her out of any chores, India emerged from the bathroom feeling quite a bit better.

Sourceless light bathed the room in a golden haze, pooled and swirled, shimmering. It gave the room the appearance of shifting, which unsettled India.

'Ah, there you are,' said the woman, coming back into the main room through the door India had noticed earlier. 'Come give me a hand with the silverware and napkins.'

With a small sigh, India moved to help her set the huge oak table.

16

'I just came over Shark's Tooth Pass from the Level One Hostel,' India volunteered, wondering where that information had come from.

'Of course,' said the woman disinterestedly. She continued placing bowls and plates at intervals around the table.

'Didn't they tell you I was coming?' asked India.

'Of course,' she repeated. 'Come help me lift the kettle off the fire.'

Puzzled, India followed the woman to the hearth.

A deep gong reverberated through the hostel and doors began opening all around the room. People filed in, taking seats around the table and reaching for platters and bowls. India stood and stared, her mouth hanging open. She had seen there were no doors in this room besides the front door, the bathroom door, and the kitchen door. The cottage she'd seen in the woods wasn't big enough to have any other rooms. So many people would have made more noise behind all those doors getting out of bed in the morning and washing up for breakfast. Wouldn't they have come in here to use the bathroom, she wondered?

'Well, come on.' The strange round woman patted India on the shoulder. 'If you don't grab the platters as they pass by, you won't get any breakfast at all.' She pushed India toward an empty chair and headed back to the kitchen.

India sat and reached for a bowl, but someone else grabbed it before she could get a hand on it. The next platter that passed by was empty. She looked around the table and saw that pretty much all the food she had seen cooking earlier was gone.

India's belly rumbled again. She had the remains of her trail rations in her pack, at least. But everything had smelled so good! She reached for the coffee pot, but it was also empty. With a sigh, she pushed back from the table and sat for a moment watching everyone.

The entire meal was being consumed in silence. People

were gesturing to each other, and their faces were animated by expressions appropriate to conversation, but no one said a word.

No one noticed her. They left the table as they finished, one by one, taking their plates and silverware to the kitchen. This done, they went back through the doors they had entered the room by, and India was left alone in the large room. Breakfast seemed to have lasted about five minutes. Standing slowly, India went into the kitchen.

Dirty plates, bowls and cups were stacked high on the counters and several large pots were soaking in what appeared to be an enormous trough.

'You wash, I'll dry,' the woman said, handing her a rag. India sighed and rolled up her sleeves.

'Do they always eat so quickly?' India asked.

The woman laughed. 'It doesn't take them very long to decimate all that food, does it?' she asked. 'Were you able to get anything?'

'No,' India said in a small, wobbly voice. She was feeling very hungry and very sorry for herself.

'Well, then you can eat with me after we get this mess cleaned up.' The woman smiled at her understandingly. 'Tomorrow you'll know what to expect, so you can fend for yourself at the table.'

Cleaning the kitchen took the better part of an hour. By the time they were done, India's fingers were raw and bleeding again.

'Come here,' the woman commanded. 'Sit down and let me bandage your hands before we eat.'

Obediently, India sat at the small table in the corner of the kitchen and held out her throbbing, bloody hands. 'What is your name?' she asked timidly.

'Anara,' said the woman as she collected salve and bandages from the cupboard under the sink. She returned to where India sat and inspected India's wounds.

'I've never in my life been taller than anyone but

little kids,' India ventured, unsure what else to say.

'How did this happen?' Anara asked, ignoring the comment and turning India's hands over to examine her palms.

'I was climbing Shark's Tooth Pass last night,' India explained. 'This great big old hairy spider-crab-thing jumped out at me and knocked me off the path. I caught the edge as I fell and had to do a bit of rock-climbing to find another path.'

'You were extremely lucky,' said Anara as she smeared salve onto India's hands.

It stung abominably, but India bit her lip and kept silent.

'So, you met Mama,' Anara commented.

'Mama?' India echoed curiously.

'The great big old hairy monster,' Anara clarified. 'Her name is Mama.'

'Why?' asked India, incredulously.

'That's how she thinks of herself,' said Anara. 'We've never seen any children, but you never know.' She wrapped the soft bandaging material gently around India's hands.

'How do you know that?'

'I asked her once,' said Anara with a smile.

'You *talked* to her?' India shuddered. 'How long has she been up there?'

'Oh, as long as anyone can remember,' said Anara as she gathered up her first-aid supplies and took them back to the cupboard. She got two bowls from another cupboard above the counter and went to the stove. There was a small pot on the back burner. Anara lifted its lid and ladled porridge into the bowls. 'Here,' she said, placing one in front of India. 'There's milk and sugar if you want it. Let me get you a spoon.'

'Thank you,' said India, staring at the gelatinous mess in her bowl. She leaned over and sniffed it when Anara had her back turned. It smelled wonderful, so India ignored the distasteful appearance and poured milk over it.

Anara dug into her bowl in silence. India looked down

at her bowl, then at her bandaged hands. She held the spoon awkwardly, since her fingers were wrapped together, but the salve had numbed the pain. India took a mouthful and discovered the mess tasted as good as it smelled. She ate in silence for a while, reluctant to bring up a subject which had been bothering her since her encounter with Mama. She continued to spoon up the glutinous porridge, glancing at Anara surreptitiously.

'What was it you wanted to discuss with me?' Anara asked her finally.

'How did you know?' asked India, surprised.

Anara smiled. 'There is something troubling you. Can I help?'

India noticed that Anara hadn't answered her question, but she let it pass. 'I've had a strange feeling since I ran into Mama,' India began. She searched Anara's plain, broad face for reaction, but there was none. The woman smiled at her, encouraging her to continue. 'There is something wrong with my being here, but I don't know what it is,' said India at last. She spooned up another mouthful of the distasteful-looking mess and looked back at Anara.

'Why do you feel it's wrong for you to be here?' Anara asked her.

India felt uncomfortable under Anara's searching eyes. She looked back down at her hands. 'I don't know,' India whispered. 'Most of the time, my mind tells me this is where I'm supposed to be, but then I remember something from last night that tells me this is wrong. When I was in the mountains, I wasn't aware of being there until suddenly this claw came out of nowhere and slashed through my candle flame. The next thing I know, I'm falling over the edge of a cliff, and I have no idea where I am, or what I'm doing there.' India paused to look at Anara again, but still there was no reaction.

India took a deep breath and continued: 'When I stopped to think about it, there was a reason in my head, but it didn't feel right. I hadn't expected to be where I was, but when I try to think about where I ought to be, this is it.' She looked around the kitchen and shuddered.

'Well,' said Anara, frowning slightly. She stood and picked up the bowls. 'What do you think the reason is?' she asked, taking the bowls to the sink and turning on the water.

'I don't know.' India shrugged helplessly. 'Every time I try to think about it, my mind kind of slides away from the questions. Why is there running water in the kitchen and not in the bathroom?' India asked.

'Nothing about this place is what it appears to be,' Anara told her. 'Think about that. Then think about your dilemma. I have no answers for you. You will have to find your own.'

'But . . .' India began.

Anara shook her head. 'I'm not here for that,' she said sharply. Softening her tone a bit, she continued: 'After I've finished here, I will show you to your room. You will have tasks here that you will be expected to perform on a daily basis. I will explain those to you tomorrow. Obviously your hands will have to heal before you can be of much use to us. Tomorrow will be soon enough.'

The room was behind another door India hadn't noticed earlier. 'How large is this cottage?' she asked curiously.

'Large enough,' Anara said.

India couldn't get an answer out of her that explained the phenomenon any better. With a sigh, she walked through the door and looked around. The room was larger than she had expected, given her apparent status in this place. It had two large windows on the outside wall with curtains opened to show a meadow. A double bed stood against the wall to her right. A small table with a drawer and a lamp was next to it. Against the wall next to the door was a large armoire. Along the wall to her left was a long, low bureau with a door on the far side of it.

'That isn't what's outside the cottage,' India said, indicating the windows.

'No,' Anara said. 'It isn't. Through that door is your bathroom. This one has running water and a shower. You will be expected to keep it clean yourself, and your room as well. Tomorrow we will discuss your other chores, but for now, I suggest you get some sleep. You look exhausted.'

India nodded and approached the bed. She didn't hear the door close behind her. She pulled back the patchwork quilt and prodded one of the feather pillows. Inhaling sharply, prepared to ask another question, India turned back toward the door and discovered she was alone. With a small shrug she turned back to the bed and began stripping off her trail-dirty clothes. Without another thought, she climbed into the bed and fell promptly asleep.

Ashraf?

Don't you ever check the time zone of the dimension you're calling? came the irritable reply.

India just showed up here, Anara said.

What time is it there? Ashraf asked, his telepathic 'voice' already much wider awake.

Just before noon. Ashraf, you wouldn't believe the mess she's in.

She's been a mess for almost a year, Ashraf said impatiently. *That's why we were sending her to you.*

I don't mean just mentally, said Anara. *She was on the path past Mama's lair and completely out of her mind.*

She's gone crazy?

No. Her mind was gone from her body, Anara clarified. *She came back to herself when Mama attacked her. She fell off the cliff.*

Gods, she caught herself? he guessed.

I dressed and bandaged her hands and put her to bed. That was the easy part.

The blocks were reinforced? asked Ashraf.

I don't know how they looked before, said Anara. *But I'm surprised she can function at all given the state she's in. Her telepathy has been cut off completely. She has no memory of any of the previous year, and no knowledge of the psi-talents she possesses. She doesn't even remember being sent to me, really. Just that the order was given, and she obeyed it.*

That sounds worse than what we got a year ago, he admitted.

I may have to ask for Henry's help on this, she said.

Do what you have to, said Ashraf. *Thanks for the call. I'll sleep better now.*

I'm sure you will, said Anara as she broke the contact. She felt a small shiver of relief as she did so.

When India awoke, light shone through the windows still, but it was late afternoon light. India was certain she had been sleeping much longer than just a few hours; she felt well rested. Sitting up, she pushed back the covers and remembered the bandages on her hands. In order to shower and change, she would have to remove them.

She sat and stared at her hands for a moment. Her fingers had been wrapped together, and her thumbs were also padded with gauze. She fumbled at the fastened ends for quite a while before finally loosening one of them enough to actually undo it. India took a deep breath and began unwinding the bandage. She didn't realize she was holding her breath until she reached skin and tried to gasp.

India hiccoughed several times as she gaped in disbelief at her hand. The raw wounds had healed completely. There was no scarring. There were no traces of her night in the mountains or the ordeal of the cliff. Quickly, she unwrapped the other hand. It too was healed.

'How long did I sleep?' she asked rhetorically.

'All day yesterday and most of today,' Anara said from the doorway.

23

India looked up in surprise and held out her hands.

'I let you sleep yourself out,' Anara continued, as though that would answer India's unasked question. 'Did you dream?'

India shook her head. 'I don't think so. Why?'

'After you shower and dress, I'll have a meal for you. Then we'll discuss your chores.' Anara nodded toward the bathroom door.

'But . . .' India began.

'First your shower,' Anara said firmly.

With a sigh of resignation, India climbed out of bed.

The bathroom looked surprisingly modern and out of place in this peculiar hostel. The tiled floor and porcelain fixtures were comfortingly familiar. The ceiling light responded when India flipped the switch, unlike the unexplained glowing in the bathroom she had first used here. The shower was a small stall, but she had not expected luxury, and the water ran hot when she tried it. 'This won't be so bad after all,' she decided, climbing into the shower. She reached for the soap and began working the bar in her hands to create lather.

The steam billowed upward and the odor of the soap assailed her nostrils. India staggered and fell heavily into the wall. The smell jogged an especially sharp sense of memory she couldn't quite reach.

'I should know this,' she mumbled, but the harder she searched her mind, the further away that fragment of memory receded. With a shrug, India washed her hair, finished showering, and toweled dry briskly. *Nothing about this place is as it appears to be*, she heard Anara telling her.

'Well, you got that right,' India said to her reflection as she wiped the steam from the mirror. Staring back at her were her own green eyes. She wasn't quite sure if she had expected them to be different, but her face was the same as she remembered it to be: a small, pale oval with large eyes and a pointed chin. Freckles scattered across her cheekbones and the bridge of her short, straight nose. Her mouth was rather wider than it should have been for the size of her face and her lips were not as full as she would have liked them to have been, but overall it was not an unattractive face. It was framed by a riot of red-gold curls which refused to be tamed even when wet. It was longer than she had expected it should be. That change was easier to deal with than the unexplained holes in her mind, though.

Her face was at the right height in the mirror, she noticed finally. India was small. She stood five feet tall in her socks and weighed ninety pounds only after a large meal. It was a small comfort to find herself physically as she remembered herself to be. If she could only find out what was wrong with her memory, she'd feel a lot better.

India found a comb in her knapsack and pulled it through her wet curls, flinching as it caught in the snarls. Some of her clothing had bloodstains on it from her midnight climbing, so it took a while to find items clean enough to wear. At last, India felt she could face Anara. She grasped the knob firmly, took a deep breath, and pulled the door open.

Anara was nowhere to be seen.

India looked around the large room. The kitchen door was the only other door in the room besides hers. The front door had disappeared, as had the bathroom door by the fireplace.

India was afraid to close her own door, for fear she would never find her room and her stuff again. She pulled a chair back from the table and propped it against the door before heading to the kitchen to find Anara.

Anara wasn't in the kitchen either.

India returned to the main room and looked more closely, hoping she had overlooked the smaller woman somehow. She happened to be looking at a portion of wall

25

when it became a door and opened. Anara walked through with an armload of folded garments and pushed the door closed behind her with her foot.

India gasped and startled Anara.

'Oh, there you are,' said Anara. 'Did you find your lunch in the kitchen?'

'N–no,' said India. 'I was looking for you.'

'There's a plate on the counter covered with a cloth,' Anara told her. She indicated her burden. 'I have to distribute these.'

India watched in amazement as Anara reached for the wall and a doorknob appeared under her hand. Anara disappeared from the central room, leaving India staring, open-mouthed, at a blank wall.

'Well, I guess that explains the lack of pictures and windows,' she muttered as she returned to the kitchen.

Lunch turned out to be a plate stacked high with tomato sandwiches and a glass of milk. India liked tomato sandwiches, but they were that sort of strange item most people wouldn't think to fix for a guest, so they surprised her. Also, there were so many of them she wondered if Anara would be joining her when she finished the laundry.

India got herself another plate from the cupboard and put a sandwich on it, then took her plate and glass over to the small table in the corner.

Nothing about this place is as it appears to be.

'The next question would be what *is* this place, then?' India murmured to herself. She took a bite of her sandwich. 'How did I get here? What am I doing here?'

Anara came into the room at that moment. India turned to ask her these questions, but Anara shook her head slightly and gave India a look that made her close her mouth again.

'Not yet,' she said quietly. Then, more briskly, she continued, 'I see you found lunch. Are you ready to discuss your responsibilities here?'

India took another bite and nodded. Then she remembered her hands. 'How did these . . . ?' she began.

'Modern medicine.' Anara put a sandwich on a plate for herself and came to sit with India. 'First and foremost,' she began, 'you will keep your own room and bathroom clean and picked up. Also, you will help me prepare meals and clean the kitchen. You will do minor cleaning in the rooms of our guests.'

'What constitutes minor cleaning?' India asked, feeling a bit overwhelmed by the scope of her chores. Level One had someone who did all of these things for her. She'd only had her lessons to concentrate on . . . but she couldn't remember what they were.

'Sweeping, dusting, cleaning the bathrooms, making beds. The usual,' Anara responded. She took a bite and chewed thoughtfully for a moment. 'Also,' she continued around her mouthful, 'you can help me in the garden.'

Can I? India thought to herself. Gee, swell! Aloud, she said, 'What about my lessons?'

'This is part of your lessons,' Anara said, rather more sharply than India would have expected given the question.

India looked at Anara, but the woman's plain, broad face revealed nothing. India finished her sandwich and took her plate back to the counter for another.

'The tomatoes came from the garden,' Anara said pointedly.

India nodded, puzzled. This woman was strange; probably partly because of the strangeness of living in a place like this. India could already feel the strangeness rubbing off on herself.

After lunch, Anara suggested India take some time to explore outside the cottage before returning to help with dinner.

India walked to the place the front door had been when she first came in. She reached for the knob, and was delighted when one materialized under her hand. So the rules were consistent so far. She opened the door and stepped through. The forest outside was the same one she'd found herself in the morning she arrived.

Looking about, she decided to find out what really surrounded the strange little hostel. She set out to her right, and continued around the building until she returned to the front door. There was nothing but forest all around. The trees were mostly deciduous, but there were a few evergreens also. There was no meadow, and nothing resembling a garden.

Confused, India walked back out to the path and stood in the middle of it, looking back the way she had come. She remembered nothing about the trip here, except the encounter with Mama. She looked at her hands again in disbelief. With the other holes in her memory, India was beginning to doubt that she had actually been in Shark's Tooth Pass. She couldn't even remember where she knew this bit of geography from.

Turning her back on the direction she had been facing, India set out along the path, going farther into the woods.

For several miles, nothing changed. By then, she was getting tired, and the sun hung lower in the sky. She turned round and headed back to the hostel, determined that she would ask Anara some of the questions that had been bothering her, and not be put off by the woman's peculiar manner.

'Oh, good!' Anara exclaimed as India walked through the door. 'I lost track of time when I was working in the garden this afternoon, and I'm a bit late getting started. Do you know anything about baking bread?'

'No.' India shook her head. She opened her mouth, but Anara talked right over her.

'Well, go wash up, then, and come stir this. I'll have to explain bread to you on another day when we have the time. Come on!' Anara brandished her long wooden spoon.

India came around the table quickly and rushed to the

strange little bathroom and splashed water hastily into the bowl. She scrubbed her hands and face and returned to the dining room. 'Anara,' she began with determination. 'I wanted to . . .'

'Thank you,' Anara interrupted, handing India the spoon. She disappeared into the kitchen, leaving India standing with her mouth open.

'Anara?' India called as she stuck the spoon into the seething mass in the huge kettle. She stirred vigorously for several moments, but there was no response from the next room. 'Anara?' she persisted.

'I can't really hear you,' Anara called back. Bowls clattered on the counter in the kitchen, and India could hear Anara running back and forth.

India continued to stir until Anara came back out into the main room.

'Anara, can I . . .'

'We can probably pull that away from the direct fire now,' said Anara, and reached into the fireplace to move the huge arm the kettle was hanging from.

'But . . .' India tried again.

'I have to finish up some laundry while the bread is baking. Why don't you set the table. Keep an eye on this' – Anara indicated the stewpot – 'and don't forget the napkins.' She rushed from the room.

India frowned and watched the door Anara had opened disappear. With a shrug, she went to the kitchen and began counting out silverware and plates.

She had just finished the table when Anara came back into the room. She nodded approvingly at the job India had done and smoothed the front of her apron with hands that India noticed shook slightly.

'You can peel the potatoes out here and keep an eye on the stew for me while I get started on the salad,' Anara said. She went quickly to the kitchen before India could say anything.

Anara came back with two bowls full of vegetables and handed them to India along with a knife. 'Just peel them and slice them into the stewpot,' she instructed and left again.

She's deliberately avoiding my questions, India thought to herself as she set herself to the task. She managed not to cut herself, but she hated peeling vegetables.

India sat sullenly at the table with the guests and vented her frustration in her efforts to get her portion of the meal. She chewed and swallowed, but she tasted nothing. If any of her dining companions sensed her anger, they said nothing.

She sat in silence and watched the animated faces around her, wondering just what was going on. Distantly, she thought she heard voices and laughter, but her ears told her nothing was being said.

While they were doing the dishes after dinner was over, India tried again to ask Anara her questions.

'Anara, I've been wondering . . .' she began.

'No!' exclaimed Anara. 'I've told you, not yet!'

'What, not yet?' India yelled in frustration. 'You don't even know what I want to talk about. You won't let me get a word in edgewise!'

'I know exactly what you want to ask,' Anara snapped. She dropped her dish-towel on the counter and gripped India by both shoulders. She looked up squarely into India's eyes. 'Say nothing out loud. It might not be safe here.'

'What?' India gasped. 'But I just . . .' She looked into Anara's eyes and saw something there that told her the small, broad-faced woman knew exactly what she wanted to ask.

'Not yet,' Anara said again.

'When?' asked India.

'You'll know when the time is right. You'll sense if it's safe.'

'How?' India persisted.

Anara shook her head and picked up her dish-towel. She finished drying the dishes in silence.

'Sleep well,' Anara said as she left the kitchen. 'Your day will start early tomorrow.'

Chapter Two

It was still dark when India awoke.

She was certain someone had been calling her, but there was no one in the room, and no sound from beyond her door. With a shrug, India rolled onto her side and stuffed her fist into the pillow to buoy the feathers under her head. She was drifting back to sleep when she heard the voice.

India? Did you dream?

'Huh?' India struggled back to the surface of her thoughts, trying to remember where she'd heard that voice. 'No.'

It's time to begin your chores.

'Anara?'

There was no answer, but now she was completely awake. With a sigh, she rolled out of bed and staggered to the bathroom.

She felt more human after a shower, but that wasn't saying much.

India dressed mechanically and went out to find Anara.

'I'm in here,' Anara called from the kitchen before India's door had shut behind her.

India frowned slightly and went to get the silverware and plates.

'Why do you cook meals out here in the fireplace if you have a stove in the kitchen?' India asked as Anara heaved the full porridge-kettle onto the iron hook that protruded from the back of the fireplace.

'Why do you ask so many questions?' Anara countered.

'I just wanted to know,' India said defensively.

'Because this is where meals are cooked,' Anara responded.

There was a finality about her tone that stopped India's line of questioning. With a frown of irritation, she turned her attention to the plates and silverware, placing them at intervals on the huge oak table. 'Where are our guests?' India asked, unable to restrain her curiosity completely.

'That's their business, isn't it?' asked Anara.

India sighed. 'Yes, ma'am.'

'Either they will come when the gong is rung,' Anara continued, 'or they won't.'

'Yes, but . . .' India began.

'You will learn more through observation,' Anara said.

India closed her mouth and stalked off to the kitchen for the serving-platters.

The trick was finding the rooms to clean them.

Remembering Anara with the laundry, she started at one end of the large main room and held out her hand. Then she walked slowly along the wall, waiting for a doorknob to materialize. When one did, she knocked on the door and entered the room.

First, she cleaned the bathroom and put fresh towels on the racks.

Anara had left large piles of towels and linens on the table while India had been doing the breakfast dishes, and was now in the garden while India was up to her elbows in toilet water.

When she had finished in the bathroom, India washed her hands and set about stripping the bed of sheets and blankets. She had never been particularly good at making beds, but she'd never really been required to, either. The maid had always done it when she was little. When she had her own apartment, it was her small rebellion against being grown up to leave the covers rumpled each morning. She always straightened them before climbing in at night, though.

Now she found herself faced with *having* to do the job well.

The first bed took her a very long time to make, but she was fairly well pleased with the result. She briefly dusted the dresser and chair. Looking around the room, India decided she was through. She left in search of the next room.

Apparently the guests were on their own for lunch. After India and Anara had a quiet lunch in the kitchen, Anara said they would spend the afternoon working in the garden.

On hands and knees in the dirt, India pulled weeds and pruned dead leaves from the various plants in Anara's 'garden'. They had gone out through another previously unseen door, this one in the kitchen, to get there. The woods India had walked through to get to the cottage were not outside this door. The garden was several acres planted with rows of almost every vegetable that would thrive in the rich, loamy soil. There were several rows of fruit trees along the back acreage. The sun shone brightly overhead, and sweat dripped down India's forehead and into her eyes, obscuring her vision. She rubbed her forehead against her upper arm to dry it, but her arms were sweaty also.

'There must be some point to this,' she muttered as she crouched among the tomatoes, checking each plant for worms and other parasites. Her fingers were turning black from the leaves. Disgusted, India moved on to the next row and began weeding. She glanced around and found Anara over in the middle of the lettuces. The cottage stood to her right.

Although it wasn't far away, there was a distortion about it that made it appear larger than it had been when India had first encountered it in the woods. India tried to focus on the structure, to determine why there was a difference, but she couldn't bring the edges together completely. Just as she got a clear view of one side, the other would slip out of alignment.

India shook her head and blinked several times in an effort to clear the sweat from her eyes, but when she tried to concentrate on the hostel again, she found she had the same trouble. She looked over at Anara again, and found no difficulty focusing clearly on the small woman.

'Where in hell am I?' India muttered under her breath as she turned back to the weeds and worms and bugs. She shuddered slightly, sighed, and set her mind on her work.

The afternoon passed swiftly, and India was surprised to hear Anara call her in to begin supper. The sun was low in the sky and the trees cast long shadows on the ground. India had finished the tomatoes. She stood up and looked back over the rows she had worked. They were straight and green. The dirt between the rows was free of weeds and the plants looked healthier than when she had started. At least, India thought they did. With a happy sigh she wiped her black hands on her hips and set off for the house.

'There,' Anara greeted her at the door. 'That wasn't so bad, was it?'

'No,' India agreed. 'Do you do all of that yourself?'

'Oh, a bit every day and it doesn't seem like so much,' she grinned. 'And now I have you to help me, it will go much faster.'

India grinned in spite of herself, then she went to the bathroom to wash up.

Dinner passed in its typical frenetic silence. The dishes were waiting in the sink for her when she finished.

By the time India fell into bed that night, she was too tired even to think about the questions that had plagued her since morning. She snuggled into the down of her pillows and fell promptly asleep.

India stood in a vast, grey plane.

She was completely alone in a place that wasn't a place. The plane was devoid of feature. There was no light, but no darkness either. There was no feeling of enclosure. Nothing recognizable as ground, or sky, or even distance separated where she stood from any other place in the No-Place.

Far away, an obelisk surged into being.

35

India took a step toward it, but the structure subsided as quickly as it had erupted.

Gods, this is weird, she murmured to herself. The sound of her voice fell dead at her feet. There was nothing for it to echo off; similarly, there was no place for it to go. She recognized she was in a dream, but she was curious where it might go, so she kept looking around for any changes that might have occurred without her noticing.

The No-Place remained empty save for her presence. She began to doubt she was really there at all. *What is this place?* she asked the emptiness around her.

There was no answer. Then the dream shifted and she was no longer standing on the vast grey plane.

India stumbled out of bed early the next morning. Anara's voice was still in her ears as she climbed into the shower, hoping the hot water would wake her, hoping the smell of the soap wouldn't trigger any memories this morning.

Yes, she had dreamed. Maybe that would help.

There were several layers of what India had come to refer to as 'Glop' in her mind. They were memories given to India that had nothing to do with the occasional flashes of truth she received from her blocked subconscious. These she had classified as 'Real Stuff'. These were what frightened her by surfacing when she was most vulnerable.

By the time she had filled the porridge-kettle with water and hung it on the hook above the fire to boil, India was moving less stiffly and feeling a little more wide awake.

'Here,' said Anara, handing India a cup of coffee and sitting down at the table with her own.

India smiled and sat down too. She sipped the hot liquid and stared meditatively into the flames under the kettle.

'A watched pot never boils,' said Anara.

'Does it count if you're not really looking *at* it?' asked India.

Anara chuckled. 'I have no idea. Grandmother never

said anything about that. She just wanted to keep me from being idle.'

'I'm not being idle,' said India slowly, 'I'm thinking.'

'Grandmother never believed me when I told her that,' Anara mused.

'When are you going to ask me what I dreamed about?'

'When the time is right,' said Anara, standing up.

'What can I do while I wait for the water to boil?' asked India. She took another sip of her coffee and sat up straighter in her chair.

'You could break eggs into a bowl for me,' Anara suggested. She went into the kitchen.

India rose and followed her. She took the bowls and eggs back into the main room and sat down in her chair again. The kettle steamed gently, but there were no bubbles forming on the bottom of the pot yet. With a small sigh, India set out her bowls and began breaking the eggs one at a time into a small bowl, looking for rotten ones, before dumping the egg into the large bowl with the others. She tossed the shells into a third bowl. Anara had gathered the eggs that morning. They were still warm from the laying.

India was almost through breaking the eggs when the kettle reached the boil. She cracked the last few eggs unhurriedly and then gathered the bowls. 'Here,' she said, giving Anara the bowl full of eggs. She put the small bowl in the sink and put the bowl full of shells by the back door to be taken out to the compost heap after breakfast.

'Here,' said Anara, handing India a bowl full of grain.

India took the bowl and a long-handled wooden spoon with her back to the main room and the furiously steaming kettle. She began slowly pouring the grain into the water, stirring all the while to prevent lumping. When the cereal had begun to thicken, India pulled it away from the direct flame and banked the coals under it to provide low, steady heat to finish cooking the porridge.

'Now what?' she asked, returning to the kitchen.

'Biscuit dough,' said Anara, pointing to the counter. All the ingredients were laid out for her, so India started spooning flour into the sifter. Periodically, India went into the main room to stir the porridge, making sure it hadn't burned or gotten lumpy.

Once the biscuits were in the oven, India scrubbed the dining table and laid out the silverware, napkins and bowls. She went back to the kitchen and measured out the cream, butter, jam, sugar, salt and pepper, placing them around the table.

As she turned to go back to the kitchen, Anara came out and handed her a huge skillet and a paper package of bacon. India accepted the items and returned to the fire. She stirred the porridge again, and then set about scattering coals over the hearth, building up the fire a bit. She laid out the bacon and placed the skillet over the bed of coals. As the skillet heated, India realized she had nothing to turn the bacon with, so she went to the kitchen to get a fork. Anara had squeezed the orange juice, so India took the pitchers with her to place on the table.

Once the bacon was cooked, India removed it from the skillet and placed the strips on a clean cloth to drain. Anara brought the egg mixture out and poured it onto the hot, greasy skillet.

'Here,' she said, handing India a spatula. 'The pancakes can't be left alone too long,' she explained as she went back to the kitchen.

'What about the biscuits?' India called after her.

'They'll be done in about five minutes; I'll take them out of the oven,' said Anara.

India nodded. 'Thanks,' she said. She began carefully pulling the cooked egg in from the sides of the skillet, allowing the liquid to run off the top of the mound and onto the hot surface to cook. Not quite scrambled, not quite an omelet, she thought, working slowly and methodically.

Anara brought a large pitcher of syrup out to the table and came to check the porridge. She nodded approvingly as she stirred. 'No lumps,' she said.

India shook her head. 'I hate lumpy cereal. Our cook taught me how to do that when I was a little girl.'

'She must have taught you quite a bit else,' said Anara, watching India moving the eggs carefully, so as not to scramble them.

'He,' India corrected. 'One of my father's men. He happened to be an excellent cook and a pretty lousy shot, so he was kept in the household to keep an eye on the servants. Make sure no one was stealing or spying, or anything like that,' she explained. 'I used to love spending the afternoons after school in the kitchen. He'd help me with my homework, then I'd help him with supper.'

'That sounds very pleasant,' said Anara.

'Yeah,' said India, smiling slightly at the memory. 'Do I have to eat in the dining room with the guests?' she asked. 'I'd much rather eat in the kitchen with you.'

'Believe it or not, it serves a purpose,' Anara smiled at her sympathetically. 'Otherwise, I would like to have the company.'

'What purpose is that?' asked India.

'That would be telling,' laughed Anara. 'You'll understand when it happens.'

'Aren't your pancakes burning or something?' India asked pointedly.

'I know it's frustrating,' said Anara sympathetically. 'But I can't prejudice your learning by telling you what to expect. You have to find your own way to the knowledge.' She was still laughing, however. 'It really won't even take that long. It will just seem like it is. It's worse than waiting for Christmas when you were a kid, because you don't have any idea what you're looking forward to.'

'It's a good thing, then?' asked India skeptically.

'Seems pretty hard to believe, given what you've been

through, but yes, it's a good thing,' Anara reassured her. 'But in the meantime, why don't you get those eggs onto a platter while I put the porridge in a bowl. Then we can ring the gong.'

India ate her meal in silence, sitting at the corner nearest the fireplace, and thought longingly of her luncheon-place at the kitchen table. As she glanced up, toward the kitchen door, her eye was caught by a young man she hadn't seen the evening before. He wasn't looking at her. He was trying to snag the plate of pancakes and was very intent on the task.

Something in India's mind wobbled and, for a moment, she was looking at a very different young man who had been reaching for a plate in just that manner . . . who knew how long ago now. Then the wobble righted itself and India was again looking at the man at the breakfast table.

He glanced at her and smiled before returning to what was apparently an ongoing conversation with the woman sitting next to him.

That shook India up more than the unbidden fragment of memory. How had he known she was staring at him? Why did his smile seem understanding? She wished she could ask Anara, but India had the feeling this came under the heading of unsafe to talk about right now. With a small gesture of frustration, India returned to her meal, eating mechanically and with no appetite.

She waited until everyone had left the table before clearing her place and finishing clearing the table. The kitchen was its usual mess after the meal, and it took India the better part of an hour to clean it up, even with Anara's help.

At last, India let the dishwater drain out of the sink. 'I'm ready for a nap,' she said ruefully.

Anara chuckled and handed India her cleaning equipment. 'We made a pretty good team this morning.'

India nodded, accepting the broom and bucket of cleaning fluid. 'It felt like we'd worked together before.' To her dismay, India could hear the hopeful question in her words.

'It did,' Anara agreed. 'But we never have. I'd remember it, even if you couldn't.'

'Well, it was a thought,' she said.

India left the kitchen in search of the first room to be cleaned, finding it much more easily than she had the day before. Cleaning also went more quickly than it had the previous day. There were no fewer rooms, and they were in no better condition, but India had developed a system for doing each room quickly and thoroughly. Knowing where to start and what needed to be done made the cleaning easier. India finished sweeping the last room well before lunchtime.

'Good job,' said Anara when India came back to the kitchen with her broom and bucket.

'You checked my work?' asked India as she put the broom back in the small closet behind the kitchen door. She took the bucket to the door and put it beside the bowl of eggshells.

'Of course,' said Anara as she set a bowl of yellowish powder on the counter. 'I think I'll teach you to make bread this morning.'

India nodded and went to the sink to wash her hands.

'Get the water running warm and we'll adjust the temperature for the yeast,' Anara instructed as India fiddled with the taps.

'It's lukewarm for yeast, isn't it?' asked India as she rinsed the soap off.

Anara came over and ran her hand under the faucet. 'This is perfect,' she said. She held the bowl under the water and filled it part-way. The yeast fizzed a little as it dissolved. 'This is a good sign,' said Anara, showing India the contents of the bowl. 'Now let's measure out the flour.'

Once the dough was kneaded and shaped into several huge rounds, Anara set them aside and covered them with clean, damp cloths.

'Now what?' asked India.

'Now we let them rise until they double in size,' said Anara. 'How about some lunch?'

India grinned. 'I'm starved,' she confirmed.

'And after lunch, we can put in a little time in the garden,' Anara suggested with a sidelong glance at India.

'What about the bread?'

'Oh, it will take a few hours to rise as much as it needs to. We can punch it back down after we finish in the garden, and after it's shaped into loaves you can go do a little more exploring before helping me with dinner.'

'Sounds like a plan,' said India, grinning. She pulled a small bowl of left-over soup out of the refrigerator and put it in a pot on the stove. 'What have we got to make sandwiches out of today?'

After lunch, India spent a couple of hours on her hands and knees pulling weeds from the rows of carrots and strawberries. Anara worked nearby on the rows of peas, tying the plants to the stakes, pulling weeds and checking for parasites.

'How long is the growing season here?' asked India as she rocked back on her heels and stretched her arms over her head to relieve the crick in her back.

'Oh, no longer than usual,' said Anara. She swiped at her temple with the back of one hand and looked over at India. 'Spring and summer, mostly. Some of the vegetables are still producing in early fall, and of course the apples ripen then. We have beautiful apples in the fall.'

'What do you do during winter? Are we going to have to can any of this?' asked India, gesturing at the acres of garden and orchard.

'Oh, no!' said Anara. 'This garden produces only enough for us to run the Inn and live on without buying from the outside. When these plants have finished producing, we will plow it under, mulch it with the compost, and let it lie fallow for the winter. There is another dimension and another garden. Right now, it's under several feet of snow, but I prepared it for winter so, once the snow melts, it'll be ready for planting.'

'How many dimensions are we hooked up to?' asked India. 'How many dimensions are there?'

'Only as many as are useful to us at the time,' said Anara. 'The dimensions are infinite, so we tend to stick to the ones closest to us because they're generally most like us and easiest to deal with. Get too far away and things get strange.'

'Aren't most of the places we're hooked up to just different locations in the same dimension?' India asked.

'Most of the places we use for our own purposes in running the Inn are located in the same dimension, yes,' said Anara.

India couldn't be sure, but she thought Anara sounded pleased.

Anara's face didn't change. 'Most of our guests, however, are from other dimensions, here on business with our own.'

'What sort of business?' India tried again.

'Still none of yours,' Anara smiled. 'When you finish that row, why don't we go clean up and punch some bread dough. Then you can check out another location in our dimension.'

India grinned and got back to work.

Punching down the bread dough turned out to be quite a bit more fun than India had expected. 'Just picture someone you're not happy with and take a good whack,' said Anara as she slammed her fist into a huge wad of dough.

India had been amazed at how large the smooth rounds of dough had become while they were working in the garden. Damp cloths which had covered the bowls were distended by the risen dough, but a good punch reduced it to its original size in no time, and India found she enjoyed it quite a lot. When the loaves had been shaped, she was vaguely disappointed that there was nothing more to do but bake them.

'Why don't you go and do some exploring,' Anara suggested once the bread was done. 'I won't need you for a couple of hours. I know that isn't much time, but as I recall, that was enough to get in trouble.'

'If you know someone to get in trouble with,' said India slowly. 'I don't know anyone here and it's kind of lonely. I mean except for working with you . . .' she finished lamely.

Anara laughed. 'I know exactly what you mean,' she said. 'And I'm sorry I can't help you, but I can point you in the right direction. Go through that door.' She pointed.

India looked, but of course there was no door, only a blank wall.

'Shouldn't I at least wash my hands?' she asked.

Anara laughed. 'You could do that,' she said. 'But dough doesn't really get them dirty like gardening does.'

'No, but I seem to recall getting flour on my face from baking when I helped Sal in the kitchen. Checking a mirror before I go might not be a bad idea.'

Anara chuckled. 'Suit yourself, but you look fine.'

'I look mostly the way I expected to,' said India, making a face. 'That's good enough for now.' She went to the odd little washroom and poured water into the bowl. The brackish mirror showed the same face she'd been looking at all her life; no flour smudges. India washed her hands and went back to the kitchen. 'Out that door?' she asked, pointing to the blank wall.

'Mmhmm,' said Anara as she picked up a very large cleaver.

'What are you going to do with that?' asked India.

'I thought we'd have chicken for dinner,' said Anara. She hefted the grip in her hand.

'You're going to *kill* them?' asked India incredulously.

'Plucking's the nasty part,' Anara replied.

'I think I'll go check out this new location,' said India, heading toward the blank wall with her hand outstretched. The doorknob didn't appear immediately, so she cast about in one direction then the other looking for it.

'To your left,' said Anara helpfully. 'Be back here in a couple of hours, okay?'

'How will I know when it's a couple of hours here?' India stopped in the doorway and looked back at the small woman.

'I'll call you,' Anara responded.

India laughed. 'Right. The chronometer keeps the same time in both locations?'

'If you'd rather,' said Anara.

India noticed the funny expression on Anara's face, but said nothing. 'I'll be back in two hours,' she said, walking out and shutting the door behind her.

She turned and studied the side of the cottage. The door was in the middle of a lean-to-like structure attached to a much larger building. Like the Inn, this building was only one story, but it was considerably bigger than the building she had just left.

Or, more specifically, it was much larger than the cottage in the woods that she had first approached the morning after her run-in with Mama. Setting off, India walked round the corner and down the side of the building. There were windows every few feet along the wall she walked beside, but she couldn't see into any of them. They weren't covered or blocked in any way that she could tell; she just couldn't see anything through them.

Giving up on getting a glimpse inside, India turned her attention to the area surrounding the building. She walked on a narrow gravel path through a pretty little garden that bordered a vast expanse of well-manicured lawn, the deepest velvety green India had ever seen. The lawn sloped down a gentle hill to a wrought-iron fence. Beyond the fence was a pale grey road and beyond that was a field that went on to the horizon, unbroken by trees. The sky was the kind of overcast grey that seems to make the colors beneath it that much more vivid.

The building she walked beside was freshly painted white. The windows were trimmed in black, and wrought-iron shutters stood open beside them. This Inn looked very wealthy and prosperous. The Inn in the woods looked much more casual and cosy.

Rounding the corner, India noticed the same phenomenon she had seen in the garden. The building didn't seem to be quite in phase with itself. When she focused on one side of the corner, it was clear. When she tried to focus on both sides of the corner, they didn't appear to quite meet.

On this side of the building, the lawn sloped down toward a large swimming pool with two diving boards, a cabana, and several tables and chairs on the cement deck. There was no one there, probably because of the grey sky and the cool breeze that stirred the trees growing around it. Ahead of her, India could see a rather dense forest curving just outside the wrought-iron fencing. The gravel path she was on continued around the building and the flower-bed followed it.

As she turned the next corner, India noticed the curving driveway leading up to the front door of the Inn. It wandered down the lawn to the base of the hill and left through a gate in the fence, joining the road not much further on. Since there didn't appear to be any more to explore on the outside of this unexpected building, India decided to follow the driveway and find out where the road went.

After half an hour of walking down the road to the right, India came on a small road-sign that announced 'Bishop 12'. She stood wondering for a moment '12 what?' before turning round and heading back to the Inn. She figured whatever unit of measure was used here, it wouldn't be minutes and she didn't have enough time to get to Bishop and back before Anara needed her to help with dinner.

The walk back didn't seem to take as long as the walk out, but her chronometer told India it had been about the same length of time. Since Anara had sent her here knowing

46

she wouldn't make it to Bishop and back in the time allotted, India decided either there was a town in the opposite direction that was much closer, and she'd had the misfortune of going in the wrong direction to explore, or Anara had the pool in mind as entertainment.

'Can't hurt to take a look,' India murmured to herself as she walked back up the long, curving driveway to the impressive building on the top of the hill.

The pool was a hundred feet long and fifty feet wide, and beautifully tiled in blues and greens with long, narrow, black tile lane-marks on the bottom. At the far end were the two diving boards. The pool was twelve feet deep. There were ladders on either side. At the shallow end, off to one side where India stood, a broad stair began above the water-line and continued out several feet into the four-foot depth in a semi-circle. From there it was only a couple of feet to the main body of the pool. India crouched down and stuck her hand in the water; it was warmer than the air by a couple of degrees. On a hot day it would feel very refreshing. Today it was too cool to really want to swim.

India stood up and decided to go explore the cabana. Several trees grew around it and azaleas had been trimmed into a hedge underneath the windows on either side of the Dutch door. A small flagstone path led from the pool deck, across a wide swath of tan-bark to the door. When India tried the knob, the door was unlocked.

As she stepped across the threshold, India was aware of leaving the dimension the pool was in. Just like the Inn at the top of the hill, what was inside the cabana had nothing to do with the outside. There was a low, round table in the middle of several chairs, and two couches just to her right, and a wet bar along the wall behind them. Beyond that were several changing rooms with louvred doors and benches inside. To her left was a large whirlpool bath, tiled in the same manner as the pool outside, and beyond that a cedar sauna. Against the back wall on this side of the room were shelves with stacks of clean bath-sheets.

India couldn't resist. She grabbed a towel and went to the spa. Shucking off her clothing, she set the timer and was in the churning water in moments. She checked her chrono: twenty minutes. With a sigh, she leaned back against the side and closed her eyes.

Something in her mind broke loose.

She stood on a vast, grey plane; a place that wasn't really a place. A man stood in front of her. Seen in a crowd, this man would never be remembered. He was exactly average; there was nothing remarkable about him. He didn't look menacing, but India was certain she feared him.

India gasped and sat up in the whirlpool. The image was gone. She searched her mind, but she couldn't find it anywhere. Shuddering, India climbed out of the water, toweled dry, and got dressed. She didn't care that she was going back to work early. India just knew she would feel safer around Anara. She left the cabana and ran back up the hill to the kitchen door.

'Well,' said Anara as India burst back into the room. 'You look like you've seen a ghost.'

India shook her head. 'I think this one is still alive,' she said. She told Anara what had happened.

'This sort of thing will happen from time to time,' Anara told her when she had finished. 'It will be pretty disturbing, but I don't think you need to be frightened by it.'

'But who was he?' India demanded. 'I *was* afraid of him.'

'Yes,' Anara confirmed. 'You *were* afraid. Anything you encounter when the blocks slip like this is something you've *already* handled. It may be knowledge *they* don't want you to know you have, but the knowledge can't harm you.'

'Are you sure?' asked India. She wanted very much to believe Anara; wanted to be reassured.

Anara chuckled. 'Why don't you get started cleaning those birds,' she suggested, pointing at a pile of chickens on the counter. 'Yes, I'm sure. Knowledge isn't dangerous, only how it can be used may be dangerous.'

India picked up the first carcass. 'You do a good job plucking,' she observed as she carried it to the sink.

'Do as good a job cleaning and we're in business,' said Anara.

India made a face at Anara over her shoulder and got to work. While India cleaned out the entrails and cut the chickens into pieces, Anara peeled and chopped the vegetables they had harvested that afternoon.

'Why does the exterior of the Inn look so different outside that door?' asked India, gesturing with her head, since she was up to her elbows in raw chicken parts.

Anara worked on in silence for so long that India began to wonder if she hadn't heard the question. 'Appearance has a lot to do with what you expect to see,' she said finally.

'That's not what I mean,' said India impatiently. 'The building that stands in the woods outside the front door seems to belong with the interior we work in. The building out that door' – again India gestured with her head – 'doesn't look like it would house a kitchen and common-room that are as simple and utilitarian as these.' She placed another chicken on its back on the cutting board and sliced into it with the long blade of her knife.

'Outside that door, this is a private residence in a very wealthy neighborhood,' Anara told her.

'Yes, but why?' India pressed. She scooped out the innards of the chicken and dropped them into a large bowl on the counter. Then she set about butchering the carcass.

'It suits our purpose,' said Anara. She finished slicing the potatoes into a bowl and began peeling the onions.

'How?' asked India, setting a drumstick on the counter with the other chicken pieces. One more chicken to go, she thought, slapping it onto the cutting board.

'There are things in Bishop that we need to keep our hand in,' said Anara slowly. She quartered an onion and tossed it into another bowl.

'Like what?' asked India as she finished scooping out the last chicken's guts and began parting it out on the counter.

Anara chuckled. 'It's nothing you need to concern yourself with,' she said, cutting up another onion. Her eyes were streaming tears, and she swiped her eyes against the shoulders of her blouse. 'Ought to keep your mouth shut when you slice these things,' she muttered.

India laughed. Her eyes were tearing too. 'Okay, fine: it's none of my business. Does anyone else use the pool or cabana?'

'The guests have it available to them,' Anara confirmed. 'But I've noticed that their work usually keeps them too busy to be able to enjoy them much. I don't have the chance to swim as much as I would like, but I often go down in the evening to use the whirlpool or sit in the sauna for a little while before going to bed.'

'Who mows the lawn and does the gardening there?' asked India, her curiosity getting the better of her.

'We employ a man to take care of that,' said Anara, smiling. 'Maintain appearances, you know. I doubt the neighbors ever check on these things, but the more complete the disguise, the more likely it is to be believed.'

India ferried the chicken pieces over to the sink and began washing them thoroughly. 'Is that the way it is in every dimension or location?' she asked.

Anara nodded. She covered the bowl of onions with a clean, damp cloth and pushed it aside. 'It would be dangerous for us to advertise our points of contact.'

India frowned. 'Why would it be dangerous? What do we do here besides run an Inn?'

'It's not just what we do,' Anara clarified. 'It's also who we are.'

India thought about that as she put the chicken into the huge kettle and filled it with water. She took a handful of each vegetable that Anara had cut up and added some salt, pepper, and a few bay leaves. Lugging the kettle out to the hearth, India hung it on the great iron arm and built up the fire beneath it. Returning to the kitchen, she asked, 'Who are we?'

'That's not a question I can answer for you,' said Anara. 'You have to find your own answers.'

India set the table and wondered why she had been sent here; wondered again why she felt so strongly that she wasn't really supposed to be here at all, in spite of the knowledge in her mind that contradicted this feeling. She had so many questions and so few answers.

The kettle bubbled and India stirred it. She tended the fire beneath it, spreading it out so the contents of the kettle wouldn't burn. She worked mechanically while her mind turned over her problems and their inconsistencies, wondering what she would eventually have to do about regaining her mind and independence.

'Why don't you go take a shower and change your clothes,' Anara suggested from the doorway of the kitchen.

India jumped at the sound of her voice. 'What?' she asked, turning round. 'Take a shower?' she repeated.

'And change for dinner,' Anara said with a small smile. 'By the time you're done, the chicken will be ready to come out.'

'Okay,' India nodded. She gave the kettle one last stir before going in search of her own doorknob.

'To your left,' Anara called from the kitchen.

India moved to her left and located the knob. 'Thanks,' she called as she pulled the door open and stepped inside.

As she stood under the water, letting it take all the day's work down the drain, India decided Anara's suggestion had been a good one. The brief time in the whirlpool had served more to upset her than to relax her. 'You've got to stop letting these memory jolts scare you so much,' she told her reflection as she combed the tangles from her hair.

Rummaging through the bureau, India discovered that Anara had washed all of her clothing and managed to remove all the bloodstains her ragged hands had caused while looking for the extra candle. 'See? You're in a safe place where people care about you,' she told herself as she pulled a tunic over her head and thrust her arms into the sleeves. 'Everything is going to be okay.'

But as she pulled the bedroom door shut behind her and moved toward the hearth to check on the chicken in the kettle, India had misgivings she didn't want to admit even to herself.

'Here's a platter to put the chicken on,' said Anara from the doorway to the kitchen.

'Thank you,' said India automatically, moving to get it, but Anara didn't let go immediately. India looked up and into Anara's eyes.

'We're doing what we can,' said the small woman as she released the platter.

India nodded. 'I just get so scared,' she whispered. Her fingers clutched convulsively on the edges of the platter. To her dismay she felt a lump growing in her throat and tears gathering around it.

Anara covered India's hands with her own and gave them a gentle squeeze. Then she turned and went back into the kitchen, leaving India alone with her thoughts as she fished out the pieces of chicken from the bottom of the kettle. She rebuilt the fire under the pot so the broth would reduce while she pulled the meat from the bones.

India and Anara worked in companionable silence. Only the sounds of knives cutting and chopping filled the air between them. India finished boning the chicken and took the meat back out to the kettle, adding it carefully to avoid splashing the hot broth on the hearth or herself. 'So if I were to walk in the opposite direction from Bishop, I wouldn't see anything more than what I saw on the way to Bishop?' asked India, returning to the kitchen. She set the cutting board on the edge of the sink and picked up the bowl of onions.

'Eventually you'd reach the city of Evanston,' said Anara. 'But it's considerably farther away from us than Bishop is.'

'And that sign,' India continued. '"Bishop 12". Twelve what?'

'Kilometers, of course,' Anara answered. 'That door leads to a location on Earth Prime.'

India went back to the common-room and added the onions to the soup. 'What about the rest of the doors?' she asked as she came back into the kitchen. She put the onion bowl on the cutting board beside the sink and reached for the carrots.

'That depends on where we've focused the threshold,' said Anara with a smile. 'And that depends on why we need a door in a particular location.'

'It changes often?' asked India. She smiled back at Anara.

'Often enough,' Anara replied. 'I left the barley soaking overnight, there on the counter.'

India picked up that bowl also and headed back to the cauldron on the hearth. First she put in the carrots, then she added the barley and gave the whole mess a thorough stirring with the huge wooden spoon.

'What sort of teaching do you do?' India changed the subject.

'I don't really do any teaching any more,' said Anara slowly. She didn't look at India, and she seemed to be measuring her words carefully. 'I used to do a lot of what Shannon does now.'

'Shannon?' asked India blankly. 'Is that someone I should know?'

'Not right now, no,' Anara said even more slowly.

India felt a small stab of pain in her heart with those words. 'Someone I used to know very well and who was important to me?' she asked.

Anara nodded, but said nothing.

As the tears welled up and threatened to overflow the

rims of India's lower lids, she suddenly squared her shoulders and threw back her head. 'Everything will be okay,' she said with determination. 'Everything is going to be fine.' She picked up the bowl of potatoes and went out to add them to the soup.

Anara watched her go and sighed quietly to herself, wondering.

When at last supper was over and the dishes had been washed and put away, India dried her hands on a dish-towel and leaned wearily against the sink.

Anara finished mopping the floor and put the mop and bucket back in the tiny broom closet. 'Would you like to go down to the cabana and take a sauna with me before you go to bed?' she asked.

'That sounds wonderful,' said India. She hung the dish-towel on its hook and pushed herself away from the sink.

'It *is* wonderful,' Anara agreed. 'One of the perks of working here.' She grinned. 'You've had a long, hard day, and tomorrow you'll feel it if you don't take care of yourself tonight.' She opened the door India had gone through that afternoon and India followed her out onto the well-kept gravel path down the vast expanse of manicured lawn.

Lights were on around the pool, creating the illusion of an oasis in the dark night, but when India glanced back at the Inn, expecting to see it lit as well, she was surprised to find the building in darkness. A light was on over the kitchen door, but the rest of the building was the same dark blank she had experienced that afternoon.

'You've done a lot of listening today,' Anara observed as they stretched out on the platforms in the sauna.

India adjusted the towel she had wrapped around herself and lay back on the second towel she had brought in as a pillow. 'Mmhmm,' she murmured as she closed her eyes and gave herself up to the penetrating heat.

'You've also asked a lot of questions,' Anara observed.

India chuckled. 'Mmhmm,' she agreed. 'But it's not safe to talk about them here either, is it?'

'No,' said Anara, sounding surprised. 'I wasn't going to talk about them. I just wanted to tell you that, believe it or not, your lessons started today. The first lesson is in listening to what is, and more importantly to what *isn't*, said. The second is in observation of everything around you.'

'Doesn't seem like much,' India said softly.

'It doesn't,' Anara agreed. 'But this "not much" task may take you weeks to complete, and you'll get frustrated in the interim. I just wanted to tell you in advance, so if you think I'm putting you off, you know up front: I can't tell you what you're listening for, or observing. These are things you have to figure out for yourself and it's going to take patience.'

'Okay,' said India.

They lay in silence for quite a while before Anara finally got up and blotted her face with the towel she had been using as a pillow. 'I think maybe a little time in the whirlpool now, and then I'm for bed.'

India sat up and got lethargically to her feet. 'I think I need a water-jet right in the small of my back,' she announced.

'That does sound good,' Anara smiled. 'We have a long day ahead of us tomorrow.'

India groaned and opened the sauna door. The comparatively cold air outside was bracing and she found herself suddenly wide awake.

'That will change the minute your head hits the pillow,' Anara reassured her.

They stayed in the whirlpool long enough to work out the day's kinks, then went back to the Inn and to bed. Anara was right: India was asleep almost as soon as she climbed into bed.

Chapter Three

India rose in the dark of early morning, stumbled through her shower, dressed slowly, and went to the kitchen for a cup of coffee.

Anara was already there. Breakfast was just started and the coffee was fresh and hot. 'I let you sleep in a little,' she said. 'I knew you were pretty tired after yesterday.'

Sleep in? India gaped to herself. She had no idea what time it was, but it wasn't even light yet! With a shake of her head, India went to fill the kettle and begin her morning chores.

By the time breakfast was ready, India was so hungry she snagged and ate her meal with fairly single-minded concentration. She paid little attention to the people around her.

They continued their silent conversations, not giving her a thought either. They gestured with utensils as if making points in conversation, but no sound accompanied the meal except the clicking of silverware against plates and bowls.

Once the food was gone, India sat back in her chair and watched until the last guests had left the table and gone off to wherever it was they went off to. They were an odd lot in appearance as well as behavior. They seemed costumed, rather than dressed, as if wearing uniforms, but no two were alike and there was no military suggestion about them. They were all of like age, only a few years older than her, and between them seemed to represent every race from several planetary groupings, but there were only about twenty of them, so she knew that was impossible.

Finally, she got up, cleared the rest of the table, and started washing the dishes.

'Our guests,' she began, as Anara took up the cloth to dry.

'Are on assignment and don't need us prying into their work when we should be doing ours,' said Anara, putting an end to that discussion.

India slipped into the routine of her chores, using only a small portion of her mind to actually perform the tasks. The greater part of her thoughts was taken up in probing the corners of her brain, hoping to find the blocks everyone was so concerned about. There didn't seem to be anything there out of the ordinary, which frustrated India no end. Everyone else could see and feel the blocks but her. If she couldn't find them, she couldn't hope to remove them.

Anara knew where they were, but couldn't, or wouldn't, do anything about them yet. What were they waiting for?

With a small shrug, India finished sweeping the last bedroom floor and went to the kitchen to put away her cleaning supplies and get started making lunch for herself and Anara.

Anara came in from the common-room just as India set two bowls of left-over stew on the table. Anara brought a fresh loaf of bread and sweet butter to the table with her and sat down.

'Why can't I feel the blocks?' India asked as she sat down opposite Anara. The window between them showed a cloudy day, but India knew now that had no bearing on the weather outside any given door in this odd place.

'You've been looking for them all morning,' Anara stated.

India was surprised that it hadn't been phrased as a question. 'Yes,' she said slowly. 'I couldn't find anything out of the ordinary. If I didn't know better, I'd say there was nothing wrong with me.'

'You've had a very professional job done on you,' said Anara.

She ate in silence for a while and India waited, watching

her face, hoping for a glimpse of anything that might help her get a handle on what she was doing here. Somehow, India knew it wasn't yet safe to talk about her presence here except in the most oblique terms.

'But whoever did it was either in a great hurry, or has a sore conscience about having to do it,' Anara said at last. 'For all the blocks are seamless, the overlaying memories that have been implanted are thin and shoddy.'

'What does that have to do with the blocks slipping?' India asked. Her stew was forgotten, and she still held a piece of bread she had meant to butter.

'If the memories were rich enough for you to believe them unquestioningly, they would help strengthen the barriers by preventing the kind of questioning you are currently engaging in,' said Anara, feeling slowly for the right way to phrase the explanation. 'Since you are able to see through what has been arbitrarily given to you, the barriers aren't as strong and won't continue to hold up over time.'

'I guess I just don't really see how artificial memories could affect a block one way or the other,' said India.

Anara sighed. 'You have a very strong mind. When it runs up against these inconsistencies, it begins immediately trying to root out the problem. Unfortunately, this is a bigger problem than most, and it keeps coming back even after we think we've dealt with it.'

'But . . .' India began.

'Enough!' laughed Anara. 'Eat your lunch. We've got a lot to do this afternoon in the garden, and if you want any time to explore or go for a swim before it's time to start supper, you'd better hop to.'

India heaved an exaggerated sigh and doused her bread in her stew. 'You just needed a slave,' she accused.

'Of course,' said Anara comfortably. 'This is all just an elaborate scheme to get cheap help.'

India laughed and dug into her lunch.

Working in the garden that afternoon was difficult for

India. The sun beat down hot on her back and arms. A huge straw hat protected her head and neck, but the warmth made her drowsy. A swim was beginning to sound more and more attractive. 'But what do I do about a bathing suit?' she asked suddenly.

Anara was across the garden, several hundred meters away, but she turned when India spoke as if she'd heard clearly. 'You'll find one in the bottom drawer of your bureau,' she said. 'It isn't elegant, or even very pretty, but it will fit and should suffice.'

India's jaw dropped open and she gaped across the acres at the small woman, whose face she couldn't even really see clearly. Anara hadn't shouted, or even raised her voice, but India had heard her clearly.

'As soon as you finish the strawberries, you can go change and get in a few laps.'

'How did you do that?' India gasped.

'If you fall asleep, I'll call you when it's time to come in,' Anara continued, ignoring the question. 'The faster you finish up here, the longer you'll have to yourself this afternoon.'

'How are you doing that?' India demanded.

'The same way you are,' said Anara.

'I'm not doing anything!' India protested.

'And yet I can hear you as clearly as you can hear me,' Anara chuckled.

'But that's impossible!'

'Okay.' Anara shrugged. She returned to her gardening, and no amount of cajoling on India's part would engage her in conversation again.

India finished weeding the strawberries and went back into the Inn to change.

The swim felt good. The sauna felt great. The whirlpool felt better. Lying in the sun on the edge of the pool, India fell asleep.

* * *

A pretty blonde girl stood in front of India in the middle of a large green field. The sun shone warm and insects buzzed in the tall grass around them.

'You can do it,' she said encouragingly.

India looked doubtfully at her. 'Why do I have the feeling it's not as easy as you say it is?'

'Because you never believe what I tell you the first time around,' Shannon laughed. 'Sometimes it takes you forever to figure out that I mean what I say.'

'Sometimes what you say makes no sense,' India countered. She eyed the object doubtfully.

'True enough,' Shannon said. Her blonde hair shone in the sunlight and her blue eyes sparkled at India. 'But I always mean what I say, and I've never lied to you, have I?'

India inclined her head in grudging assent.

'Then do it!' snapped Shannon, all patience gone from her voice.

India glared at the canister.

It winked out of sight.

'You see?' Shannon giggled, delighted. 'Where did it go?'

'How in hell should I know?' India demanded. 'You just said send it. You didn't say where.'

Shannon sighed. 'You've got to learn to control your temper if you're going to learn control of your craft.'

'I didn't choose this!' India yelled. She'd had just about enough. 'None of this is my fault. I refuse to accept responsibility.'

'Whether or not you accept responsibility, you are currently in this situation and under my tutelage,' said Shannon sternly. 'And you *will* learn to control your temper.'

'Or what?' asked India. 'You'll spank me?'

'Okay,' said Shannon. She reached out with her hand and India felt a swat on her butt.

'Oh, ow,' she said sarcastically.

An invisible hand tightened around her throat. 'Ow, indeed,' Shannon said softly. 'You're here for a reason, even if we don't know what it is. I want to find out. How about you?'

India nodded, eyes wide.

Shannon loosened her grip. 'Someone took your life from you. This is what should make you angry, not what I do to help you regain it.'

India nodded again. 'I'm sorry,' she whispered.

Shannon tilted her head toward India. 'Where did it go?' she asked again.

'My apartment,' India replied slowly. 'I think.'

'Bring it back,' Shannon instructed.

India closed her eyes and concentrated.

The canister appeared in front of them.

'Thank you,' said Shannon. Once more, she seemed a young girl who could pose no threat to anyone.

India shuddered and sat up. 'What?' she asked blankly.

India?

'Anara?' she asked.

It's time to come back to the Inn, Anara said.

'Where are you?' asked India stupidly. She sat on the edge of the pool rubbing her eyes. The sun was lower in the sky now, and the shadows from the trees were longer.

Where do you think? came the amused reply. *Come on. I need your help now, not in a while.*

'But how . . . ?' India began.

Now! said Anara.

'Coming,' India muttered as she scrambled to her feet and grabbed the towel she had been lying on. 'What should I do with my towel?' she asked, not really expecting an answer.

Bring it with you, Anara suggested. *Who do you think does the laundry for the pool?*

'You're spooky,' said India, heading up the cinder path toward the Inn.

*   *   *

India and Anara began the dinner preparations in their customary silence. India worked mainly in the common-room, tending the fire and the pots on the hearth. Anara worked in the kitchen. India set the table in between pokes and stirs.

'Can you remember anything at all?' Anara asked unexpectedly when India went to the kitchen for condiments.

'No,' said India automatically. She reached into the cupboard. 'Wait,' she corrected herself. 'I had a dream this afternoon at the pool. I dreamed about a blonde girl. She made me use my mind to move something; make it disappear. Then I brought it back.'

'You remember how to do this?' asked Anara.

India shook her head. 'Only that I did.'

'It will take time,' said Anara. She turned back to her work.

India gathered the condiments and returned to the common-room.

Time.

Time seemed to be something India couldn't count on any more. Time could be manipulated around her by snatching her from it and changing her memory of it. Time was the one thing she didn't *know* she had.

'What else did I know?' asked India, coming back into the kitchen for serving-platters.

'I'm afraid you'll have to rediscover that for yourself,' Anara said thoughtfully. 'I wish I could tell you more, but I really don't know the answer. Even Shannon doesn't know. Your blocks were so strong when you were working with her that she was only able to teach you a little bit. We have no idea if this means you have no other abilities beyond what she was able to teach you, or if you have abilities far beyond our capacity to instruct.'

'Can you even hazard a guess?' asked India.

'A guess,' Anara repeated. She stood silent for a long

moment. 'Yes. We figure you wouldn't have been put here if you had only a little more ability than you demonstrate or recall right now. Your skills would be of no use to anyone if that were the case. Abilities beyond ours we tend to doubt because they would most likely have manifested themselves in awkward and readily apparent ways during your adolescence. We don't rule this out, however, because there are cases on the records where the individual showed no sign of talent until much later in life. The slower these gifts are in developing, the more powerful they are when fully realized.'

'So you figure I'm more in the middle ground?' India prompted. 'Enough talent for this to have been considered worthwhile, but not enough to attract attention?'

'We hope so,' said Anara briefly. She returned to the salad she was making and began to tear lettuce into the bowl.

'What do you mean by that?' asked India, puzzled.

'When I say much later in life, I mean *much* later. People in their twelfth decade, sometimes even later than that, but almost never sooner.' Anara paused again for a moment, weighing her words carefully. 'If you were one of these late bloomers, then someone has used a criminal and extremely dangerous means of waking and developing your abilities.'

'How could they do that?' asked India.

Anara shrugged. 'It would take a tremendous amount of power. The last time it was tried, virtually every telepath they could find was used. They linked gifts and focused their combined energy on the subject, and it was still barely enough power to do the job. The poor woman they tried it on went immediately into Opening Sickness and everyone was so wiped out from waking her gift that no one had the reserves to protect her from the Disembodied. She went to them without question and never regained consciousness.'

India shuddered. 'At least that's not what happened to me,' she said.

'How do you know that?' asked Anara.

'What?' demanded India.

'We have no idea what happened to you. We only know what's happening now, so that's all we can work with. Now' – she handed India the salad bowl – 'go fill the platters and call our guests.'

That evening during supper India wasn't able to ignore the conversations she was excluded from. She tried to focus on her meal, but sounds she couldn't quite hear kept interrupting her concentration. When she looked up to see who might have spoken, no one was paying any attention to her at all. And still no one spoke out loud. Grimaces, laughter and gestures took place in silence.

India shuddered and tried to return to her thoughts, but that non-existent sound kept interrupting. It was a relief when the meal was at last over and the guests had returned to their rooms. India finished clearing the table and went to her customary position in front of the sink. She fell into the rhythm of washing dishes and emptied her mind of anything but her hands performing their task.

You still remember self-hypnosis? asked Anara from a great distance.

India was surprised that Anara's voice didn't intrude on her mental state. *Mmhmm,* India murmured.

Good, said Anara. *Come sit over here, but keep doing the dishes.*

India left the sink and walked over to the lunch table, but she left her hands at the sink to continue washing the dishes.

Since you're already here, we might as well have a lesson, Anara said, but she phrased it as a question.

I thought I heard sounds during dinner, said India. She felt light and dreamy, as if asleep. Talking in her sleep. *It kept coming and going, but I couldn't really find it. I guess it wasn't really there,* she concluded, sounding rather disappointed.

Maybe it was and you just aren't ready to hear it? asked Anara. *I bet if you keep trying, you'll find you can hear it someday.*

You've heard it? India asked, eagerly. *You know what I'm talking about?*

Anara nodded. *I've heard it. You'll hear it soon.*

How can you be sure? asked India.

Because you can hear me now, said Anara. *How about you get back to those dishes and I'll get a drying cloth.*

What about the lesson? India remembered.

We just had it, said Anara.

Really? Wow, that was easy, India said enthusiastically. *Much easier than Shannon's lessons.*

Oh, give it time, laughed Anara. *Now, come on.*

India swayed and came to with a start. She stood in front of the sink, and her legs had been locked in the same position much too long to allow for time sitting at the table by the window. Too many of the dishes had been washed and Anara had already put most of them away.

'What just happened here?' India asked uncertainly.

Anara was still laughing. 'Your first lesson with me. What did you think?'

'I think I need to sit down,' said India shakily.

'In a bit,' said Anara. 'We're almost done here. Then you can go back down for a swim if you want.'

'Will you go too?' asked India.

'Not tonight,' Anara said smugly. 'I have a date.'

'A date?' India echoed blankly. 'With whom?'

'A gentleman friend,' said Anara primly. Then she grinned. 'None of your damned business, kid.'

'Fine,' said India with a laugh. 'Have fun anyway!'

'I will,' said Anara as she put the last pan in the cupboard. 'Don't wait up.'

'I won't,' laughed India. 'But a soak in the whirlpool sounds like a fine idea. If your date has a friend, send him down.'

'You don't have a boyfriend?' Anara sounded surprised.

India shrugged noncommittally. 'No one special,' she admitted. 'At least, no one who would have waited through whatever's happening to me.'

Anara came over to India and squeezed her shoulders gently. 'We're here to help you,' she said softly.

India put her hands on Anara's. 'I know,' she whispered, tears thickening her voice. 'I just get so scared. None of this is what I would have chosen for myself.'

'So now you know how I feel.' Anara gave India's shoulders one last squeeze and let go.

India turned to face her. 'No. I don't know how you feel. I don't even know how I feel!'

'Frustrated?' Anara suggested.

'Yes,' said India. 'And angry.'

'Outraged?' Anara asked.

'How could one human being do this to another?' India demanded.

'Until we know who, we can't know why,' said Anara. 'And we can't know who until some more of those blocks have come down. Now, this isn't getting me ready for my date, or getting you into the whirlpool. Self-pity isn't going to answer our questions.'

'Self-pity?' raged India. 'I've had my life . . .'

'Yes, yes. We all know what happened,' Anara interrupted. 'That doesn't change the fact that until we know who did this to you, we can't do anything about it except try to help you regain your memory and learn to control the psi-powers you'll be redeveloping.'

'But I . . .' began India.

'I have a date to get ready for and you have a kitchen to finish cleaning,' said Anara pointedly.

'Yes, ma'am,' said India resentfully.

'Ma'am, indeed,' said Anara as she paused in the doorway. 'I'm doing all I can for you,' she said quietly.

'I know,' India whispered. 'I'm sorry.'

'Enjoy your whirlpool. I won't be too late.'

India nodded.

Anara left the kitchen and India returned to her clean-up.

He came for her that night in her sleep.

He entered her dreams like a thief, skirting the periphery of her mental images, remaining apart from them until she noticed he was there.

Seeing him was a backhand slap across her face, and probably showed in her expression, but he smiled and came to her confidently, arms opened to embrace her.

So, of course, she entered them and turned her face up for his kiss.

She hated herself for doing that, but she couldn't refuse him. She hated him for knowing her so well, but his lips on hers seemed to suck the will out of her. His arms, tight and low around her waist, held her up as much as against him. The smell of his skin was intoxicating, and the ground fell away from her feet as he kissed her deeply and insistently.

Her body responded to him unquestioningly, but her mind was a jumble of outrage and desire, hurt and need.

This isn't even happening, she told herself sternly. *I'm asleep and this is a dream.*

He chuckled low in his throat and reached up to where her hand was on his shoulder. *This is real,* he said softly, moving her hand down and placing it on his erection. *Oh, I've missed you,* he moaned, moving slowly against her hand.

You're the one who left, she reminded him in a small, hurt voice. She wanted to let go of him, push him away, certainly let go of his penis, but her body didn't respond to her commands. When she was with him, her body wasn't her own. She did exactly what he wanted her to do because, somehow, he always did exactly what she wanted him to do.

Everything except stay. How long had it been? She couldn't remember. She couldn't think. When in hell had they gotten naked? Then he touched her *there*.

You're wet, he said in a voice that sounded smug in her ears.

I know, she wailed. *I hate you!*

Laughing gently, he lowered her to the ground. *Are you comfortable?* he asked, kneeling between her legs and looking directly into her eyes.

Where are we? she asked. She was mesmerized by his eyes, so dark and bottomless she was afraid she'd fall in ... so she shifted her gaze and noticed that his penis loomed large and hard before her. Had he really been that big? she found herself wondering as her hand reached out to stroke it.

Oh, does it matter? he asked.

He lay down beside her and pulled her to him. As he entered her, the ground fell away from them and they made love suspended in mid-air, moving together unimpeded. The surreal quality of their surroundings seemed to heighten her response to him and telescope time until she was certain they had been making love for hours.

Why did you go? she asked him finally. The ground had reappeared when they finished and they lay for a long time silently in each other's arms.

I'm here now, he said.

And this is a wildly erotic dream, and since I don't know why you left I can't supply myself with an answer? she half asked, half told herself.

Did it feel like a dream? He sounded pleased with himself; as if he were asking, Was I that good?

It was *a dream,* she said. *This* is *a dream,* she clarified. *If I don't know where I am or how I got there, how on earth could you just show up?*

Think about it and let me know what you come up with, he said as he disengaged from her and stood up. *I have to go now, but I'll be coming back*. He started to walk off.

I hate you! she shouted after him. *I don't want you to come back!*

But he didn't turn round; he just kept walking.

She lay where she was and sobbed until the dream evaporated and she was asleep once more.

India sat at the breakfast table feeling emotionally drained and physically ill. Her dream of the night before was etched sharply in her mind, and she could still feel his touch on her skin, feel him inside her. Mostly she felt angry with herself for responding to him.

He'd never been particularly kind to her, and when he'd left the first time, she hadn't even known he wouldn't be back until several days had passed. Instead of resigning herself to his absence and writing off what was obviously a bad relationship, she had continued to replay scenes from their love-making in her mind.

'You have such tiny breasts,' he'd said on one particular occasion.

She lay in her bed and he lay beside her, propped up on one elbow, stroking her body with his other hand. 'All of me is tiny,' she pointed out rather defensively. She hated being small, looking young, constantly being mistaken for a child.

'Not your eyes,' he'd said, surprising her. 'And not your heart.' He'd kissed her and then . . .

India sat at the breakfast table, masochistically playing the scene over again in her mind, superimposing last night's dream over it and wondering what was wrong with her. She hadn't even noticed that the young man she'd seen during earlier meals had sat down next to her this morning; hadn't noticed that he was filling her plate for her as the platters and bowls were being passed. She wasn't even paying attention to the ebb and flow of conversation around her, since there was still no sound to impinge on her consciousness. She heard the voices, muffled in the distance, but paid no attention to them as she wallowed in her misery.

A hand closed gently on her shoulder, startling her. India looked up and saw the young man looking at her; saw the concern in his soft brown eyes. Who *was* he? she wondered. She smiled a timid smile at him, one that didn't touch her eyes, and started to turn away, but he stopped her. He cupped her chin between his fingers and thumb and turned her head toward him again. Smiling gently, he nodded toward her plate, indicating she should eat something.

'But . . .' she began.

He moved his thumb and put it over her mouth, stopping her voice. India glanced around the table guiltily, but no one else was paying any attention to them. *Why?* she wondered to herself.

You already know why. You just need to rediscover the answer, the young man told her, silent and smiling. *Now, eat your breakfast.*

Thank you, said India, shocked to her socks. The young man let go of her chin and turned his attention back to his own meal, leaving India with her own thoughts and several very big questions.

'Who is he?' she demanded of Anara as they were doing the dishes.

'Who?' asked Anara. Her own thoughts taken up with her date the night before, she was only marginally aware of India's distress.

'The guy at breakfast?' India clarified. 'He's smiled at me before, but he was always across the table from me. Today he was sitting beside me and he put food on my plate and talked to me inside my head.'

Anara laughed. 'I've done that and it never bothered you before.'

'Huh?'

Your wake-up calls? When I'm across the garden from you? When you were down at the pool the other day? I don't know why it took a young man at breakfast to break through that particular barrier for you, but I'm grateful it happened this quickly. You've been in denial mode for quite long enough, said Anara as she stacked a bunch of plates in the cupboard.

So, how was your date? asked India experimentally. She looked over her shoulder at Anara.

Anara turned to look at India, and grinned. *I think it's time for your next lesson.*

After the dishes were finished, they went out to the garden as usual, and Anara assigned India to tend the squashes before going over to the tiny cornfield at the far side of the acreage.

How are we going to conduct a lesson like this? asked India as she crouched in the wide furrow between the first and second rows of squash-mounds and began pulling weeds.

Distance is a relative thing with telepathy, but you need to practice, and we can do that while we work, said Anara as she reached the cornfield and set to work.

What do I need to practice for if I'm obviously doing it again? India wanted to know.

You'll be surprised at how tired you'll be when you finish practicing today, and how glad that young man made you eat your breakfast.

You never did tell me who he is, India pointed out.

Just a guest, said Anara mildly. *And apparently one who's taken an interest in you.*

You don't think he's . . .

No, said Anara, cutting off that line of speculation. *If he were one of them, do you think he'd be guesting here?*

But how can you be sure? We don't know who they are.

India cut a ripe squash from the vine and carried it over to the lawn behind the Inn.

Did he strike you as guilty of kidnapping and brainwashing you?

Well, no, said India thoughtfully as she went back to her weeding. *But I'm not sure my judgement is the greatest these days.*

Anara laughed. *Listen to what your heart says and you'll never go wrong. What does your heart tell you about this young man?*

India laughed too, but she didn't answer the question. *How are we going to go about finding the people who did this to me?*

I don't think we'll have to look too hard, said Anara. *I think they'll find us.*

India shuddered. *What if they do?*

We'll just have to be prepared.

Why doesn't that make me feel any safer? India asked dryly. There were only a few ripe squashes, so she mostly tossed weeds over the furrows onto the bare ground beyond them.

You're safer here than anywhere else right now, said Anara. *And your blocks are coming down faster and faster, even if it's only in your dreams.*

What do you know about that? India demanded, disconcerted.

Anara laughed gently, kindly. *You're an untrained telepath at this point, even though you've been trained before. Everything you think or dream is projected into the environment around you. Those of us who are sensitive to it can't help but receive your transmissions.*

Oh, said India in a very small voice.

Oh, indeed, laughed Anara. This time her laughter was unapologetic. *That was quite a dream you had last night. Henry and I got a little carried away on it ourselves.*

Well, that would explain why you were so goddamned

cheerful this morning, drawled India, trying to cover her embarrassment about the night before. She was even more embarrassed by some of the other things she had been thinking since she'd gotten to this odd place.

Don't worry, said Anara. *One of the things we'll be working on is how to control what you spew into the environment. For now, just remember that none of this is personal for any of us.*

Except you and Henry, said India. To her dismay, she blushed. At least she was all the way on the other side of the garden and Anara couldn't tell.

Of course I can. Anara was laughing hard by now.

Well, at least I'm a fine source of amusement! India was beyond indignant. She had been stripped of any sense of privacy she might have cherished and there was nothing she could do about it yet. *Do you think the young man from breakfast knows?* she asked timidly.

Everyone in a ten-dimension radius knows, Anara assured her.

Oh, gods! India wailed. *What am I going to do?*

Learn some control, Anara suggested blandly.

How am I going to do that?

Well, first of all, why don't you try picturing yourself surrounded by a barrier that can't be penetrated unless you want it to be. You've been using this method to prevent voices from coming in to you. Reverse it and prevent your voice from going out to other people when all you're doing is thinking about things. Save the barrier penetration for your real voice and the voices of people around you. Listen for the mental voices of our guests at the table, but concentrate on what they are saying, not how you feel or what you're thinking about. Anara paused for a long moment. *You have to become less self-centered.*

Self-centered? India gaped in disbelief.

Concerned about self, Anara clarified helpfully.

I am not self-centered, said India. She finished the squash in silence and moved on to the potatoes before Anara responded.

Not deliberately, no, Anara said at last. *But you have to admit that your current circumstances have caused all of us to concentrate on you pretty much to the exclusion of all else.* Your *problems,* your *mysterious pursuers. Who are you really in the infinite scheme of things? Of course, we've let it happen, because it was necessary for you to maintain ego integrity through this, but you have to admit that sharing erotic dreams with everyone in the area isn't what you really want to be doing, yes?*

India sighed. *The barrier you described; it works?*

As a start, Anara agreed. *There are other, more sophisticated methods you'll learn as your concentration increases and your talent reasserts itself.*

Promise? India asked. She wasn't pleased to hear the wobble in her voice.

I promise, said Anara gently.

India could hear the smile in her voice, but she couldn't bring herself to resent it.

Why don't you go for a swim when you finish up here, suggested Anara. *There is someone at the pool waiting for you.*

The young man? India asked hopefully, half seeing the picture in Anara's mind.

His name is Peter.

India hurried through the rest of the squash, hoping Peter wouldn't leave before she finished and got to the pool. Finally reaching the end of the last row, India stood up, brushed the dirt from her knees with the dirt on her palms, and ran back to the Inn to change. She wished she had a nicer bathing suit, but it couldn't be helped, so she pulled it on and glanced at herself in the mirror over her bureau. Her eyes sparkled back at her in a rather dragonish way from a very dirty face. 'Oh, bother,' she murmured, running into the bathroom to splash her face with cold water.

Feeling at last presentable, India left her room and went down to the pool.

Peter looked up and smiled as India approached. 'They keep you working pretty hard around here?'

'You spoke?' India asked, half coy, half genuinely surprised.

'It's allowed,' he admitted. 'Just not often done. You've been working hard all morning, though, and I remember what it was like for me when I was just getting a handle on the telepathy. An hour of practice and you're bushed.'

'Evidently I'm relearning,' India admitted. 'But it doesn't feel like that.' She dropped into the chair next to his and sighed. 'It feels like I've never done any of this before.'

'It's tough,' he agreed. He sat back and closed his eyes against the sun.

India studied him through squinted eyes. His hair was dark brown, wavy and longish, falling away from his face, which was nicely tanned with regular features. He was handsome, but in a quiet way. His good looks didn't reach out and grab you from across the room, just settled in and made you feel good about looking at him, she decided. Most of it was in his eyes, which were closed right now. They reflected a gentle soul, and India found herself immensely attracted to that. Especially given my current record, she thought wryly to herself.

'It can't be that bad,' said Peter. He didn't sit up or even open his eyes.

'Oh, gods!' India wailed. 'How am I going to learn not to dump all this garbage all over the place?'

'First of all, stop worrying about it,' Peter suggested. 'By the way, I think you're very pretty, too.'

'Yeah, but the whole civilized world isn't aware of it, are they?'

Peter laughed and sat up. He turned to look India in the eyes. 'Who was that guy in your dream last night?'

India flushed hot red and looked away.

'He was a fool to let you go,' he said intensely.

India looked back into his eyes, amazed. 'Who *are* you?' she asked.

'Just a guy,' Peter responded glibly.

'I'm sorry,' India apologized immediately. 'I keep forgetting I'm not supposed to ask that.' She looked away again miserably.

'No, I'm sorry,' Peter said. 'I didn't mean to put you off. I just meant, I'm no one special. I'm just a guy sitting here by the pool talking to you.'

India reached out and gave his hand a squeeze. 'You're special enough to me. You're the only person who's been kind to me with the exception of Anara, and she has to be because she's my teacher.'

Peter smiled and squeezed her hand back. 'Let's go for a swim,' he said, changing the subject completely. 'You must be pretty hot after all that work this morning.'

India grinned. 'You talked me into it.'

The cool water felt wonderful, but India was feeling a lot better about having someone to talk to who was completely unrelated to her current situation. The subjects of kidnapping and brainwashing never even came up. She and Peter paddled around in the pool, soaked in the whirlpool, and sat in the cabana drinking a mixture of iced tea and lemonade. Mostly they flirted with each other, laughed at each other's stupid jokes, and enjoyed each other's company. India was reluctant to break the spell when Anara called her back to work, but she knew she would see Peter again at supper, so she went back to the kitchen without complaint.

'Well,' said Anara, looking at India as she came back through the door. 'You look much better than you did this morning.'

India grinned. 'I'll go change and be back in a minute,' she said as she swept through the kitchen and out into the common-room. Then she popped her head back round the door for a moment. 'I feel great,' she announced, and disappeared round the corner again.

Marinda was waiting for her that night.

It felt like she had only just closed her eyes. Her head hadn't even warmed the pillow and she was caught in another dream.

Where have you been? Marinda towered over India. She stood almost six feet tall and always wore spiked heels. *When you didn't show up last night like usual, we got worried.*

Well, I'm here now, said India defensively.

Yeah, but you're not even dressed. Are you okay? Marinda frowned and fussed with her bright pink wig, pulling it further down on her high forehead.

I just didn't feel like hooking last night.

What about tonight? asked Marinda. *You gotta eat, you know.*

I know, but a night or two off won't kill me, India responded. *What are you doing here?*

Marinda gave a short, high bark of laughter. *Well, honey, what do you think?* She snapped her pink suspender against her left breast and wiggled her ass. *I thought I'd do a little shopping.*

No, I mean here in my dream.

If this is your idea of a dream, honey, I feel sorry for you, said Marinda. *Hey, baby! You want a date?* she called to a man on the other side of the street.

India suddenly noticed that she was on 'her corner'. It had been raining, and the sky was still a dull, heavy grey, made pinkish with the reflected lights of the city. The night security gates had been pulled across the shop windows, making the block look like a row of prison cells, but neon lights glared and blinked all around her, shining on the glass and the wet pavement, a garish, demented Christmas display. *What am I doing here?* she asked.

77

Marinda laughed again. *It sure ain't working,* she said, surveying India from head to toe. *You look almost wholesome. Are you going for the innocent schoolgirl look tonight? Older men sometimes faze on that, but you picked the wrong night for it.*

Wrong night? asked India stupidly. She looked around at the people on the street; mostly male, young, single.

Marinda put her hands on either side of India's face and turned it up toward her own. *Honey, you sure you're okay? No one gave you a roll?* Her hands moved to feel India's skull, checking her forehead for fever.

I'm okay, she said impatiently, pulling away from Marinda's ministrations. *I just don't know why I'm here.*

Same reason as the rest of us, I expect, said Marinda bitterly. *Make a buck and try not to get rolled. That's what we always said. Hey, Carol!* she interrupted herself. *Come over here a sec.*

India, where were you last night? demanded Carol, coming over from where she had been leaning against a parked car. *That guy you went with last week was here again asking for you. You remember, the one who kept saying how he never does girls like us? I asked if I would do, but he insisted on waiting for you, only you never showed up.* Carol was wearing her own hair, but that was about it. Her entire body had been redone in a chop-shop; lifted, stretched, padded, tucked and sucked. She looked gorgeous, but fragile, like if you touched her she'd fall apart. It often worked to her advantage, because guys thought they could use her and then roll her, but she was tough and strong. She got more money that way, because she'd empty their wallet after she beat them up. Of course, she didn't have many repeat customers, but she was so beautiful, she never had trouble finding new ones. India wondered what had happened to make Carol that way, but the girls had a policy: you *never* talked about who you had been before you hit the streets. Hooking was how you survived, not who you were.

Did he say if he would come back? India asked. There was a strange feeling of déjà vu about this whole scene. She knew the answer, knew that he would be back, knew that he would change the course of her life, but couldn't say how she knew all this. The scene was so vivid, India had forgotten she was dreaming.

No, honey. He didn't say and I didn't ask. I got my own living to make, and a guy came by to tap me just then, so I split.

He waited a long time, supplied Marinda. *But he didn't want to talk with the rest of us, so we just left him alone. So you working tonight or what?*

I guess, sighed India. She took off her coat and surveyed what she was wearing. Not exactly working clothes, so she stripped off her skirt and blouse, leaving on her opaque black leggings, high heels, and a black lace bra. *Better?* she grinned up at Carol and Marinda.

Just so long as you're okay, they said.

India smiled at them. *I'm okay.* She watched them wander back down the street in search of tricks before turning away to drum up her own business. She stuffed her clothing into her oversized shoulder bag and fished around for her compact mirror to see what needed to be done about her hair and face.

She stopped under a street light and effected repairs before getting to work. It wasn't long before he showed up, just as she'd known he would. Driving slowly, looking for her, window rolled only halfway down.

Girl, it's your lucky night! called Marinda as she saw Mr Standish drive by.

India grinned. *You have no idea!* she called back as the car stopped in front of her. This guy paid *well*, and didn't make kinky requests. Still, she approached the car with trepidation. She was beyond this now! She had moved past this! This wasn't how she made her living any more.

She opened the door slowly and climbed in, still not believing she was back here doing this.

Peter sat behind the wheel.

India gaped at him, recognizing that he didn't belong here even before placing his face. *What are* you *doing here?* she stammered finally.

You aren't this girl any more, he said. *Come back to the Inn.* He reached out and took her hand. *You're dreaming.*

Oh, yeah, said India, finally understanding the feeling of déjà vu. *But what about . . .*

They belong in the dream, Peter said. *They'll still be here if you ever need them.*

Okay, said India. She allowed Peter to drive her down the street and out of her dream. *Thank you,* she murmured as he tucked her back into her own bed.

Sleep well, he said, kissing her on the forehead.

For the rest of the night she slept deeply and dreamlessly.

India awoke feeling muzzy and slightly embarrassed, as though she had done something she needed to apologize for. 'This is ridiculous,' she told herself as she climbed out of bed and stood for a moment, getting her bearings. 'I didn't have anything to drink last night, so I'm not hungover.' She stumbled into the bathroom and examined her face in the mirror over the sink. Nothing was apparently wrong, so she stripped off her tee-shirt and panties and climbed into the shower. Hot water was her favorite cure-all. Hot water and lots of soap, but as the steam billowed upward, the scent of the soap hit her nostrils and triggered the same fragment of memory she'd been unable to grasp that first morning here.

India staggered and fell against the door. Losing her balance, she went over backward and hit her head on the faucet. She landed hard on the floor of the shower, but she retained the shred of memory. The block was down now and she could see the tiny room; the cot and chair, no windows and only the one door. Dim light came from no particular source and didn't do much to push back the darkness. A man sat on the chair, but she couldn't make out his features. A girl lay on the cot and India knew it was herself huddled under the thin blanket. The blanket smelled of soap. The same smell as the soap she was using here in the shower.

Then the realization hit her. This was one of the men who had done this to her. She strained against the darkness to see his face, but was unable to distinguish his features. She couldn't even be sure how big he was because he was dressed in dark clothing. It was impossible to determine where he left off in the dim light. Similarly, there were no salient features in the room. Nothing hung on the walls, there was no furniture besides the chair and cot; no window, no view, nothing to place where this room might be located. She had no way of knowing what was beyond the door.

Who are you? she asked the image. She didn't expect a response, and she wasn't disappointed. Slowly, the image faded. With a sigh, India shook her head to clear it and stood up. There was a small lump forming on the back of her head that stung a little as she washed her hair, but except for a few bruises she was uninjured by her fall. She had no idea how long she had sat on the floor of the shower, so she hurried to finish washing and get dressed.

Are you okay? Anara asked from the kitchen.

Yeah, did you catch that image? India asked back, unconsciously responding telepathically as she tucked in her shirt and buttoned her pants. *I just wish there were more information behind the barrier.*

It's a start, said Anara. *I'm just glad you didn't get hurt in the fall.*

You're just glad I can still help with breakfast and get the rooms cleaned and the gardening done, India shot back with joking overtones. She left her bedroom and came out into the common-room. *Was there enough information for you to try and find out who that guy was?*

No. We're just going to have to give it time. I know that's not a very popular suggestion right now, but it's the best I can do, said Anara.

India sighed. *So what do I do in the meantime?*

How about you get the porridge started?

Ma'am, yes, ma'am, said India as she took the kettle from the spider-arm in the fireplace and went to the kitchen to fill it with water.

Oh! Anara pretended pain. *Please*, never *call me ma'am!*

India grinned. *Shot to the heart?*

A mortal wounding. Now get to work.

During breakfast, India finally heard some of the conversations taking place between the guests. The distant voices had grown close enough that she could actually hear words. Or, more specifically, she told herself, she heard what the guests didn't mind her hearing. Some of the conversations were obviously taking place between a guest and someone not present in the room. These were damped and she couldn't hear a thing, but some of the more general breakfast talk between the guests she could finally understand. She didn't participate, but it made her feel less left out to be able to listen.

Peter sat beside her again and insisted she eat, even though she insisted she wasn't hungry. *You work hard around here. You have to keep your strength up.*

India grumbled good-naturedly, but she ate everything on her plate to please him. *Will this give me the strength of ten men?* she asked.

Ten women, maybe, he smiled back at her. *I have a lot of work to do this morning, too, but maybe I'll see you at the pool this afternoon?*

That would be nice, India agreed.

In spite of her hot shower cure-all, India felt as if she were at half-speed. The rooms didn't really take her much longer than usual to finish, but by the time she and Anara sat down to lunch, she felt exhausted. She ate her sandwich mechanically and spooned her soup, unaware of what she was eating.

'Would you prefer not to work in the garden?' Anara asked, breaking through India's preoccupation.

'Huh?'

'You could take a nap instead,' Anara suggested. 'You look a little the worse for your shower this morning.'

'I don't know,' said India slowly. 'I woke up feeling a little hung-over, even before the shower. I think maybe spending some time in the garden will bake this thing out of me, if it's a bug of some kind.'

'Well, you don't have to if you don't feel up to it,' said Anara. She stood up to clear her plate. 'Maybe we won't have a lesson. That'll make it a bit less taxing.'

'I'm okay. This'll pass,' said India with more confidence than she felt. She cleared her place and they quickly washed the dishes.

India worked mechanically on the rows of melons, playing the scene over and over in her mind, wondering if there was any detail she had missed that might provide a clue. She lifted the long tendrils back in order to pull weeds and dead vines out of the dirt, her eyes turned inward to the small, dark room, and the man on the chair. None of the fruit was ripe enough to pick yet, but she wouldn't have noticed if it was. It was a surprise when she came at last to the end of the final row. Her hands ran out of things to do and went to her mind for instruction. Her mind was still focused on the man in the chair and only reluctantly came back to the garden behind the Inn.

Why don't you go to the pool? Anara suggested from a distance.

India jumped. Turning slowly to locate Anara, she became aware of her surroundings. *Don't you want me to pick blueberries?*

Another day won't hurt them. Anara waved a dismissive hand. *Go rest for a while before dinner. You need it. Besides, Peter is waiting for you.*

India smiled and nodded. She left the garden and went in to change.

'I dreamed about you last night,' said India. She lay on a chaise, soaking in the afternoon sun and enjoying the luxury of doing nothing at all.

'I know,' said Peter quietly.

'How could you possibly know?' India rolled toward where he lay and opened one eye to squint at him. 'I thought the barrier Anara taught me would hold even in my sleep.' She stopped for a moment, embarrassed. 'I was broadcasting, wasn't I?'

'No.' Peter yawned and sat up. 'I was there.'

'But it was a dream!'

'It was another block coming down,' he corrected. 'You needed help to break out of it. You got dragged in too quickly.'

'What do you know about this?' she demanded, sitting up as well. 'Did I broadcast the whole thing before Anara taught me to shield myself? Does everyone know?'

'No, everyone does not know. You were directing a pretty tightly focused call straight at me.' He paused for a moment and rubbed his eyes with the heels of his palms. 'I guess subconsciously you knew you were getting into trouble and you trusted me enough to ask me for help.'

'So you know?' India asked quietly.

'That you used to be a whore?' he asked bluntly. 'You did what you had to in order to survive. You don't do it any more, so you must have found a better way.'

'Yeah,' sighed India, thinking about it. 'But I still wound up getting rolled.'

'Yeah, well.' Peter looked at her, appraisingly.

'Indeed,' India agreed.

84

Peter laughed. 'You feeling better?'

India thought for a moment. 'I always feel better when I talk to you.'

'Good.' Peter stood up and stretched. 'Feel like another swim?'

India shook her head. 'Anara's going to call me in about two minutes and I feel so warm and sleepy . . . Hey! Put me down! No! I don't want to get wet . . .' She hit the water in a modified cannonball, with a huge splash and a shrieked protest. As she surfaced, another huge splash rocked her.

Peter came up grinning. 'You can't go to work half asleep. You'll burn the stew.'

'I'll burn your butt,' said India, and she dove under the water and grabbed for his suit.

India!

Damn. *Coming, Anara!* she called. 'Saved by the bell,' she told Peter when they surfaced. 'But just remember: I owe you big-time, so when you least expect it, expect it.' India swam to the edge of the pool and pulled herself up and out in one smooth motion. She scooped up her towel and dried herself off as she walked back up the hill to the Inn.

'Have you gotten any more insights into the image you had this morning in the shower?' Anara asked as India was passing through the kitchen to go change out of her wet suit.

India shook her head. 'I just can't see enough,' she said. 'I think the real meaning is buried much deeper, to keep it safe from me. It seems to be the stuff that's more minor that they didn't bother to cover very well.'

'How are you feeling?' Anara changed the subject.

India shrugged. 'Okay, I guess. Up to about three-quarters speed. I don't think it's a cold, though. I'm probably just tired today. I'll go to bed early tonight and I should be fine tomorrow.'

Chapter Four

The next morning, India woke slowly. Sunlight pressed against closed curtains, brightening her room only marginally. As she turned toward the windows, she began feeling slightly dizzy. When she shook her head to clear it, she noticed a dull throb in her temples, behind her eyes, and in the back of her neck. It had no particular center and it made her head feel stuffed with cotton. She rubbed at the grit in her eyes, but the pressure stabbed at the backs of her sockets. She gasped at the pain, setting off popping, flaming fireworks along her jaws and throat. Her inner ears burned in the aftermath.

'Oh,' she groaned. Her voice echoed loudly in her head. She pressed her hands against her cheeks and felt the heat of her face. What's wrong with me? she wondered. She tried to think of what she might have come down with, and where she might have picked it up, but the thoughts wouldn't stay in her mind.

There seemed to be a crowd in there with her. There was no sound, but somehow India knew she wasn't alone. She blinked myopically, but couldn't keep her eyes open long enough to actually see anything. Moving her head again seemed an unwise thing to do, under the circumstances. Why did she feel so awful?

Then the voices became audible.

At first, India was too involved with her discomfort to notice the change, but gradually they became loud enough to cut into her misery. She couldn't distinguish one from another. There were too many of them.

This isn't one I've heard before.

Where is she?
Is this the tiny bit? Is that all?

They were coming from all sides. At least sides as she perceived them in her mind. She was at the center of a slowly shrinking sphere. Emotions contrasted with voices; even though India couldn't understand words or thoughts, she understood the emotional content which the voices directed at her. There was nowhere she could go to escape them. Even if she had not been physically ill, she couldn't have warded them off. There is no physical protection from an attack inside the mind.

Anara? India's voice sounded small against the ever-increasing din of the intruders. *Peter?* She didn't hold out any hope of being heard.

Anara? Can you hear me? India managed to put a bit more force into her call for help.

Laughter echoed in volleys across her mind, trying to drown out her voice. The others were growing steadily closer. India could feel them now as a tangible presence in her head. They pressed around her, shutting off her contact with herself.

Leave me alone! she shrieked at them. The laughter grew louder. The volume of the voices increased. India could only understand their thoughts in snatches here and there. What she heard terrified her.

She's by herself!
So young! This will be easy.

Greed and joy were the emotional content of these thoughts. They were happy she was unprotected. India had no way to defend herself. She was vulnerable to their attack.

What do you want me for? she cried in terror.

They are the Disembodied, said a quiet voice beside her.

Anara? India gasped. She had not felt the small woman's thoughts enter her mind; was surprised to find her so close in the middle of the shrinking sphere. *Who are they? What do they want?*

The Disembodied, Anara repeated. *They are the lost souls. They have gone past the point of reclamation. They no longer exist on the physical plane. They want to take your soul from you.*

India shuddered violently. She felt a vague physical reaction, but she was oddly detached from actual awareness of her body. She knew she was still feeling really rotten, but she wasn't affected by it any more.

What will I do? India wailed.

First of all, calm down, Anara instructed. *It's my job to see they don't succeed. We'll worry about the rest of it after we stave off this advance.*

Will they come again? asked India.

They're never far, Anara replied. *Now concentrate. Form a barrier around us that they can't penetrate. Build it of anything you can think of that you know will make us safe from them. It must be completely impermeable.*

With a frantic nod, India began setting up her barrier. It was difficult to imagine something into being. India had never been particularly creative and this was a stretch for her.

Not a brick at a time! said Anara impatiently. *This isn't the three little pigs. The Disembodied will be here before you're half done. See the barrier as done. Picture it completed and it will be.*

Can't you show me? India pleaded. *Can't you just do it for me? I'm not sure what you want me to build.*

No, Anara said gently. *No one can do this for you. Just picture a place where you feel safe and imagine we are in it. Lock the Disembodied outside. Seal all the entrances.*

The voices were much closer now. India could feel them pressing around her. They sent off waves of emotion that she found difficult not to give in to. She thought about where she felt safe.

Her apartment.

It was small, all she could afford really, but entirely her own. Paid for with her own money, which she earned working as a secretary for a relatively minor planetary official in the Orion sector. It was the first constructive thing she had ever done entirely on her own. It didn't have the stink of her father's money, and no one had died so she could have it. She treasured that apartment and wondered where she was now in relation to it; wondered if she would ever see it again.

Shutting her ears to the discordant clamor of voices in her mind, India pictured the small living room in her apartment. The pale, sea-foam green sofa against the wall with the teak-wood table and Dresden china lamp beside it, the VidCon opposite. On the hardwood floor between was the oriental rug she had saved up for two years to buy. A low, glass-topped table stood on it, and a deep, overstuffed chair that matched the couch. Walls of off-white with prints of impressionist art. The window screens were set for spring meadows with woods in the background. Very old-fashioned and antique, but India liked it better than the sterile, functional environments preferred by her friends.

Where were her friends now, she wondered. Were they worried about her? Or had whoever had done this to her also provided a convenient excuse to discourage curiosity?

What a lovely room, Anara exclaimed.

The sound of her voice brought India back to herself and an awareness of her surroundings. She had managed a very neat reproduction of her home. A quick glance revealed the doors leading to kitchen, bedroom and building hallway. Beyond that she knew was outside, but she had sealed the door. No one could come in; neither could anyone leave. There was no other way in or out of that small apartment.

The voices, India noticed, were gone. *Are we safe?* she asked.

You tell me, Anara replied.

India nodded slowly, walked over to the couch, and slumped down on it. *So, where's my body, then? Am I safe?*

Still in bed, said Anara. She sat down in the chair. *It would be a good idea if you stayed there for the next few days while you get over the Opening Sickness.*

Opening Sickness? Is that what this is? asked India, testing the words on her tongue.

Your mind has just re-opened to the other senses you will develop.

Re-opened? India echoed.

Another one of your blocks has come down, Anara explained. *It concealed most of your other senses. I think all this telepathy practice acted as a catalyst. It takes a while for the body to adjust to the shock. Most physical symptoms originate in the brain. That's why you have a headache and sore throat. When they come in a rush like this, it's painful, but it may be easier than the first time.*

India grimaced. *The first time was worse?*

Anara smiled sympathetically. *I can still feel it when I think about it*, she said. *I try not to think about it very often.*

I bet, said India dryly. *If I have to stay in bed, should I stay in this room, as well?*

Only if you want to, though I can't imagine you'd be very comfortable in your conscious state right now.

I'm not conscious? India was surprised to hear that. She had assumed that as long as she was aware of what she was doing, she was conscious.

You aren't exactly asleep, but you're mostly unaware of your physical existence. You can do some pretty amazing things in an alpha meditation. Eventually your lessons will be done here, but we'll have specific tasks, Anara told her.

When do we begin those? India asked again.

When your mind and body have meshed again, said

Anara. *Until then, there isn't much point; no energy to draw on.*

Do you have some time? Perhaps we can discuss what's going on now? India suggested.

I only know a little, Anara admitted. *Maybe we can compare notes and see if it adds up to anything.*

Swell, said India. She took a deep breath. *Suppose you go first. Most of what I know, I've already told you.*

They watched each other rather expectantly for several moments. Then India sighed.

I really don't have much to add, she said tiredly. *I 'came to' on the mountain in the middle of the night as I was going over the edge of the cliff. I keep having flashes of memory that contradict what my mind tells me I should remember. I have no idea why I'm here. I can't even tell you why I haven't made any effort to leave. My memories of where I was before I came here are sketchy, and I remember my home, my job, and my childhood only in flashes.* She sat back and studied Anara's face for reaction.

Anara sat quietly for several minutes longer. Then she closed her eyes and rubbed the bridge of her nose with her index finger and thumb.

I realize none of this makes sense, she began. *You were on a reservation of sorts. It's a place where people's minds are trained in the use of their other senses, those beyond the first five. There are a few such places scattered among the known planets, but they're largely unknown and the concept is scoffed at by nearly everyone. We try to maintain a low profile to protect ourselves. Mostly we're patronized by rich crackpots who fancy themselves gifted, but on occasion someone like you turns up who has a real talent.*

India looked startled, and somewhat skeptical, but she said nothing.

You were there for almost a year, Anara continued.

India surged to her feet, mouth gaping open. *What?* she demanded, incredulous. *What's the date today?*

Anara told her.

I've missed two birthdays! India fell back onto the couch, staring at Anara and feeling the tears well up in her eyes. *I thought I was still twenty-five. It's been just over a year and I'm twenty-seven!*

Anara held up a placating hand. *You haven't become an old lady. I'm telling you what I know. The teachers in the Level One Hostel spent most of that time trying to break down the barriers in your mind, but they didn't succeed. They were able to teach you a great deal of theoretical information, but the barriers prevented you from actually completing much of the practical-application work.*

India slumped back down on the couch, and stared at Anara silently.

Finally, Anara continued, *the decision was made that nothing more could be done for you there. The night before you were to be sent here, you disappeared. They had no way of tracing you, and no idea where you might have gone. Judging from the barriers, you were not there voluntarily, but they hadn't been able to find out who was responsible for you. Every avenue of information was completely sealed off.*

India sat forward, forgetting to glower. *Did they find anything out after I disappeared?*

Anara shook her head. *They were going to send you to me anyway, but when you showed up on my doorstep, everyone was surprised. We hadn't expected to see you again.*

That explains the joyous greeting, said India wryly.

With a shrug, Anara said, *I was shocked by your appearance. You were a mess. I didn't want to frighten you by making too big a deal of it. You had been told about the journey here, to prepare you for it, but to get here, you had to cross time and space. This 'hostel' is a house between dimensions. There is no conventional way to get here.*

Then how . . . India began.

Anara shrugged again. *But you made it to me, so I will have to teach you what I am able, and what you can learn. We will still have those blocks to contend with. They seem to have been strengthened during your week-long absence, and the memories of your stay at the Level One Hostel have been largely blocked off also.*

'Have' to teach me? India was sensitive to the implications of Anara's word choice.

Anara chuckled wryly. *You could say this is punishment for not playing nice with the other kids,* she said in explanation.

I don't get it, India complained. *Why don't you hate me, then?*

Have you done something I should hate you for? asked Anara, amused.

If you got me as punishment I think you'd have good reason to hate me.

Well, Anara mused. *I'll have to think about that.*

Why doesn't that make me feel better? India asked.

Is that what you think I'm here for? asked Anara.

No, India said quietly. *I have no idea what any of this is about. I guess I was hoping you would tell me everything was going to be okay. If you're not, then I have no way of knowing that I'm safe here. I guess I was hoping for some reassurance.*

I'm sorry I have none to offer, Anara said apologetically.

What happens now? asked India.

I have no idea, said Anara. *I guess we wait and see.*

What about my lessons? asked India.

Do you want to continue?

Yeah. India sounded surprised with herself. *I guess I do. Will you teach me?*

Anara grinned. *That's what I'm here for,* she said.

Well, okay, then. What happens now? India asked again. This time she grinned back.

You have to recover, said Anara.

India nodded. *How long will that take?*

I have no idea, Anara frowned. *You've had this before. That may make it easier; it may have no effect at all.*

Swell, said India. *When can I leave this room and go back to my body?*

You haven't left your body, Anara chuckled. *This room is inside your mind. It's a safe place for you to come when the Disembodied harass you.*

Does that happen often? asked India, horrified.

They're part of the Collective Unconscious, whether we want them to be or not, Anara responded. *Everyone who has passed through corporeal existence contributes to this phenomenon. If you search long enough, you will even find the trace of your own soul and be able to follow its path through this and other lives. You wouldn't have time for anything else, though, so I don't recommend it. Most of them are souls who will never again assume flesh, and most of those are bent and twisted beyond human recognition.* She stood and looked down at India. *However, this doesn't get beds made and supper on the table. You rest and I'll come talk to you if I can. I'll be pretty busy.*

I'm sorry, said India, almost automatically. She hated herself immediately for saying it, but the words were so conditioned as a response to that kind of statement that she was unable to stop herself.

Anara understood. *Don't be,* she said. *I ran the hostel before you came here. I can do it again for a few days while you get better and back on your feet.*

India nodded timidly.

Good. As long as we understand that. Anara stood up and walked to the door. *Let me out, please? You can come with me if you want.*

India shook her head. *I guess I'll stay here for a bit,* she said. Then she pictured the door open and smiled at Anara. *Thanks,* she said quietly. *I'll see you again in a while?*

Anara nodded and left, closing the door softly behind her.

India drew a deep breath and looked around the room. It was nice to be in her apartment again, even if it was only in her mind. She wondered what had become of the real one. If she had really been gone a year, her landlord had surely rented it to someone else by now. Did anyone wonder what had happened to her? Had someone told her boss that she was quitting her job?

Somewhere deep in her soul, India felt a kernel of resolve harden and grow. Whoever had done this to her would be made to pay dearly for the damage they had done to her mind and her life.

India stayed put for a small eternity, only peripherally aware of what was going on with her body.

She reread every book she possessed in her 'apartment-in-her-mind', and paced the floor a lot.

She slept in her own bed again and wore the clothing she had left behind her when she left the real apartment over a year before.

India still wasn't sure she believed Anara on that point. It didn't feel like she had been away that long. Or, more specifically, there didn't seem to be any memory of activities spanning a year. She was certain time had passed; she had been at the Level Two Hostel over two months already, but what had happened to her in the meanwhile?

India wandered into the kitchen and found a box of soda crackers in a cupboard. She munched absently as she continued her pacing through the small apartment. She knew there was no real point in eating anything in this peculiar environment, but it made her feel better, so she saw no harm in it either.

Then she had a thought that halted her in mid-stride.

Oh, gods, she murmured, and reached absently into the box for another cracker. *What if I'm in on whatever is going on? What if the people I'm involved with have removed my knowledge of this operation to protect us all from whoever might find out?*

She thrust the fear into the back of her mind, but she was unable to dismiss it.

India?

A familiar voice broke into her thoughts and she paused a moment, trying to place it. *Peter?* she asked at last. *Peter, is that you?*

May I come in?

India ran to the door and jerked it open. *What are you doing here?* she asked as she dragged him inside.

Peter laughed. *I thought I might come for a visit. Anara told me you were laid up for a while and I missed our talks by the pool, so I came looking for you.*

But how did you know where to look? India persisted.

Anara told me, he admitted. *I'm telepathic, not psychic!*

India giggled. *Well, I'm glad to see you in any case. Come in and sit down.*

This is really nice, said Peter as he sat on the couch. He patted the cushion next to him and smiled at India. *You like antiques?*

India glanced around guiltily, as if she had something to apologize for. *Well, it's home,* she said noncommittally.

Peter grimaced. *Did you decorate it or did someone come in and hold a beam to your head, forcing you to do this?*

I did it, India admitted. She looked all around the apartment, anywhere but at him.

Then why do you belittle it?

India shifted her gaze and stared at him. *That is what I was doing, huh?*

Why is what other people think so important to you? he asked gently.

India shrugged, staring at her hands, folded in her lap.

Peter reached over and covered them with his hand. *What I think isn't important. What Anara thinks isn't important. What you think is important. If you listen to what your heart tells you to do, you'll never go wrong.* He paused. *Unless, of course, your heart is hopelessly twisted and sick, and I just can't believe that of you.*

India looked up and met his eyes. He smiled down at her and her heart lurched sideways. *I was just wondering . . .*

He cupped her chin in his hand and tilted her head up. No. *You already know you aren't involved in this.*

But I . . .

A victim is a different thing. He cut her off again. *You aren't responsible for what's happening to you.* For a long moment, he stared into her eyes. *You are responsible, however, for getting yourself out of this situation. Anara can help you a little, but you have to do most of the work.*

How do you know this? she asked, suddenly a little afraid.

Because I lied about not being psychic, he chuckled. *Do you trust me?*

India nodded.

Then you know I'm not responsible for your situation?

India nodded again.

He leaned forward and kissed her gently. *Then I won't ever lie to you again.*

India fell against him and buried her head in his shoulder. *Why do you care?* she asked softly, trying not to cry.

His arm tightened around her shoulder and she could feel him laughing gently. *You know a reason I shouldn't?*

India laughed in spite of herself.

I have to go, Peter said regretfully. *You'll be okay?*

India nodded. *I appreciate your coming,* she said a little shyly. *Will I see you on the outside?*

Count on it, said Peter. He leaned forward and kissed her.

Eventually, there was a knock on the door which took India completely by surprise and pulled her mind from her problems for the moment.

Wh—who is it? she quavered. She stood poised in the middle of the living-room floor, as though there were someplace she could run to that would be safer than where she was.

Anara, came the immediate reply. *May I come in?*

Sure. India sighed in relief. She reached the door in two strides and pulled it open. *Is it safe to come back yet?* she demanded, scanning the hallway behind Anara, looking for the Disembodied.

They've gone for now, said Anara. *But they never go very far away or for very long once a new mind enters the Collective Unconscious. Always keep on your guard for them.*

The Collective Unconscious? India asked, a trace of disbelief in her voice. She remembered Anara saying something about it a while ago, but her mind had been in no shape to understand what she had been hearing. *You mean Jung was right?*

In part, Anara acknowledged. *It's sort of the medulla oblongata of humanity; a kind of societal id. It's everything basic to life and socialization. The Disembodied are never far from it. They never reach contact with the Greater Consciousness.*

What is the Greater Consciousness? India asked curiously. *That's not something we covered in Psych. 101.*

I'm not surprised, Anara laughed. *May I sit down? And are there any of those crackers left?*

Sheepishly, India nodded and proffered the box. *I know it's silly to be eating here, but I couldn't help myself. It felt sort of comforting to be doing something so normal in such a strange place.*

That's fine, said Anara as she took a handful of crackers and handed the box back to India. She munched one thoughtfully before she answered India's question. *The Greater Consciousness is comprised of the Higher Souls. It's what we all strive to become a part of.*

India had no idea what Anara was talking about, but she wasn't willing to pursue the subject at the moment. She nodded in what she hoped was a sage manner and prayed to whatever deity might be listening that Anara would leave the matter alone.

Anara smiled slightly. *There is time enough later,* she said. *In the meantime, you may leave here whenever you like.*

Great! India jumped to her feet. *Let's go.*

Anara stood and gestured toward the door.

India pulled it open and they both stepped through into the hallway beyond.

You're back! Peter said as she sat down to dinner that night. He pulled out the chair next to her and sat down.

India grinned at him. *You missed me?* She snagged a passing bowl of vegetables and spooned generous helpings onto both of their plates.

It's been very quiet around here with you all shut up in your center, he teased, putting pieces of chicken beside the mounds of succotash.

You missed Radio Free India? she teased back. *Hey, where's the biscuits?* she called. The basket was passed down the table to them.

Well, your broadcasts did liven up the place, he admitted. Then he touched her cheek. *You look awfully thin and tired. Do you think you'll be up for a swim later?*

Maybe a sauna or a whirlpool, she suggested. *Warmth and inactivity sound really good to me right now. I have to do the dishes, but after that, I'm free.*

I'll wait for you there, then. Peter squeezed her knee under the table and turned his attention to his plate.

India washed the dishes in record time that evening in spite of the fact that she still felt muffled and padded from her Opening Sickness. Her headaches and joint pains had vanished, but the cotton between her skin and nerve endings had not gone. She found she had to really concentrate on the task at hand. If she forgot, she dropped things, and that just made the job seem more interminable.

'How come you're so quiet tonight?' India asked Anara while she was washing out the huge roasting pan.

The tiny woman smiled serenely and continued drying plates.

'Date tonight, huh?' India guessed. She ran clear water over the pan and put it on the counter for Anara to dry as well.

Anara's smile deepened.

'Me too,' said India, grinning in spite of herself.

Peter was already in the whirlpool when India arrived.

'Come on in, the water's fine.'

India stepped in and was surprised at how hot it was. She felt so muffled, she hadn't expected to feel hot or cold much. She stood on the first step, allowing herself to get used to the temperature in stages. 'So what are you still doing here?' she asked, easing herself down another step.

'That's partly why I wanted you to myself tonight,' Peter said slowly.

India looked at him, waiting. Her newly reawakened senses told her what he was about to say, but she wanted to hear it from him.

'I've been stalling as long as I could, but I have to leave tomorrow. My employer has another job for me and it's planetary, not dimensional.'

India nodded. 'You've been here much longer than anyone else. Most of our guests stay only a few days.' She eased her way onto the last step and began to sit equally slowly on the seat next to him. 'I guess I knew you couldn't stay, but I was hoping you might be here a little longer.'

'This isn't forever, you know,' Peter chuckled. 'Just for now. Besides, you have too much to do here for me to be underfoot distracting you, and I do have a living to earn.'

India laughed harshly. 'Yeah, so did I once.'

'And you will again,' said Peter confidently. 'Everybody's got to pay taxes.'

India gasped and moved away from him, holding up crossed index fingers to ward off the evil eye.

Peter laughed and reached out to pull her closer to him. 'I'll be back before you know I'm gone.'

'I'm just going to miss you so much,' said India.

'I'll miss you too,' he said, and kissed her.

India felt his mouth on hers and the heat of the whirlpool rising up around them, but even as she began to kiss him back, the weakness in her body betrayed her and she fainted.

'Wow,' thought Peter to himself as he caught her slumping form, preventing her head from going under the water. 'I've never done *that* to a woman before!' He chuckled to himself over his vanity and picked up the tiny, inert form. He wrapped her in a towel and carried her back to the Inn to put her to bed.

When India awoke in the morning, Peter was gone.

India moved through the day on automatic pilot. She was weak and suffered occasional disorientation, but she managed her chores by herself, even if at half-speed. She spent all afternoon in the garden, doing much more than Anara had set for them. She didn't want to go down to the pool, knowing Peter wouldn't be there. His absence was a dull ache under her ribs and in the back of her neck, and pulling weeds was the right kind of mindless task for the thinking she needed to do.

Reading it in her thoughts, Anara left India alone in the garden, doing the laundry instead, but she checked on her periodically, knowing it was more than Peter's leaving that India was brooding over.

In a better frame of mind, India could have looked at herself that afternoon and laughed. She was so ferocious in her concentration it was comical, but there was nothing funny about what she was doing. She started at one end of her mind and worked her way to the other, sorting out what felt real from what felt like artificial implants, attempting to discard as much of the Glop that had been dumped in her mind as she could. The longer the task took, the angrier she got. They had done a terrible job on her. Hell, even now she could have done better herself. What angered her most were the remaining blocks. There was no way to eradicate them herself. The best she could do was clean up the debris around them.

Once the clean-up was done, India set about testing her psi-powers to determine what changes had occurred since the Opening Sickness. First, she set a pile of dead leaves and old weeds in a clear area. Eyes closed, frowning in concentration, she visualized the pile burning. Acrid smoke reached her nostrils and she opened her eyes. The pile was already mostly incinerated. *Wow,* she thought to herself as she backed away rather belatedly.

Feeling pretty good about that, she decided to start testing her psychokinesis by lifting a pumpkin, but try as she would, she couldn't get the thing to budge. Rather disappointed, she scaled back her sights and tried a tomato. It was heavy, but she could keep it aloft. Suddenly, she remembered a lesson with Shannon, in which she had kept chairs, books, candles and herself aloft simultaneously. *Why can't I do that any more?* she wondered. *I should to be able to do what I used to, shouldn't I? Or did they block it all off when they took me in last time?* No answer was forthcoming, but it seemed probable, so she moved on to the next phase of testing herself.

By the time Anara called her in to start dinner, India had determined that her psychokinetic abilities were only marginally better than when she had come over Shark's Tooth Pass levitating the candle. She couldn't lift much more than that even after the Opening Sickness. Her pyro-kinetics were just fine. She could start a flame, and that was the only important thing as far as fires were concerned. Her telepathy was much improved. She could hear everything going on in the immediate area, but she had no idea what qualified as immediate. She thought she might be hearing at quite a distance, but since the Inn was at the apex of several dimensions, she didn't know if that had anything to do with it or not. If she could hear interdimensionally, she was prepared to be impressed, but there seemed no way to test this theory, so she contented herself with adding telepathy to the catalog of talents she possessed.

By the time the dishes were put away after supper, India was feeling a little more ready to face Peter's absence, so she went down to the pool and swam a few laps before bedtime. She lay in the spa, letting the water-jets pummel her body and soak away her pain. Tomorrow she would ask Anara about starting some serious lessons.

Can't we start today? I really want to get going. Or are you too busy? India asked Anara as she passed by the large table on her way from one room to the next. She had asked Anara about lessons that morning while they were making breakfast, but Anara hadn't answered.

Anara didn't look up from where she was cleaning the fireplace. She swept the ashes deliberately into a small pail and set down the broom. *You aren't fully recovered yet,* Anara said finally as she carried the bucket to the garden door. The door swung shut behind her.

But we can at least practice telepathy, can't we? India called after her.

Anara didn't answer.

Puzzled and disgusted, India went on to the next room. 'I thought she was supposed to be my teacher,' she grumbled as she made the bed. 'I don't know how to teach myself, or I'd do it,' she muttered as she swept the floor.

'I feel fine. How much more recovered am I supposed to get?' she demanded as she scrubbed the toilet and shower.

By the time she had finished the room, India had worked off most of her frustration, but the puzzlement remained. She gathered her cleaning supplies and went on to the next room. She finished her cleaning and wandered out to the garden.

As she picked peas and weeded among the vines, she slowly relaxed and began to enjoy the fresh air and sunshine. A gentle breeze stirred the leaves and lifted her tangled curls off her back. The sun warmed her back and darkened her bare arms.

Slowly she came back to her conversation with Peter, and an earlier one with Anara. *Listen to your heart. Pay attention to what it tells you.* Lost in thought, India picked up her full basket and walked back to the small porch. Settling on the stoop, she put the basket beside her. She had brought a large pot out with her earlier. She put this on the step below her and began shelling peas into it. 'If that's the case, then I don't really believe I'm part of what's happening to me,' she continued talking out loud to herself.

It was an old habit her father had been unable to break her of. Probably that was why she still did it. India had vague recollections of her mother talking out loud to herself. It was one of the few memories she had of her dead mother. India was unsure if she had picked up the habit because she knew it made her father angry, or if she had always done it and continued to spite him.

India knew from pictures that she resembled her mother closely. Old friends and family who had known Dannie never failed to point out how much India's speech and gestures mirrored her mother's.

Dannie was the only thing her father had ever really cared about. He had been amused to watch her ramble about the huge old house keeping up a steady monologue as she worked. He had allowed her to have a baby, but had no interest in the child himself. India had been Dannie's pet, and when Dannie died, India became a constant reminder to her father. Everything she did angered him. She tried to stay out of his way as much as possible, but when he caught India talking to herself, he beat her.

He had never managed to beat it out of her, though.

Her mind began wandering again, away from the mindlessness of the task her hands were performing. Even though she didn't think it was beyond him, India didn't believe that her father was responsible for what was happening to her. All her life, he'd had as little to do with her as possible. It didn't seem right that he would begin manipulating her life now in this bizarre way. He had too many other ways of achieving his goals.

India reached absently into the basket and found it empty. She put the pot of shelled peas up on the porch and stood with the basket. The sun hung just above the trees and the sky was paling with late afternoon. Soon the pink and orange streaks of sunset would light the horizon. She gathered the empty shells into the basket and headed off to the compost heap to dispose of them, still thinking about what Anara and Peter had said.

India stood again in the vast, grey plane.

She was completely alone in a place that wasn't a place. The plane was devoid of feature. There was no light, but no darkness either. There was no feeling of enclosure. Nothing recognizable as ground, or sky, or even distance separated where she stood from any other place in the No-Place.

Far away, a skyscraper surged into being.

India took a step towards it, but the structure subsided as quickly as it had erupted.

Gods, this is weird, she murmured to herself, unable to shake the feeling of déjà vu. The sound of her voice fell dead at her feet. There was nothing for it to echo off; similarly there was no place for it to go. She recognized the strangely familiar dream, but she was curious if it might go further this time, so she kept looking around for any changes that might have occurred without her noticing.

The No-Place remained empty save for her presence. She began to doubt she was really there at all. *What is this place?* she asked the emptiness around her.

There was no answer. Then the dream shifted and she was no longer standing on the vast grey plane.

India came awake talking. 'Do you know where the poison is? If we're out, I know where we can get more.' As she finished this, she realized that she was sitting bolt upright in bed, in the dark, discussing who-knew-what in her dreams. She had no idea where this had come from, nor what dream might have sparked it.

She felt a cold touch in the back of her mind and shivered. The touch was unpleasantly familiar, but as she searched for an association in her mind, the feeling slipped away, leaving India with the conviction that she must have been having a nightmare. Sliding back down under the covers, she pulled the blanket up under her chin and lay very still. Her heart was beating rapidly and her skin was flushed.

Then she heard a soft scraping from the corner by the bathroom door.

'Hello?' India quavered, cringing further back into her pillow.

The door opened and a dark shape passed through it silently.

Oh, gods, she moaned to herself. This was no nightmare. Who or what had been in here with her and what was it doing in her bathroom? India could feel a barrier weaken a bit, but it continued to hold.

By sheer act of will, India reached out and turned on the lamp beside her bed. Blinking myopically in the sudden light, she looked quickly around the room.

She was alone.

India pushed back the covers and started to swing her legs over the edge of the bed.

She froze.

What if there was something under the bed?

There was no noise in her room, and none in the bathroom, but whoever had been here with her was in there now. India reached deep into herself and found the courage to look under the bed. First, she pulled the covers back up over her legs and then rolled onto her stomach. She pulled the covers the rest of the way up over her back and then balanced her hands on the edge of the old-fashioned wooden bed frame.

Cautiously, she eased her weight forward onto her hands as she leaned out off the mattress and lowered her head toward the floor. Her legs and body on the bed helped balance her, but the wood cut into her palms and they burned from the pressure of her weight. Finally, she was able to see under the bed. Squinting into the darkness under it, she carefully checked all four corners.

Nothing was there.

Feeling very silly, India eased herself back onto the mattress and rubbed her palms to restore circulation to her hands. There was still no sound from the bathroom, though, and this was beginning to scare her badly. She was finally awake enough to realize what was happening.

Marshalling her much-abused courage, India stole out of bed, picked up her small, ladder-backed chair, and moved as silently as she could to the bathroom door. She twisted the knob slowly and raised the chair up in front of her so the legs faced the door. Then she pulled it open and reached inside to switch on the light. The bathroom was empty.

The shower curtain was pulled open, showing there was no place to hide. India lowered the chair and switched off the light.

Had she really only imagined the whole thing?

India put the chair back and climbed into bed. She turned out the light and pulled the covers back up to her chin. She lay in the dark trying to calm her heartbeat, but sleep didn't come for the rest of the night.

'Are you doing this deliberately, Bob?'

'No, sir,' said Bob.

'If you're doing it deliberately, it'd really piss me off, you know?'

'This one just keeps getting away from me,' said Bob.

'I don't pay you to screw up, Bob. Usually you don't. Why is this one different?'

Bob shrugged. 'You tell me.'

'Control yourself. This is a job. You just do your job. You don't have any feelings one way or the other, is that clear?'

Bob didn't answer.

'You couldn't have announced our presence more clearly.'

Bob still didn't answer.

'Just do your job.'

'Well, you did say you weren't entirely awake,' Anara said as she lifted the large kettle onto the spider-arm in the fireplace. 'How can you be so positive you saw something go into your bathroom? And if that's where it went, how did it get out without you seeing it again? How could it have left your room?'

'I don't know,' India sighed. She put a huge pitcher of fresh orange juice on the table and started back to the kitchen to take the bread from the oven. 'I also don't know why I would be discussing poison with it. Do you think it has something to do with the blocks in my mind and my absence from Level One? I felt a block weaken a little bit last night, but it's still holding.'

'What do you think?' asked Anara, following India into the kitchen. She picked up a basket of eggs and headed back to the fireplace.

'Where did those come from?' India asked curiously. She had never seen a chicken coop in this peculiar place.

Anara chuckled. 'There are many dimensions around us you haven't been to.'

'I think it *must* have something to do with the blocks and my disappearance, but I can't think what it could be. I don't know where to get poison and I can't imagine why I would want to,' India said as she gathered silverware from the drawer and followed Anara out of the kitchen.

She had been over the strange incident again and again in her mind as she lay awake in her bed, waiting for the dawn. Her recollection of the feeling she'd had as she finished speaking was that she was talking to someone she knew well but didn't particularly like. Something about him made her uncomfortable and this fact came through her dream-state.

How could she be so certain it was a man who had been talking to her?

Pay attention to my heart. Then why did she feel that her father was somehow involved in, but not responsible for, what was happening to her? She hadn't been troubled by thoughts of him for several years.

India had moved out of her father's house as soon as she was able, and ended her dependence on his financial support. She couldn't bear the thought of being indebted to a man who made his money on others' blood, and who hated the sight of her.

She had started running away at the age of eight, but her father always managed to find her and bring her back. She would stay for a few months, or until he beat her again. Then she would leave, only to be tracked down and forcibly returned.

On the streets, she had seen the effects of her father's 'business': junkies, strung-out and trying desperately to sell themselves for just one more fix. India had sold herself also, to survive, and had begged and stolen as well, but she stayed clear of her father's drugs. She wanted nothing to do with him.

India had thought on occasion that it would be ironic if she had become a junkie. What would her father have done then? But her life was worth more to her than that. At sixteen, she left home for good.

She got herself off-planet as quickly as she was able and went as far away as she could get. Orion sector was just opening up, so she was able to work her way through school with the help of scholarships and the government official she later went to work for.

India had been lucky when she propositioned Mr Standish as he walked past her corner late one evening. He took her up on her offer and discovered, in talking to her, that there was more to her mind and ambition than being a mattress-back. He encouraged her to go back to school and paid her first semester's tuition. Later he hired her as his assistant. She wondered where he was now, and if he missed her at all.

'My heart says Father is capable of manipulating me this way, but I don't think this is his doing,' she told Anara. She laid out the last place-setting and leaned against the table, watching Anara stir the eggs in the skillet.

'I don't think so either,' said Anara. 'I also believe that there was in fact someone in your room last night. Your thoughts when you discuss it recall the shape and noise specifically.'

'Then I wasn't dreaming it?'

'It may have been a kind of hypnotism,' Anara suggested. 'Perhaps your subconscious is breaking through some of the blocks in your mind. If that's the case, we will have to be especially careful that no one manages to take you from here and reinforce them. I think we need to give you the chance to overcome them. I don't like the idea of anyone being used against their will and without their knowledge, especially in this manner.'

'But how can we do that?' asked India. 'What if they have a way of coming in from another dimension like our guests do, and hooking up their room to mine? How do we stop them?'

Anara smiled broadly. 'We are innkeepers here. There are always ways of keeping guests from leaving without paying, and of preventing the chronically delinquent from attaching themselves and becoming a drain on our resources.'

'People *pay* for our services?' India demanded incredulously. She had never seen a unit of pay for the work she did.

'Well, of course. Did you think we did this out of the goodness of our hearts?' Anara laughed. 'You don't get paid because you're taking it out in trade. You're working for your education.'

'What's the hour-for-hour exchange?' India asked. 'I think I'm getting rooked!'

Anara laughed. 'Well, so far, I'd have to agree with you, except for the matter of some sick days you hadn't earned yet . . .'

'Okay!' India gave in laughing. 'How do we keep strangers out of my room?'

'You leave that to me,' said Anara. 'Go ring the gong to call our guests. Breakfast is ready.'

India slogged through the day hoping Anara could really do something to make her room safe from intrusion. A sleepless night and a day of hard work made the nocturnal visitor seem all the more malevolent to her tired mind. It also put a fine point on just how little recovered she was from her Opening Sickness.

What would she find, she wondered, when the barriers remaining in her mind at last came down?

In the afternoon, after finishing the rooms, India found Anara in the garden.

'You look dreadful,' Anara said cheerfully. She was on her knees among the strawberries, picking the ripe ones.

India grimaced. 'I love you too. Have you sealed off my room yet?'

'Of course. I did that first thing after breakfast. Did you want to take a nap instead of working out here today?' Anara asked.

'Would you mind?' India asked. She twisted her fingers into her coppered curls, feeling a twinge after Anara's comment about unearned sick days. If she was working for her lessons, she thought she should put in the time and energy, but she could hardly keep her eyes open.

'Mind?' Anara demanded incredulously. 'A scare like that so soon after Opening Sickness? You're doing better than we had any right to expect. Certainly I don't mind. Shall I wake you for dinner, or would you rather sleep yourself out?'

'If you wake me before, I could help you get it,' India offered diffidently. She shifted from one foot to the other and shoved her hands into the pockets of her grey work-pants.

Anara waved her out of the garden. 'I'll wake you if you want to eat, but I can manage without your help quite nicely if I have to. You seem to think I'm a helpless old woman!'

'Well, you're older than me,' India grinned. 'You know that's not what I meant!'

'I know,' Anara smiled at her. 'Just go rest. Worry about yourself. I'll be fine. Sleep sweet dreams, okay?'

'Okay,' India smiled back. She wandered out of the garden and back to the Inn.

In spite of Anara's reassurances, India left her door open

while she checked in the armoire, under the bed, and in the bathroom. Her room was empty of unwanted presences. With a sigh of relief, India closed the door and pulled off her dirty work-clothes.

After a quick shower, she ran a comb through her wet, tangled hair, pulled on a tee-shirt, and climbed into bed. She was asleep in moments.

India stood on the vast, grey plane.

She was again completely alone in a place that wasn't a place. The plane was devoid of feature; there was no light, but no darkness either. There was no feeling of enclosure. Nothing recognizable as ground, or sky, or even distance separated where she stood from anywhere else in the No-Place.

Far away, a mountain surged into being.

India took the inevitable step towards it, but the structure subsided as quickly as it had erupted.

Gods, this is weird, she murmured to herself. The sound of her voice fell dead at her feet. There was nothing for it to echo off; and there was no place for it to go. She knew she was having the recurring dream, but she was wondering if it would go any further, so she kept looking around for any changes that might have occurred without her noticing.

For quite a long time, the No-Place remained empty save for her presence. For so long, in fact, that she began to doubt she was really there at all. *What is this place?* she asked the emptiness around her.

'No-Place' will do just fine, said a familiar voice at her elbow.

India jumped and turned toward the unexpected sound. *Anara?* she asked stupidly.

Anara in the No-Place looked nothing like Anara on the physical plane, yet all of the features and details came from her physical being. She smiled at India. Her face was thinner and younger than the one India knew. Her brown hair fell loose down her back instead of being pinned out of the way of her work. The same oddly content aura surrounded her, though. This India recognized. It made her feel a little less strange in this strange place.

India wondered what she herself looked like in the No-Place. She smiled back at Anara and looked into her eyes . . . and fell through!

There had been no reflection, not even iris and white. Her eyes seemed to be all pupil, dilated impossibly wide. There was nothing to catch and hold India on the surface as she was accustomed to, so she just kept plummeting.

Anara, help! she screamed as she fell. This had to be worse than Alice's trip down the rabbit hole, she thought as she flailed in the darkness for something to hold on to.

A hand reached out of the black and caught India. Her plunge came to an abrupt halt without any sensation of stopping at all. *Anara?* she asked.

I was about to warn you about this place, Anara said as she drew India back up out of herself. *You can guard against falling into the trap, but you can't really do much about other people falling into yours unless you keep looking away from them. Mostly, no one here wants to fall through, so they guard themselves against it, but if someone wants to do you harm, it's a good way for them to accomplish it.*

Gods, I'm sorry, India murmured as she withdrew apologetically. There had been entirely too much to beware of recently. She made a mental note to be careful with eyes in the No-Place. If this trick could be embarrassing between friends, between enemies it could be deadly.

Why do you look different in my dream? India asked, curious.

In an odd sort of way, this isn't a dream, Anara said.

It wasn't the explanation India was looking for, but she was interested in the directions this dream was taking, so she smiled. *In what way is that?*

This is a place I would have brought you soon. Instead, you found it on your own. Were you taught what to look for? There was a curious probing tone in Anara's voice.

There isn't anything here to find! India laughed. *I've been here before,* she mused. Her glance swept the empty, dense grey around them. *What were you going to bring me here for?*

We'll be doing some of our work here. This is the level at which the Greater Consciousness can be tapped. The dispossessed can't come here.

Why not?

They aren't able to reach it. They gave up their claim on the Old Knowledge when they lost themselves, Anara explained. *Perhaps your mind came here instinctively, knowing it would be safer for you than the normal levels of consciousness.*

Maybe, India grinned. She didn't buy a word of this, but it was definitely a more entertaining version of the dream than she'd had before. Also, it was better than the one she had awakened to the night before.

Have you been listening to your heart? Anara wanted to know.

The question brought India back to the subject which had been troubling her for the last couple of days.

I've tried, she said seriously.

I only want you to pay attention to what you know to be true within yourself, Anara tried to explain. *I haven't been a teacher in a long time. I'm more than a little rusty at going back to the basics. You have to believe that what you intuitively know to be true probably is.*

You mean like when I get a flash of Real Stuff come up through the Glop? India asked tentatively.

Anara laughed. *Not very eloquent, but that's pretty much it,* she said finally. *If you can tell the difference between 'Real Stuff' and 'Glop' when you run into it, you're pretty much on your way. Perhaps that's how you got here on your own?*

India shrugged and looked around again. *Are we in my mind like when I made that copy of my apartment?*

Yes and no, Anara replied. *This is your mental access to a place where anyone can go if they seek the Old Knowledge.*

Then how did you get here? India wanted to know. This dream no longer seemed much like a dream.

Through my own access, Anara told her. *I sensed you here while I was working in the garden.*

Where are you now? asked India.

Still in the garden, said Anara. *I'm just not getting much work done!*

Well, maybe I ought to go back to my dreams and let you get back to work, India suggested.

This is the stuff dreams are made of, Anara replied mysteriously. *Why don't you see what you can create with it?*

India looked again at the unchanged, unchanging grey. *What . . .* she began.

Anara was gone.

Well, bother her! India exclaimed. She set out to experiment with her peculiar surroundings.

Chapter Five

India stood on the plane of the No-Place for several minutes without moving. Nothing around her moved either. The grey didn't become less dense, nor did it become further populated.

More out of boredom than curiosity, India began to walk. There was no resistance to her steps, but there seemed to be no progress either. Nothing about her environment changed in the least. India continued walking.

If this is a place where people come for higher learning, why isn't anyone here? she asked as she traveled through nothing on her way nowhere.

Does that mean you think I'm no one? asked a voice behind her.

India turned quickly, but there was nothing behind her.

Who said that? she asked, frightened.

I did, said a young man's voice. It was pleasantly low and rich, but still disembodied.

Where are you? asked India. The voice sounded vaguely familiar, but she couldn't place it. She glanced around to see if he was playing games with her, but the area around her was still empty. There was a touch, soft as a breath on her cheek. India jerked her head back from it. *That wasn't funny!* she exclaimed, fearful and indignant.

The only response she got was laughter. The laugh was infectious, but India was unnerved by her dreams in the No-Place, and the presence in her room the other night. She was in no mood for game-playing. Turning away from the voice, India resumed her walk.

Hey! Where are you going? the voice demanded of her

retreating back. *I'm sorry. I didn't mean to scare you!* He sounded truly apologetic.

India turned back slowly and found a rather pleasant young man facing her. He had straight brown hair falling over his forehead, high cheekbones, and a long, straight nose over a full mouth which curved into a playful grin. His shoulders were wide and straight. He wore nothing but a pair of blue shorts. He had nice legs, India observed.

His grin widened. *Thanks,* he said.

India blushed and looked away. She wasn't sure what color his eyes were. She didn't dare find out. *Is this what you really look like?* she asked instead, remembering how different Anara had looked in the No-Place.

Roughly, he replied easily. *Is this what you really look like?*

India looked down at herself. Without a mirror, she could only guess that her face was the same one she carried about with her daily. *Roughly,* she grinned back. *What's your name?*

Tyler, he said. *But call me Ty.*

My name is India, she told him, smiling a little shyly.

Ty nodded. *I know,* he said.

How do you know? Do I know you?

Ty shrugged. *What are you doing here?*

I didn't come here on purpose, India said. *I dreamed myself here, and my teacher came and talked to me for a little while. Then she went away, and you arrived. What are you doing here?* she countered.

I heard you, so I came over, Ty said, explaining nothing. *Come on, let's play!*

Play? India echoed rather disdainfully. *Aren't we a little old for that?*

Nah! Ty exclaimed. *This stuff you play with till you die. Come on!*

With a sigh of resignation, India followed his retreating

back. Maybe he wasn't really as old as he looked here, but as long as she avoided his eyes, she figured no real harm could come of humoring his childish request. *Where are we going?* she called. Who was he? Why did she think she should know him?

Back to where I was working before I heard you, he called back. *Hurry up!*

I'm coming, India said. Her voice sounded condescending even in her own ears, but Ty ignored her and ran on ahead.

Since time and distance didn't really exist in the No-Place, India had no idea how long it took her to travel the indeterminate stretch to where Ty had been 'working'. She recognized it when she got there, though.

A sandcastle? she asked derisively.

Sure! Ty threw himself to his knees on the sand and set back to work on the wall he had been constructing. *Isn't it great?*

Swell, India replied without enthusiasm.

Aw, come on, lighten up, Ty demanded, rocking back on his heels and looking up at her.

India quickly averted her eyes.

You're way too tense, Ty said.

India could feel his eyes on her, appraising her. She could imagine he found her wanting.

What's the matter? he asked gently.

Nothing, India mumbled. She studied the sandcastle, hoping Ty would be sidetracked by her attention to his work.

Seriously, he persisted. *You look uptight and unhappy. What's wrong?*

Ty's voice was soft and warm. India could hear his concern. She could feel it speaking to something inside her that wanted to tell someone else what was happening to her. Someone besides Anara. Someone besides Peter who, it seemed, already knew everything about her. Someone who wouldn't tell her that she was learning from all of this. She wanted some plain old sympathy. She wanted a hug.

Wondering briefly what it would be like to feel his arms around her, India shook her head. *It's just not something I can talk about right now,* she said, hoping that would hold him off. With a smile she didn't feel inside, she dropped to her knees on the sand beside him. *Got floor plans for this?* She gestured at the castle. *Or can anybody play?*

Ty grinned. *Use your imagination,* he invited with an expansive gesture.

Do you come here a lot? India asked as she scraped sand together to add a turret on the side of the castle nearest her. Looking around, she saw no water to wet the sand with.

Just imagine a puddle, Ty instructed, seeing her dilemma. He was almost finished with the first side of the wall that would surround the castle. *Yeah, I come here pretty often,* he said finally. He patted the sides to strengthen them and then crabbed around in a half-crouch to find a better position in which to begin the next side. *I guess it's the place I'm happiest. Here, I can do anything I want. There's no one to stop me, or tell me what they think I should be doing.* He looked over at India, but she looked away before he could meet her eyes. *Any place can get lonely, though, if you don't have anyone to talk to.*

Why aren't there any people here? India asked. Her puddle had appeared on command, and she was constructing an elaborate tower from the ground up, with an internal curving stair and windows at intervals. If the sand were real, this little bit of architecture would never stand, but she imagined it would, so it did.

Hey, that's really neat! Ty said enthusiastically as he watched her build a rounded, peaked roof over the small structure. He threw himself onto his stomach and peered in through one of the tiny windows. *We ought to do that with the whole castle!*

Ty jumped up and ran a short distance away. *Stand back!* he cried as he began to run back toward India.

Hey! Wait! she protested. *What about all the work you did?*

We'll just do it again! Ty sailed through the air and landed feet first in the middle of the castle proper. He danced around, kicking the sand out to the sides and laughing maniacally.

India dove away from the decimated castle, covering her eyes with her arm. *Not my tower too! I don't want to play with you any more.*

Ty stopped his mad dance and stood in the center of the ruined castle. *Why not?* He sounded genuinely puzzled by her reaction. *I thought we were friends.*

How can we possibly be friends? India demanded angrily. *I don't even know if I know you! I've got enough weirdness in my life right now, thank you. Go back where you came from and leave me alone.* India stood up and brushed the sand off her. It never occurred to her to imagine it gone. There was a quality of realness to this place that was disorienting. During the course of working on her tower, India had begun to imagine she was at a beach on a bright afternoon. Now she noticed that there were waves lapping the sand beside her. Her exit was blocked by an ocean that had appeared from nowhere. Angry at herself now too, India turned her back on Ty and stomped away from him. She tried hard to imagine the ocean gone, but the solidity of so much water didn't seem a thing to be banished by imaginings, so the sea stayed where it was and India was forced to go in a direction she hadn't planned. The further she walked, the madder she got.

She was so furious, in fact, that she didn't hear footsteps on the sand behind her.

This is great! Ty said gleefully as he caught up to her. *Did you imagine all this?* He flung his arm out and described the scene around them with a sweeping arc.

India imagined again for a moment.

A seagull wheeled out of the sky and shit on Ty's head.

Okay! he laughed. He ran down the sand and jumped into the water.

As he splashed around, India tried again to imagine the ocean gone. When she opened her eyes, Ty stood knee-deep in a desert, flinging sand around him as though he were still in water.

Why don't you come out of there? she asked.

Come on in, the water's fine! Ty called back.

I changed the water to sand, India protested.

I choose not to see it that way! Triumphantly, Ty threw himself onto his back and began paddling around in what still looked like sand to India.

She shook her head. *You aren't just weird, you're crazy.* She continued her walk away from the beach, hoping she would find her way back to herself in the conscious world.

See you later! Ty yelled after her.

Somehow, she figured, he was probably right.

'Did he say anything else to you?' Anara asked, narrowing her eyes suspiciously.

India shrugged. 'No,' she said. She felt uncomfortable and defensive. 'He's harmless enough. He's just a little crazy.'

'We don't know that,' said Anara. 'After what happened in your room the other night, I think we can safely mistrust everyone for a while.'

'Does that include you?' India asked. She immediately regretted it, though. 'Sorry. I don't know where that came from.' She turned her attention back to the array of cast-iron cookware displayed at the shop they were in.

Anara was finally showing India another dimension. The

dimension included the livestock and a small village where supplementary shopping could be done. The village contained only a few shops, all of which were devoted to useful items. There were no extras to be found anywhere.

Anara led India into a scullery shop. 'Henry?' she called.

A tall, slender man with a tremendous growth of white hair poked his head through the doorway at the back of the small, crowded shop. 'Anara!' he said. His face creased in a grin and he came out into the shop. He reached out and took Anara by the hand. 'Who have you brought with you?' he asked, catching sight of India.

'This is my apprentice, India,' Anara said.

Henry looked India over with sharp grey eyes that missed nothing. He nodded, but said nothing to her. He turned back to Anara instead. 'She's a troubled one,' he said.

Anara nodded also. 'I've spoken with her previous teachers. They seem to feel that she has no real talent besides telepathy and some minor levitation skills, but they can't be sure because of all the blocks. I thought I would bring her to you; see what you could find out.'

India was irritated that Anara and Henry were talking about her as though she weren't there, but interested enough in the conversation that she kept her mouth shut and listened.

'Can you leave her with me for a few days?' Henry asked, looking at India critically.

'Given the nocturnal visitor, I don't feel safe doing that,' said Anara.

Henry pulled at his lower lip for a moment as he thought. 'Tell you what,' he said finally. 'I'll send her back to the Inn at night, but I really need a few days to work with her.'

'That won't interfere with running your shop?' Anara asked.

'Is she a good worker?' Henry smiled and winked at India.

India tried to resent the suggestion, but she found that she liked Henry and didn't really mind. Selling pots and ladles would be a pleasant change from making beds and cleaning bathrooms.

Anara understood India's feelings. 'Her safety is my responsibility,' Anara cautioned Henry.

'I'll look after her,' he reassured.

'Fine.' She turned to India. 'India, do you remember how to get back to the Inn?'

'It was the back door to the barn at the end of the street, right?'

Anara smiled. 'I'll see you this evening, then.'

Suddenly, India remembered. 'Will you be okay without my help this afternoon?'

Anara laughed. 'How many times must you be told? I'll be fine. You just look after yourself and don't give Henry here a hard time.'

'I'll see you this evening, then,' India grinned. *So this is the mysterious 'date'?* she asked Anara impudently.

Anara smiled, but said nothing.

Once Anara had left the shop, Henry turned to India and handed her a broom. 'You can start by sweeping out the shop,' he said.

India wasn't sure, but she thought she caught a glint in his eye as he turned away. With a sigh, India began to sweep.

Henry went behind the counter at the back of the store and leaned on his elbows against it. 'Would you like to tell me about the problems Anara described to me earlier?' he asked conversationally.

India felt her grip on the broom-handle tighten. 'You mean about the guy in my room the other night?' she asked, deliberately ignoring the question Henry was asking.

Henry shrugged and waited.

India swept under a display table and thought again of the missing year. 'Just after I came to the Inn . . .' she began. She hesitated for a moment, trying to decide what exactly she was trying to say. She could feel Henry in the back of her mind, but he was only observing her. In spite of the fact that she was certain he was seeing more of her than she was entirely comfortable with, she did her best to ignore him. 'There were a couple of incidents where the smell of the soap in the shower triggered a kind of jolt of memory. A thought that made me make an association that my mind told me afterward wasn't accurate.' She stopped to consider this. 'During the flashes of insight, I was absolutely certain the insight, and not the thought that replaced it later, was the memory I should pay attention to.' India stopped sweeping and turned to face Henry. 'The trouble with all of this is the memories of Real Stuff are usually so brief I can't really even get a glimpse of what they're about. I have no idea if they come from the year that's missing, or from the time before.'

Henry nodded silently.

'I've been thinking about my father a lot recently. I haven't really thought about him in years. We never got along well. Hell, we hated each other, but I get the feeling he's mixed up in all of this. I think he may be in as much danger as I am. Gods, I just realized that as I said it.' India fell silent and resumed sweeping the floor.

'Your father is involved in some questionable activities?' Henry asked.

India snorted. 'You could say that,' she laughed bitterly. She swept the tiny pile of dirt out the door and off the porch into the road. 'And I wouldn't want to run into most of his employees in a dark alley if they were looking for me,' she added, coming back into the store and carrying the broom to the back room. 'What next?'

'Dusting,' Henry said automatically. He pulled cloths and a bottle of lemon oil from under the counter and handed them to India. 'The wood gets oiled. How could your father be vulnerable with such a crew around him?'

'That's part of what I don't get,' India said, clearing off a table and setting to work. 'The people who work for him often have their own agenda, but usually that involves schemes to curry favor.'

'And you think this is different?'

India placed the pots back on the table and moved on to the next display. 'I don't know what to think about all of this. Anara tells me to listen to my heart, but there are so many gaping holes in my mind, I'm not sure what I should pay attention to, and what I should ignore. I'm terrified part of the time, and working my ass off the rest. Isn't there supposed to be some happy medium in here somewhere?'

Henry laughed. 'I expect there is,' he said.

India worked the rest of the day in silence, feeling Henry in the back of her mind, but he didn't say anything, and neither did she.

'I'll see you tomorrow,' he said finally.

'Bye,' said India. She let herself out of the shop and walked down the middle of the dirt road toward home. 'This is for the birds,' she said to herself as she let herself back in through the door in the barn. Henry watched her closely, though, and she had to admit she felt safe in his shop.

India helped Anara wash dishes and clean the kitchen and dining room after the guests had departed that evening, then went to bed exhausted.

That night, she found herself back in the No-Place and Ty was waiting for her.

Hi! he said cheerfully.

How did you know where I would be? India asked suspiciously.

It's where you always are, he responded, unconcerned by her tone of voice. *I knew you'd be back. Wanna play?*

Where I always am? India echoed uncomfortably.

Are you mad at me or something? Ty asked. He still didn't sound upset.

I'm not mad at you, exactly, India said, trying to sort out her feelings about him. She was having trouble articulating them. *But you aren't exactly relaxing to be around.*

You like Henry, Ty said matter-of-factly.

How do you know about him? India demanded. Suddenly, she felt a little frightened.

I know lots about you, Ty explained. *Your thoughts are sort of all over the place.*

What do you mean by that? asked India.

Everything you think just comes out of you and announces itself to anyone who's listening, he explained.

India felt herself blushing. *I thought Peter and Anara taught me how to control it!*

It's okay, he told her. *You learn how eventually.*

But I thought I already knew! India wailed.

Wanna play? Ty asked again.

Suddenly, India knew what he meant by projecting thoughts and feelings. He didn't have sandcastles in mind this time.

Can you . . . she gasped, turning back to him. *Is it possible . . . I mean, here . . .*

Can, and is, he grinned at her. *You want to, don't you?*

But I don't . . . India began.

You do, he said softly. There was an urging tone in his voice.

. . . know you, she finished miserably. This wasn't turning out right. She hadn't meant to come here. She didn't want to have to deal with Ty's innuendoes. She was still trying to figure out where she knew him from. She was certain she knew him from somewhere.

I'll wait, Ty said. *But I won't wait patiently.* He grabbed her hand. *Come on. Let's imagine horses and ride for a while instead.*

Okay, India said. She was only marginally relieved by

his change in tactics. She had managed to sidestep the issue temporarily. She was certain he would bring it up again.

But hopefully not that night. They imagined two beautiful bay thoroughbreds and another endless stretch of beach. Ty and India galloped along the water's edge far longer than real horses could possibly have endured.

In spite of herself, India found she was relaxing in Ty's presence.

What do you usually do here? she asked him when they stopped for a moment, more to rest themselves than out of concern for horses that didn't really exist.

Well, sometimes I play with other people, he said grinning wickedly at her.

India twisted her mouth into a grimace and kicked her horse into a canter. Rocking against his bare back, she could feel the splash of water on her bare feet. She held the reins tightly, but there was really no need. The horse wouldn't do anything she didn't tell it to do. There was no problem with running toward the barn on the way home. The warm, rippling muscles felt good between her legs.

Not much of a substitute, though, said Ty as he caught up. She could hear his laughter as he passed her at a gallop.

Men, India thought to herself, and tightened her heels against the horse's sides. He lengthened his stride and she crouched against his neck, urging him to a run.

How would you know? she shouted as she sailed past Ty and his horse. *At least he doesn't talk back!*

When they finally got back to the far end of the beach, where they had created it to begin with, India swung down from her horse and patted his nose. *Thank you,* she said as she unimagined him. Turning to Ty, who was still mounted, she said: *Good night.*

See you later, he said.

This time, India was certain she would.

* * *

'They've taken her to a specialist,' said the Captain. He looked pointedly at Bob.

Bob looked at the four other men seated around the table in the conference room, trying to ignore the Captain.

'The blocks in her mind are giving way again,' the Captain continued. 'We can't have him finding out anything inconvenient, can we, Bob?'

Bob glared at the young man and chafed under his superiority. 'Are we bringing her in again, sir?'

'No, Bob. You're bringing her in again. This time you'll do what needs to be done?'

Bob nodded. 'Her mind can't take too much more tampering,' he said.

'Motivation for doing it right this time, then,' said the Captain, dismissing Bob.

The other four men remained seated as Bob left the room.

As the door closed behind Bob, the Captain turned to the four men. His voice deceptively pleasant, he asked, 'Are we always such a well-oiled team? You've left Bob pretty much out on his own here.'

'We don't know how to do that mental stuff,' one of the men mumbled.

'But you are familiar with many of the drugs he uses and could help him with some of the less technical aspects of his activities.'

The men nodded.

'You could ask questions,' the Captain continued. 'You could show some initiative.'

The men nodded.

'You could do your jobs?'

Recognizing this as a dismissal, the men rose and filed silently out of the conference room.

The two men stood again on the plane of the Disembodied.

We'd better make it quick, said the younger man,

nervously. He shifted from one foot to the other, even though he didn't really stand where he appeared to be. His body was in a small, cramped and dirty room with no windows and only one door. He lay on the floor, but he was unaware of how hard the surface was under his head.

The older man sneered at him, but only a little. He was scared too, but he was trying not to show it. He ran his fingers through his thick, dark hair and stood a little straighter. *Fine, let's get on with it,* he drawled, as if he had no problem being where he was, doing what he was doing.

The two men opened their minds to each other and then reached out for the energy of the Disembodied, gathering around like spectators at a grisly accident.

Power surged through the two men and, for a moment, they were staggered by it. It became more difficult to control the contact each time they made it, and both men were growing uneasy, though neither would admit it to the other. There were ways to conceal these emotions from each other, even in such close contact as they were right now.

Find the focus, one of them said. They reached out for the ship, feeling the throb of power from the interstellar engines. They could feel the police escort in the periphery, but they were incidental to what the men were doing. The concentration of their energy was the freighter.

You're sure it's his? came a thought. It was the younger man, groping for reassurance.

Check the cargo, snapped the older. *What do you find? Only Gilbert would have the balls to use a police escort to transport this stuff. Now quit stalling. She'll be here any minute.*

The two men focused their combined and augmented strengths on the freighter. They stunned the crew and tossed the ship halfway across the galaxy, toward their own ships. The police escort immediately went on alert, but there was nothing to direct their attention on. There were no psi-mechanics on board, and even if there were, there was nothing anyone could have done.

Our men will take over from here, said the older man. *The cargo won't be traceable. Crazy old man Gilbert is smarter than that. He wouldn't have anything aboard that could get back to him. Just in case.*

You're sure no one knows what happened? asked the younger man uncertainly.

We've done this before, said the older man derisively. *Has there been a problem yet? Any complaint?*

The younger man shook his head and withdrew his mind from the joint contact. *We'd better get out of here,* he said, turning apprehensively toward the distant sound of rattle and hiss.

You were an exceptional student, said the older man appraisingly. *You've gotten soft since taking this job.*

The younger man glared at the older man, but said nothing. At last, he turned and left the plane of the Disembodied. With a chuckle, the older man followed. In their wake, a huge arachnid-like creature screamed and hissed, snapping and rattling her crab claws in anger and frustration.

You still haven't told me where all these people you play with here are, said India. She stood on the dense grey plane of the No-Place. Ty stood near her, grinning as usual.

With here are? he teased. *Is English your second language?*

If it was, would you make fun of me anyway? she asked.

Probably, Ty said affably. *There's people all over the place up here. They just don't always choose to be seen.*

Why not?

For the same reason you won't look me in the eyes, he said. *Or maybe what they're doing is private. This is a place to work, too, you know.*

Okay, India conceded. *What do you want to do tonight?*

Ty grinned lasciviously.

Besides that, said India.

Boy, you're no fun, Ty complained good-naturedly.

Then why do you keep hanging around? India shot back. *Go play with someone else.*

I'm a masochist at heart, he said.

Don't do me any favors, she said. *What sort of work do you do here?* she asked, trying to change the subject.

Private, Ty said briefly. *Never ask people what their work is here. It's none of your business, and it's rude.*

Well, sorry! India exclaimed. *I'm not familiar with No-Place etiquette yet. Next time just gently tear my head off.*

Ty grinned. *You're right. I forgot. Why don't we take a hike. You enjoy hiking. Imagine some mountains with trails. Maybe we'll find a nice, secluded clearing off one of the paths.*

Do you ever stop? India asked in disgust. *How do you know I like hiking? And why can't I shake the feeling that I should know you?*

But Ty was imagining mountains. He paid no attention to her question.

Is it rude to ask who you are when you aren't here? India asked sometime later as they hiked up a broad, smooth path on the imaginary mountain.

Not generally, said Ty briefly. He didn't look at India as he considered his answer. *I'm just a guy. I work nine to five for a living and I like to cut loose on weekends.*

That doesn't tell me much, India protested. *How did you find your way here?*

That's none of your business either, he said. There was no anger in his voice this time, though. *Everyone has a different way here, and a different reason for coming. Telling you mine wouldn't do you any good. Besides, it's not*

something I want to share with you right now. He lengthened his stride, as though by increasing the pace he would
terminate the conversation.

Okay, fine, India grumbled, hurrying to keep up.

India awoke the next morning feeling surprisingly good.

'It's really not uncommon to feel relaxed and refreshed
after spending time in the No-Place,' Anara told her as
they worked to get breakfast on the table.

India, who was beginning to feel like her life was a never-
ending series of meals to be prepared and floors to be
swept, nodded absently as she set the table. Then the words
sank in. 'Why?'

'Because in spite of the amount of "work" you seem to
be doing, what you actually accomplish is relaxation of
the mind. How exhausting is it really to build a sandcastle
or ride a horse or climb a mountain if you haven't in fact
used any muscle?'

India said nothing. She wandered into the kitchen and
came back with a large bowl of fruit. 'Doesn't it use up
energy, though?'

Anara laughed. 'Thinking uses negligible energy, at least
in that respect. If you're not accustomed to it, I guess it
can be pretty painful, but that's not the problem. At least
Ty doesn't seem to be doing you any harm. How do you
feel about him?'

'Oh, he's okay, I guess,' India said, feeling a little uncomfortable. 'I do get a little tired of the grade-school sexual
innuendoes. Other than that, he's good company. When
do you and I start work there?' she asked, changing the
subject.

'Soon,' Anara said.

India said, 'I guess that translates to "when hell freezes
over"?'

Anara grinned.

'She's right,' Henry said as India walked through the

door to his over-crowded shop. 'You aren't strong enough yet.'

'Good morning,' she said sarcastically. 'I'm fine. And how are you? I trust you slept well?'

'Piss off,' he said cheerfully. 'Finish up the inventory this morning and you'll be free to spend the afternoon wandering about the village if you want before going back to the Inn.'

India rushed through the inventory and finished counting the last spatula just before noon.

Henry checked her work and dismissed her. 'Have a little fun,' he said, giving her some coin. 'There's a bakery at the far end of the street.'

India smiled. She felt like a small child being given a reward for being cute. 'What was my reason for being here after all?' she asked.

'I was doing an evaluation on the blocks in your mind,' Henry said. 'Tell Anara that I'll contact her later about them.'

'What about them?' India persisted. 'It's my mind. Don't I have a right to know?'

'In good time,' Henry said. 'Now run along.' He turned and walked back into the shop.

India went down the two steps to street level and set off in the direction of the bakery. Anara would answer her questions soon enough. For now, she wanted to enjoy her rare afternoon of leisure.

With the introduction of new dimensions, India had more places to go, but no more time in which to visit them. Most of the opportunities had come with chores attached. Setting off down the wide dirt road that functioned as the main street for the village, India pocketed her coins and breathed deeply of her freedom. She caught a whiff of freshly baked cinnamon rolls. Henry had certainly known where she would end up. It was nice to have the price of some rolls in her . . .

'Hey!' called a familiar voice.

India's head jerked right, her thoughts interrupted. Where had she heard him?

'India, wait up.'

India stopped. She turned toward the approaching figure.

The man was of medium height and build. He had brown hair and brown eyes. His face was pleasant, but wholly unremarkable. India was certain she knew him from somewhere, but had no frame of reference to place him in.

'You gonna buy me one, too?' he asked as he caught up to India.

'What?' she asked, wondering if he might be one of her father's men. That didn't seem right, though.

'You were focused pretty hard on the cinnamon rolls when I found your thoughts,' he explained. 'You were thinking about how nice it was that Henry had given you some credit to buy a few. They smell pretty good.'

'I know you from somewhere, don't I?' India asked bluntly. 'I feel like I should know who you are, but I can't place you anywhere.'

The familiar stranger grinned. 'You don't remember anything?' he asked. He sounded rather pleased by that.

She hadn't known him at Level One Hostel, she was certain of that.

'How certain are you?' he asked, grinning comfortably.

'I guess I'm not certain of anything these days,' India laughed shakily.

'Why don't you tell me about it over cinnamon rolls; they smell really good,' he suggested.

'Sure, you want one?' India asked. 'Let's go.' She started walking up the street, motioning him to follow. Then she stopped again. 'What are you doing here?'

'You ask too many rude questions,' he responded.

Something in his face had changed, but even as India

started to be afraid of it, she felt her mind darkening and closing in around her.

Bob saw the look of terror and laughed. 'We'll have those blocks strengthened again soon enough,' he said. 'You shouldn't fight against the post-hypnotic suggestion. It'll take effect in a moment anyway. You ask too many rude questions,' he said again. His gaze was intent on India's face, watching for signs that the suggestion was working.

India felt her mind shutting down and tried to scream for Henry or Anara, but something was preventing her from making any contact with either of them.

Henry was sitting in the back of his shop reconciling his inventory to the work orders and raw materials on hand. He had been keeping his mind partially focused on India. He was alerted when she recognized the strange man, and sent a call to Anara. Then India's mind disappeared. Henry called again frantically to Anara and dropped his inventory sheets. He sprinted out of the shop and into the main road. No one else was there.

'India!' he shouted. *India, are you there?*

There was no answer.

Anara arrived shortly, and together they searched the village thoroughly, but there was no trace of India.

'I'm sorry,' Henry said as they walked back toward the barn.

Anara said, 'I just wonder where she will turn up next, and what will have been done to her this time.'

Henry shrugged and said nothing. He pushed the barn door open and followed Anara inside.

'We've got to find these people and stop them. Her mind can't take any more abuse,' Anara said. 'Whoever would go to all this trouble and obvious expense must have some pretty big plans. I'm not at all comfortable being a party to this in any way, shape or form.'

'How can I help?' Henry asked.

'I think we need to talk to Ashraf and Shannon. Between us, maybe we can come up with something resembling a plan,' said Anara.

'Let me go close my shop and I'll come with you,' he said.

Anara shook her head. 'I can't shut down the Inn that quickly. Let's talk to Ashraf and Shannon before we go off half cocked and do more damage than good. Who knows, she may even show up before then.'

Henry didn't believe that. Neither did Anara. They both hoped they could do more than just wait to find out what would happen.

Chapter Six

India returned slowly to consciousness. She was in darkness. Her temples throbbed and her mouth tasted thick and sticky. She lay on her side on a hard surface. Her arm was twisted underneath her and felt numb.

India figured she had been lying in this position for quite a long while. She rolled over slowly, freeing the pinned arm, and sat up. Her head banged hard against a sharp edge.

'Ow, shit!' she cried softly to herself. As she spoke, her jaw popped back into joint. Tears welled up in her eyes, but she blinked them back and began flexing her fingers and wrist to restore circulation in her numb arm. With her other hand, India reached out and felt for the object she'd hit. It turned out to be the edge of a desk.

The feeling in her arm returned with an oddly seizing sensation, as though all her muscles were tensing against the returning flow of blood. India groped in the darkness to find a chair, but there wasn't one within her reach. Carefully, she felt about her to make certain, if she stood, she wouldn't hurt herself again.

Slowly, she rose. With the exception of her arm and head, India felt pretty good. She remembered she was in an office. It didn't have any windows, and only one door. The desk and two chairs were the only furnishings in the room. There was a lamp on the desk and a few pictures of mostly-naked, sad-eyed women on the walls.

India reached out and found the desk, touching items on its surface until she found the lamp. She switched it on and blinked back more tears as the bright light stabbed into her eyes, blinding her momentarily.

His chair lay on the floor against the far wall.

The man had been angry. He had leapt up and kicked the chair backward. His eyes bulged at her and his face darkened several shades. India had stood before him with her head thrown back in defiance, a strong sense of déjà vu tickling the back of her mind. She knew this man. He came toward her with hand upraised and struck her hard across the side of her head. She didn't remember hitting the floor. That must have been hours ago now.

'Hey!' said a voice on the other side of the door, startling her. 'Why don't we just use the hypo again? It did real good last time.'

'We can't do that again. After the first couple of times, it stops working and begins to disintegrate the brain. She'd be no use to us at all then,' said another voice that sounded familiar to India.

Her brain was too muzzy to concentrate on what the actual conversation meant, but she moved silently to the door and pressed her ear against it, straining to hear everything said in the room beyond.

'What about experts, then?' asked a voice from the opposite side of the room.

'The damned experts are the ones who are helping her to break down the barriers we're trying to maintain,' explained the familiar voice with exaggerated patience.

This sounded to India like a conversation that had taken place before.

'Well, what about other ones?' demanded the first voice.

'Aw, come on, use your brain. Think about it!' said a new voice very near the door India was pressed against.

She started away from it before realizing they didn't know she was listening to them.

'The more people we have in on this, the greater the likelihood that a leak will occur,' the new voice continued.

'We already have entirely too many "experts" involved. We're going to have to make do with what we have already. Now, does anyone have a constructive suggestion to make?'

There was a long pause, during which India stood holding her breath and pressing her ear harder and harder into the door, straining to hear anything that might be said quietly. As the silence grew, so did India's trepidation.

'I don't see the point of any of this,' snapped a previously unheard voice. 'Why don't we find another way that doesn't involve innocent girls.'

'Carl, you're such a pussy!'

'I may have an idea,' said the familiar voice. 'It'll require some pretty heavy sedation for the girl, and some hard work on my part, but I may be able to get the results we've been looking for.'

India gasped. That was where she knew Bob from!

She should have paid attention to her heart. India was fairly certain it wouldn't have prevented this from happening, though. She doubted even Anara could have prevented this from happening.

The next question was where in hell was she? The one after that was who in hell were these people, and how was Bob associated with them? The foremost question in India's mind since she had become aware of a problem was what on earth did they want from her?

She was relieved at least to hear they wanted her alive and with a functioning mind, but that was small comfort. How would she be able to avoid the proposed tampering?

'Fine,' said the first voice. 'You do that. But you'd damned well better make it work. We don't have lots of time to be wasting here.'

'Everyone knows that,' said the voice nearest the door. 'You should stop ingesting the substances you confiscate. They cloud your brain.'

There was some incoherent grumbling, and a door slammed.

'S'pose she's awake yet?' asked a voice India hadn't heard yet.

India moved quickly to turn off the lamp and lay back down on the floor in roughly the same place and position she had awakened in. Muffled footsteps approached the door and India heard the knob turn. Light came in as the door opened, and India stirred in what she hoped was a convincing manner.

Two men came into the room and picked her up roughly.

India protested wordlessly, but didn't struggle much as they marched her into the outer room. She glanced at the men seated around her. Bob wasn't among them. India frowned. He must have left while she was being brought out of the stark office.

'What?' she demanded of the staring faces. She recognized the man who had struck her earlier.

He chuckled. 'For now, nothing,' he said. 'You will be taken down the hall and shown to a room. You will stay there for a while.'

'And?' she prompted in the rudest tone of voice she could summon.

The man smiled unpleasantly. 'Use your imagination,' he said, and waved to the men who held her to take her away.

Hands closed on India's upper arms and she was propelled out of the room and into a long corridor of dirty white walls and institutional marbled, green-tiled floors. The ceiling was old acoustic tile, yellowed and stained in places where the roof had leaked during the rainy season, or perhaps it was from utilities on other floors. It didn't look like any place India could recall. The doors were spaced about every five meters on both sides of the hall. They finally stopped in front of one. The man on her right let go of her arm long enough to unlock the door. He pushed it open with his foot. India was then thrust through the door and it was slammed shut behind her.

With a sigh of resignation, India looked around her, again hoping for some jolt of recognition.

The room from her memory.

It was a tiny cell of a room. Like the office, there was no window, and only one door. A small cot stood in one corner. It sagged in the middle and the blanket looked thin and poor. A chair stood beside it. The walls were bare. Looking at it, India could see herself lying on the cot; could see Bob sitting in the chair. She was certain now that it had been Bob sitting in the chair. She couldn't see him any more clearly, but she knew in her heart that it was him.

India moved to the bed and sat down. The door was locked from the outside. There was nothing to do. No books, no VidCon, nothing. Then the lights went out.

It seemed they were determined she sleep.

India had been asleep on the floor of the office for some time, but she would eventually grow tired of just lying on the bed. She would inevitably find herself on the plane of the No-Place.

India wondered if there was a way she could find to go to the No-Place on purpose. She lay down and closed her eyes. Her forehead drawn down in concentration, she forced her breathing into a slow, steady pattern and tried to imagine the dense, grey plane.

Her fists gripped the scratchy blanket and she lay rigid on the cot for a very long time before boredom began to relax her face and posture. After an equally long time of trying hard to see herself at her destination, India found her mind wandering.

Once she stopped trying, India found herself in exactly the place she had been trying so hard to get to.

She stood in the vast, grey plane.

Hands clenched into fists, India stood and screamed, long and loud.

What the hell was that for? Ty asked from behind her.

India started guiltily. *You could say I'm having a really lousy day,* she said, turning to face him. *Oh, put some clothes on. You aren't helping things any!* In spite of herself, India laughed.

Ty pranced around in front of her for a moment before his customary shorts materialized around his hips. *I just wanted to cheer you up,* he said, grinning at her. *Do you want to talk about it?*

No! I want to forget the whole thing, at least for a while, she said. *Let's play.*

Really? Ty sounded delighted.

Not that, India protested. *I mean, play.*

What do you want to do?

I need an excuse to scream my head off and not scare anyone. How about a roller-coaster ride? India created the most tortuous roller-coaster she could imagine and stepped back to examine the results. *What do you think?*

Still running away from your problems? he asked.

Spare me the psychology, she said.

Can I make it scarier? Ty asked.

Feel free. India shrugged.

The gigantic structure of wood, metal and imagination warped and twisted silently as Ty increased drops and added some loops and curves.

Wow! India exclaimed when he was done. *Think we'll get to be the first ones in the car?*

She ran toward the entrance and Ty followed.

How long do you think they'll let us ride for? he asked as he sprinted past her to get into the car first.

India climbed into the car beside him and held up a roll of old-fashioned carnival tickets, waving them gleefully. *As long as we want! Start the thing!* she yelled.

The car lurched forward on the track and the safety bar lowered itself across their laps. India threw the tickets over the side and grabbed the rail on the front of the car as it gained speed. They started up a steep incline and the car slowed. Lying on her back, India watched the chain pulling the car up the long slope, listening to the grind and click of the gears. She sent a thought to strengthen everything, feeling grateful that she could.

As they reached the top, India looked down and gasped. *It didn't look this high from the ground.*

It never does! said Ty gleefully.

The car went over the edge.

India screamed. The downward plunge took forever. She was held in the car only by the safety bar. Her butt never touched the seat as they fell from the sky. Ty was whooping and hollering, laughing and holding his hands in the air above his head. India just screamed.

The car reached the bottom just in time to swoop back up and around in a tight curve that took them up and over a small bump. India's knuckles were white and her fingernails dug into her palms as they careened around in loops and curves, up and down, in and out.

By the time they reached the beginning again, India's voice was hoarse and her throat sore.

How long did that last? she rasped as the car came to a halt on the platform.

Time is a relative thing here, Ty responded unhelpfully. He was grinning broadly and flexing his hands on the safety bar. *Want to go again?*

I think my throat has had all the screaming it can take, she said, making a conscious effort to pry her fingers from the rail on the front of the car.

You don't have to scream, he pointed out. *Let's go again.*

It isn't a matter of wanting to or not, India tried to explain as she climbed out of the car. *That's the scariest roller-coaster I've ever been on. I can't help it. Besides, I'm over the immediate symptoms of today's tension. You go ahead if you want. I'll watch from here.*

Nah! Ty climbed out of the car after her. *It's no fun to ride these things alone.*

They descended the stairs and the roller-coaster disappeared.

Now what? Ty demanded.

Oh, I don't know, India said as she created a meadow and threw herself down in the grass. She lay on her back and felt the sun beating down hot on her. *Maybe I'll just sleep here for a while.*

I can help with that! Ty said enthusiastically, making his shorts disappear again. He was hard.

Damn, said India, sitting up. *I forgot. You're in perpetual heat.*

Ty did his best to look offended. His shorts reappeared.

I think I just want to be alone for a while, if you don't mind, India said, squinting up at him.

And if I do mind? he asked, joking.

Go away anyhow, she said, waving him off.

Are you sure you're all right? he asked with sudden genuine concern.

She wasn't sure if he really meant it, or if it was a ploy to lower her guard. She nodded.

If you need me, just call, okay?

Thanks, said India as she rolled over onto her stomach and closed her eyes. She felt him leave and relaxed. Shortly, she fell asleep.

Sleeping, she dreamed.

It was a Sunday afternoon, and she lay on her couch in her apartment, reading a book and listening to music on the VidCon. Books were pretty rare, but she had collected some, preferring the aesthetics of holding one and turning the pages to pressing the screen to advance the text.

The music was interrupted by an insistent buzz, so India called to answer. 'Hello?'

'India? Hi! It's Jan. Listen, Carrie and Hallie and I are

going out to brunch. Why don't you join us?'

'Oh, I don't know . . .' she'd started.

'Come on!' Jan wheedled. 'It won't be any fun without you.'

India remembered the afternoon in detail. They'd wound up doing a lot more than getting a meal. They'd spent too much credit, had too much wine, and enjoyed themselves thoroughly. She replayed the afternoon in her dream, anticipation enhancing the enjoyment. She knew what happened. That wasn't the issue. What she wondered now was: where were her friends? What were they doing and did anyone miss her at all?

The door opened at last. The two men who had brought her to the room were standing shoulder to shoulder in the open doorway. They looked unhappy, but determined.

'You guys get all the plum assignments,' India observed as she stood and held out her arms to them.

They came through the door and walked toward her. India ducked between them and ran out the door. She turned down the hallway, away from the office and her cell, and opened her stride. About a hundred yards away, the corridor made a left turn and continued away from her captors. India fled along the slick green floors, praying for an exit sign, or evidence of a stairway.

She could hear heels thumping behind her, and muffled curses. The two men seemed to want to keep her escape quiet. India frowned and kept running.

At the end of the next hall, double doors marked 'exit' stood in front of her. India glanced over her shoulder and saw the men were gaining on her. She plunged through the double doors and sprinted up the stairs. Her lungs burned and her muscles ached to stop, but she drove herself upward, away from the labored breathing of the men behind her. She guessed most people in the building must take the lift. The stairwell was empty. Glancing upward,

India could see at least a dozen floors rising above her. Risking a look down, she could see almost as many floors descending. The two men were almost a level below her, but they were still in pursuit.

Why wouldn't they have called for assistance? Would they get in that much trouble?

India rounded another landing and began the next flight. Her hand gripped the banister and pulled her up the stairs in an effort to take some pressure off her legs. Her knees ached from the unaccustomed strain, but her muscles were finally settling into the rhythm: fifteen stairs, a landing, fourteen stairs, another landing, repeat.

The men fell behind her. India lost track of time and place. Nothing existed for her but the stairs and her need to climb them as quickly as possible. She ran, not daring to slow her pace. Her breath rasped loudly in her ears and her feet pounding the stairs were drowned out by the sound of it. Sweat dripping into her eyes blinded her, but the rhythm was all she paid attention to.

She ran right into the door to the roof.

India could feel the blood start from her nose and saw it splatter when she shook her head to clear it. She managed to stay on her feet, but the effort cost her. Abused muscles cramped in the effort to keep her standing. India ignored them as she fumbled for the knob.

The two men were still climbing, but they had slowed considerably and were puffing loudly on the stair behind India. She found the doorknob and twisted it. Her heart pounded in fear and she sent a small thought to whichever deity might be listening.

The door swung open and India bolted through. The cold hit her with tangible force. It took the breath from her tortured lungs and chilled her over-worked muscles. The door slammed heavily behind her and she turned to look at it stupidly for a moment. Dusk cast long shadows across the rooftop, but she could see the lock clearly. She slapped the bolt home and turned to take stock of her surroundings.

The roof was deserted. It was flat and rectangular, perhaps a mile in length, but only a quarter of a mile across. India started toward the edge, arms wrapped around her, teeth chattering. She could feel her nose still bleeding, but the cold had slowed the flow somewhat.

A heavy weight hit the door behind her. The lock wouldn't last long against both men. They were large and had bulk to put behind their shoulders.

India stumbled to the low wall that ran round the edge of the roof and looked over. It was a long way down, but the roofs of the nearby buildings were close enough to jump to, if she could find one about the same height. Most of the buildings in the neighborhood were much taller.

The pounding increased behind her. On the building to her right was a ladder extended below an old-fashioned fire escape. She ran without stopping to think about what she was doing. She leapt off the edge of the roof and reached for the metal rungs.

She overshot her goal and slammed into the ladder.

'Christ!' she screamed as she grabbed for any hold on a rung or supporting pole. Her hands closed on the rusty metal and she hung in mid-air for a moment, collecting her wits. 'Sonofa . . . Man, that hurt!' she gritted between clenched teeth.

India found her bearings and climbed up to the rickety metal platform. The window on the platform was ajar. She stepped through and onto the occupant's kitchen table. The occupant was having dinner.

'Hey!' he objected as India upset a bowl of peas; they rolled across the floor, under the stove and table.

India looked up, startled, and right into eyes the same green as her own. 'Uh,' she said, brilliantly. 'Sorry.' She scrambled down off the table and stood on squashed peas in the middle of the kitchen floor.

'You're bleeding all over,' the man said. He glanced out the window and pulled the curtains shut. 'You okay? I guess it was you hitting the fire escape that scared me so bad. Hell of a noise!'

'Yeah, uh . . .' India said. She couldn't help staring.

She was probably more of a sight than he, but he was definitely the oddest man she had ever seen. He had an amazing abundance of long, snow-white curls, and fiercely bushy white eyebrows above eyes of clear emerald. His fat face was wrinkled, but each line looked like it had been created by a smile or a laugh. His pointy chin was made more so by a small white goatee. A moustache was just beginning to droop over his full, red lips. He was not a particularly tall man, standing only a few inches taller than India, but he was round and comfortable and familiar.

'Santa?' India's addled mind asked.

He laughed and shook his head. 'Perhaps you would like to clean up while I make you some tea?'

India nodded dumbly and allowed herself to be led to a small, clean bathroom. The strange man gave her a fresh towel and left her to herself.

'They'll be looking for you soon,' said the odd man as he sat and watched India sip her tea. 'Why were they chasing you?'

'I don't know,' said India. 'They let me get away. They let me run between them without even making a grab for me. They never called for help.' She blew reflexively on the tea to cool it. 'Where am I?'

'Continental Americas,' the man told her. He pushed a plate of cookies closer to her.

'On Earth?' She gaped at him, disbelieving.

'And in the kitchen of Mr Theodore Winslow,' he said with a flourish. 'You may call me Theo.'

'My name is India Gilbert, and I'm a very long way from home,' India said in a small voice. Actually, that wasn't exactly true. She had lived with her father here in the CAs for most of her life, but she had come to think of Giles Three in the Orion sector as home.

'Well, India, what are we going to do with you?' asked Theo practically.

'I guess get me out of here as soon as possible. If I stay here, I put you at risk. Besides, I don't know you.' India picked up a cookie and bit into it. Suddenly she was ravenously hungry. She devoured that cookie and then wolfed down two more.

'Where will you go?' Theo asked, watching India attack the cookie plate. 'How about I make you a sandwich?'

'Yes, please,' India said politely. 'I don't know where to go. I'm not sure where I came from.'

Theo chuckled. 'Misplace yourself regularly?' he asked genially.

India watched him move about the kitchen, building an impressive sandwich for her. 'No,' she said at last. 'I was in a hostel between dimensions. I don't know how I got there and I don't know how to get back.'

'Between dimensions?' Theo repeated. He seemed vastly amused. 'Well, I've heard stories about places like that, but I never figured to hear from anyone who claimed to have been there!' He brought the sandwich to India and took his seat opposite her again.

India wasn't sure what to say to Theo about myths and legends. She couldn't remember if this was an unusual thing to have experienced, or if this was commonplace. There was nothing in the Glop or the Real Stuff to indicate what the thinking on this was. Damn the holes in her mind!

India grappled with her sandwich, temporarily putting off the question of Theo's skepticism. She could remember being surprised by the oddness of the Inn, but she didn't remember any feeling of disbelief.

That didn't help much.

'Do any of the stories you've heard say anything about

how to get to these places?' India asked around her mouthful.

Theo looked thoughtful for a moment. 'Not that I recall,' he said. 'Did they have you locked up for chasing rainbows?'

'They came back for me because the blocks they had put in my mind were disintegrating,' India explained. 'Who are they, exactly?' She nodded her head toward the window she had come through as she took another bite of her sandwich.

'That's a government building. There are lots of branches of different agencies housed there. No telling just who grabbed you, or who let you go. At least, not without asking. And I get the feeling anyone asking too many questions about something no one is supposed to know about is going to put several people in immediate danger.'

'Probably you're right,' India sighed. 'I've put you in danger already. I'm sorry. I just needed to escape.'

Theo dismissed her apology with a wave of his hand. 'Is there anyone you can contact from this dimensional place to come get you, or tell you how to get to them?' he asked practically.

India thought for a moment. 'I could ask Anara,' she said finally. 'I would need to borrow a quiet room for a while though.'

'Okay, then you can use the VidCon. Don't worry about the bill. I kind of like playing hero to a damsel in distress,' Theo chuckled comfortably.

With a flash of homesickness, India thought how comfortable she was sitting in Theo's kitchen talking with him. 'Actually, the VidCon wouldn't do any good,' she admitted. 'That's the reason I need a quiet place. I have to go to the No-Place and see if I can't find Anara there. Even if I thought she might have access to a VidCon somewhere at the Inn, I wouldn't know where to find her address.'

'Sounds pretty complicated,' Theo observed casually.

'How do you go to a place that isn't a place from a quiet room of my apartment?'

India grinned. She polished off the remainder of her sandwich and stood up. 'Just show me where I can lie down, and I'll do the rest.'

Theo took India to a back room and left her to her work.

India was grateful he didn't ask any questions. She stood in the center of the room and breathed deeply in and out, trying to clear her mind of the turmoil of her escape. Eventually, she figured she had done as much clearing of her mind as her mind would allow. She lay on the floor with a pillow under her head and closed her eyes.

Remembering that trying hard got her nowhere earlier, India focused her mind on a meditation exercise from a gym-equivalent course she had taken back in college.

When at last the dense grey of the No-Place surrounded her, India looked around to make sure she was alone. Shielding herself as best she could, India began to call for Anara. For a small, frantic eternity there was no answer.

Then an unfamiliar face loomed out of the nothing and held up both hands, palm out.

India stopped calling. *Who are you?* she asked.

The woman looked a little hurt. *I was one of your teachers on the first level,* she said. *I will go and tell Anara you're here. Please try to stay in this place until she comes.*

The woman evaporated.

'People come and go so quickly here!' India murmured to herself. She sat down to wait.

Anara wasn't long in coming. *Where in heaven's name are you?* she demanded as she rushed up to India.

India jumped to her feet and threw her arms around Anara. *I've been so scared!* she cried. *I managed to get away, but they let me go. At least two of the guys let me go. The rest of them will be after me pretty soon, I guess. I'm somewhere in the Continental Americas. I'm in some guy's apartment. He looks like Santa. I trust him, but I don't know him. I'm afraid I've put him in danger. How do I get back to you?* India sobbed.

They've taken you back to Earth? Anara asked, surprised. *Do you have any idea who they are?*

No—o, India hiccoughed. *Theo says there are too many agencies housed in the building I escaped from to tell which one was responsible for taking me. How do I get back to you?* she repeated.

Where in the CAs are you? It's a big country. Anara set India away from her and gave her a cloth to wipe her eyes with.

I don't know, India wailed.

Anara considered for a moment. *It's rather dangerous, but we do have one door in the CAs right now. In Old San Francisco there is a large structure, called the Arboretum, in Golden Gate Park. You'll know which door it is once you find it.* Anara looked at India for several moments. *Be very careful,* she said at last. *Be certain you aren't followed.*

I will, India said in a small voice.

Take care of yourself, Anara said, giving India a warm hug. *We hope to see you back here soon.*

Isn't there anything else? India asked, hoping there might be more.

We risk a lot giving you that much, said Anara regretfully. *Hurry. I don't think you have much time.*

India turned away. *Thank you,* she said. *I'll be as quick as I can.*

India left the No-Place.

'Did you make your connection?' Theo asked as India emerged from the room.

'Yeah,' she said, blinking her eyes in the glare of lights. 'I didn't take too long, did I?' she asked, wondering just what time of night it was.

'Only about half an hour,' Theo told her. 'What did you find out?'

India slouched into an overstuffed armchair and rubbed her eyes for a moment with gentle fingertips. 'I have to get to Old San Francisco,' she told him finally. 'That's the best they could tell me.'

'You mean the original peninsula?' Theo asked incredulously. 'No one can get in there now. They have the whole area walled just inside the landfill. You have to have a special pass to let you in the gates!'

'I don't suppose you know how I can get a hold of one, do you?' India asked rhetorically.

'Well, yes,' said Theo. 'But how do you propose to get there? You can't take public transport; they'd find you in a moment.'

'Why don't we start with where we are in relation to the old city?' India suggested. Then she paused. 'How on earth *do* I get a pass?'

'We'll worry about that once we get there.' Theo brushed aside her question. 'We're only about 2500 miles northeast of San Francisco in the state of Canada, just west of Quebec City.'

'Wait a minute,' India said. 'I can't take you with me!'

'Why not?' asked Theo.

'I've endangered you enough just by being here!' India objected.

'Then what further harm if I accompany you to San Francisco?' Theo asked pragmatically. 'My daughter and her family live in northern San Francisco, just outside of the Vintners' Quarter. It would be nice to see them again, and it would help you at the same time. Her husband could probably get you a pass into the Old City, since that's where he works.'

'Are you *looking* for trouble?' India shook her head. 'I can't say I wouldn't be grateful for the company, but I couldn't ask you to risk yourself for my safety.'

'I can also rent ground transport. It's not a hundred per cent safe, but it's better than taking the capsule and risking turning up on a passenger manifest. Also, your friends have probably staked out the ports.'

'Doesn't it follow that they'd do the same thing for the belts?' she asked.

'They can't check every one, and they can't check every person on every one. We can pad you up with extra clothing and change your hair. With some make-up your features can be made to look different. No one would recognize you if they did check us,' Theo said with studied carelessness.

'You've thought this through pretty thoroughly, hmm?' India grinned at him. 'Why are you doing this? I interrupted your dinner and squashed peas all over your kitchen floor. You don't even know me.'

Theo shrugged. 'I enjoy adventure,' he said simply. 'Fleeing across country with a hotly pursued, possibly dangerous young woman is more exciting than eating dinner in the kitchen alone every night.'

'Well, put that way . . .' India giggled.

'Did they teach you anything useful in this mythical Inn between dimensions? Anything that might help us in our escape?' asked Theo, changing subjects rather abruptly.

'I can set a mean table and scrub a bathroom, if that's what you mean.' India pulled a face.

'That's not what I mean,' Theo reproved her. 'I should know a little better what I'm getting into, don't you think?'

India sighed. 'Okay,' she said, her eyes focusing on a pillow on the couch opposite her chair. Theo had seated himself on the other end of the couch.

India concentrated for a moment. The pillow rose slowly into the air, turned on its point, and spun for a moment before sailing out of the room and into the hallway. 'You'll find it on the bed in the room you let me use earlier.'

'Can you move it into the other bedroom?' Theo asked.

India shook her head. 'I can only do that in places I've been in before,' she said. 'If I don't have a picture of the place in my mind, I can't move the things in it.'

'Well, I guess if we need to move any pillows in a hurry, you're the one for the job,' Theo chuckled. 'But I don't see any practical use for that while we're on the lam.'

'Well, probably you're right,' India sighed. 'What do you propose we do with my hair?'

Theo grinned wickedly and rubbed his hands together. 'Leave that to me. I promise you won't recognize yourself!'

India stood in front of the bathroom mirror with a towel wrapped around her head. Theo had finished his ministrations in the kitchen, washed her hair in the sink, and swathed her with the towel. Now she was reluctant to find out what the effect was.

'No, I thought I'd like to drive out and see some of the countryside along the way,' Theo was telling his daughter over the VidCon in the other room.

India returned her attention to the towel and removed it hesitantly. She shook her head, feeling the strangeness as she looked into the mirror.

She gasped.

Her long, red-gold curls were gone. She had known this. She was awake and aware of Theo cutting them off. She had given him permission to do so. She had also been there when he applied the peroxide and then washed it out. All of this had done nothing to prepare her for the face in the mirror.

Damp curls of white-blonde clung closely to her scalp. She certainly didn't look much like herself. 'Oh, Theo!' she wailed.

'Who was that?' asked Theo's daughter on the VidCon.

'A girl I met recently. I want you to meet her. We thought we might come out and visit with you,' Theo said quickly.

'Daddy, what are you up to?' asked his daughter in a

knowing tone of voice. 'Are you adopting stray puppies again?'

'Jenny! The things you accuse your poor old man of!' he protested jokingly. 'We'll be there as soon as we can. Good night, dear.' Theo rang off and came to stand in the door to the bathroom. 'You don't like my handiwork?' he asked India, trying to sound hurt.

'It's just . . .' She turned to him tearfully. 'My hair!' she wailed, bursting into tears. 'I was always so proud of it.'

Theo laughed outright at that. 'It'll grow back,' he said. 'And in the meantime, if I didn't know who you were, I wouldn't recognize you. Our objective is for you to remain anonymous.'

'By scalping me?' she cried.

'I've made up the bed in the spare room,' he said, ignoring her tears. 'Get some sleep. I'll knock before dawn. We'll want to get an early start.'

'Okay,' India snuffled.

Theo had also left a clean pair of pajamas on the bed for her. As she changed, he locked up the apartment and turned off the lights.

'Theo?' India called as she heard him pass by the closed door. She opened it and smiled up at him. 'Thanks.'

'Sleep well,' he said gruffly, and went down the hall to his room.

India turned off the light and snuggled down under the covers, falling asleep almost immediately. She slept deeply and dreamlessly all night.

It was still dark when Theo knocked on the door.

India sat upright with a start of terror. 'Hello?' she quavered, glancing wildly around the room.

'India, it's Theo,' he said softly through the door. 'It's time for us to get under way.'

'You scared me to death!' India exclaimed, climbing out of bed.

'Sorry,' said Theo. 'Bathroom is free, and breakfast will be ready in ten minutes.'

'Do you keep black-out shades as a matter of course?' India asked as she sat down at the kitchen table.

'When it's dark, I want darkness,' Theo explained. 'Not this flood of street lights the city sees fit to inflict on us at night. It gives me a feeling of isolation and privacy, I guess.'

'Sounds like you ought to be living in the country,' observed India as she helped herself to scrambled eggs and toast. 'Where do we go to get the vehicle?'

'It's already in the garage downstairs. I got up a while ago and went to get it,' he said. 'Didn't want you out and around the streets rousing suspicion.'

'You trusted me not to walk off with the place?' India was surprised. 'I could be anyone! You shouldn't leave strangers alone in your house.'

'I trust you,' said Theo. 'I'm a pretty good judge of character. I like you. You're a bit off-center, and you've got some pretty strange ideas, but you're a nice girl. I don't like to see nice girls show up bloody on my kitchen table scared half out of their wits.'

India laughed. 'Stray puppies!'

'You heard Jenny, then?' Theo shook his head. 'Well, I guess she's right. Most puppies know not to bite the hand that feeds them.'

'Especially when the hand feeding them is also paying to get them out of danger,' said India only half jokingly. 'Theo . . .' She became serious. 'I have no way to repay you for this. If I ever get to Anara, she will probably reimburse you for your troubles, but I have no credit at all, and no way of getting any.'

'And you were going to take off on your own?' Theo's tone was incredulous, but his eyes twinkled at her knowingly. 'What were you planning to do? Hitchhike?'

India grinned sheepishly. 'Well . . . Okay. I had no idea what I was going to do. I'm glad you're coming with me.'

While India cleared the table and recycled the dishes, Theo hunted up some of Jenny's old clothing and set it out for India to put on for extra padding.

'Where did these come from?' India asked as she pulled a sweater on over three tee-shirts and her own clothing.

'I just never quite got around to throwing them away, or sending them out to Jenny. Well, I guess she hasn't got much use for them now, but we'll leave them with her once you go back to your job at the Inn.'

India climbed into a pair of sweats and trousers, and zipped them up. 'I can't move,' she complained. 'I feel like a scarecrow: stuffed and padded.'

Once the make-up had been applied, India was completely unrecognizable. 'I look dreadful!' she gasped, taking in the whole effect in the full-length mirror on the back of the bathroom door.

'You don't look much like you, that's for sure,' Theo said solemnly. 'Are we ready?'

'No,' said India decidedly. 'I have small-child-just-bundled-into-snowsuit syndrome.' She made shooing motions at Theo and shut the bathroom door. 'I'll be out in a minute!'

The garage was deserted so early in the morning. Sunrise was still half an hour away as they entered the beltway and put the ground capsule into the computer's automatic pilot. Very few vehicles were on the belt with them at that hour.

'You might as well take a nap,' Theo suggested. 'I'll keep an eye out to make sure we aren't followed.'

India took him up on his suggestion, and slid down in the seat to find a more comfortable position. 'Wake me if anything happens,' she said. Then she dropped off to sleep.

Ty was waiting for her on the plane of the No-Place.

Chapter Seven

What are you doing here? India asked.

I was waiting for you, Ty started to explain.

Don't you have anything better to do? she demanded. *Why don't I ever see anyone else here? How come whenever I get here, you're already here, or you show up just afterward?*

Ty shrugged. *Just lucky?*

India narrowed her eyes and stared at him. He grinned disarmingly.

I just wanted to keep in touch. You seem like you could use a friend, he continued.

Don't do me any favors, she said rather ungraciously.

Got up on the wrong side of the bed?

Just out of a strange one, India replied.

Oh, ho!

It's not like it sounds. I met this man . . .

And you accuse me of overactive hormones? Ty interrupted.

No! I mean . . . I don't know what I mean. India turned away and began walking.

You mean you met a guy and went to bed with him in real time, but you won't give me a tumble in the No-Place? Ty trotted to catch up with her.

India stopped abruptly and turned to face him. *I don't know you. I don't have to justify my behavior to you. I have nothing to apologize for. I didn't ask you to be here. Why don't you go away?*

I'm sorry, Ty said. *I was just teasing you. Sometimes you don't have much of a sense of humor.*

India shrugged.

Is it anything you want to talk about?

She shook her head. *How come you're acting like you care?* she asked.

I do, he said gently. *Look, sometimes it helps to have someone to talk things out with. If you feel like talking, I'll listen. That's all.*

India studied Ty for a long moment. *Thanks,* she said softly. *Right now, I think I just want to forget it, though.*

That's what you said last time when you screamed through the entire roller-coaster ride. You're still upset, he pointed out.

It's just . . . India began.

Ty cocked his head to the right and looked intently at her.

I was kidnapped and I've escaped, but they're chasing me and I'm scared to death, India said at last, the words coming out in a rush.

Oh, gee. Is that all?

India knew Ty was only trying to be lighthearted about a serious problem, but his response still rankled on her raw nerve endings. *You're acting more like a court jester than a friend,* she said shortly.

I was just trying to take some of the heat off!

I know. Look, I've been seeing too much of you recently. It would help a lot just to be by myself for a while.

You've said that before, too, Ty said softly. He came closer and put a hand on India's shoulder. *I don't think being by yourself is solving the problem any more than screaming about it.*

India nodded silently.

Do you know who's chasing you?

She shook her head.

Do you know why they're chasing you?

She shook her head again. She looked up at him, eyes bright with unshed tears. *I thought for a while it might be my father,* she said. A tear spilled over her lower lid and slipped down her cheek. *He hasn't bothered me since I was old enough to be legally responsible for myself,* she laughed shortly. *Probably the only law he ever worried about!*

What do you mean? Ty asked, still holding on to India's shoulder.

She felt him start to fall into her eyes and quickly looked past him into the dull grey of the No-Place and shuddered. *Nothing,* she whispered.

(*You're playing with fire.*)

What? India looked up at Ty.

I said: What do you mean? Ty repeated.

I heard something, India said, staring past him again.

His grip tightened on her shoulder and she shuddered, tugging herself loose.

Don't do that, she whispered. *I have to go.*

Why? Are you sure you're okay?

India's anger flared. *Stop asking me that! If I were okay, would I be here?*

Yes, Ty answered frankly. *Lots of people come here to work. They're all just fine.*

Well, good for them, India snapped.

When she woke up, the beltway stretched before her. The buildings of Quebec had been left far behind. Theo smiled over at her and returned his attention to a game he was playing on the VidCon. India relaxed. She was safe here.

'How long do you figure it'll take us to get there?' India asked much later. She shifted in her seat, trying to find a more comfortable position. Buried under so many layers of clothing, she felt uncomfortable most of the time. 'It's hot in here.'

Theo smiled. 'Barring incident and assuming we don't stop too often, I figure it'll take us about four or five days.'

'That's what I was afraid of,' India sighed. She squirmed again.

'Why don't we pull off at the next stop,' Theo suggested, watching her contortions. 'We can stretch our legs and get a bite of lunch.'

'Do we dare?' asked India.

'We won't take long.'

'You *let* her go?' Bob couldn't believe what he'd heard. He glared at the two men standing in front of him.

They stood stolidly, returning his look with unfocused, noncommittal gazes.

'Deliberately?' he demanded.

'Well, yes and no, sir.'

Bob glared at them, waiting for elaboration. The silence grew louder. 'Well,' he said sarcastically. 'Would you like to build on that?'

'I expect you'll have to fire us, sir.'

'Fire you? Hell, I'm going to assign you to track her down and bring her back.'

'Then I expect we'll have to quit, sir.'

Bob laughed unpleasantly. 'A little post-hypnotic suggestion will change your minds,' he said.

'I thought you didn't like this either, sir.'

'I don't. But it's part of the job.' He looked thoughtfully at each of the two men for a moment. 'And the job is more than this one incident. It's more important than this one stupid situation. The job is what's important to me.'

'Yeah, but what about what . . .'

Bob cut him off. 'What he wants is a big score. It's our duty to see that he gets it.'

The two men grumbled under their breath.

'You screwed up,' he said to them. 'Now go make it right.'

Harry and Grindle left the office.

'How the hell are we going to find her now?' asked Grindle.

Harry shrugged. 'Check the roof first. See if we can't find a clue about where she went?'

'Door's still barricaded,' Grindle pointed out.

'We didn't try very hard to break it down, did we?' asked Harry.

The footsteps were still clear in the snow on the rooftop, leading to the edge where India had jumped.

The two men stood at the edge and looked down.

'I didn't hear anything about a body yesterday,' said Grindle.

'Me either,' said Harry, looking up. 'Guess she was scared enough. She coulda made the jump.'

'What floor is this?' asked Grindle.

'Twenty-second?' Harry guessed.

'Let's go talk to the landlord.'

'He ain't home! What do youse two want?'

The woman's sharp features were drawn together in anger and mistrust. She peered at Harry and Grindle through the crack the door-chain allowed.

'We need to talk with your husband, ma'am,' said Harry with exaggerated patience. 'Do you know when he'll be back?'

'He din't tell me. He never tells me nothin'. Jus' said he'd be back when he was damn good and ready.'

'Could we wait for him, then?' asked Grindle.

'Sure! You wait. You wait till hell freezes over. He's out chasing skirts. He'll be home when he wants his supper, most likely!' She slammed the door.

Grindle sighed and called through the closed door, 'Did he leave you the pass key?'

'No!' she shouted back at them.

They weren't able to get any further response from the woman.

Harry settled himself on the front step. 'I guess now we wait,' he said, nodding to the stair next to him.

Grindle sat down. 'What time is it?'

'Two.'

'Shouldn't we come back?'

'Grindle, what happens when a landlord finds out we want to talk to him?' Harry asked rhetorically. He patted the stair next to him.

'What if he calls home? What if she tells him?'

'Did she sound like she expected a call?'

Grindle shook his head and sat down.

It was close to midnight when the man finally came home.

'Sure, I got the pass key. Twenty-second floor, you think? Let's go see if anyone's home.'

The lift was incredibly slow. Harry and Grindle studied the landlord as they rode upward.

He looked surprisingly like his wife. His sharp features seemed to draw to a point at his nose, and recede from there. He had no chin to speak of, and a long, sloping forehead bereft of hair. His Adam's apple bobbed up and down as he swallowed uncomfortably. His narrow shoulders gave way to a spreading middle and rather womanish hips. He didn't look much like a man who spent his time chasing women.

'What is it you're looking for?' he asked uncertainly.

'We'll know when we get there,' said Harry, still staring at the man.

The lift ground to a halt with a shudder and the doors opened on to a dark hallway.

'Keep meanin' to fix the lights,' the landlord muttered as they walked down the hall to a window to get their bearings.

'One floor down,' Grindle said, craning his neck to see out the window. 'Two fire escapes over.'

'Twenty-one, twenty-one,' mused the landlord. 'That'd be old Theodore Winslow's place. What'd he do?'

'We don't know yet.'

The lift had been called by someone on another floor. The three men waited an eternity for the next one to come.

No one answered their knock on the door. The landlord pressed the doorbell and a recording responded.

'Gone to visit his daughter,' the landlord repeated. 'Guess he won't be gone long. He didn't tell me to shut off the electric or nothin'.'

'Where does his daughter live?' asked Harry.

The landlord shrugged. 'Maybe he told me, but I forgot. Can't keep track of everything.'

'Grindle, we got anything to help his memory?' Harry asked casually.

A shrewd gleam came into the landlord's eyes.

Grindle nodded, reached into his coat and pulled out a gun. 'Don't remember?'

The man's eyes widened. 'S—San Francisco. She lives out west.'

'And her name?' Grindle prodded.

'Jennifer,' said the man, backing away from the gun Grindle had leveled at him.

'Jennifer Winslow,' said Harry.

'No!' the landlord started. 'She don't go by Winslow. I don't know what her husband's name is. All's I know is they live north of the Old City. Theo don't talk to me often. Quiet guy, you know? Is he in trouble?'

Grindle put his gun away. 'Maybe.'

Harry grinned. 'You know how it is with those quiet guys. Here's my card. Call me if you hear anything, okay?'

The landlord accepted the card, visibly relieved that the gun had disappeared. 'Yeah, sure, okay, no problem.' He started to back down the hallway.

'We'd still like to take a look around Mr Winslow's apartment.' Harry smiled.

'Need a warrant or something, don't you?' he asked.

'Grindle, show the man our warrant,' said Harry, still smiling.

Grindle reached into his coat again.

The landlord flinched. 'Okay, okay. Here, just let me find the key.'

The apartment was clean. Harry and Grindle moved into the living room with no idea what they were looking for. Nothing seemed amiss. They wandered through the apartment, each taking separate rooms.

'Hey, Harry!' Grindle called from the kitchen. 'Come look at this.'

Harry found Grindle standing in front of the open refrigerator. 'You looking for a snack?'

'Guy has an open carton of milk and fresh vegetables and stuff in here.' He stood back to show Harry the contents of the refrigerator.

'So?'

'So, when we go away somewhere for a while, my wife always cleans out the fridge. That way nothing goes bad.'

'So?' Harry repeated.

'So, look at the rest of the apartment. This guy doesn't look like the kind who would forget to clean out the fridge. Maybe he left in a hurry. Maybe he didn't expect to make this trip at all before last night.'

'What happened last night?' asked the landlord from behind Harry.

'India,' said Harry and Grindle together.

'No,' the landlord complained. 'I said she lived in San Francisco. Why would he go to India?'

'Maybe the VidCon recording from last night will tell us something?' suggested Grindle.

There were no VidCon recordings. 'A man who habitually erases all his transactions?' asked Harry.

'Costs to store them,' said the landlord. 'I can't afford the top-end models. Most of my tenants erase their transactions at the end of the day.'

'Damn,' said Grindle. 'If we think of anything else, you'll hear from us,' he told the landlord. Then he and Harry left the building.

India emerged from the restaurant bathroom tugging at her clothing. Theo was nowhere in sight.

India panicked and ran out into the parking lot. The car was still there, but Theo wasn't inside it. He was nowhere in the parking lot either. India turned and walked slowly back into the restaurant. Standing by the register, she looked about.

Theo sat in one corner on the CrediVid, talking earnestly to the screen. He looked up and saw her staring at him. Quickly, he disconnected and came over to her.

'All set?' he asked heartily.

'Sure,' India said. 'Who were you talking to?'

'Just a friend,' he said, taking her arm and steering her toward the door. 'We'd better get back on the road.'

'I thought you called everyone you needed to talk to last night,' she said as they went out into the parking lot.

'I just had some business to take care of,' he said, opening the car door for India.

'What kind of business?' India persisted. 'I thought you said you were retired.'

'I am,' Theo admitted. 'That doesn't mean I don't keep my hand in. I like to stay on top of things.'

'You weren't calling to let them know where I was?' she asked.

Theo laughed outright. 'Why on earth would I do that?' he asked. 'They'd get me for aiding and abetting, remember?' He gestured at her hair and clothing.

India thought for a moment. His reaction seemed genuine to her. She relaxed slightly and permitted herself a grin. 'Yeah, sorry.' She climbed into the car and they re-entered beltway traffic.

*　　*　　*

'They didn't take a tube or shuttle out of here,' Grindle announced. 'No matching prints, no one matching their general descriptions on any of the departures since last night.' He sat back from the VidCon and watched Harry shaving himself in front of a small mirror he had propped on his desk.

Harry swished his blade around in his coffee before dragging it down his lathered cheek.

'God, I hate watching you do that,' Grindle complained. 'Why can't you use a depilatory like everyone else?'

Harry washed his razor in his coffee again before answering. 'You know I'm allergic to the chemicals in those damned things. The coffee tightens my pores.'

'Cosmetic tips from Auntie Harry,' Grindle said, disgusted.

'Look, you don't like it, don't watch,' Harry said, returning to his task. 'Why don't you start on ground-vehicle rental to take your mind off it.'

'Think they'd do that?'

'How else they gonna do it? Walk?' Harry finished shaving and began cleaning up his desk. 'You take the first half of the alphabet, I'll take the last half, and we'll access every rental agency until we find what we're looking for.'

'It's a long drive from here to San Francisco,' Grindle observed.

'Yes, it is,' said Harry. 'And they already have a good lead on us, so I guess we better get to it.'

Two hours later, Grindle jumped to his feet. 'Yeah! Got him! This guy's no pro. He even used his own name!'

'When did they pick up the vehicle?' Harry asked tiredly.

''Bout five this morning. This says he picked it up alone, though. Guess he went back to his apartment to get our girl.'

'Is there a homing device on the vehicle?'

'Standard on every vehicle they rent. Humming along

nice as you please.' Grindle smiled broadly. 'Just look at this.' He swung the VidCon screen toward Harry. A tiny red light pulsed on a highway route south and west of Quebec.

'Let's go pick them up,' said Harry. He switched off the screen.

'Shouldn't we tell the Captain we're going?' Grindle reminded him.

Harry pulled a face. 'Yeah. Come on, let's go.'

'Do you have other family in Quebec?' India asked Theo idly as they traveled south through a long corridor of tall buildings. Everything outside the windows seemed grey. The sky was overcast; the same color as the man-made structures surrounding them. It fitted India's mood. She wished she had some needlework or a good book. Reading the glowing VidCon screen hurt her eyes in this kind of light, so she was bored and restless.

'No,' Theo responded thoughtfully. 'I've often thought of moving to San Francisco since Jenny and her family settled there, but I just never got around to it.'

'What about Jenny's mother?' India pressed. She knew it was none of her business, but she asked anyway, figuring if he didn't want to tell her he wouldn't.

'We signed a twenty-year contract. When the twenty years were up, we decided not to renew,' he said. 'Jenny was eighteen and had moved out to go to college, and we discovered we just weren't interested in each other any more.' He shrugged. 'Jenny keeps me up to date on what her mother is doing. I suppose she also does the reverse and keeps her mother up to date on me.'

'So what have you been doing?' asked India.

'Not a lot really,' said Theo diffidently. 'Some volunteer work with troubled kids downtown, a little freelance writing for magazines and newspapers; enough to keep me out of trouble. How about you?'

'I was a secretary in a governmental office in the Orion sector,' she said briefly.

'I meant where did you come from?'

'Berkeley District,' she said softly. 'Up in the hills.'

'I've heard about that area,' Theo said, obviously searching his memory for the reference. 'Wasn't there some crazy mobster kind of guy living up there building twelve-foot stone walls around whole neighborhoods and tearing down old houses and re-landscaping with grass, trees and laser turrets?'

India nodded.

'What was his name? Gilbert. Franklin Gilbert. Neighbor of yours?'

'My father,' she said.

Theo was quiet for a long time. 'India Gilbert. You told me that, didn't you?'

India stared out the window at the passing buildings and tried to feel what Theo's emotional reaction was, but she couldn't. She was upset and he was blocking himself somehow.

'Is he the one who's chasing you?' he asked finally.

'I don't think so,' said India. She gave up trying to probe his mind. 'He's there at the bottom somewhere, but I can't quite reach the memory. My impression is that he's unaware this is happening.'

'Is it possible his men are acting without his knowledge?' asked Theo.

India shook her head. 'I don't think so.'

'I didn't mean to uncover old wounds,' he apologized.

India shrugged and looked at him directly. 'No one said it would be easy; no one said it would be fair. I just want my life back.'

They rode for a long time in silence.

'Will you go back to your old job?' Theo asked finally.

India gave a short, mirthless laugh. 'I don't even know if it's still there. After a year, my boss has surely filled the position. My landlord has probably evicted me as well. Who knows if I'll ever find my stuff again. There were some pieces of jewelry that belonged to my mother; some pictures of her. Everything I had, everything I was, has been taken from me. That makes me really angry.'

Theo nodded, watching her face closely. 'That's not all, though.'

'No.' India was silent again for a long moment. 'In a funny way, I'm glad I've had the chance to discover my mind in different ways. I like the people who've helped me learn these new things.' India squirmed inside her many layers of clothing, shifting positions in her seat. She looked outside again, watching the buildings and the other traffic on the beltway.

Something in her mind slipped.

'Gods!' she gasped, and sat up straight in her seat.

'Are you okay?' asked Theo.

'Yes!' she exclaimed. 'Bob kept bringing me back because he kept screwing up the blocks and they're slipping again. One just breached a bit and I got a glimpse of Ashraf.'

'Who?' he asked interestedly.

'The administrator for the Level One training facility,' India explained. 'He was the one who insisted I be sent to Anara. What would he have been doing behind one of my blocks?'

A vehicle drew level with theirs on the beltway and matched their pace. Distracted, India looked over at the occupants and gasped again. 'Theo, we've got to get out of here!' she cried. 'They've found us!'

'Who?' asked Theo, looking over at the vehicle.

'Those are the two men I escaped from back in Quebec.'

'Damn,' he said, thumbing the auto control to manual and shifting down a belt to a slower lane. The dash display showed an exit coming up. 'I didn't think to check the vehicle for a homing signal.'

The two men shifted their vehicle down a lane and matched pace again.

'Gather our stuff together and be ready to abandon the pod quickly,' Theo told her as he pulled off onto the exit. He wove through surface street traffic, increasing speed as he went.

'Can't we shut off the device?' asked India.

'Try,' said Theo, not taking his attention from the road.

India logged into the VidCon and located the homing beacon. There was no way to disable it through the computer. 'It's in the trunk,' she said, dismayed.

'Go through the back seat,' suggested Theo, taking a corner very quickly.

India crawled over the front seat and landed with a thump as the vehicle righted itself in the next street.

The seat-back posed little problem, and India stood out of the way to lower it onto the back seat, exposing the opening to the trunk. 'Is there a light back here?' she asked.

'Can't help you,' said Theo shortly, treading hard on the accelerator again.

India swayed against the surge of power and then braced herself to crawl into the dark space. Little light was cast by the grey skies, so India fumbled blindly in the area of the homing device until she came across what felt like a panel door. The compartment sprung open at her touch and she reached inside before her imagination could supply images of the things she might encounter. It felt like a small, solid-state logic board. She reached around until she found the edge, but behind it she found nothing to grab on to or tear out.

Abandoning that for a moment, India searched the trunk space with her hands, looking for a tire iron. There was nothing resembling anything useful. 'Damn,' she muttered to herself. She relocated the homing beacon, took off her outer shirt, and wrapped it around her fist.

Pressing her padded fist against the logic board for a

moment, she drew back a bit and then punched it as hard as she could. 'Dirty words!' she hissed as the pain blossomed in her hand. 'Theo!' she yelled. 'Did that knock it out?'

'No,' he called back to her.

The vehicle lurched sideways again and India rolled in spite of herself.

'Damn,' she muttered, blinking back tears and reorienting herself in the dark trunk space. She unwound her shirt from her hand and wrapped it around the other. She punched the small board as hard as she could. Then, ignoring the pain, she punched it again.

'That got it!' Theo yelled.

Gratefully, India climbed out of the trunk, pushed the seat-back into place, and tumbled over into the front. 'They know about my disguise now,' she said as she examined her knuckles. They would bruise, but the skin was unbroken.

Theo nodded and slowed his pace. 'We lost them.'

'Now what?'

'Now I think we find another rental place and disable the homing device before we return to the beltway, but I think we should take surface streets to the next district before we do that,' said Theo, glancing over at India. 'You okay?'

India smiled at him. 'Once I swallow my heart, I'll be fine.'

Theo chuckled. 'Me too.'

It took several hours to reach the next district. Theo and India traveled in a zig-zag through the city streets, hoping to avoid Harry and Grindle, who were no doubt still searching for them. It was getting dark when they pulled over near a rental agency.

'Keep it out of sight of the clerk,' India advised as Theo inched forward along the curb. 'What name should we use to rent this one?'

'I have to use my own,' Theo said. 'They check licenses

and credit cards before just turning a vehicle over to people.'

'Bother,' she said. 'I'd forgotten about that. Well at least we can disable the homing device before we get back onto the beltway.'

'How about a bit of supper before we get back on the beltway?' Theo asked. 'All that adrenalin got my appetite up.'

India grinned. 'Yeah, I could live with that.'

'Her father is that guy from Berkeley, you know the one I'm talking about? The one with the drugs and prostitutes? Yeah, the crazy guy with the guns and the real-estate fetish.' Theo looked up and saw India approaching from across the restaurant. 'I gotta go, George. See what you can do, okay? Yeah, thanks, you too.'

Theo rang off and stood up.

'Who was that?' asked India as she joined him.

'Just calling the Youth Center to let them know I won't be in for a while,' said Theo easily. 'Are you ready to go?'

'Yeah,' India nodded. She didn't look convinced, but she didn't question him. She turned and walked out of the restaurant.

Once on the beltway, Theo put the vehicle into auto pilot and sat back. 'Do you want to play a game?' he asked, indicating the VidCon.

India shook her head.

'It'll help pass the time.'

'I think I'll sleep for a while,' India said. 'I'm still feeling a little tired and beat up from rolling around in the trunk.'

'Okay.'

Theo activated the screen and turned on the news.

India lay back in her seat, closed her eyes and went instead to the No-Place.

Anara? she called, doing her best not to summon Ty. *Anara!*

While she waited for Anara to appear, India decided to imagine a comfortable living room where they would be able to talk safely. As she worked, the room began to resemble the central room at the Inn, except that where the table and chairs took up most of the floor India set up two couches and a small table between them. On the table, she put two cups of fresh coffee.

This looks very nice, said a familiar voice behind her.

India turned and saw the same blonde woman she had contacted when she was in Theo's apartment. *Shannon!* She grinned and gestured toward the couches. *Come sit down. Where's Anara?*

Shannon smiled. *You remember me this time?*

India stood still for a moment and searched her mind. *Gods, another block must have slipped. That's what I was calling Anara about.*

She couldn't come to you right now. That's why I'm here. Is that okay? Shannon still stood uncertainly in the doorway.

Sure, said India enthusiastically. *Come on in.*

Shannon sat gingerly on the edge of one of the couches and looked at India, who sprawled on the other. *Your blocks are still slipping? It must be pretty erratic. Sometimes you know who I am and sometimes you don't. Anara said to expect it, but it's so strange when it happens.*

Mmhmm. Have some coffee. India reached for the mug closest to her and took a sip. *I know it's silly, but it makes me feel more at home.*

Shannon relaxed and sat back with her mug. *How have you been?*

India wrinkled her nose. *I miss you guys.*

You're coming back, aren't you?

I'm trying, said India. *That was one of the things I wanted to talk to Anara about. I don't know if I should be worried about Theo.*

What do you mean?

He keeps making calls every time we stop and then lying to me about who he's talking to, but his mind is blocked in a way I can't read through.

Then how do you know he's lying? asked Shannon practically.

Body language, mostly, India admitted. *He never looks comfortable with the answers he gives me.*

Do you think this is a good enough reason to distrust him?

That's what's so weird, said India. *I feel like I should trust him.*

Didn't Anara tell you what to do about things like this?

Yes, said India, a trifle sullenly.

Shannon waited silently.

Pay attention to my heart, India said at last. *But what if . . .*

Shannon shook her head. *You can second-guess yourself, or you can learn to trust yourself. It's your choice. Now tell me about the slipping blocks.*

I saw Ashraf behind one for a moment. The block didn't come down entirely, so all I got was the one glimpse. I don't understand why he would be there. I only met him the once. India looked at Shannon. *Any ideas?*

I think this one we keep to ourselves, for a while, anyway, said Shannon. *I'll talk it over with Anara and Henry as soon as I can.* She stood up. *Will you be coming back here again?*

Should I? asked India, also standing.

Shannon nodded. *I think we should keep in touch. We may be able to help you along the way.*

Anara said you couldn't.

I think she meant physically assist you on your journey to San Francisco, Shannon clarified. *We may find ways to help you that don't require our actual presence. Anyway, come here when you can and one of us will always be able to answer your call.*

India stepped forward and gave Shannon a hug. *Thanks for answering this time. I'll see you soon.*

They left the room and went in opposite directions.

The room disappeared as India walked away from it, toward her contact with the No-Place. An obelisk surged into being far off on her right, and India felt a presence behind her, but when she turned no one was there. Shannon had vanished and India was alone on the vast grey plane. Shuddering slightly, India found her contact and left the No-Place.

Harry made a face at Grindle. 'We have to tell him,' he said.

'You tell him. You were driving,' Grindle said. 'I didn't lose an old man in the streets of Montreal.'

'Right. Like you could've kept up any better,' Harry grumbled as he keyed the VidCon. 'Maybe we could get Winslow's daughter's address and get there before them.'

Grindle nodded hopefully.

The Captain's face appeared on the screen before them. 'Well?'

'We caught up with them okay,' Harry began.

'But you lost them,' finished the Captain.

'They managed to disable the tracer while the old man was driving like a lunatic on the surface streets. We found the car parked on a side street near another rental agency,' Harry explained. 'They got another car, but we can't find its signal.'

'You'll find them on beltway 81 heading south through New York,' said the Captain. 'You did get the license number from the rental agency?'

'Yes,' said Harry. 'How do you . . .'

'And the color and make of the vehicle?' the Captain interrupted.

'Yes, sir. Thank you, sir.'

The connection was broken. Harry looked at Grindle.

'Well?' Grindle looked at Harry. 'Let's go get them.'

Shannon stood in the middle of Anara's vegetable garden and looked up. Tall, dark green trees stood against the deep blue, cloudless summer sky. The heat made her feel slightly dizzy as it rose in waves from the cultivated earth, and the smells of growing vegetables and compost stirred on the small, warm breeze.

Henry stood near her, watching Anara who knelt between the rows, weeding.

'That was all she had to say?' asked Anara. She rocked back on her heels and wiped the sweat from her chin with a towel she kept for that purpose.

'Were you expecting something else?' asked Shannon. 'Her body language only revealed tension, and that was to be expected.'

'No,' said Anara, returning her attention to the lettuce. 'Nothing else. I was just hoping she might have found out more.'

'But Ashraf . . .' said Henry wonderingly.

Shannon shuddered involuntarily, remembering the feel of his contact in her mind.

Henry saw this and grinned. 'Not an easy guy to warm up to.'

'He gives me the creeps,' Shannon complained. 'He's the only part of the job I don't like.'

'I know what you mean,' said Anara, looking up again. 'I was grateful for the transfer out of there after a few years. I was never very comfortable working for someone younger than me who made me feel as if I'd done something wrong even when I was sure I hadn't.' She looked around at her garden. 'I really like working for myself.' Smiling warmly at Shannon, she said, 'Give yourself the time to get out from under him and you'll like this organization a whole lot better.'

Shannon sighed. 'Yeah,' she said. 'In the meantime, what do we do about India? I told her we'd try to find a way to help her if we could.'

'You shouldn't have given her a false hope,' Henry admonished. He hunkered down among the lettuce and began pulling weeds.

'I couldn't just let her go back without any hope at all!' Shannon protested.

'I did,' said Anara pointedly. 'She has to believe she's the only one she can rely on if she's going to make it back here.'

'What about Theo?' asked Shannon as she also dropped to her knees to weed.

'You said she wasn't sure whether or not she could trust him,' said Henry, tossing a weed into the basket.

'We can't do anything?' pleaded Shannon.

'What?' asked Anara. 'What could we possibly do that would make any difference here?' She paused for a moment to let Shannon think. 'We can give her emotional support. Period.'

Chapter Eight

'Hey, the VidCon says the junction for 80 West is the most likely place for India and Mr Winslow to start heading west toward San Francisco. It's the most direct route,' said Grindle, squinting at the small display screen in the dashboard.

'You think they might have taken that?' Harry asked.

'Probably. Think we ought to call the Captain?'

Harry winced. 'I really don't want to, but he was so sure they had taken 81, we ought to tell him we didn't catch up with them yet.'

'He'll be pissed,' said Grindle.

Harry nodded. 'They did have a few hours' head-start on us,' he pointed out.

'That should carry a lot of weight,' Grindle said sarcastically as he punched in the numbers.

'Why don't you go ahead on that interchange and I'll check on their location for you,' the Captain said.

Grindle and Harry stared at the tiny screen.

'Really?' Harry asked finally.

'You can change to another belt later if it's necessary, but for now it makes sense they would go by the most direct route. They think they've lost you. Maybe they won't be as cautious.'

Grindle disconnected the line. 'Damn,' he said. 'That was too easy.'

Harry shrugged. '80 it is.' He entered the change in the computer and sat back. 'I guess we just keep an eye out and wait for the call?'

'Sure. Wanna play Galaxy Pirates?' Grindle handed

Harry a remote and called up the game on the dash screen.

'My kid plays that,' said Harry derisively.

'It's a good game.'

'It's a kids' game.'

'Yeah, but it's fun. Come on, loosen up. You've been wearing a tie too long. Boss won't see you take it off,' said Grindle. 'The rules are simple. Anything you can get away with is okay. If you get caught, you die.'

'Democratic,' said Harry, giving in. 'What are we actually doing?'

'What pirates usually do: rape, pillage, plunder. Just be sure the cops don't catch you,' Grindle said impatiently as he moved his cruiser across the screen toward a huge starship.

'But the starships are always escorted by cops. How do you get past them?' objected Harry. He watched Grindle maneuver his cruiser into position on the screen.

'That's the point of the game!' Grindle paused the program for a moment. 'You have to figure it out. We can double-team them, or you can go after your own quarry. I'm going after this one if you don't blow it for me.'

'That's what these games are teaching my kid?' Harry gaped. 'How to attack a starship?'

'Right. Like he's going to go out to get his ass thrown in jail by the cops for doing something so stupid.'

'But this might give him the idea!'

'Harry, how dumb is your kid?' asked Grindle bluntly.

'He's not dumb at all,' said Harry defensively.

'Then why do you think he's dumb enough to do something so incredibly stupid as think this game is telling him to get a space cruiser and attack a starship?'

Harry shrugged. 'No harm in being cautious,' he said a little sullenly.

Grindle chuckled to himself as he maneuvered his cruiser around the vanguard of the cops and attacked the starship.

Harry picked up his remote and blasted a few cop

cruisers himself. A small detachment of cops broke away from the main force and came after him. Harry leaned forward and thumbed the control, intent on avoiding getting blasted out of the vacuum.

Grindle glanced at Harry and grinned. They'd find the girl soon enough. Might as well enjoy themselves in the meantime.

India stood in darkness, disoriented.

She had been expecting to go to the No-Place, but this was something entirely different. She felt she should know where she was, but there was no way to get her bearings. In the dark, she couldn't see what surrounded her.

Hello? she called tentatively.

No one answered, but India thought she could hear voices in the distance.

Hello? she repeated, starting toward the sounds. As she moved, the noise grew louder. The darkness also lessened, and she began to see shadows around her. *Is anybody here?* India called.

A sudden light flared in front of her, and the voices became loud and clamoring. *It's this one again! She's alone! Catch her this time! Don't let her get away!*

Panic froze India's heart. The Disembodied. How had she wound up here? The bright light remained in front of her, somehow, not moving to surround her as she had expected. The voices grew louder, but no closer.

Slowly, two shapes resolved themselves between her and the light. She was unable to see more than silhouettes, but she felt she should know who they were.

What are you doing here? rasped one of the shadows.

Before she could answer, the shadows raised their hands toward her. India found herself moving backward at an alarming rate, unable to stop herself. *Hey!* she shouted. *Put me down! Who are you? What's happening?*

Laughter echoed back to her. *Go play where it's safe, little girl,* whispered another voice in her ear; a voice she was sure she knew, if she could only place it.

'Oh!' India sat straight up in her seat.

Darkness shut off the grey view she and Theo had been traveling through all day. The dash console glowed a dim green, showing Theo what he was doing, but not illuminating the interior of the vehicle.

Theo glanced over at India, but didn't comment.

'Wow,' India said, hoping Theo would ask her what had awakened her.

Instead, he shut off the VidCon and sat back in his seat. They traveled silently for several long moments.

'The strangest thing just happened,' India said finally.

Theo scratched his chin reflectively; said nothing.

'Do you want to hear about it?' India asked tentatively.

Theo shrugged. 'I expect if you want to tell me about it, you will,' he said.

They rode for several more minutes in silence.

'I had a sort of dream,' India started. She stopped for a moment and thought about it. 'I guess it wasn't so much a dream as a block shifting or something,' she clarified.

Theo said nothing. He sat in his seat and stared out the windshield at the beltway.

The darkness grew deeper, separating India from reality as she thought about the thing that had awakened her. She shuddered involuntarily.

Theo glanced over at her, but she was so wrapped up in her vision she didn't notice.

'I saw two men standing between me and the Disembodied,' she said, still testing the reality of the event in her mind.

'I see,' said Theo.

'Do you know what that means?' asked India.

'No,' said Theo.

India stared out the window at nothing for quite a while before saying, 'Me either.'

'Were you hoping I would?' Theo asked.

India shrugged. 'I guess I was hoping someone might.'

'Why don't you ask those friends of yours at the Inn?' suggested Theo.

India thought she heard a trace of laughter in his voice. 'You don't believe me, do you? You don't believe that place exists?'

'I'm not saying it doesn't,' said Theo slowly. 'I haven't been there. How would I know?'

'You could believe I'm telling the truth,' said India.

'I could, but what difference would it make? Whether or not I believe you isn't the point.'

'No, but it would help,' said India.

'In what way?' asked Theo. He seemed genuinely curious.

'I guess maybe I would have less self-doubt.'

'You don't need me for that,' Theo said.

India laughed shortly. 'I need everyone I can get for that. Who do you call when we stop?'

'Do you think I'm one of the men who are after you?'

India's mouth twisted bitterly. She was trying not to cry. 'I don't know what to think any more.'

'Do I seem like someone you can trust?' asked Theo.

'Yes! You do,' said India forcefully. 'That's what I don't get! I can't read you and even when you're lying I don't feel like I should mistrust you, but that's just it. I can tell when you're lying, but you don't do anything to make me feel like you're telling me the truth.'

'Would it make you feel any better if you couldn't tell the difference?'

India shook her head. 'Then I'd *know* I couldn't trust you.'

'What does your gut tell you?'

'Oh! You and Anara and Peter! Don't tell me you work

with them?' India turned halfway round in her seat and faced Theo. She studied his profile.

He grinned. 'This Anara sounds like my kind of woman!'

'Men!' India turned back in her seat and stared out the front windshield. 'I guess what I don't get,' she said slowly, 'is that I trust you in spite of having almost no reason to.'

'Then why don't you tell me about these two men who are standing between you and the dismembered?' suggested Theo.

India laughed. 'Disembodied!' she corrected. 'They exist in the Collective Unconscious, and I have no idea who might be on that level and still be in their body.'

'Are you sure they still have bodies? You aren't just picturing them that way?' asked Theo. He turned to face India.

'No. That's what surprised me so much. They were solid and real compared to the massed energy of the Disembodied. Like shadows in the light. That was why I couldn't see their faces. I couldn't see who they were, but I was certain I knew them and I was afraid of them.' India turned to look at Theo. 'I know that doesn't make sense, but that's what I saw.'

'Whether or not it makes sense isn't for either of us to judge. Have you told Anara this yet?'

'No,' admitted India. She avoided Theo's eyes.

'Well, maybe you ought to?' he suggested.

'Yeah, maybe,' said India.

'Why does that suggestion make you uncomfortable?' asked Theo.

'Two reasons,' India started slowly, trying to think. 'If I go to the No-Place, I might run into Ty. I just don't feel like seeing him right now and having to fend off his adolescent advances.' She stopped.

'That's one,' Theo prompted.

'When I left Shannon last time, I was certain I was being watched, or followed. There wasn't anyone there, but I could feel eyes on the back of my neck. It gave me the creeps. If I go back, there could be someone else waiting for me and that could be worse than Ty being obnoxious.'

'Isn't there any way for you to defend yourself in the "No-Place"?' Theo suggested diffidently.

'I don't know,' said India. 'I haven't even learned how not to broadcast everything I'm thinking when I'm there.'

'Couldn't you just imagine you're surrounded by a shield that won't let anything out but lets anything in that you want?'

India frowned. 'I don't know,' she said. 'Anara suggested that for everyday stuff, but no one ever said there was a specific way to solve the problem in the No-Place. I guess I sort of did that when I created that copy of my apartment, and the room from the Inn in the No-Place. I sort of shielded the places from anything outside them.' India grinned hopefully. 'It could work!'

Theo grinned back. 'Why don't you try it, then?'

'I still don't want to run into Ty,' said India.

'You're making excuses.'

India grinned sheepishly. 'There's enough time to screw up my courage. In the meantime, why don't you tell me about your daughter and her husband. Why do you all live so far apart? What do they do for a living? Do you have any grandchildren?'

'Do you ever take a breath between questions?' Theo countered. 'Yes, I have grandchildren. Four of them. All Jenny's. I didn't have any other children. I guess she was kind of lonely growing up, so she had lots of her own to compensate.'

India leaned back in her seat and closed her eyes. 'What do they all look like?' she prompted.

'Tall,' said Theo, his voice softening as he pictured them in his mind. 'Jenny's mom was a big woman and so is Jenny. Taller than me, anyway. Jenny has brown hair and brown eyes, and looks like I would imagine Earth would look if she were a woman. Everything about Jenny is big: her body, her heart. Her husband is the same way: brown and big.' He chuckled.

India opened her eyes and looked at him.

'Their kids are the wildest bunch of little savages,' Theo continued. 'I guess they're growing up now. I haven't seen them in too long. They send pictures now and then, but it isn't the same thing as seeing them. David is in high school now, I think. And Sandy looks more like her mother every day.'

'Why don't you visit them more often?' India asked. 'You're retired. What keeps you in a tiny apartment so far away from the people you care about?'

Theo shook his head. 'Kids need room to grow,' he said. 'Freedom from parents in order to find their own path in life. I didn't want to interfere.'

'There's a difference between grandparenting and interfering,' India said impatiently.

'You wouldn't want your father hanging around telling you what to do with your kids,' Theo countered.

'That's different!' India objected.

'How?' demanded Theo. 'Every kid, if they've been raised half right, wants to get as far away from their parents as possible, to prevent them from messing up a new generation!'

India giggled.

'What's so funny?'

'You must have been a great dad,' she said.

'Jenny might tell you differently.'

'So she's the perfect parent?' asked India. 'She who raises the wildest bunch of little savages?'

'You see?' demanded Theo. 'That's my opinion of her brood. She would disagree with me. Probably thinks her kids are wonderful.'

'Aren't they?' asked India.

'Yeah. Best kids in the world,' Theo said. The pride in

his voice was evident. 'I just say that to keep people from thinking I'm a besotted grampa.'

'Nothing wrong with that.'

Theo shrugged. 'You want to see pictures?'

India grinned. 'I thought you'd never ask!'

Miles slipped past in the dark as India looked at Theo's grandchildren. It was cheap holography. The images were blurry and faded. India squinted at the faces, but she wasn't exactly sure what any one of them looked like. She guessed she would find out when they got to the Vintners' Quarter.

'What does your son-in-law do?' India asked as she scrutinized his holo.

'I'm not sure,' said Theo, handing her another. 'This is Jenny just after Sandy was born.'

India looked at another faded holo and nodded as if she saw it clearly. Theo obviously did. 'Haven't you ever asked him?' she asked.

'Sure,' said Theo, taking back the holos. 'It's classified. Everyone who works in the Old City proper is working on some project or another that requires secrecy and can't be talked about even to close family members. Jenny doesn't know what her husband does. Or I was never able to pry it out of her. Anyway, they don't trust an old man, I guess, or they'd have told me.'

'What about San Francisco is so hush-hush?' India pressed.

'After the big earthquake when the government moved in, they just never moved out. Bought up all the properties on the peninsula and closed access to civilians. It was as if the Presidio just took over the city. George says it's beautiful now, but I've never seen it myself. I don't know how he's planning to sneak you in, but he said leave it up to him. Passes are issued only to special visitors and permission is required by several levels of authority, but George said he could swing it. I told him it was a matter of life and death.'

'That's very kind of him. He runs as big a risk as I do if we're caught. He has more to lose.'

'We don't know that,' said Theo. 'My football-knee is telling me you have a lot of secrets. Some of them I may not want to know.'

India laughed softly. 'You may be right.'

'So,' Theo said slowly. 'Are you going to talk to those people of yours about your dream now?'

'No, I think I'm going to panic,' said India, pointing.

Theo looked over his shoulder out the window.

In the darkness it was difficult to see, but the man staring back at him from the next vehicle was familiar.

'Theo, we have to get off the beltway now!' India gasped, punching the map up on the VidCon.

Theo accessed the pilot program. 'What are the coordinates of the nearest exit?'

'There isn't one!' India moaned, frantically checking additional maps. 'The next exit is in twenty miles. What are we going to do?'

Theo looked back over at the man in the next car.

The window was down and a rather large gun was leveled at Theo's window.

'Quick! Get your head down!' He grabbed India by the back of the neck and shoved her to the floor.

The shot cracked loudly and the window shattered, but remained intact on the sheet of plastic laminated between the panes. The small round hole was in the wrong place if the man had been trying to shoot the driver. The bullet wouldn't have hit the passenger either. Theo frowned and flipped the controls to manual.

As he maneuvered onto the next-slower belt, he risked a glance at the next car. The gun was still leveled at the window. Another shot cracked at the window.

'What's happening?' India screamed from the floor. 'Why are they using a gun instead of a laser?'

The window fell out of its frame onto Theo. He pushed

it back out and let it fall out of the vehicle onto the beltway. 'You're asking me?'

The men had moved down a belt also, and this time the weapon was a dart gun.

'Tranquilizers? These guys are serious about keeping you alive?' Theo asked India.

She nodded, but was too frightened to speak.

'Hang on,' Theo instructed. 'I'm going to engineer a crash.'

'But that's impossible!' India gasped.

Theo ignored her. He moved down another belt, slowing even more. The dart gun wavered and was pulled back inside the other vehicle for a moment. Then the vehicle moved down a belt also.

This gave Theo the time to override safety programs and the steering mechanism. He wrenched the vehicle across several belts of traffic and over the edge of the beltway. 'Hold tight!' he shouted.

They fell for an endless moment in silence.

They hit with a sickening squeal of twisting metal and glass.

India screamed.

Theo was silent.

For several long moments, they lay in the wreckage. The silence pressed against the vehicle.

India could hear Theo breathing. 'Are you okay?' she asked finally.

There was no answer.

'Theo?'

Still no answer.

'Theo? They could be here any minute. Can you get out?'

When he didn't respond, India climbed up off the floor and put a hand on Theo's shoulder. 'Theo?' she repeated, pulling him back from the crouched position he was in.

There was blood on his forehead. He was unconscious.

India started to panic.

What is the first thing you do when someone is injured? she heard a voice in the back of her mind ask.

Shannon?

No one was there, but the question had jolted India out of her self-pity. She had been taught healing on Level One as a part of her training. Quickly, India ran the checklist on Theo and found that the only injury to him had been the blow to his head on impact. She was able to lessen the pressure and stop the blood flow, but she couldn't raise him to consciousness.

She also couldn't drag him out of the vehicle by herself. After several attempts, she gave up and stood back to take stock of the situation. She was acutely aware of Harry and Grindle. They could be along any minute if they chose the same escape route she and Theo had used.

If only Theo weighed less! She could levitate him out if she were strong enough, but she wasn't. The blocks had kept her from tapping the core of her strength.

'But the blocks are slipping,' she said out loud. 'Maybe . . .' She grabbed his arms and levitated as much of him as she was able. Then she tugged.

He moved!

Working slowly in this manner, she eventually had him lying on the ground beside the wrecked vehicle.

Then she heard the sirens in the distance.

At the very least it was police coming to investigate the crash. India didn't want to imagine what the worst could be. Grabbing Theo by the arms again, she exerted every force she could think of on him.

Something in her mind slipped and Theo's body shot skyward.

'Oh, gods!' India cried, stopping his flight and bringing him back down to her level. 'Where on earth are we going to go?'

A quick search of the car showed nothing in it belonging

to either of them. India grabbed Theo's arm and began to run, towing him behind her.

The sirens grew louder.

She rounded a corner just as lights strobed the area. It would take the police several moments to discover the vehicle was empty. Then they would search until they found something. India ran through unfamiliar streets, holding tight to Theo's hand and drawing reassurance from him, even though he was unconscious.

Something probed the periphery of her mind.

The police had a psychic tracker? She threw up a barrier around herself and Theo, hoping no one would notice the hole where they were supposed to be.

'Theo, what are we going to do now?' she cried as she ran.

The buildings stretched up into the darkness, but the streets were well lit. At this hour, there were few people out: the ones who had nowhere else to go, the ones who lived on the fringes, outside the law. They saw India coming full-tilt down the street with a levitated Santa Claus in tow and decided not even to touch that illusion.

They drifted out of the way, into alleys and doorways to avoid the apparition.

India took no notice. She just ran. She had no destination in mind, no idea what she might do once she got there. She just wanted to put as much distance between herself and the wreck as she could before Theo woke up and could explain why he felt such drastic measures were necessary.

'I trusted you!' she sobbed, running blindly.

He didn't betray that trust, said a voice in the back of her mind. *He might have saved your life.*

Shannon? India gasped and pressed her free hand against a stitch in her ribs.

You screamed pretty loudly for one of us when the vehicle went over the side, said Shannon in the back of

India's mind. *I thought I should come and find out what had happened.*

I don't know! wailed India. She did not slacken her pace, or loosen her grip on Theo. *He shoved me onto the floor; there were gunshots and we crashed.*

Gunshots?

Yeah. Two of them. Loud. Then we dropped forever and smashed into the ground, said India.

Who would be using such old-fashioned and inefficient weapons? asked Shannon.

What? asked India blankly as she rounded another corner, hoping she wasn't accidentally heading back to the site of the wreck. She had a terrible sense of direction.

Why bullets? Why not lasers? asked Shannon.

I dunno, said India. *Neither did Theo when I asked him. Who cares? What am I going to do now?*

Hole up somewhere until Theo regains consciousness, I guess, said Shannon diffidently. *He will probably know what to do next.*

Can't you help me? asked India. She could feel panic rising.

No, said Shannon reluctantly.

But you said . . .

I was wrong, Shannon interrupted firmly. *Anara was right. I can talk to you, but there isn't any physical assistance I can give you.* She paused for a long moment. *You'll have to figure out this one on your own. Just remember, we'll be waiting for you at the door in the Arboretum.*

Great, said India. *If I make it there.*

You must, said Shannon. *I have to go now.*

Fine, bye, said India brusquely.

In the distance, she could hear Shannon sigh. She could also feel the probe in the back of her mind. They wouldn't rest until they had found her and Theo.

India felt she couldn't run any further. She had a cramp burning in her side. She was lost and frightened and essentially alone. She was also feeling very sorry for herself.

What would Theo do?

India ducked into an alley and stopped for a moment. Her breath was coming in gasps and her hands shook, but she managed to pry Theo's wallet out of his pocket. He had a few credits on him. Enough for a cheap hotel room if she could find one. They would be able to lie low for a bit, while India tried to heal Theo's head injury.

Finding a cheap hotel posed the problem, though. This was mostly a business district, and the hotels were very expensive. It was several more blocks before India found something more in their price range.

The smell of urine in the doorway was almost enough to turn her back, but they needed a room, so she pulled Theo through the door after her and tilted him ninety degrees to an upright position. She pulled one of his arms around her shoulder and approached the desk.

'How much is a room for the night?' she asked the clerk.

'¿Qué?' asked the clerk. He didn't look Spanish, but you never could tell.

'A room?' India repeated loudly. She rubbed her thumb against her first two fingers in the internationally accepted symbol for 'expensive'. She didn't speak Spanish.

The clerk looked blankly at her and said nothing.

India pulled out the credits and showed them to the clerk.

He grinned, showing stained brown teeth. He reached out for the small sum.

'No.' India shook her head and withdrew her hand. 'How much?' she repeated.

'¿Qué?' asked the clerk again.

'Oh, never mind,' said India. Feeling defeated, she pulled Theo toward the door. There had to be another place nearby.

'You wait,' called the clerk, suddenly learning English.

India turned.

'Twenty for the night, twenty for sheets and towels. You get that back if you don't take them.'

India looked at the handful of credits she hadn't yet pocketed. Figured. That was it exactly. He could count okay. Fast, too. She sighed.

'Night is half over,' she pointed out. 'I'll give you ten for the room. Twenty for sheets and towels, but you have to give me a receipt.'

'Fifteen,' he said, grinning.

'Fifteen and a receipt,' she said.

'Okay, you give me money now,' said the clerk.

India shook her head. 'Sheets, towels, receipt and key. Then I give you thirty-five credits.'

'Your friend don't look so good,' the clerk observed as he wrote out the receipt for India. He looked at her, inviting her to explain.

She looked back, said nothing.

He shrugged and continued writing. 'Okay,' he said at last, handing her the paper and the sheets and towels.

'Key?' said India, holding out her hand.

The clerk grinned and dropped the huge plastic disc into her hand. 'Top'a stairs, go lef'.'

'Thanks,' said India, rather more graciously than she felt. She turned with Theo and plodded up the stairs. She didn't expect the key to work, but when she inserted it in the slot the door opened. She pushed Theo inside and tossed the sheets and towels onto the dirty mattress. There were no pillows, she noticed, but she was too tired to care.

She made the bed, trying not to notice how bad it smelled. She put Theo into it and again probed gently at his injuries with her mind. He was hurt badly, but he would live. India decided she had better get some rest before trying to do any healing on either of them. She climbed into the bed and turned her back on Theo. She was asleep almost instantly, in spite of the smelly mattress.

*　　*　　*

'Shannon, how many times do you have to be told that we can't help India?' asked Anara. She stood in the middle of Henry's store with her arms crossed and a stern expression on her round face.

Henry stood behind his counter and polished his glasses with a large cloth. Shannon sat in a chair in front of Henry's counter and stared at her hands, folded in her lap.

'I didn't help,' she mumbled. There was a small note of defiance in her voice.

'You answered her call for help. Don't you think Henry and I heard her? Don't you think we wanted to go to her?' Anara demanded.

Shannon raised her head. 'Why didn't you? Why can't we even talk to her? I'd really like to understand.'

Anara glanced at Henry before responding. 'She's being watched in the No-Place. Every contact she makes with us, every contact we initiate, she is observed. We don't know by whom, but it all seems related to her journey across the Continent. If this is true, you endanger her more than you help.'

Shannon craned round to see Henry's face. 'Is this true?' she asked.

Henry nodded.

'It's twofold,' said Anara.

Shannon turned back to face her.

'The blocks are coming down faster now. She needs time to discover what's there by herself, discover how to use that knowledge to help herself.' Anara uncrossed her arms and took a step forward. 'You are probably more attached to her than the two of us are, but we still love her a great deal. We don't want to see any harm come to her either.'

'Have you had any ideas about why Ashraf might be behind one of India's blocks?' asked Shannon, changing the subject.

'No,' said Henry. 'But if what you said about India levitating Theo was accurate, she's dropped a big one there.'

Shannon giggled. 'The best she had been able to do before was combinations of lightweight objects. You should have seen the image of her running down the street towing this man behind her! Scary-looking people were getting out of *her* way. I didn't dare laugh. I knew it would offend her, but it looked so funny!'

'Where is she now? Do you know?' asked Anara.

'Not really. Somewhere near Lake Michigan, I think,' said Shannon. 'Why?'

'They're traveling rather slowly,' said Anara.

'What do you expect for beltways on the Continent?' asked Shannon. 'They couldn't take the tubes or shuttles. They would have been spotted right away.'

'I just hope they hurry, is all,' said Anara. 'I'd feel a lot safer if she were here.'

'How in hell did he manage to crash a vehicle off the beltway?' asked the Captain. 'And why didn't you go down after him?'

Grindle looked at Harry.

Harry shrugged. 'We got off at the next exit and went back for them. They weren't there. The police said there wasn't anyone at the site when they got there and a psychic search came up negative. They couldn't have gotten far on foot. There was blood in the front seat, too.'

'They haven't gone far from where you are now. Keep searching Michigan City until you come up with something.'

The VidCon flickered and went out.

Harry looked at Grindle. 'I guess we search. Where do you want to start?'

Grindle sighed. 'The beginning, I guess.'

India woke after a few hours of restless sleep. The light in the room was as dingy as the room itself, coming in through one very dirty window.

She sat up and looked around, trying to orient herself. Her entire body ached and she couldn't think why.

Something stirred beside her and she was surprised to find Theo. With a small frown, she stared at him, trying to remember what had happened.

The crash.

No wonder. She hopped out of bed and grabbed a towel.

The bathroom was as bad as she had expected it to be, but at least it was private. She showered as best she could without actually touching anything except the soap and water. She hated putting on the same travel-worn clothes, but she didn't have anything else. She was lucky to have Jenny's old clothing. One last look in the mirror depressed her completely. The short, blonde curls just didn't belong in her picture of herself. With a sigh, she left the bathroom.

Theo was still asleep, but seemed to be resting easier now than he had before. She climbed onto the bed to get a better look at his forehead. The wound had scabbed, but it looked pretty awful, in India's considered medical opinion.

She went back to the bathroom and wetted a towel with water and got the soap. She washed the wound as best she could, and blotted it dry on the other end of the towel. Then she sat back to admire her work. It looked much better. Now she could heal him internally.

Sitting cross-legged on the bed beside him, she closed her eyes and imagined herself in her old apartment. Then she imagined Theo was there with her. She sat him on the couch and then sat down in the chair opposite him.

How do you feel? she asked.

Confused, he said. *What happened? Where am I?*

You're in a place I imagined, if you can believe that, said India, trying her best to explain the strange situation to him. *I'm going to try to heal you.*

Heal me? he echoed. *Is that why I feel so funny?*

You feel 'funny' because you deliberately crashed our

vehicle off the beltway last night, said India rather severely. *You banged your head and are unconscious.*

How can I be unconscious if I'm talking to you? he wondered.

Never mind. Just tell me what I can do to make your head stop hurting.

Do you have any aspirin? asked Theo, abandoning the consciousness issue. *My head aches.*

India brightened. *Aspirin I have. Stay there. I'll bring it to you.*

She ran to the bathroom and opened the medicine chest. Aspirin was there, and so was a large bottle of orange liquid. She poured a cupful of the liquid and shook two tablets from the aspirin bottle.

Here, she said, handing Theo the cup and the pills. *Drink them down with this in one swallow.*

What's in the cup? asked Theo, frowning at the contents.

Something to make your headache go away faster, she said. Actually, she wasn't sure what the liquid was, but something told her it would do more for his internal health than the aspirin would. Something Shannon had said about always finding what you needed most in the medicine chest in your inner workplace had stuck with India, so she supervised while Theo drained the cup.

Theo sat for a moment, staring into space. Then he sat up and looked India in the eyes. *Are you all right?* he asked anxiously.

India cocked her head to one side. *What do you mean?* she asked.

The crash. Are you all right? he repeated.

Sure, she said. *A little sore, I guess, but okay.*

Go drink a cupful of that orange stuff, he ordered.

India grinned and stood up. *I'll be right back.*

Theo was right. After the liquid took hold, India felt great. She returned to the living room and sat down.

What do we do now? she asked, leaning forward expectantly.

Let's start with where are we? Theo suggested.

A dive, said India dryly. *It was the best I could do last night after the crash. I had to use most of your credits, since I figured if we thumbed anything, we'd have our friends on us, and probably the cops, too.*

Theo nodded. *That's okay. We can always get more. You were right to be so cautious. How did you get me here, anyway?*

I levitated you, said India.

I thought you could only do that with pillows, said Theo.

I thought so too, but last night, while I was trying to levitate as much of you as possible, something slipped in my mind and you shot straight up into the air. I guess I'm stronger than I thought. It was a good thing, too, or we would never have gotten out of there before the cops arrived.

You floated me here? asked Theo, beginning to smile.

Half floated, half dragged, yeah. India giggled. *You were floating horizontally behind me and I was pulling you by your arm as I ran.* She laughed outright. *We must have been a sight!* she howled.

Theo was laughing so hard he shook. *I can imagine.* He sobered slowly. *But such a sight would be easily identified to anyone searching for us.*

India stopped laughing also. *I didn't see very many people on the streets last night. Come to think of it, the few I did see were quick to get out of our way. They looked mostly like vagrants, though. Not the kind who would give a reliable report even if they were questioned.*

Still, we can't take any chances, said Theo.

What? she asked, flinching away from his hand, reaching toward her hair. *You can't cut it any shorter; I won't have any left!*

Theo shook his head. *Dye it,* he said.

Oh, no! India protested.

I'm afraid we not only have to dye your hair, but mine as well, said Theo. *And I'll have to shave my beard, also.*

India gasped involuntarily. *You can't do that!*

Can and must, I'm afraid, said Theo, stroking his beard fondly. *I will grow it back as soon as I can, but in the meantime, looking like Santa is just too easy for anyone trying to locate us.*

India nodded sadly. *Shall I go out for supplies?*

You're still the one they want, Theo said. *It's safer for me to go. I can also get more credits while I'm at it. I won't be gone long.* He stood up and looked around. *How do we get out of here?*

India laughed and opened the door.

It was a real come-down to find herself on the bed in the filthy little hotel room. Theo lay on his side with his back to her. India reached over and shook his shoulder.

Theo rolled onto his back and made an odd snuffling noise. His eyes opened slowly and he looked around the room.

'It was the best I could do,' said India defensively.

'I'm not criticizing,' said Theo. He sat up and rubbed his eyes. 'How did you get us here after the crash?' He got out of bed and put on his shoes.

India opened her mouth and then remembered that Theo's conscious mind would remember none of their previous conversation. Quickly, she told him again, trying to remember everything.

India handed him the remaining five credits. 'You might also check with the front desk about check-out time. I didn't cover that with the clerk last night. I was more concerned with getting out of sight.'

Theo nodded and stuffed the credits in his pocket. 'I'll be back as soon as possible,' he said, and pulled the door shut behind him.

India remained cross-legged on the bed for a long time after he left.

She stood on the plane of the No-Place, seeking with her feelings, trying to locate the presence that was following her.

No one was there.

She searched farther, straining her senses against the nothingness surrounding her. There was nobody near. No one was paying any attention to her at all.

With a shuddery exhalation, she created the room at the Inn and closed the door behind her.

Anara? she called. *Shannon? Henry?*

She waited.

Shannon?

She paced for a while.

I need to talk to one of you, she called. *Please. It's important.*

She pulled a wooden chair out from the table and sat down. She propped her elbows on the table and her chin on her fists.

I need to tell you something that might be important! she called more urgently. *Shannon?*

She folded her arms on the table and lowered her head down onto them.

Anara yelled at you for the last time, didn't she? India thought conversationally to Shannon's absence. *She said you shouldn't have told me you might be able to help. She knows about the person following me up here, and she said it would be dangerous to contact me.*

How did you know? asked a voice behind her.

India jumped. *I didn't hear you come in!* she gasped. *Shannon, I'm so glad to see you.* She reached out and hugged Shannon around the waist.

How did you know what Anara said to me? Shannon

repeated. She was looking at India strangely, but she returned the hug.

I didn't, India chuckled. *That just sounded like Anara to me. I didn't think you could hear me. I was just supplying her dialogue.*

Well, you hit it dead on, said Shannon. *It scared me. I was certain you knew more than you were telling.*

Maybe I do, said India. *In the meantime, I need to tell you about a dream I had the other night. I was going to contact you sooner, but we sort of had an accident and I got sidetracked.*

Shannon sat down. *Okay. I'll listen, but you have to remember, I did get lectured just like you imagined. This time it's going to be worse. Nothing gets by Anara and you can bet she knows I'm here right now.*

I'll make it fast, said India. *I checked before I created this place. I wasn't followed this time as far as I could tell. No one else knows we're here. Except Anara. Anyway, in this dream I saw the Disembodied massed in front of me. Their massed energy shone like a bright light and in front of them, between me and them, stood two men. They were like shadows in the light; silhouetted. I couldn't see who they were, but I was certain I knew them. I was certain I was afraid of them.*

Standing between you and the Disembodied? Shannon frowned. *Do you have any idea what it means?*

I was hoping you might know, said India.

Is there anything else?

No, I guess that's it. Time for you to go get lectured again? asked India wryly.

Shannon grimaced.

I'm sorry, said India. *I didn't mean to get you in trouble. I just really needed to tell one of you about that. It seemed important enough to take the risk. I won't come back here unless I absolutely have to, okay?*

India, I'm a big girl, said Shannon, giving India's hand

a squeeze. *I can take responsibility for my own actions. No one forced me to come here. I think Anara might even consider this important enough. I'll see what I can find out about it, and next time we have an emergency I'll let you know. Deal?* She stood up.

India stood up also. *Deal. Tell Anara I apologize.*

Shannon smiled. *Keep your eyes and ears open and come home to us soon.*

Soon, India echoed as Shannon disappeared.

India left soon after, letting the Inn disappear as she walked away from it.

When she returned to the dingy hotel room, Theo had come back with breakfast and sundries.

'That was fast,' India observed as she climbed off the bed.

'Not really,' said Theo. 'You've been gone a while. Did you finally tell your friends about your dream?'

India nodded.

'And?'

'Nothing,' she admitted. 'Shannon had no idea what it might signify, and on top of that, she can't talk to me except in an extreme emergency any more. Anara gave her a talking-to about the dangers of my being followed there. She's going to look into it, anyway. We just have to keep our heads down and get to San Francisco as soon as possible.'

'Well, we can have breakfast first,' said Theo, putting sandwiches out on the table. 'Then we have a little altering of ourselves to do before we're ready to face the day. The clerk said we could check out any time after I paid him for another night in this charming establishment. You do have expensive taste, my dear. How on earth did you manage to locate this place?'

'It's a talent I have,' grinned India as she picked up a sandwich. 'What sort of dive did these come from? I think someone is already in here enjoying my meal.'

'No roaches in this place,' said Theo, managing to look offended. 'I checked the kitchen myself. Now shut up and eat. Then you get to become a brunette for a while.'

India made a face at Theo and took a bite of her sandwich. 'This is wonderful!' she exclaimed through the mouthful. 'I didn't realize how hungry I was.'

Theo glared at her.

'Okay, okay. Shut up and eat,' said India.

She polished off two sandwiches and an entire container of milk before she began to slow down. 'How are we going to get out of here?' she asked at last.

'That's what I wanted to talk to you about,' said Theo, setting down his milk. 'They'll have every exit from the city watched, including tube, shuttle, and vehicle rental.'

'What are we going to do, then?' asked India.

'I thought we'd get a couple of bicycles,' suggested Theo diffidently.

'It would get us out of town inconspicuously,' said India.

Most downtown traffic anywhere was bicycles. More practical in the streets, easier to park, and free of pollutants. Just not very practical over the long haul.

'You don't think they'd catch on?' she asked.

'Eventually,' said Theo. 'If we can think of it, so can they. But it would give us a good start while they're checking all the other possibilities first.'

'Then I guess that's what we do,' said India decisively.

'I was hoping you'd see it that way,' said Theo.

'Because there happen to be two bicycles locked together in the lobby waiting for us to finish making ourselves beautiful, right?' India grinned.

'Just so happens,' said Theo, eyeing the last sandwich. 'Split it?' he asked.

'Help yourself,' said India, leaning back in her chair. 'I'm stuffed.'

* * *

India surveyed her dull brown curls in the mirror. She made a face and turned her back on the image. 'Theo, I think this is even worse than the blonde,' she called to him. 'It looks awful. It's also completely ruined by your tender ministrations.'

'Stop whining,' said Theo, rubbing his bare chin. 'Your hair will grow back. Would you rather suffer my ministrations, or have Bob playing in your brain again?'

India looked at Theo. His curls were similarly shorn and the same awful shade of brown. His chin was naked-looking without the pointed goatee. He looked odd; certainly unlike himself. India felt a pang of guilt. 'You're right. I'm sorry. Are we ready to go?'

Theo glanced around the room. 'Let's pick up this garbage and take it with us. We can recycle it somewhere else. That way, if anyone tracks us here, they won't know any more than the clerk can tell them. The one downstairs isn't the same one who saw you check in last night. He won't know you came in here as a blonde last night. He may wonder about me, but that doesn't matter as much.'

India had already begun collecting their trash and was stuffing it into a bag. 'How far do you figure we'll have to pedal?'

Theo shrugged. 'We'll see about alternate transportation as soon as we reach the next city. I bought a map, but we'll have to take surface streets. It could be a few days.'

They finished gathering their belongings in silence and took a last look around.

'I'll be glad to leave this place far behind,' said India, shuddering. 'I was certain there were spiders and cockroaches all over the place.'

'Probably are,' said Theo, opening the door. 'Come on.'

Downstairs were the two bicycles locked together. Three-speeds. Old and ratty-looking. Theo would have checked them, though, made certain they were safe and serviceable. Inconspicuous. They would be just two more cyclists in the city streets. It wouldn't be until they hit the open roads between cities that they would start to stand out. These roads were more often traveled by electric vehicles.

Theo came over and unlocked the bicycles. 'We're all checked out,' he said, winding the chain around the stem of his seat. He snapped the lock shut and put his hands on the handlebars. 'I can't remember the last time I rode one of these contraptions.'

'Neither can I,' said India. 'We'll both be sore tonight.'

'Good thing you have that healing technique down pat,' he said, pushing his bike out the door.

India followed. 'Yeah, if I'm not too tired to do it!'

They climbed on gracelessly and pedaled off toward the other side of the city.

Chapter Nine

Harry stood at the main desk of the shuttle port and tried again to explain what it was he wanted to a pretty but rather dim boy who stood behind the counter and clutched the disc of passenger manifests.

'You'll have to ask my boss,' he repeated. 'I'm new at this. I don't know what I should do.'

Harry sighed. 'Where is your boss?' he asked.

'He's at lunch, sir,' the boy said.

'When do you expect him back?' asked Harry, trying not to lose his patience.

'He just left, sir.'

'We've been having this conversation for almost half an hour. Do you think he left just now, or just before we began this pointless exercise?' asked Harry.

'I guess he'll be back in about half an hour, then, sir,' said the insipid youth.

'Will you tell him I'll be back to talk to him then?'

'Yes, sir. You understand my position, sir?' he asked anxiously.

Harry turned and walked over to where Grindle was using the VidCon. 'Any luck?'

Grindle looked up. 'No. You?'

'The kid's boss will be back from lunch in a bit. How about we grab a bite and come back here to talk to him then?'

'Eat here?' Grindle asked. 'Be serious. Port food is lousy. We can grab a lift into town and get something decent. He won't leave again right after he gets back from lunch.'

'I'll go ask what time the boss's shift is over and meet

you back here. Keep looking on the tube bookings.' Harry went back to the desk again.

Grindle punched up the next manifest and began to run down the IDs.

'Was she able to give you any description beyond men she knew and was afraid of?' asked Anara.

Shannon was relieved. She had been expecting a more forceful version of the earlier lecture about allowing contact with India. 'No. She said they were in silhouette against the power of the Disembodied.'

'This was a dream?'

Shannon nodded. 'That's what she said. I got the feeling it was more than that, though. The blocks in her mind have been slipping at a faster rate lately. It may be this image came loose while she was asleep and worked its way into a dream. She might not have been able to accept the information without it being couched in dream symbols.'

'This and the levitation, and a brief glimpse of Ashraf. That's not all that rapid,' said Anara.

'Well, at least it's happening. They haven't gotten a hold of her to reinforce them,' said Shannon defensively.

Anara nodded. 'Is there anything you can do in the Collective Unconscious to find out who these two men are?' asked Anara. 'I realize what I'm asking is extremely dangerous, but you're the best person for the job.'

'You mean most expendable?' asked Shannon.

'That's *not* what I mean,' said Anara sternly.

'I know,' Shannon recanted. 'That level scares me, though. I'd almost rather submit to mind-to-mind contact with Ashraf.'

'Interesting comparison,' Anara said mildly. 'I know what you mean. You're the best person for the job because neither Henry nor I have easy access to Level One's tools. Our presence there would raise questions.'

Shannon nodded. 'I'll do it, but I'm not happy about it.'

'Thank you. I'm also asking you to do this to remind you that I would rather you didn't respond to India's calls for help.'

'I know,' said Shannon miserably. 'I can't help being a soft touch; especially where India is concerned.'

'*I* am a soft touch,' Anara corrected. '*You* are a push-over. Now get to work. Let me know as soon as you've found out anything.'

With a wobbly start, Theo and India pedaled slowly down the street, gripping the handlebars tightly and forgetting to breathe. After a while they gained a bit of confidence and began to ride better. They eased their fingers and flexed tight muscles in their necks and backs. They remembered to breathe, and relaxed, making the entire process easier.

'I guess what they say is true,' said India. 'About riding a bicycle. You never forget how. Just don't ask me to make a sharp turn or ride no-handed!'

Theo grinned. 'It isn't as bad as I thought it was going to be,' he admitted. 'I memorized the first few turns to make it easier on us. At the next intersection turn left and we'll be right on course.'

'How is your head this morning?' India asked. 'I forgot to ask before you went out. Is the bump gone? The wound seems to have healed completely.'

'If I didn't know there had been an accident last night, I would have thought you were kidding about my having a head injury,' said Theo. 'I feel more than fine. I feel better than I have in several years. Whatever you did worked wonders. As long as you can do it this evening when we have to get off these contraptions, we're all set.'

'I'm not sure what that orange liquid was, but I feel really great too,' said India. 'By the way, where are we?'

'What do you mean?' asked Theo.

'I mean, where are we?' she repeated. 'Last night when we crashed, I didn't know where on the beltway we were.

How far are we from the Old City? Did we get very far?'

'Not as far as I would have liked,' said Theo. 'Michigan City. We only had a few hours on the beltway before those goons caught up with us again. It felt like we should have gone further, but beltways are almost the slowest way to travel. If it had been the old highway still, and if we had been in a fuel-driven vehicle instead of on a solar-electric beltway, we would have been far past where we are.'

India sighed.

'No use thinking about what might have been. What could have happened did,' said Theo. 'Isn't it a beautiful day? We'll ride along the lake for a bit of our trip. Did you know there was a time when the lakes were so polluted it wasn't safe to swim in them?' He glanced sideways at India. 'Cheer up. We'll get there. It'll just take us a little while longer, that's all.'

India looked at Theo.

He made a comical face at her.

She laughed. 'It *is* a beautiful day. I'll concentrate on that.'

They pedaled across the city and out onto the road which would take them to the next one. As they rode beside the lake, India stared at it, trying to imagine the waters as Theo had described them.

A block in her mind dropped for a moment.

He had been hard; big inside her, slow and deliberate. Her hips ached to move, but he controlled the pace, looking into her eyes with an expression of wonder and triumph. Finally she knew *who* he was.

India gasped and fell off her bike.

The block slipped back into place.

Theo leapt off his bicycle and ran back to India. 'Are you okay? What happened?' he demanded, kneeling beside her.

India looked up at him blankly. 'What?' she asked. 'Why am I down here?'

'You fell,' said Theo. 'Don't try to sit up yet. What happened?'

'Another block slipped for a moment. This time I saw Ty behind it. It's back up now, though,' said India. She sat up slowly and felt the back of her head. 'I'm fine,' she said, sounding surprised. 'I guess I was more surprised than hurt by the fall.'

'Will you be able to get back on?' asked Theo solicitously.

India stood up and flexed her legs and arms. She smiled. 'I'm fine. I just want to know what Ty was doing behind another of those damned blocks. First Ashraf, now him. I'm confused.'

'Well, Confused, get back on your bike and you can call those people you talk to when we stop for the evening,' said Theo, walking her back over to her fallen bicycle.

'I can't risk getting Shannon in trouble again for something that trivial. He's just a pest who hangs out in the No-Place waiting to torment me when I show up there,' India dismissed the suggestion as she picked up her bike and climbed back on.

Theo climbed onto his own and they set off down the road again. 'Maybe you ought to go there tonight and ask *him* about it,' said Theo.

India said nothing, but secretly she decided to do just that.

It was extremely late in the afternoon when Theo decided they couldn't risk stopping in Chicago for the night.

'Why not?' India complained. She was hot and dirty and sore and tired. 'All I want is a hot bath and a soft bed.'

'So do I,' said Theo ruefully. 'But we're still too close to Michigan City for my comfort. If those two charming gentlemen who shot at us last night are anywhere in the neighborhood, I don't want them finding any trace of us in a hotel.'

India said nothing as they left the road and pushed their bicycles across a meadow to a stand of trees. She leaned her bike against the trunk of a tree and sat down. The tall grass hid them from the road. It gave India an idea, so she stood up again. 'Do you have a pocket knife?' she asked Theo.

He shook his head. 'Sorry.' He looked thoughtful for a moment. 'If you need a blade, you could try to find a sharp rock, but you'd better hurry. It'll be full dark soon. What did you have in mind?'

'You'll see,' India grinned. She set about looking for a sharp rock and soon found what she needed. She returned to the tree Theo sat under and showed him the stone. 'I thought I'd make a bed.'

'Then I'll make supper while you do that,' he said.

India grabbed a handful of the tall grass and began sawing through it with the sharp edge of the rock.

'Might be faster if you pulled it up by the roots,' said Theo.

'Might,' agreed India. 'But then we'd have dirt in our bed. I don't want to sleep in dirt.'

By the time India had a sizable stack of grass cut, Theo announced dinner.

'I thought you were kidding,' said India. 'Did you pick up this stuff when we had lunch?'

'Give the girl a medal,' Theo laughed.

'I'd rather have the chest to pin it on,' said India mournfully, looking down at her tiny breasts.

'You'd look pretty silly with knee-shooters,' said Theo, handing India a sandwich.

India giggled and sat down to dinner.

'When do you figure we'll be able to find faster transportation?' she asked around a mouthful.

'It's too dark to see the map now,' said Theo. 'But I figure we should stick to bicycles until we reach Davenport. We should be far enough away by that time to escape notice by Tweedle Dum and Tweedle Dee. Unless, of course, they've caught up with us by then.'

You didn't make a call when we stopped for lunch, India thought to herself. She wondered why it bothered her so much. In her heart, she trusted Theo completely. In her mind, she was confused. Still, she figured, if he hadn't made a phone call during lunch, the Brothers Grimm might not catch up with them for a while.

'Eat up,' said Theo, offering India another sandwich. 'I expect another first-rate healing job tonight. I don't know what that orange stuff was, but I could use another swig of it.'

India waved away the sandwich. 'We'll need something for breakfast,' she said. 'I'll see what's in the medicine chest tonight. Maybe more orange stuff, maybe something else fun. Whatever it is, Shannon told me it will always be what I need.'

Theo nodded. 'That's good enough for me, then.'

India shot a sideways glance at him. 'Does that mean you're starting to believe in what I'm telling you?'

'India, I don't disbelieve you. I've just never before encountered anyone who could honestly say all this stuff existed. I'm learning you're really not crazy. They really are out to get you, for whatever reason, and you really do have powers of the mind I thought were a hoax. I'm not too old or too stubborn to admit I'm wrong. Just old and stubborn enough to be extremely cautious.'

'Are Jenny and her family going to be worried that it's taking so long for us to get there?' asked India, changing the subject.

'I told them to expect us whenever we showed up. I expect she'll worry a little if I don't phone soon and let them know where we are, but that can wait until we reach civilization.'

'Well,' said India, standing up, 'the sooner the better, as far as I'm concerned.' She began spreading the grasses she had cut, beating down a large area and padding it with the cut lengths.

When she finished, she turned to Theo. 'And now for a little healing, and a little talk with Tyler-the-dead-president.'

'Do I need to be asleep for you to do the healing?' asked Theo. He started putting away the remains of their dinner.

'Nope,' said India. 'You could do a dance while I work if you felt like it. Just do it quietly. I need silence to concentrate.'

'Well, then, I bid you good night,' he said. He lay down on the grasses and wriggled around for a moment, testing the comfort of the makeshift bed. 'Not bad,' he murmured, and was asleep immediately.

'I wish I could do that,' said India.

Instead, she closed her eyes and concentrated on going to the apartment in her mind. She attended to the healing she had promised both of them. The medicine cabinet had more of the orange liquid, and a green powder as well.

Drink me, eat me? she asked, puzzled. *What am I supposed to do with the green powder?*

It lay in a small pile on the second shelf. There was no container, and no instructions of any kind accompanying it.

Theo? she called. *Theo, come in here please.*

Theo wandered in the door and looked around. *Mix it with something?* he suggested. *Eat it? Sniff it?*

She poured him a glass of the orange liquid. *At least we know what this is for. Drink up.*

Obligingly, Theo swallowed it. *I thought I went to sleep,* he said, puzzled. It was as though the thought was only just occurring to him. *When did I wake up and how did I get here?*

You aren't really here, said India. She poured herself a glass of the orange stuff and drank it. *This isn't really a place. At least not in the physical sense.*

What do you mean? Theo demanded. *I'm here, and you're here, and this is most certainly a place.*

I invited your energy into a place inside myself and allowed it to take a familiar shape for the purposes of the healing, but you are still asleep in the meadow. You never left. She turned to consider the contents of the medicine cabinet. The powder remained a mystery. *I don't get the feeling that any of those suggestions are right,* she said at last.

Have you touched it? asked Theo, evidently giving up on the question of his reality.

India reached out and placed her index finger on the tip of the small pyramid. *Oh!* she gasped. She jerked her finger back and looked at it closely.

That wasn't it? asked Theo, also looking at her finger.

That was exactly it! she said. *But the wrong place to put it. Lie down.*

Theo looked at the floor and back at India.

Okay, out on the couch in the living room, she relented. She scooped up a handful of the powder and giggled. *This feels really strange.*

Theo lay down and waited expectantly. India stood over him and poured the powder onto his solar plexus. It disappeared immediately.

Oh, my! said Theo. He lay still a moment longer, then sat up and frowned.

Are you okay? asked India anxiously.

Theo stood up and stretched. *Whatever that was, it worked. You next?*

You bet! India lay down on the couch.

You realize it will be difficult to do this, since I'm not actually here. Theo grinned and went into the bathroom for a handful of the strange green powder.

When it hit her solar plexus, India felt a slight burning sensation, but as it sank in it bloomed in her nerve endings, healing all the little raw places the bicycle and the unaccustomed exercise had created. *Oh, boy, does that feel wonderful,* she sighed. She didn't want to move, but she felt like jumping up and down.

Theo gave her a delighted smile. *Anything more, boss?*

That's it, she said. *You're free to go. Sleep well.*

You too, said Theo. *Thank you very much.*

When he was gone, India braced herself to go to the No-Place and find Ty.

He was waiting for her.

Once again, India faced Ty on the grey plane of the No-Place.

Hey! Where've you been? he asked as he approached.

Busy, said India stiffly. *But I could ask you the same question. The last two times I've been here, you've been nowhere in sight. Find a girlfriend?*

Nah. I'm still waiting for you to come around, said Ty expansively. *Wanna play?*

No, said India. *I want to ask you something important and I want you to tell me the truth.*

Ty sobered. *Ask.*

This afternoon a block slipped in my mind for just a moment. I didn't see much behind it before it moved back into place, but I did see you, she said bluntly.

Ty raised an eyebrow and said nothing.

What were you doing behind one of the blocks in my mind, Ty? she asked.

This time, she stared him down and was surprised to find no danger in his gaze. His eyes didn't reflect the emotions she sensed behind his voice. He made no effort to fall into her eyes. Once again, she was confused by the mixed signals she read from him.

Who are you? she asked finally.

Don't you remember? he asked softly.

India was made uncomfortable by the degree of familiarity in his voice.

He moved slowly toward her.

You were making love to me, India accused. She shrank away from him, but her eyes were riveted by his face, searching closely for a clue. She shook her head. *I don't think you're telling me the truth.*

What else would I be doing inside your head? he asked. He looked a little hurt. *Did they take everything about it from your mind? You can't recall anything?* He came closer.

India fell back a step. *No.* She frowned and shook her head again. *This doesn't feel right.*

Look, you've had your brains ground into hamburger. It's not surprising you wouldn't feel right about something you barely remember. It's true, though. Ty reached both hands out and took her face between them.

This was familiar suddenly. As his face neared, India tipped her head back. His kiss sucked the breath from her and left her limp and dizzy in his arms. *It was always like this,* she moaned against his chest. *You consume me. When I spend any time with you at all, you just use me up. There's nothing left when you go away.*

His arms tightened around her gently before he reached with one hand and tipped her chin up, making her look at him. His eyes were dark pools, no longer reflective. They projected his feelings at her as he bent to kiss her again.

No, India gasped, pushing away from him. She could feel his penis growing hard against her. *I can't let you do that to me any more.*

You used to, Ty insisted. He thrust against her, holding her tightly. His breath was loud in her ears. *Please? You need it, too.*

Stop! India cried. She didn't know what to feel. He sounded so wild and urgent. Her heart was beating loudly in her ears. She was afraid. *Why did you leave? Where did you go? Don't you care that you hurt me?*

(You're playing with fire.)

What? asked India.

Mmm? Ty mumbled against her neck. He tried to kiss her again, but she evaded him. *What did you say?* he finally asked.

N–nothing, India lied. She knew he could see right through her, but she had the feeling she shouldn't tell him.

India, please come play with me, Ty begged. He brushed his hand gently against her cheek.

I can't do this again . . .

(Listen to your heart.)

Who's there? India asked.

What? asked Ty. His mouth was inches from her own. India was fascinated by his gaze. *Stop,* she pleaded.

Ty laughed, baring his teeth in an unpleasant smile. *You don't really want me to,* he insisted.

India reached up with both hands and caressed the back of his neck, winding her fingers into his hair. *Yes,* she whispered. *Yes . . .*

Her fingers tightened in his hair. Her knee came up hard. *Yes, I do.*

Ty gasped and sagged against her hands.

India eased him to the ground and stood for a moment looking at him. *I can't let you do that to me any more,* she explained; then she fled the No-Place.

India awoke to discover Theo already up and making breakfast. The sun shone brightly and insects buzzed in the grass. She felt warm and safe.

Theo noticed she was awake. 'Did you sleep all right?' he asked.

'Mmhmm,' she said, stretching luxuriously. 'Deep and dreamless. How about you?' She stood up and stretched again.

'Best night I've had in years. I don't know what you did by way of healing last night, but it was wonderful. Come have some breakfast.' Theo indicated his preparations.

'Uh, nature calls,' said India. 'I'll be right back.'

When she returned, Theo handed her a sandwich.

India wrinkled her nose, but took the food without comment.

'What kind of treat did you find in the medicine cabinet last night?' Theo asked.

'The same orange liquid and a strange green powder. You were really funny, though,' India told him. 'You didn't want to believe that I had created your energy for the purposes of the healing. You kept insisting you were real.'

'Well, I am,' said Theo seriously.

'Of course you are! But how much do you remember of what happened in my apartment while we were doing the healing?' she asked.

'None,' said Theo. 'That doesn't mean I don't exist.'

India sighed. 'That's not what I meant. When I call you into my workplace – my apartment – your consciousness isn't what comes to me. I don't think it's even your subconscious that comes to me. I couldn't explain that to you last night in my apartment because you were so certain you were there.'

'I probably was,' said Theo. He finished one sandwich and started on another.

India picked a bit of crust from her sandwich and tossed it at a small bird that was watching her intently. It hopped over, grabbed the crumb, and flew off.

'How many days do you think it will take to reach Davenport?' she asked idly.

'Map's in my coat pocket, over there. Why don't you get it and we'll look at mileage.'

India retrieved the map and spread it out between them.

'I figure we're about here,' said Theo, pointing at a spot outside Michigan City.

'Boy, we sure didn't get very far, did we?' said India. 'Where's Davenport?' She traced Beltway 80 through Illinois County and stopped when her finger reached the City.

'Oh, my word!' She looked back to where Theo's finger marked their location. 'That's impossible!'

'Inconvenient,' Theo corrected. 'There's quite a difference. But it could be the difference between those goons catching up with us now, or not finding us again.'

'Shouldn't we switch to another beltway?' asked India, eyeing the distance they had to travel on bicycle according to Theo's plans.

'That would be what they might reasonably expect us to do,' said Theo. 'Which is precisely why we aren't going to do it. They'll have to check all the tube and shuttle manifests looking for our IDs, and all the vehicle rental places, before they start checking bicycle stores. We may even be able to get to Davenport before they suspect that's how we got out of the city and out from under their noses.'

'But it could take weeks!' India whined.

'And if we put some effort into our pedaling, it could take only days,' said Theo reprovingly. 'You're younger than I am. It should be easy to keep up.'

India grinned. 'You're right. Shall we strike camp and get on with it?'

Theo grinned back and began to put things away, starting with the map.

They pedaled hard all morning and made good time, but India had to be convinced to stop for lunch.

'We'll lose time,' she said impatiently.

'You'll lose energy if you don't. Fatigue doesn't lend itself to good performance,' Theo pointed out. 'Besides, I need a rest. You probably do too.'

'We had a big breakfast,' India pointed out. 'We can push through to an early dinner and find a campsite just before dark.'

'We will stop now for lunch and a rest, and purchase dinner and breakfast to eat in camp as we did last night,' said Theo.

'But . . .'

'Period,' said Theo.

They found a small restaurant with a good menu and locked the bikes.

'I'm going to go take a shower in their sink,' said Theo as he pulled the door open. 'You can wait for me at the table if you want.'

India suddenly discovered an urgent need for the ladies' room and followed him in that direction. When she came back out, after a bath of sorts, and feeling much fresher in spite of not having had a change of clothes in several days, she found Theo on the CrediVid.

This time, instead of disconnecting as soon as he saw her, he called her over.

'George, this is India,' he said to the screen as he drew her into the booth. 'India, this is my son-in-law, George.'

'How do you do?' she asked politely.

'I'm pleased to meet you,' said George.

Theo had been right. George was a large man, if size could be gauged on a small video screen. He had straight brown hair and a moustache. His eyes were wide and deeply set, the sort of brown India liked best, like a puppy or a deer. His mouth was straight and wide, like her own, but she liked it anyway. On him it fit. His face brightened when he smiled, but normally he looked a little sad.

'Dad has told me about you. We'll look forward to seeing you when you get here.'

'Thank you,' said India, not knowing what else to say.

Theo squeezed her shoulder and India felt better.

'Well, George, I'm going to go buy this lady some lunch. We'll get there as soon as we can. I just didn't want Jenny to worry.'

'Thanks, Dad. We appreciate the call.'

Theo disconnected the transmission and drew India out of the booth. 'You look a little better,' he observed.

India smiled. 'You were right. We needed the break.'

'Of course I'm right. I'm always right.'

India giggled.

After lunch, loaded down with their next two meals, they set off again. It was a hot afternoon. India gradually peeled off one layer after another and put them in the basket behind the seat. In a controlled environment like the rental vehicles, the extra layers hadn't really bothered her, but on a bicycle they hampered her movement and became unbearably sticky.

Theo pedaled along, apparently unaware of the temperature. His round face was red, but that was its usual color.

Traffic was light, and they had the road to themselves most of the time. They had a lot of time with their own thoughts, since talking took too much breath and energy.

India pedaled doggedly and wondered.

She found no answers, but wondering did help pass the time. She was surprised when Theo finally called a halt.

'But it's still light out,' she objected.

'Only for about an hour more,' said Theo. 'We have dinner to prepare, and you may want to make another bed like the one you made last night.' He paused. 'I would certainly like it if you felt like making another bed like you did last night. I'll even make dinner again.'

'How can I pass up an offer like that?' she asked as she dismounted.

They walked across another field much like the one they had been in the night before.

'Everything looks the same out here,' she said as they headed toward a stand of trees.

'Well, we aren't that many miles from where we were. If you go far enough, you leave the prairie and begin climbing mountains. That's why I want to be in a vehicle before we reach Colorado County. They've got some mean mountains there; and snow. I'd rather not be pedaling when we get there.'

'Me either,' said India.

She made camp much the way she had the night before,

but didn't need to search for a sharp stone. Theo had purchased a knife for that purpose. Also for sandwich-making and self-defense, he claimed. India just cut the tall grass and made a huge bed for them.

By the time dinner was finished, it was dark. Stars flickered, hard white points in the blackness. The moon was in half-phase, chunky and unfinished, low in the sky. India and Theo lay under the vast sky, not talking.

At last, Theo fell asleep, breathing deeply and evenly.

India performed a quick healing on them both, making sure to take care of the little aches and pains so they could make good time tomorrow.

She avoided going to the No-Place. She wasn't ready to see Ty again. She didn't want to get Shannon in trouble. Mostly, she didn't know what to make of the information, and needed time to assimilate it, make sense of it. She would be able to contact Shannon later. Assuming, of course, that Shannon would be allowed to respond to India's call.

Still wondering about it, India fell asleep.

She dreamed she was floating in space. Her entire body was muffled, as though cotton batting was wrapped around her, between her nerve endings and her skin. She was in darkness, but moving toward a bright light that shone as a small point in the distance. She was alone, but there were people jostling against her.

The light opened up and beat on her eyes like a sun. Squinting against the intensity, India began to see the people around her.

They had no faces, only mouths. Gaping mouths. Yawning maws. They were reaching toward her with shapeless hands, pawing at her body. She couldn't really feel them, though, because of the cotton batting. She was aware of their touch on her skin, but the feeling didn't penetrate to her nerves. She shuddered, and the people laughed and pressed against her in greater numbers.

Then they were drifting away from her, leaving her alone in the stark light. She felt naked, but she couldn't really see herself. She tried to look around, but her head was immobilized. She couldn't even rotate her body to see what was behind her.

She began to imagine all sorts of creepy-crawlies behind her, but there was no way of verifying it. Just as she was about to panic, two shadows appeared in the light before her.

Hello? she asked. She couldn't speak out loud. She wasn't even sure telepathy would reach the ears of anyone who might be out there.

There was no answer, but the shadows kept advancing.

India squinted against the bright light, but was unable to see features, or even distinct shapes.

Hello? she asked again.

What are you doing here? came the gruff question.

I don't know, she replied. *Who are you?*

Go away, the voice said.

India thought she recognized it, but before she could repeat her question a force from the two shadows was pushing her away from them.

(You're playing with fire.)

What? she cried. She was helpless to stop the backward movement.

She began to worry about the creepy-crawlies again, but she still couldn't control her own movement. Just as she was about to panic, she jerked round and saw there was nothing there.

With a deep sigh of relief, she put her feet down on the ground and stood for a moment, just enjoying the feeling of something solid in her environment.

Then the ground ruptured and swallowed her.

India screamed and fell into the fissure.

She kept falling.

She screamed again and sat up.

Theo was holding her by the upper arms and was talking to her gently, constantly.

'You're having a bad dream, India. Wake up now. It's okay; you're right here with me and nothing bad has happened. It was just a dream. You're safe and sound, and everything is all right. Are you listening to me?'

India nodded and drew a deep, shaky breath. 'I'm okay,' she said at last. Her voice sounded strange in her ears. 'I'm sorry I woke you.'

'Don't be silly,' said Theo, letting go of her and sitting down. 'Will you be able to go back to sleep?'

'I'll try,' she said. 'Maybe I'll see what the medicine cabinet has for dreamless sleep.'

'Good idea,' said Theo. 'Or maybe sweet dreams?'

'Yeah,' said India. 'Maybe. Good night, Theo. Thank you.'

She slept quietly for the rest of the night.

The two men stood on the plane of the Disembodied, minds joined, energies tapped into the power surrounding them. Their attention was focused on the task they were performing. The cargo of the freighter had proven much more lucrative than they had originally thought, but it also meant shipment to several different locations, all of which were dangerous. Protection would come at a much higher cost, and they were having to provide it themselves.

Pirates had of course heard of the snatch, and were keeping a close eye on when the cargoes would be moved, hoping to capitalize on it in much the same way, which was why the two men were using the forbidden power again.

That was the sixth load? asked the younger man.

Two more to go, said the older as their concentration shifted to the seventh ship.

In their minds, they could see the small cargo carrier in its docking bay. They pictured its destination and shifted it quickly. The scream and hiss they dreaded was coming closer. Closer than it had ever been before. Fear closed in on them, too, making them hasten the last ship into its berth carelessly. No warning had been issued, and several people were killed as the carrier dropped to the deck.

The two men shuddered against the rattle and snap of claws, and started to disengage from each other when they noticed someone watching them.

Hello? she asked.

They made no answer, but started to move toward her.

Hello? she asked again.

What are you doing here? demanded the older man.

I don't know, she replied. *Who are you?*

Go away, he said.

They exerted their combined energies against her and pushed her away from them. They didn't have any time left now. They released the power of the Disembodied and disengaged from each other. The scream and hiss, rattle and snap was all around them now. Without looking back, they fled, each secretly hoping never to have to do that again.

Shannon padded down the hallway of the Level One Hostel, looking in each door as she passed, straining her ears and senses to find out who was in range and what they were doing.

As she came to the door to her room, she paused a moment, hand on the knob, and waited.

No one was following her, and no one seemed aware of what she was doing. Holding her breath, Shannon opened the door and slipped inside. She pushed the door shut as silently as possible and stepped away into the center of the room. There was no lock on the door, so she pushed a chair up under the knob and hoped no one would have reason to come looking for her.

Anara had given her a dangerous and almost impossible

task. There was no privacy here for her to do the necessary work. If she got caught, she risked expulsion from the hostel and her position within the organization. She didn't want to lose either.

Quietly, she sat down on the floor and crossed her legs under her. She took several deep breaths and tried to slow the pounding of her heart. When she felt ready, she began dropping her consciousness down to the level of the Collective Unconsciousness and the Disembodied. On the way, she tried to imagine herself shielded from the seductive and destructive energies of the Disembodied. There really was no way to protect herself from them and still be able to do the observing she needed to do, so the shield consisted mostly of positive thoughts about her life on Level One. She needed to come back from this to help India.

Slowly at first, but then more and more, Shannon heard the voices of the Disembodied as they discovered her presence. Calling to one another, they gathered around her, pressing against her.

They had no faces, only mouths. Gaping mouths. Yawning maws. They were reaching toward her with shapeless hands, pawing at her body. She couldn't really feel them, though she was aware of their touch on her skin. The feeling didn't penetrate to her nerves. She shuddered and the people laughed and pressed against her in greater numbers.

Shannon, she thought. My name is Shannon. I have a life. I will not allow them to suck me in. I can't allow them to drain me of myself.

A bright light sprang up all around her and the Disembodied shrank away from it. They moved from her, leaving Shannon shivering and alone.

Where is this coming from? she wondered. She looked around her, but the light made it impossible to see anything. She squinted against the light, trying to see where the Disembodied had gone, but she was alone, feeling pinned in the spotlight.

Is anyone out there? she asked timidly. She didn't want the Disembodied to come back, but she felt extremely vulnerable alone on the plane.

What are you doing here? asked a familiar voice.

Shannon couldn't place it. *Who are you?* she asked. *Where are you?*

A shadow flickered briefly past. It was human-shaped, but that was all she could tell. India had said there were two of them. Two men, and she was afraid of them.

Shannon followed the shadow for a little way before it discovered what she was doing.

Go away, said the familiar voice.

Who are you? Shannon repeated. She started to move forward again.

The shadow gestured and Shannon found herself moving backward. She tried to stop, but couldn't. She had no control over her movement. She was pushed backward until she found herself resurfacing to consciousness in her room in the hostel.

Shannon shuddered and called for Anara. This was too strange to wait.

What do you make of it? Anara asked.

I have no idea, said Shannon, perplexed. *I'm as puzzled by it as India was. I feel like I should know the voice, but I can't place it. It was distorted, I'm sure, but not enough that I couldn't recognize it at all. And the power it commanded! It wasn't one person's power. It was far too strong for that.*

Are you suggesting whoever this is has managed to control some of the power of the Disembodied? asked Anara harshly. *Do you know what that would mean?*

Shannon nodded, but Anara couldn't see it. *Yes,* she said finally. *But who? And why?*

I guess that's your next step. Call me when you have anything more.

Anara broke contact.

Shannon continued to sit on the floor of her room for a long time. She was terrified and she didn't know why.

The Captain sat back from the VidCon, but Grindle could tell he was tired. His shoulders weren't set square the way they usually were; instead, he slouched over his desk leaning heavily on his elbows. He was also in a very bad mood.

'You two really don't want to catch this girl, do you?' the Captain asked.

The question took Grindle off guard. The two men had been staring at each other through the screen for so long, Grindle had wondered if he should just disconnect.

'No, sir,' he answered truthfully. 'But it's my job. I like my job. I just don't like this assignment.'

'Gee, that's too bad, isn't it?' asked the Captain. He sat up straighter and glared at Grindle through the screen. 'We don't always get the plum assignments, now, do we?'

'No, sir,' said Grindle, unconsciously standing straighter in front of his own screen.

'How do an old man and a young girl keep managing to elude you?'

'There was no way to get off the beltway after they crashed, sir,' Grindle started to explain.

The Captain waved him silent. 'This is sometimes a dangerous job, Grindle. You knew that when we hired you. You were one of the most enthusiastic recruits we've ever had. One little girl makes you go soft?'

Not a little girl, thought Grindle. India had nothing to do with this. But the Captain was an outsider hired in above deserving men.

'You think Bob should have gotten my job?' asked the Captain.

Grindle started. It was creepy how the boss always seemed to know what you were thinking. 'He worked hard for it, sir,' he temporized.

The Captain nodded. 'That doesn't change the situation, though.'

'No, sir.'

'So you'll find the girl and bring her back?'

'Yes, sir.'

'Good,' said the Captain. 'What progress have you made in locating her?'

'We found the hotel they stayed in that night,' Grindle said. He fell into recitation easily. 'It was a real dump. The clerk said a guy left in the morning with white hair and a beard. When he left in the afternoon, he had shaved and dyed his hair. He was with a tiny brunette. They had bicycles locked in the lobby. I figure they'll ride to the next city and find another rental vehicle. Maybe switch to Beltway 70 or Beltway 40.'

'They are past Gary already,' said the Captain, sounding faintly amused.

'How do you know?' asked Grindle.

'Because my contact told me they are outside of Joliet. They are still on bicycle and using a surface street that parallels Beltway 80. I suggest you and your erstwhile partner get your respective asses in gear and get out there to find them. I don't care what you do with this Winslow character, but I want the girl alive and well, and I want her soon. Do I make myself clear?'

'Yes, sir,' said Grindle. He broke contact and turned to Harry. 'Your ass in gear?'

'You bet,' said Harry unenthusiastically. 'Wonder who the hell his contact is.'

Grindle shrugged and put on his coat. 'You wanna maybe arrange to give him a heart attack?'

Harry grinned and picked up his coat from the back of the chair. 'An unfortunate accident, maybe?'

'Well, Joliet, here we come,' said Grindle.

'Shit,' said Harry.

Chapter Ten

India sat up and looked around.

The sun was up and a bird sang in the tree near where she had made the bed the night before. Theo was watching her. That made her feel irritable, but she couldn't say why. She got up and stumped off to the bushes, saying nothing.

Theo watched her go, also saying nothing.

When she returned, he had a sandwich waiting for her. He held it out silently, but he smiled at her, hoping to mitigate her mood.

India took it and looked at it for a long time. 'I'm so sick of sandwiches,' she said. 'Just once I'd like pancakes for breakfast.'

'Have pancakes for lunch,' Theo suggested.

India sat down and took a bite of the offending sandwich. She chewed it sullenly and swallowed.

'I'm sorry you had such a rotten night,' said Theo.

India shrugged. 'There've been lots worse,' she said, taking another bite.

'Not that I've been through with you,' said Theo. 'Are you always in such a good mood after a nightmare? Or is this a special occasion?'

'Special occasion,' said India. The question struck her as funny, but she tried not to laugh. It irritated her that he could make her want to laugh when she felt so lousy.

Theo chuckled. He ate his breakfast in silence and packed away their things while India finished her sandwich. They pushed their bicycles out to the road and got on. Theo took the lead and set a brisk pace. India had to pedal hard to keep up.

'I shouldn't do such good healings on you,' she complained almost an hour later.

Theo glanced back and saw she was red in the face with her exertions. He wasn't feeling any better, but he didn't want to give in to her temper. He increased the speed and pulled away from her.

India swore under her breath and pushed a little harder to keep up.

They rode like this until Theo decided to take pity on both of them and call a halt for lunch.

'Feel like some pancakes?' he called over his shoulder.

'You're enjoying this, aren't you?' called India.

She was breathing heavily, and looked even more tired than she had when she awoke. Theo felt a twinge of guilt as he pulled into the parking lot of a chain restaurant and stopped.

'What if I decided not to do a healing on you tonight?' asked India as she pulled up beside him and got off her bike.

'You wouldn't do that, would you?' asked Theo. 'We should be in Davenport by tomorrow if we keep up this time.'

'Really?' asked India, forgetting to sulk. She pushed her damp hair out of her face and looked up at Theo. 'Tomorrow?'

'If we can keep up this morning's pace,' said Theo. 'So you better eat a good lunch and cheer up some. Being angry all the time takes up too much energy.'

India smiled a little guiltily. 'What if I did an extra healing after lunch?' she asked, trying to make up for her temper.

'Wouldn't that take too much of your energy also?' asked Theo as he locked the bikes together. He started toward the door of the restaurant without waiting for an answer. He was hungry and wanted to sit on something he didn't have to pedal.

'No!' said India, dancing beside him.

Kids today have too damned much energy, he thought to himself as he watched her out of the corner of his eye.

'No, really!' said India again. She tugged at his sleeve to stop him. 'It would strengthen both of us. It wouldn't even take very long.'

'Well, then, it seems like it might be a good idea,' said Theo as he pulled the door open and shooed her through. 'Can you get enough quiet to do it effectively?'

'No one ever goes into the ladies' room while I'm in there. I don't know why, but I always seem to have a public rest-room to myself.'

Theo hid a grin. 'Would you rather do this before or after lunch?' he asked. 'Two, please,' he told the host.

They were led to a table at the back of the restaurant and seated.

'After, I guess,' said India. 'I'm too starved to concentrate right now.'

'After, then,' said Theo, studying the menu. 'Do you know what you want?'

'Pancakes,' India grinned.

Theo smiled back at her.

After lunch, India went into the ladies' room and locked herself into a stall. True to her luck, there was no one else in the rest-room. A quick glance around confirmed that she wouldn't sit down here. Instead, India braced herself against the door to make sure she didn't accidentally fall down while she concentrated. She dropped her consciousness to the level she had created her apartment on, and went inside.

Nothing had changed since the night before. She hadn't really expected it would be different, but the nightmare had been so real she wasn't really sure what to expect. Without hesitating, India headed straight for the bathroom and the medicine cabinet.

Theo? she called as she pulled the cabinet door open.

Right here, he answered. *Unless you're going to tell me I'm not.*

I know better, said India as she poured two cups of the familiar orange liquid. *Here.* She handed one to Theo and raised her own as if in toast. *Drink up.*

They drank down the fluid and threw the cups away.

Anything else? asked Theo, now familiar with the drill.

India looked. *Green powder. Go lie down.*

When they had administered the powder to each other, she checked the cabinet again. One small blue tablet lay next to the bottle of orange stuff. India picked it up and examined it for a moment before popping it into her mouth.

Only one? asked Theo.

Only one, said India. *That nightmare shook me up more than I realized. Blue is for mental health. At least that's what Shannon told me. I guess this will improve my temper a bit.*

Let's hope so, said Theo.

India made a face at him. *Let's go do some bicycling,* she said. They both left the apartment. This time, India locked the door behind her as they left.

When India came back to the waiting area of the restaurant, she saw Theo disconnect from another CrediVid and stand up. She frowned, but said nothing when he came over.

'Success?' he asked cheerfully.

'Success,' she confirmed. 'Are we ready to go?'

'Ready and waiting,' said Theo.

'Ready and making another contact,' said India. 'Who do you keep calling?'

'Just calling George,' said Theo easily. 'You're not worried about that again?'

'Theo, at this point, I'm not sure what *not* to worry about.'

Theo smiled down at her. 'George asked me to keep in

closer contact while we're on the road. You were busy; I figured it was a good time to call him. If you don't trust me by now, what are we doing here together? Why haven't you done something other than healing on me and left me crippled by the side of the road? Why didn't you leave me at the crash site in Michigan City? Why do you have to keep quizzing my every move?'

India sighed. 'You're right. I'm sorry. Come on, let's go.'

'You don't sound very happy,' said Theo.

'I won't be happy until this mess is over,' she said gloomily.

Theo unlocked the bicycles and wrapped the chain around the stem of his seat.

They climbed back on and pedaled off. India felt a little better knowing they were so close to Davenport.

Late that afternoon, they rode through a smaller town and stopped on the far side to consult the map.

'This is where we are right now,' said Theo, pointing to the black dot labeled Peru.

'We did pretty good today, huh, boss?'

'Not too shabby,' said Theo. 'All we need to do is find us another field tonight and tomorrow we can rent another vehicle, get rid of these bicycles.'

'Yeah,' India sighed. 'Sleep in a bed?' she asked hopefully.

'Nope. Sleep on the road. We've been stalled long enough on this one stretch of 80.'

India sighed again. 'You're right. How much more daylight do you figure we have?'

'We can ride for maybe a half-hour more. Then we really need to find a place to sleep,' said Theo. They remounted and were about to move on when a vehicle screeched to a halt behind them. 'India, look out!' yelled Theo. He threw his bike to the ground and ran back to her.

India turned to look and screamed.

A hand clamped over her mouth and another grabbed her upper arm. The bicycle fell out from under her as she was dragged away from it. She saw Theo grab someone else and hit him hard. A compressor shot something into her arm and she screamed again as she fell into darkness.

Theo, what's happening? she asked. Not knowing what else to do, she ran through the gathering black, looking for her apartment. She managed to find the door in spite of her panic, and yanked it open. As she closed it behind her, she saw she was only moments ahead of the dark.

She leaned against the door, panting. Theo was already there, sitting on the couch, drinking a beer.

I hope you don't mind, he said, indicating the drink. *I found it in the fridge.*

Sure, said India, shaking her head. She pushed herself away from the door and moved toward him. *How did you get here?* she asked.

You've been yelling for me ever since those two charming gentlemen joined us. The door was unlocked, so I let myself in.

I left the door unlocked? She gaped in disbelief. *I was certain I locked it after lunch!*

Probably only unlocked for me. I don't have any way to test the theory, but I would expect that's how it works, said Theo. He took a long pull on the bottle. *There's more; can I get you one?*

Uh, yeah, said India. She sat down and looked around. Nothing in the apartment appeared to have been disturbed. No one else had been here while she was gone. How had Theo gotten in?

Here. He handed her the bottle and sat back down. *I take it we've had a setback?*

You could call it that, said India. She took a long swallow and leaned back into the cushions. *I'd forgotten how good this is.* She sat silent for a moment, studying Theo. *A setback. Yes. The Bobsey Twins showed up. They drugged me. I don't know what's happened to you, but it looked like you were swinging away while I went down. Do you know what's happening out there?*

I think I've been drugged, too. They threw both of us in the car, hitting me in the butt with that nasty compressor gadget as I went in. He thought for a moment. *I don't know why they didn't just leave me by the side of the road. Would have made more sense. It's you they want.*

I guess we shouldn't look a gift horse in the mouth, said India. *Is there anything we can do? They've probably turned us around and are taking us back to Quebec. I don't want to go there. Bob is there.*

Let me think, said Theo, taking another swig of his beer.

India settled down and enjoyed her beer, allowing her mind to slough away the fears of the past minutes. She closed her eyes and thought of nothing.

What's in the medicine cabinet? asked Theo suddenly.

What? asked India, stupidly. She sat up and looked at him with one eyebrow raised.

Is there anything in the medicine cabinet that could counteract the drug they gave us? he elaborated.

India shrugged. *I dunno, why?*

They really scared you, didn't they? asked Theo. Patiently he explained, *They probably don't have us tied. They probably hit us with enough of the stuff to keep us quiet until they could get back to Quebec.*

Oh! said India. She leaned forward eagerly. *If we can counteract the drug . . .*

Exactly, Theo interrupted. *Now scoot off to the bathroom and see what goodies your higher power has left for us this time.*

India jumped up off the couch and ran to the chest. *Must be a mind-suppressant of some kind,* she said, coming back with a large container of yellow gel.

Theo eyed the stuff curiously. *What is it?* he asked finally.

You're going to love this, said India. She set the container on the table between them and scooped out a large handful. *Here's to it.* She plopped the stuff on her head and smeared it all over her hair, on her face, and down her neck.

When every bit of her above the shoulders was covered, she sat down to wait.

Theo watched, partly revolted, partly curious. As India sat quietly, the gel began to be absorbed. Slowly at first, then more quickly, until all of it was gone, and India looked just as she had before smearing herself with the muck.

She opened her eyes slowly and saw Theo staring at her. *Your turn,* she grinned, seeing the expression on his face. *It really does work. It just feels completely disgusting.*

Well, if it works, said Theo, scooping up a handful of the obnoxious substance. He reached up hesitantly and put the stuff on the top of his head. *This is worse than the stuff some of these kids are doing to their hair these days.*

India giggled. *You're stalling,* she said. *Just do it and get it over with. You'll be amazed how great you'll feel.*

Almost as good as with that orange stuff? he asked, starting to spread the gel around on his hair.

Different, but yeah.

That's helpful. Theo stopped talking and smeared the yellow substance over his face and down his neck.

You need to get the back of your neck and your ears, too, said India helpfully.

Theo made a face through the muck, and grabbed another handful from the container on the table. When he had finished spreading the stuff on, he sat back and waited just as India had.

She watched with interest as the gel was absorbed into Theo. *So that's what it looked like,* she said when he opened his eyes. *Yuk!*

You looked equally charming, my dear. Are you sure this is it?

Let's go see, suggested India, picking up the container and going back to the bathroom.

Theo followed her and looked into the cabinet himself. *Two blue tablets this time.*

Yup, said India. *You get to swallow yours with some more of the orange stuff. You got more roughed up than I did and you're older.*

How rude of you to mention it, said Theo jokingly.

Just the kind of girl I am, said India, pouring him a cupful of the curious liquid. She handed him the cup and a tablet, then picked up her own.

What will you swallow yours with? asked Theo.

I'll chew mine.

Speaking of yuk . . . said Theo. He placed the tablet on his tongue and took a swallow of the orange stuff.

India chewed her tablet. It tasted like cherry. *Not bad,* she said, reaching into the cabinet again. *A little green powder for each of us, and that should counteract the poison they gave us.*

Having accomplished a cure, they sat back down on the couches.

Now what? asked India.

Now I propose we resume consciousness and find an opportunity to hit these buggers with a little of their own medicine, said Theo.

Should we grab them around the necks or something? asked India.

A little dramatic, Theo told her. *Also too much chance for something to go wrong. I think we wait until they stop for something. Then we can find that compressor syringe and zap them with it.*

Sounds like fun, said India. *What do we do with them afterwards?*

Nothing, said Theo. *We head for the nearest tube station and get ourselves to San Francisco as soon as possible. They can stay in the car and sleep off their debauch.*

Then I'll see you in reality, said India.

They left together by way of her front door. The darkness was gone from her system. The healing had worked. Together they rose up to the conscious level and waited for their kidnappers to make a stop.

Two hours later, just when India was certain she would scream from boredom and immobility, one of the men broke the silence.

'When's the next exit?'

'You can use the VidCon as well as I can.'

A sound of electronic beeps told India one of them was programming the stop.

'You hungry?'

'Gotta go.'

'Fine, but are you hungry?'

'You're hungry, aren't you?'

'I could go for a bite.'

'Okay. We'll make it a longer stop. Those two aren't going anywhere.'

India smiled to herself, taking care not to let anything show in her face or body, just in case they could see her at all. Not going anywhere but to the nearest tube station.

The next exit was another fifteen minutes down the beltway. By the time they pulled off and found a restaurant, India was so tense she was certain anyone looking at her would be able to tell she wasn't asleep or drugged. Theo was motionless and silent beside her.

One of the men reached back and poked her. She managed not to react. They got out of the vehicle and the doors shussed closed behind them.

As their footsteps receded, Theo whispered, 'Are you okay?'

Without moving, she whispered back, 'Yeah, you?'

'Fine. Give them a few more minutes before moving.

We'll have to find the compressor and get back into these positions as soon as possible.'

'Can you see anything from where you are?' asked India.

'I can see both front seats pretty well. How about you?'

India opened her eyes. 'Nope. Not a thing. I guess I'm staring at a back door.'

'It'll be up to me, then,' said Theo. He moved cautiously.

India stirred. Her muscles were cramped, but she felt fine.

'Remember that position,' Theo cautioned.

'I know,' said India. 'Don't sit up all the way. They may have gotten seats looking out at us.'

'Good point,' said Theo. He ducked a bit and wriggled into the front seat. They were parked in the darkest part of the lot, so nosy people wouldn't see two bodies in the back seat. He had to feel around in the dark, looking for the compressor.

'What about the dash compartment?' India suggested, stretching as much as she could in the confines of the back seat.

'Not there,' said Theo, shutting the compartment again.

'Under the seat?' asked India. She could hear Theo fumbling around in the dark.

'Nope,' came the reply.

'What about a secret compartment in the door?' asked India, remembering her father had a similar set-up in his vehicle. Just in case.

'What would open up a secret door like that?' asked Theo.

'Try tweaking the window button three times fast.'

She could hear the familiar click. 'That did it?'

'I'll say,' said Theo. He handed the compressor back to her. 'Look at this!' The next thing he handed back was a badge.

'Continental Police?' India's voice squeaked out. 'Who

are these guys? This looks real. Stolen? Or a really good counterfeit?'

'What if it's real?' asked Theo. He was still leaning into the front seat, so his voice was hard to hear.

'Then I'm in more trouble than I thought,' said India. She handed the badge back to Theo. 'Better leave that where it was,' she said in a subdued voice. 'And get back here and into position. Who knows when they'll be back.'

She heard the hidden compartment snap shut again, and Theo wriggled back into the back seat.

'Where's the compressor?' he asked.

'Here,' said India, handing it over. 'What do you make of the badge?' she asked.

'Anything you suggested is possible. I think we don't know enough to base an intelligent guess on,' he said. 'Now get back into position and keep quiet.'

India arranged herself the way she had been stuffed into the back seat and prepared to wait. Theo would hit them with the drug once they were back on the road. There would be no witnesses on the beltway. There was no guarantee what might happen in a restaurant parking lot.

'I wish they weren't worried about how they'd look carrying two bodies onto the tube,' India complained. 'This is bloody uncomfortable.'

Theo chuckled, but didn't say anything.

Shortly, footsteps approached the vehicle and the doors opened. The two men got in and started the vehicle.

As they pulled back onto the beltway, India felt adrenalin surge in her system. It was all she could do to hold herself down. Then Theo sat up.

'Hey!' yelled one man just as Theo stuck the hypo against his neck.

The other man turned, but Theo had already dispatched his partner. 'What the . . .' he began.

Theo smacked the hypo against his neck as well and emptied the next dosage into the man.

After that, things happened quickly. Theo jumped into the front seat and tried to push the limp bodies over the seat to India.

'This would be easier if I levitated them,' she pointed out.

'Right. Then do it! I've got some reprogramming to do here anyway.' Theo abandoned the moving to her, and began setting the course to the nearest tube station.

India moved the men to the back seat and then climbed into the front. 'Are we all set?' she asked, settling back to rest for a moment.

Theo held up a hand and pressed two more keys. 'All set,' he said, sitting back. 'We should be at the station in twenty minutes. Assuming they weren't supposed to be checking in with anyone in the near future, we should be safe enough for a while.'

'That's what you said last time,' said India wryly. 'You aren't going to make a phone call, are you?'

'Not till we get to San Francisco,' said Theo, grinning at her. 'You aren't still worried about that, are you?'

'Theo, every time you make a phone call, those guys show up again. If you were in my shoes, what would you think?'

'I'd be pretty paranoid,' said Theo, laughing. 'You've cost me too much for me to want to turn you in!'

'Good point.' She laughed too. It felt good. 'Okay, no more paranoia. Not tonight, anyway.'

'Good girl,' said Theo. 'Now, why don't you check on those two. Make sure they're really gone. We don't want the same nasty surprise we gave them.'

'Okay. Wake me if we get to the station before I'm done with them.' India closed her eyes and lowered into her meditation state to check on Frick and Frack.

They were both down and out. When Theo jostled her arm to let her know they were almost there, India had just completed the locking process. Their minds were where they wouldn't find them for quite a while. Feeling pretty good about her work, India climbed back up to consciousness and looked out the window.

They were in the parking lot of the tube station, and Theo had just eased the vehicle into a space far from any of the lights.

'Is there anything here we need to take with us?' they asked simultaneously.

They laughed. 'I guess not!'

Together, they walked away from the vehicle toward the tube station. 'They're gone?' asked Theo.

'Where they won't find themselves for a while,' India assured him. 'We should have a clear trip now.'

'Keep your fingers crossed,' Theo told her.

He purchased two tickets and they boarded the tube. At that hour it was more crowded than either of them had expected. They found their seats and belted down for the trip. The doors of the car closed and the train began to accelerate rapidly, diving to the subterranean level where they would reach travel speeds of 800 kilometers an hour.

India hated the tubes. She was always certain the cars would be derailed and kill everyone aboard. It hadn't happened in decades, but she still worried.

Theo noticed her white knuckles and put his hand over hers, giving it a gentle squeeze. 'Everything will be fine now.'

'Okay,' she said. But that wasn't how she felt.

'Well, then, where the hell are they?' demanded the Captain. He slammed his fist down on his desk, rattling an over-full ashtray. Butts and ash fell onto his desk.

Bob watched in disgust. 'I don't know, sir.'

'Why not?' demanded the Captain, slowing his pace around the office for a moment.

'Perhaps because you didn't consult with me on this,' said Bob. He couldn't stand it any more. He picked up a piece of paper and shoveled the mess off the Captain's desk. 'You really ought to quit this,' he said, tossing the butts in the trash. 'It shortens your life and harms the people around you.'

'There are other things I do that will kill me much quicker,' the Captain snapped. 'I want you to find Harry and Grindle. They may be idiots, but they're my idiots. If that makes any sense. They were supposed to pick up India and the man she's traveling with yesterday evening. They haven't reported even a failure. That isn't like them.'

'Where were they when you lost contact?' asked Bob.

'Somewhere off Beltway 80, near Peru,' the Captain said absently.

'Sir, Peru is in South America,' Bob said, puzzled.

'It's also a city in the Illinois County,' said the Captain acidly. 'They were on the trail of the girl and the old man. Go find them. Find out what happened. I can't trace them.'

'Well, of course not, sir,' said Bob. 'You aren't the psi expert.'

'That being the case,' said the Captain, 'go prove to me you're worth keeping on the payroll.'

'Yes, sir,' said Bob. He saluted and left the office. It was always easier to breathe out here. Not just the cigarettes. The Captain had a way of sucking the atmosphere out of a room.

Bob went back to his office.

'Bibi, please find the nearest tube and shuttle stations to Peru, Illinois, and find out if any passengers with these IDs used the transports during the last two days. Also, find out anything reported by the police about two men answering to these descriptions.' He tossed a stack of discs onto her desk.

'I'm not your goddamn secretary!' she protested.

Bob walked past, saying nothing more.

'Bastard,' she muttered, shoving the discs onto the floor.

'By the way,' Bob said, sticking his head back through his office door, 'Boss says to authorize double-time on anything you're willing to help me on.'

'All you had to say was please,' said Bibi, getting up to retrieve the discs. 'Who're we looking for?'

'Just a couple of our men,' said Bob. 'I'll be in here if you need me, but only knock in an emergency.'

'Sir, yes, sir!' said Bibi, returning to her seat. 'My double-time starts now; make a note of the time.'

Bob looked at his watch and nodded. 'I really appreciate this,' he said.

'Just don't start asking me to shop for your wife,' said Bibi.

'I'm not married,' said Bob.

'Don't get any ideas,' said Bibi.

'That's two minutes you don't get paid for,' said Bob.

'Your mother,' said Bibi cheerfully.

'She don't get paid either,' said Bob. 'Get to work.' He shut the door behind him and looked at the chair behind his desk. Not the right place. Looking around at the bare walls, he decided the floor would have to do.

He sat down and loosened his tie. He took deep breaths as he removed his shoes and crossed his legs. 'Lights, dim, please.' The lights lowered obligingly. 'Lower, please.' They went almost dark. Bob closed his eyes and began to drop his level of consciousness. On reaching his workplace, he called for Harry and Grindle.

The two men came right away. *You wanted to talk to us?* they asked.

Sit down, guys, said Bob, gesturing to two chairs in front of the desk in his workplace.

Harry and Grindle sat.

Where are you? asked Bob.

They consulted with each other. *Right here, sir,* they answered finally.

No. I mean where are your bodies right now?

They looked at each other again. *Right here, sir,* they answered.

Bob sighed. *You aren't here. I created you to ask you questions. Where are your bodies, really?*

Harry and Grindle looked at each other.

They didn't understand. That much was completely obvious.

We've lost contact with you, said Bob, trying another tack. *We want to know where you are in the Continental Americas, in order to find out where India and Theo went?*

We're right here, said Grindle.

'Here' doesn't exist! yelled Bob. *You're somewhere in the middle of a vast country and we don't know where! The Captain has ordered me to find you and find out what happened to the two people you were supposed to bring back here! Now where the hell are you?*

In the vehicle? asked Harry.

Thank the gods! thought Bob. One of them is catching on.

And where is the vehicle? he prompted.

I don't know, said Harry. *We picked them up outside of Peru, but I guess the drug we hit them with didn't work. They escaped.*

And how did they do that? asked Bob.

Harry shrugged. *I guess they hit us with what we hit them with.*

If you hit them with it, why did they recover and you're still whacked out? asked Bob, pointedly.

Harry and Grindle had no answer for that.

There was a knock on the door.

Harry and Grindle both started.

Bob waved them back. *It's my secretary,* he explained.

'I am not your secretary!' yelled Bibi through the door to Bob's office. 'You answer your own goddamn phone! If you want information, I got information. Otherwise, you work on your own.'

Sounds like you got her just where you want her, said Grindle. He poked Harry in the ribs and they both laughed.

If you two come around before I find you, you better find another place to be, Bob warned, kicking them out of his workplace.

Harry and Grindle left, chuckling to themselves.

Bob slammed the door behind them and resurfaced. Bibi was still pounding on the door, and still upset over the secretary remark. *How high is your psi-rating?* he asked telepathically, out of curiosity.

High enough, asshole. The idiots you're looking for are in the parking lot of the Peru tube station in the back seat of their vehicle. Any questions?

'Yeah,' said Bob. 'Did you get that from eavesdropping on my telepathic link, or from your research?'

Bibi handed him a disc. 'What do you think?' she asked, turning to walk away.

Laughing, Bob went back into his office and shut the door. *Thank you*, he called after her.

Fuck you, she called back cheerfully. *I still expect my double-time. All twenty minutes of it!*

Bob slammed the button of his VidCon. 'Captain,' he began.

'You're going to Peru; they're in the back seat of their vehicle in the parking lot of the Peru tube station,' said the Captain.

'Sir, with all due respect, what do you need me for?' asked Bob.

'I'm not going to go retrieve those idiots,' said the Captain. He disconnected the communication.

Bob stuck his tongue out at the screen. 'I guess that means I am.'

You got it, said the Captain.

Anyone else out there? Bob yelled.

Yes, came the surprising reply. *But I won't let you find me. I don't like you. I won't let you hurt me ever again.*

India? Bob called.

There was no answer.

India! yelled Bob. *Shit!*

Bob, you need a vacation, said Bibi. *When are you leaving?*

Get out of my head, all of you! Bob ordered.

He heard two women giggle, but he wasn't sure who they were. Anyone could have tapped into him by now.

India leaned back in her seat, chuckling.

'What's so funny?' asked Theo. He had been stroking his now-bare chin and thought she might be laughing at him for it.

'Another block came down,' said India happily. 'Guess what I found behind it?'

'Another strange man?' suggested Theo helpfully.

'Strange, yes, but not a stranger. Bob was having an extremely awkward interview with two men named Harry and Grindle. Guess who they are.'

'Don't tell me. Heckle and Jeckle?' guessed Theo.

'Yup!' said India cheerfully. 'He was having even less luck with them than I have with you sometimes.' She laughed again, sounding entirely more delighted than Theo thought she ought to.

'How far away was the transmission?' he asked.

'Dunno,' said India. 'Why?'

'How far have you been able to read telepathically before?'

'Not very far,' said India. 'A few miles, I guess. I'm not sure.'

'Where do you think Bob is?' asked Theo.

India thought for a long moment. 'Quebec?' she asked finally.

Theo nodded. 'Quite probably,' he said. 'Harry and Grindle were sent after you because they let you go to begin with. Probably punishment. Bob stayed behind in the office and is only now being sent out to find the men sent to find you.'

'Makes sense,' said India slowly. 'It was such a surprise to find myself listening to his conversation. I was also surprised to find out how many other people were listening, too.'

'How many would you estimate?' he asked.

'Only a few on the physical plane,' said India. 'But there were thousands of people in the Collective Unconscious listening in, too.'

'Why would they be there?'

'I have no idea,' said India. 'I got the feeling they were waiting for something, but it had nothing to do with the conversation. They were just waiting.'

'What was so funny, then?' asked Theo, puzzled.

'Bob's co-worker. She was objecting to being called his secretary,' India explained. 'She gave Bob quite a ration.' She paused for a moment, thinking. 'He heard me, too. He asked if anyone else out there could hear him. I answered.'

'Why did you do that?'

'I guess to let him know the mess he made in my mind is going away and there's nothing he can do to stop it,' she said.

'That was a pretty dangerous thing to do,' said Theo. 'You know that, don't you?'

'I guess so,' said India. 'It felt good at the time, though.'

'You've got to remember that a moment's gratification can cause lasting damage. If you can hear him and he can hear you, he can probably use that to find you as well.'

'Why can't I hear you?' she asked.

'You can't?' asked Theo. He sounded genuinely surprised.

'No,' said India. 'I've tried. I don't know why I can't get past your barriers, but I've never been able to hear your thoughts.'

'Well, that would explain why you've had trouble trusting me,' said Theo. 'I wondered why you kept questioning my intentions.'

'I still can't read you,' said India.

'Even with the new barrier down?' asked Theo.

'I'm scanning you now,' she said. 'You read like a brick wall. I can get some surface texture, but the structure and depth are missing. I can't get past the wall you've put up. Do you have any psychic talents?'

'Nope,' said Theo definitely. 'Not a one. If you can't get into my mind, it's probably because I don't let anyone in there. It's not a conscious thing. I just don't like to have my life pried into.'

'I wasn't trying to pry!' India exclaimed. 'I just have a hard time trusting people. I like to read them a bit first. Make sure I'm not making a mistake.'

'Some things you just have to take at face value,' said Theo.

'What do you mean?' asked India.

'Have you ever noticed there are some people you just don't like, right off the bat, even though you have absolutely no reason for it, and figure you're probably being silly?' he asked.

'Yeah,' she prompted.

'And sometimes you meet someone and just as immediately like them and feel you can tell them anything and not have to worry about it?' he continued.

'Yeah,' she prompted again.

'How often have you been right, either way?' he asked.

'Almost one hundred per cent,' said India. 'I have an instinct about people.'

'Then why haven't you used it on anyone recently?' Theo demanded.

'Everything is so mixed up right now!' she protested.

'How mixed up is your heart?' Theo countered.

'My heart's not mixed up,' she said. 'It's my mind.'

'Your mind isn't what makes up your heart about

people,' said Theo. 'It's the other way around.'

India thought about that for a long time as they shot through the subterranean tunnel. They would be in the Vintners' Quarter in three more stops. It had been a long night, and she hadn't gotten much sleep.

She was afraid to sleep. She didn't want to end up in the No-Place. She was afraid of running into Ty. She didn't trust him. According to Theo's definition, she had never trusted him. After the last encounter, she never wanted to see him again. She was also concerned about what he might try to do to her after what she did to him.

It was a mess, she decided. Almost as much of a mess as her mind was after Bob got through with it. Idly, she wondered if her life would ever return to normal. Or at least as normal as possible considering that everything was different now. The chances seemed slim.

Lying back in her seat with her eyes closed, India was rocked by the motion of the train. The lights in the car were low, and the hushed murmuring of the passengers around them lulled her. She found herself sliding down to her meditation level in spite of herself.

'Was Bob told to look for you also?' asked Theo.

India jerked awake.

'Or was he just supposed to look for George and Gracie?' he continued.

'Huh?' asked India, desperately trying to switch gears.

'Was Bob coming after you himself?' Theo repeated.

'Uh, I don't think so,' said India, catching up with the conversation. 'I don't know.' She was grateful Theo had pulled her out of her stupor, at least for the present.

'Will it take him long to find our little friends?'

'Shouldn't,' she said. 'Bibi knew exactly where they were.'

'How?' asked Theo.

'I don't know. I wasn't able to read that in her mind. Neither was Bob,' said India, smiling. 'Probably, she found the vehicle through a police report filed in Peru, but I couldn't tell for sure. She didn't tell Bob. She only took twenty minutes to find them, she said. They must be plugged into some kind of network to be getting that kind of information.'

'What if they really are the police?' asked Theo.

India shook her head. 'The police don't kidnap people and brainwash them,' she said decisively.

'Mmm,' said Theo cynically. 'Neither does the government, right?'

'You think so?' asked India.

'Know so, kiddo,' he said. 'I've been around a lot of years and seen all sorts of things I could have sworn would never happen. All it's taught me is not to say "never". Eventually, everything happens to everyone. It may take several lifetimes, but eventually everything catches up to your lowest expectations; especially people.'

'You sound pretty bitter about that,' said India drowsily. She was starting to fall back to sleep.

'Maybe I am,' he said. 'Get some sleep. I'll wake you when we get to our stop. We'll get to Jenny's house pretty late, I'm afraid. But I'm glad it's so close.'

'Me too,' said India, snuggling down into her seat. 'Thank you, Theo. I couldn't have done this without you.'

Theo smiled, but India never saw it. She was fast asleep and dreaming.

Chapter Eleven

India stood on the trail through Shark's Tooth Pass. She knew she was dreaming, but curiosity kept her following the images in her mind.

She was levitating the same candle Mama had slashed through. It was almost burned down, but India made no effort to replace it. She knew what would happen next.

The claw slashed out of nowhere and managed to frighten India despite the fact she was expecting it. This time, instead of falling over the cliff, she stood on the path, facing Mama. They glared at each other for a long time before India finally spoke.

What do you want from me? she asked.

I want nothing from you, the creature hissed.

Why have you attacked me, then? India persisted.

You are trespassing, said Mama.

It wasn't intentional, she apologized.

That doesn't matter, Mama breathed.

The scene shifted and India found herself inside Mama's cave. It was dark, but India could see clearly with her mind. Bodies were chained to the walls. She took a step forward and felt something crunch underfoot. Looking down, she was stepping on bones. In the distance, someone moaned. Then, without transition, India was among the Disembodied.

They plucked at her clothing, but having no real hands they couldn't get a purchase on her. She pulled away from them and started to run.

Help me! she cried.

The Disembodied pursued her. The footing became

increasingly difficult. The ground began sucking her down. Energy surrounded her, muffling her and pushing her deeper into the muck.

Help! she screamed.

India?

Shannon!

India, where are you? Shannon called.

I don't know! India cried. Something kept trying to push her words back into her mouth. *Down here,* she managed.

A hand reached toward her. She grabbed it and felt it pull her out of the mire.

Shannon, what are you doing here? she asked, wondering why that was the first thing she asked.

Come with me quickly! Shannon pulled India away from the grasping hands and muffling energy.

They ran away from the Disembodied and up to the No-Place.

India tried to pull away from Shannon when she realized where they were. *I don't want to come here!* she cried, trying to free herself.

India! Shannon stopped and held tight to India's hand. *You don't have much time. I had to find you to warn you.*

India stopped and waited.

Ashraf is using the Disembodied, Shannon continued. *But there's someone else. I don't know who. They are working together. Or at least as much together as two people can who have different goals and different means of achieving them.*

How do you know this? asked India.

I've been here, looking, on and off since I told Anara about your dream, Shannon explained. *You're dreaming now, aren't you?*

I thought I was, said India. *I was standing in Shark's Tooth Pass. I was talking with Mama. Then I was in the Collective Unconscious and screaming for help.*

Talking with Mama? Shannon echoed.

Yeah, said India. *I have no idea how I got from there to here, but the Disembodied were sucking me in and I was scared. Then you showed up. I guess I'm not dreaming any more.*

'India?'

What?

I didn't say anything, said Shannon.

Must be Theo, said India. *I guess we're there.*

Well, just promise you'll be careful. I don't know what Ashraf has to do with all this, but if he's using the Disembodied, it could be serious trouble for you.

India gave Shannon a brief hug. *Thanks for your help*, she said. *I won't tell Anara.* She chuckled. *Of course, she'll find out anyway*, she said.

You let me worry about that, said Shannon. *I'll see you again if I can find out anything more.*

India smiled and left the No-Place. They were just pulling into the Vintners' Quarter station.

'More rough dreams?' asked Theo.

'Not so bad this time,' said India. 'How far is it to Jenny's house?'

'Not far. We'll call before we leave here, though. I hate to wake her up, but we don't seem to have a choice.'

'She'd be furious with you when she found out you hadn't,' said India.

Theo nodded. 'I expect you're right. She'll probably tell me to wait here while she comes down to get us.'

'Probably,' India agreed. The train stopped and the doors hissed open. India started, glancing around involuntarily. It was the same hissing noise Mama had made.

They got off the train with the few people leaving the train at that hour. Fortunately, India didn't recognize any of them. Theo found the CrediVid booth and called Jenny.

'I'll be right down,' she said as soon as he told her where they were.

'Don't be silly,' said Theo, winking at India. 'We can grab a taxi and be there in no time.'

'That's what you said when you left Quebec,' Jenny reminded him.

'Nothing of the sort,' said Theo. 'Besides, if you come down here, we'll just pass you on the way out.'

Jenny sighed. 'You remember the address?' she asked.

'I'm old, not stupid,' said Theo.

Jenny made a face. 'You'll never be old,' she said. 'Okay, you win. I'll be here waiting. I've had the beds made up since you left Quebec. I'll turn them down and have some milk warming.'

India made a face this time. Theo grinned. 'How about a couple of brandies instead?'

'That's my Pop,' said Jenny. She disconnected.

Ten minutes later, Theo and India stood on the front porch of a huge old house, made of wood and standing on more land than India had seen since leaving her father's fortress in the Berkeley hills.

'This place is gigantic!' she exclaimed as Theo pressed the doorbell. India jumped at the sound. 'No VidBox?'

'They don't believe in such contraptions,' said Theo. 'That's why they live here. The Vintners' Quarter is almost entirely still vineyards and farms. Jenny actually grows vegetables. Spends hours in the garden all by herself.'

India sighed wistfully. 'Gardening is very relaxing,' she said.

'What would you know about it?' he asked, surprised.

'A bit,' said India.

The front door opened and India was pulled into the house by a woman who was even larger than she had expected. Jenny must be close to six feet tall! she thought.

'Our wayward travelers have arrived?' asked George, coming down the front stairs.

India looked up. And up, and up.

George came to stand beside his wife, and India began to understand what Theo had meant by large brown people. George was closer to seven feet than to six. What on earth would their children look like?

'Dad, you'll have the guest bedroom,' Jenny was saying. 'India.'

India jerked around to face Jenny.

'You'll have to bunk with Sandy. She's asleep, but a herd of rampaging elephants stampeding through her room wouldn't wake her, so don't worry about making noise while you get ready for bed. I've put extra towels in the bathroom for you, and a clean nightie on the foot of the bed. If you want to take a shower tonight, feel free.'

'Thank you,' said India in a small voice. 'You're very kind.'

Jenny smiled. It was a warm, wonderful smile and it made India feel not only welcome, but a part of the family as well. 'Do you want a glass of warm milk, or a brandy with my degenerate father?'

'I think a brandy and a hot shower sounds just fine, thank you,' said India.

'Shall I bring it up to you, then?' asked Jenny.

'Thank you,' said India.

'George, will you please show India where everything is upstairs while I pour the drinks and give my father the third degree?'

'With pleasure,' said George, offering India his arm.

He was so tall his elbow was in her ear. India giggled and reached up. Jenny giggled too. George very solemnly escorted India up the stairs and down the hallway to Sandy's room.

'The bathroom is through that door,' he said, pointing. 'Jenny will bring your brandy up in a moment. I'm going back to bed. I'll see you in the morning and we can discuss how to get you into the Old City.'

'This is very kind of you,' said India. 'I'm not sure you

understand what kind of risk you're taking by doing this for me.'

'I understand you need my help. Jenny's father trusts you. That's all I need to know,' said George. 'Sleep well.'

India smiled. 'Thanks. You too.'

When India came out of the shower, she found the snifter of brandy on the nightstand beside her bed. She pulled the nightgown over her head and wasn't surprised to find it was almost a foot too long and huge all over. She climbed into bed and tossed the brandy off in one swallow. It burned going down, but warmed her arms and legs and made a drowsy feeling rise up from her pelvis into her chest and head. She lay down and was asleep almost at once.

When she finally awoke she had no idea what time it was. The sun was well past the window, and it was bright daylight in the room.

India sat up and looked around her. The other bed was made up with an old-fashioned piecework quilt and large pillows. There were ruffled curtains at the window and rag rugs on the floor. All the furniture was wooden and sturdy-looking. She stepped out of bed onto the hard wood floor and padded down the hall to the bathroom. She couldn't believe people still lived this way.

When she went back to the bedroom, she found the bed made up and some clothing laid out across the foot of it. With a smile, she closed the door, took off the nightgown, and tried on the jeans and frilly, faded blouse. They were only a little too big, so she rolled the hems of the pants and the sleeves of the blouse and took a look at herself in the mirror.

The effect was comical. The ruffles completely overbalanced her, and the pants looked like they were about to fall off. India rummaged about for a belt and finally found several in the closet. She tried them all on, but they were all too big.

'Well, the hell with it,' she said to her reflection. She ran her fingers through her ruined curls, trying to make them look less shaggy, but it didn't really help. 'Ah!' she said, making a face at herself. She left the room and went downstairs to see where everyone else was.

Jenny looked up from her book when India wandered into the kitchen. 'Oh, my!' she laughed. 'I thought those would fit! You're even smaller than I thought.' She stood up and tossed her book down on the table. 'Let's go see if we can't find anything better than that.'

'Oh, it's okay, really,' India protested. 'I've put you out enough.'

'Nonsense,' said Jenny, taking India by the hand and leading her back up the stairs. 'I have a lot more where that came from. We can play dress-up until George and Dad have finished hatching their plan.'

India thought longingly about the coffee she had seen in the pot on the kitchen counter, but resigned herself to being Jenny's doll for the time being.

'Here,' said Jenny, pulling India into a huge closet in what appeared to be the guest bedroom. 'See if you can't find anything better while I go get you a cup of coffee.'

'Oh, thank you!' said India, looking at the racks and shelves of clothing. It was the biggest closet she had ever seen. 'But where do I start?'

'Smallest here,' said Jenny, indicating the left-hand side of the closet. 'Around to biggest here.' She pointed to the right side of the closet. 'Smallest is baby clothing. You never know when you'll need those again,' she chuckled, and ran a hand over her stomach.

'Oh,' said India politely. 'Are you planning on having more children?'

'Oh, George and I don't plan these things,' said Jenny, smiling. 'We just do them. I'm just out of the first trimester now.'

'Congratulations,' said India, not knowing what else to say. 'You must be very pleased.'

'Always,' said Jenny. 'Now get started looking and I'll be back up with that coffee.'

India found jeans that fit almost right away. The size was still on most of the garments in the closet. She guessed they had been outgrown fairly quickly. Nothing seemed to show much wear. She shucked the too-large pants and pulled on the new ones. They were perfect. She folded the others and put them on a stack of similar sizes and began looking for a shirt.

'Oh, that's much better,' said Jenny, handing India a steaming mug.

India sipped the hot liquid and sighed. 'That's wonderful,' she said. 'Thank you.'

'No,' said Jenny firmly. 'Thank you for getting Dad out here, finally. Maybe now we'll be able to convince him to move here.'

'He thinks he'd be in the way,' said India. 'He figures you came out here so you could make your own mistakes raising your kids. He says you don't need him around telling you what to do all the time.'

Jenny laughed. 'That's my Pop! Here, what about this shirt?' She held up a pretty blue blouse with black piping in a western pattern.

India took off the frilled monstrosity and slipped her arm into the sleeve Jenny held out for her. 'That's not how you feel, though, is it?'

'India, I've been trying to convince him to move out here for almost fifteen years. George agrees with me. Ever since Mom decided not to renew their contract, he's been kind of depressed. You're the best thing that's happened to him in a long time. Shook him up, if you know what I mean.'

'He didn't seem unhappy to me,' said India. 'He seems pretty self-sufficient and active in his volunteer things.'

'What was he doing when you met him?' asked Jenny in a knowing tone of voice.

'Eating dinner,' said India. She remembered the look on his face as his dish of peas crashed to the floor, and giggled.

'At home, alone, right?' Jenny pressed.

'Right,' said India.

'So what were you doing there?' asked Jenny. She sounded genuinely curious. 'I mean, how did you meet?'

'I jumped from the roof next door and caught the ladder of his fire escape. I opened the window and stepped onto his kitchen table into the middle of his dinner,' India explained, trying not to laugh.

Jenny did it for her. She laughed until tears ran down her cheeks and she had to sit down on the floor of the closet. 'You must have scared the hell out of him,' she gasped at last.

India started to giggle. 'Peas were everywhere,' she laughed, and sat down too.

'Dad was eating Green Things?' Jenny asked in amazement.

'They were on the table. I didn't notice what he had on his plate,' said India.

'Maybe he figured if he cooked them that was close enough,' said Jenny, starting to laugh again. 'Mom and Dad used to argue about Green Things all the time. He said if God had wanted man to eat vegetables he wouldn't have created cows. Since cows ate Green Things, he should be getting all those vitamins from eating the cows. It used to make Mom nuts. I tried the same argument once and nearly got grounded for the rest of my life.'

'He must have been a great dad,' said India wistfully.

'Yeah,' said Jenny. 'I'll never forget him trying to teach me how to ride a bike. He ran up and down the street behind me, holding on to the seat so I wouldn't fall and hurt myself. Mom was yelling at him that he'd have a heart attack if he kept going like that. He told her he wasn't going to quit until I could ride all by myself.' Jenny smiled thoughtfully. 'He didn't. He kept at it for days. Then finally I learned and I think that was when I stopped depending on him for everything. He gave me my autonomy and I never really looked back.'

India stood up and finished buttoning the blouse.

'Not bad,' said Jenny.

India started tucking it into her jeans.

'Tell me about your parents,' said Jenny. 'You know so much about mine.'

India shrugged. 'Not much to tell. My mother died when I was a little girl. My dad and I never really got along. I moved out as soon as I could and never went back. I hear news reports once in a while, but I don't keep in touch.'

'He's missing a lot,' said Jenny softly. Then more briskly she added, 'Well, then you'll just have to adopt mine. Dad has enough love for everyone.'

'He's been wonderful to me,' India agreed. 'What I can't figure out is why.'

Jenny put her hands on India's shoulders and turned her to face the mirror. 'You are a tiny girl,' she said. 'Tiny girls usually punch the protective-father button in guys. Besides, Dad likes helping people. It makes him feel needed.'

'Think he and George have hatched their plan?' asked India, changing the subject as much as she could. Even if it were true, India hated being called 'tiny'.

Jenny gave her shoulders a small squeeze. 'Let's go see.'

They went back downstairs and India refilled her coffee cup before she and Jenny went to the den to find George and Theo.

The two men were deep in conversation, but looked up when Jenny propelled India into the room.

'How's it going?' asked Jenny, pushing India into a chair. She sat down herself and looked at her husband. 'Any luck?'

'Some,' said George. 'Has India had breakfast?'

Jenny looked startled. 'The clothing I put out for her was so big, I got sidetracked by trying to find something to fit her.'

'It's okay,' said India. 'Coffee will be fine.'

'Nonsense,' said George. 'Besides, I want lunch, so we can talk in the kitchen while we eat.'

'George, are you ever *not* hungry?' asked Theo, standing up and stretching.

'Tell me you don't want something too,' said Jenny. 'Sandwiches?'

Theo looked at India and laughed. 'How about some pancakes?' he asked.

'No!' India protested. 'Pancakes take too much work.'

'What work?' asked Jenny. 'You forget I have three boys and a bottomless pit. Pancakes are something we have all the time. What do you think, honey? Pancakes for lunch?'

'My favorite,' George rumbled. 'Now, feed me, woman!'

'I'll set the table,' said Jenny. 'You know where the batter and the pan are. Besides, you make much better pancakes than I do.'

They all moved into the kitchen. India and Theo tried to help Jenny set the table, but kept getting in the way, so Jenny finally ordered them to sit quietly in the corner.

'See how she picks on me?' Theo complained to India with a wink. 'If I moved out here, I'd be treated like this all the time.'

India nodded. 'It's a rough life,' she agreed.

'Well, gentlemen, spill it,' said Jenny. She had finished setting the table and was ferrying plates from the stove as quickly as the pancakes came off the griddle.

Theo assaulted the butter plate, putting immense globs between each pancake. 'Pass the syrup,' was all he would say.

'George,' said Jenny in a warning tone.

'We figure I can get two University passes,' said George, not turning around to face Jenny. 'One student and one professor should do it. Theo is insisting on coming along, and you know how your father is when he sets his mind on something.'

India watched as George's shoulders slowly raised as he talked. She looked at Jenny and discovered why.

Jenny didn't look happy.

George had known she wouldn't be.

India looked at Theo. He was grinning at her. She smiled back.

'So you just caved in and said he could go?' Jenny demanded. '*I've* never seen where you work and you'll let him just waltz in there because he's a pain in the ass?'

'Something like that,' said Theo. He cut a huge wedge from the stack, sopped up as much syrup as possible, and shoved the whole thing in his mouth. He could barely chew there was so much food crammed in.

Jenny looked at him in disgust. 'The object is to enjoy, not demolish in the shortest possible time.'

'I'm the only one who has to go,' said India. 'I don't want to start a fight because George is willing to help me.'

George winked at India and brought a special stack of pancakes hot from the griddle for Jenny.

'You aren't starting one,' said Jenny, looking at the plate in front of her. 'This has been going on for a long time.'

George sighed and went back to the stove to make himself some pancakes.

'San Francisco used to be one of the most beautiful cities in the world,' said Jenny. She started putting almost as much butter on her pancakes as Theo had. 'I've never been able to see it because the military won't let just anybody in. My husband works there every day, but I haven't been able to convince him I'd really like a pass myself just to poke around a little. He always puts me off with a promise of someday, but someday never arrives.'

'Jenny, I just don't think now would be good,' said George, coming to the table and setting down his plate.

'Because I'm pregnant?' she asked.

Theo looked up at her. 'Are you really? Why didn't you tell me! Congratulations to you both.'

'That,' said George, 'and because we have no idea if Theo and India managed to shake their traveling companions. We don't know if we'll suddenly have company trying to shoot at us. I don't want you anywhere near if that should happen.'

'You're willing to risk my becoming a widow?' she asked. 'That's not a chance I'm willing to take.'

'Are you saying I should send India and Theo off to the Arboretum by themselves?' asked George patiently.

'I don't know what I'm saying,' said Jenny. She put down her fork and covered her face with her hands. When she finally looked up from them, her eyes were dry, but she looked very tired. 'I don't like this much at all.'

India looked stricken. 'I'm so sorry!' she cried. She jumped up from the table. 'This is all my fault. I never wanted anyone to get hurt. Theo insisted on bringing me here. I shouldn't have let him!' She ran from the room, but there was really no place to go. She could hear their voices rising behind her, so she went upstairs to Sandy's room and shut the door. 'What a mess I always manage to make of things,' she said as she threw herself on the spare bed.

Shortly there was a tap on the door. India ignored it.

'India?' asked Theo quietly. 'May I come in?'

'Okay,' she snuffled ungraciously. She rolled over and sat up.

Theo closed the door behind him and came to sit on the edge of the bed. 'No one is blaming you for this,' he started.

'How can they not?' she interrupted, feeling the tears well up in her throat again.

Theo put his hand on her arm. 'Shh,' he said. 'Listen to me. It's not your fault you're in trouble. You need help and we're the people in the best position to give it to you.

Maybe that makes us in the right place at the wrong time, but if you don't let us help you, you'll lessen your chances of getting out of this alive. I know that for certain. That's why I won't let you go into the Old City alone. You need protection from these people. They haven't given up. You know that. Any fighting between Jenny and George on this is old stuff. They'll get over it. Jenny may even get a chance to go into the City herself after the baby is born, but George has a point about the dangers involved.'

'So does Jenny,' said India.

'Yes, she does,' Theo acknowledged. 'But George can't let us go unescorted. The passes entitle us to a guided tour. He has to go along, or send someone else along with us. Someone else introduces a risk none of us should be willing to take. It would jeopardize George's job and his life, and they would probably come after Jenny and the kids as well. The government takes these things very seriously. Any breach of security is immediately and harshly punished. I'm not prepared to lose my family.'

'Would they go after you too?' asked India.

Theo shrugged. 'They might. I don't know. The point is, we're all in this together now. So come back downstairs and finish your breakfast. We'll go in tomorrow with George when he goes to work.'

'Not this afternoon?' asked India. Staying here any longer than necessary made her worry that Stupid and Stupider might find them again.

'Look too suspicious, George says,' Theo explained. 'Especially since he called in sick this morning.'

India nodded. 'Breakfast, then.'

'That's my girl,' he said, standing up and pulling her up with him. 'George will be disappointed if you don't put away more of his special pancakes. He's used to the appetites around here.'

India giggled. 'I'll do my best.'

*   *   *

They finished eating and Jenny kicked George and Theo out of the kitchen. 'India and I will wash up. The kids will be home from school shortly.'

Grumbling good-naturedly about bossy women, the two men had just sat down when the front door burst open.

'Grandpa!' shrieked Tommy as he hurtled across the room and into Theo's arms. 'What happened to your hair?' he demanded, pushing back from an enthusiastic hug. 'Where's your beard?'

'I was traveling in disguise,' said Theo mysteriously.

'Really?' asked Tommy, wide-eyed.

'Mmhmm,' said Theo. 'There were men chasing us, and we had to ride for a few days on bicycles to escape them, but they captured us, so we waited until they thought we were asleep and we conked 'em on the head and came here.'

'Will they come here to get us?' asked Tommy fearfully.

'No, no,' said Theo, smiling into Tommy's wide brown eyes. 'But if they did, I would protect you, just like I protected the damsel in distress.'

'There was a damsel in distress?' asked the little boy. 'Just like in King Arthur?' He craned round in Theo's arms to look for her. 'Where is she?'

'She's in the kitchen helping your mom,' said Theo, putting Tommy down. 'Where's your brother?'

Tommy didn't answer. He was running to the kitchen to see what a real live damsel in distress looked like.

Theo watched him and smiled. Tommy had been enchanted by the same stories Theo had read as a boy. Since Theo seldom visited them here, he called on the Vid-Con at Tommy's bedtime to read the stories to him. The other children had never been as interested as Tommy had been, so Theo reserved a warm spot in his heart for the boy. He didn't love his other grandchildren any less, just differently.

'Where's Peter?' he called loudly.

There was a giggle from behind the couch.

'That was the strangest thing I ever heard a couch say,' said Theo.

The giggling was a little louder and longer this time.

'Jenny!' Theo called toward the kitchen. 'There's something wrong with your couch! I think we may have to have it looked at!'

A small blond head popped up from behind the huge, over-stuffed sofa. 'It's me!' crowed Peter. 'I tricked you, huh!'

'You sure did,' said Theo. 'Do you have a hug for your Grandpa?'

With a shriek only possible for small, overexcited children, Peter launched himself over the back of the couch and somersaulted across the cushion to land on the floor at a dead run.

Only a child, thought Theo as he opened his arms to catch the tiny guided missile.

'You look funny, Grandpa,' said Peter, burying his face in Theo's chest.

Theo hugged Peter. 'I suppose I do,' he said ruefully. 'But my beard and moustache will grow back and my hair will be white again when the dye grows out.'

'I don't care,' Peter pronounced solemnly. 'Just please stay this time. I want you to live here.'

Theo hugged Peter again. 'We'll see,' he said. 'Let's go see if your Mama has some cookies for you.' He set Peter on the floor and followed him into the kitchen.

Jenny looked up when Theo walked in. 'We had the worst time getting them off to school this morning once they found out you were here,' she grinned. 'I had to promise they could come home after lunch and skip the afternoon.'

'You shouldn't let them bully you like that,' said Theo gruffly. 'These boys need cookies. Cookies and milk. All little boys should have cookies and milk when they come home from school. It makes playing much easier.'

'India, would you pour a couple of glasses of milk for the boys while I get the cookies?' asked Jenny.

'I think I need a glass, too,' said Theo, winking at the boys.

'You just had lunch,' India objected.

'You can never have too much milk and cookies. Besides, I have to maintain my image,' said Theo, patting his round middle. 'How many kids can say their Grandpa is a real live Santa Claus?'

'I can!' shrieked Peter.

'Shh!' Tommy elbowed his brother. 'We know that.' He waited until India had moved away a couple of paces before turning to Theo. 'She doesn't look like a damsel in distress,' he said. He looked a little disappointed.

'What did you think she would look like?' asked Theo. He could remember the descriptions in the books he had read to Tommy, but kids tend to embellish an idea that really grabs hold of them.

'I thought she'd have long golden hair and blue eyes and wear long dresses and lots of jewelry, not have brown hair and wear blue jeans. Everyone has brown hair and wears blue jeans.'

'Her hair isn't brown,' said Theo.

'Huh?' asked Tommy. 'Sure it is. Look at her.'

Theo chuckled. He noticed India's shoulders twitching suspiciously, but turned his attention back to his grandson. 'What color is my hair?' he asked.

'White!' said Tommy scornfully.

'No. What color is my hair now?' Theo insisted.

'Brown, but . . . Oh, I get it. So she really does have golden hair?'

'My hair is red,' said India, setting a glass of milk in front of him. 'But I was a blonde for a couple of days. Your Grandpa saved my life after I stepped in his supper.'

Jenny put the plate of cookies down in front of them

and all talk of damsels in distress and daring rescues was forgotten.

When Sandy and David came home, more introductions were made and more milk and cookies provided. The story had to be told all over again, but this time Tommy and Peter helped with the telling. Sandy stared at India, a little admiring, a little envious. David was conspicuously uninterested, and wouldn't look at India at all, except when he thought she didn't notice.

'Well,' said George, standing up and surveying the wreckage on the table. 'Why don't we wash up these glasses and go for a drive.'

'Oh, yuk,' said David loudly.

'Where?' Sandy wanted to know.

'Can Grandpa come?' asked Tommy.

'Goody!' squealed Peter.

'A little sight-seeing?' suggested Theo.

'Dinner already?' complained Jenny.

India sat quietly and waited.

'A little sight-seeing, yes, and then dinner at one of the wineries near here. They have excellent food and have preserved the original building wonderfully. You can take a tour of the facilities and see how the wine is made, and then enjoy some with a four-star meal afterward.' George smiled and clapped his hands together. 'So last call for the euphemism and we'll be off!'

India leaned toward Jenny. 'A four-star restaurant?' she whispered. 'I'm not dressed for a fancy place.'

'With this brood, we don't do fancy,' Jenny laughed. 'Don't worry. The food is excellent. The atmosphere is casual. You'll really love it. And we won't have to do dishes afterward.'

'How come you don't have a recycler?' India asked.

'No one in Vintners' Quarter does,' said Jenny. 'We just like to live the old-fashioned way, I guess.'

'I kind of like it,' said India. 'That's how things are done at the Inn. I guess I didn't know how much I would miss it, but I really can't wait to get back there.' She stopped and looked at Jenny. 'Oh! I didn't mean I don't like it here, or appreciate what you're doing for me.'

'But you're homesick, right?' asked Jenny with an understanding smile.

'Sounds silly, doesn't it?' asked India as she dried the glasses. 'I don't really even live there, but it's the place I seem to feel most comfortable.'

'Nothing wrong with that,' said Jenny. 'Now scoot to the bathroom. George doesn't like to stop for people who don't heed his first warning.'

Harry and Grindle were still unconscious in the back seat of their vehicle when Bob finally found them in the tube station parking lot in Peru. They had been reported to the local police and a tow had just pulled up behind the ambulance which was parked beside the abandoned vehicle.

'Sir, you can't go in there,' said a man in uniform, putting a huge hand in the middle of Bob's chest to halt him.

Bob reached into his coat.

'Sir,' said the man, grabbing Bob's wrist and holding it tightly. 'You shouldn't do that. Go back behind the barricade and wait with the other reporters.'

Bob smiled slowly. 'I am reaching into my breast pocket to remove a badge you want very much to see before you call me reporter again,' he said.

'I'll check that, then,' said the officer, pulling Bob's hand away from his chest. 'The left pocket?'

Bob nodded.

The officer reached into Bob's jacket and removed the small leather case, opened it, and examined the badge and ID inside. 'I beg your pardon, sir,' he said, handing the case back to Bob. 'Are these your men? They had badges in a compartment in the passenger door. They had a few other things you should probably know about.'

'Yes,' Bob grimaced. 'My men. We're chasing a difficult prisoner. Do you know when this vehicle was reported abandoned?'

'No, sir. You'll have to see my sergeant about that, sir,' said the officer. He stepped aside and let Bob through to the vehicle.

The ambulance crew had removed Harry and were strapping him onto a gurney.

Harry? asked Bob. He pushed aside several layers of drug-soaked consciousness and called again. *Harry!*

Yeah, boss?

What was in the hypo? asked Bob.

Sacronol, why? asked Harry.

Should wear off in a couple of days? asked Bob.

Depends on the dosage, said Harry.

What setting did you have it on? asked Bob with patience he didn't feel.

Normal for 200 pounds. Figured the old man would come around before the girl so we could question him first, Harry explained.

That should keep him under about two days, her about four or five days, yes?

Give or take, sure, said Harry. *I still can't figure out what went wrong.*

Bob retrieved the hypo from the back seat. The setting was still on normal, but much more was missing from the vial than should be. *Did they hit you twice?*

I don't think so, said Harry. *They may have changed the setting to inject us, and then changed it back to make you think we would come around that much faster.*

Why would they have taken the time to do that? asked Bob.

They aren't professionals, said Harry. *Who knows what they were thinking?*

Do you know where they were heading? asked Bob. He tossed the hypo back into the back seat.

Grindle was now loaded onto a gurney and both were being put in the back of the ambulance.

Theo Winslow's landlord said Winslow had a daughter in Old San Francisco. He figured the old man would head there first, said Harry.

The door to the ambulance was slammed shut and the operator came around to climb into the front seat.

Harry, the Old City is strictly off limits to anyone who doesn't work there, Bob reminded him.

North of the Old City. That's what he said. That'd probably be the Vintners' Quarter, said Harry. *That's where all those strange people live. It'd make sense.*

Well, then, I guess you two are off the case, said Bob. *When they release you, report back to HQ. The Captain will debrief you.*

Well, that's something to look forward to, said Harry sarcastically. *Either tell Grindle the same thing, or tell the guys in charge that we have to be discharged at the same time.*

Fine, said Bob. *Grindle, you want to get in on this?*

What? asked Grindle groggily. *Huh?*

How much did she hit you with? asked Bob. *I can hardly reach you.*

Who knows, Grindle mumbled. *This joy-juice hits me harder in general anyway. I don't ever use these things, even for operations.*

Swell, said Bob. *Listen, don't leave without each other, okay?*

Yeah, sure, they both agreed.

Bob broke contact, stepped back from the ambulance, and looked around. He walked over to the stile and placed his thumb against the plate.

'Destination?' asked the box.

'Vintners' Quarter.'

'Number of passengers?' asked the box.

'One.'

The gate opened and Bob stepped through to the platform.

'Follow the blue light,' the box instructed.

A tiny blue light appeared on the wall and began moving away from him. Bob started walking.

India stared out the window of the huge electric car George drove. Everyone else in the car had seen the sights, but India couldn't believe her eyes. The late 1900s had been almost perfectly preserved, just like some of the frontier towns on outlying planets. She'd even been to one on Giles Three, but the Vintners' Quarter was astonishing. One-lane roads that wound through the vineyards and huge buildings set all by themselves on acres of prime real estate ... They didn't have beltways or mall housing or office districts or anything. Just a whole lot of trees and vineyards.

'Oh, look!' she exclaimed, pointing out the window at two kids on horseback. 'This is incredible.'

Everyone else in the car was smiling at her.

'I don't think I've ever had a more appreciative audience,' said George, slowing down so India could look longer at them.

'Hey, those are friends of mine,' said Sandy. She leaned across India and rolled down the window. 'Betsy! Caroline! Hi!'

The girls waved back as the car passed by them. Sandy started to roll the window back up.

'Oh, please, does anyone mind if we leave it down?' asked India.

'Good idea,' said Jenny, rolling hers down. 'Dad, let me know if that gets to be too much for you.'

They drove around the entire Quarter until it became too dark to see anything.

'Dinner?' asked George.

'Yeah!' shouted everyone.

'Good,' George said, pulling off the road onto a small drive between growing fields. 'Because we just happen to be at the restaurant.'

'Daddy,' said Tommy seriously. 'You planned it that way.'

'No, honest. It just happened,' claimed George. 'We could go somewhere else.'

'No!' shouted Tommy. 'I'm hungry!'

'Me too!' shrieked Peter.

'Me too!' said everyone else.

The restaurant was everything Jenny had promised. 'They don't use synth here,' she explained as their food was served. 'You order steak, you get cooked cow.'

'Gee, thanks, Mom,' whined Sandy, dropping her fork onto her plate and grabbing her stomach.

Jenny made a face at her. 'You know this. I was just explaining to India.'

'Yeah, but "cooked cow"? Yuk!'

India sat quietly at her place, eating and listening to the good-natured squabbling going on around her. She felt a strange longing in the core of her being, but she wasn't sure what caused it until Theo leaned over and whispered to her.

'Pretty special being part of a loving family. I guess that's how you feel about your people at that Inn,' he said.

India smiled wistfully, but she could feel a lump rising in her chest. 'I really miss it,' she whispered back. 'I never had it until then. I didn't know how lonely I was before.'

Theo squeezed her hand under the table. 'I know what you mean.'

'Will you stay this time?' she asked him.

'I just might do that,' said Theo, smiling at her. 'I just might.'

'I'm going to have the decadent-double-fudge-death for dessert,' David announced.

'Oh!' said Sandy. 'You are so disgusting!'

'What is it?' asked India, distracted.

'He orders it every time,' Sandy explained. 'You have to see it to believe it. What are you going to have?'

'Real coffee,' said India.

'Why?' asked Sandy, baffled. 'There are so many great things to choose from.'

'Coffee,' said India firmly. 'Coffee and good company. I can't do any better than that.'

Jenny smiled at her and reached for George's hand. 'Thank you,' she said.

India shook her head. 'Thank *you*.'

Chapter Twelve

Anara?

Hmm? Anara asked in her sleep. It had been a long day and she'd only been in bed a couple of hours.

Anara?

Can't this wait? she asked plaintively. She rolled over and pulled the pillow over her head.

No, it can't, said Shannon apologetically. *I just spoke with India. They're heading for the door this morning, and I've found out what her dream meant.*

Anara sat up and clutched her pillow against her chest. *Tell me.*

Jenny woke India extremely early. The dark had only just begun to recede outside, but the curtains at the window were shut so the room was pitch dark.

'Huh?' India asked groggily.

'You have to get ready to go into the Old City with George and Dad,' Jenny explained, tugging India's arm. 'I have to go fix breakfast. If I leave now, you won't fall back to sleep, will you?'

'Huh?' India repeated. She sat up and rubbed her eyes with her fists. 'No. Go ahead. I'll be fine.' She pushed back the covers and swung her legs out over the floor. Her feet didn't touch, but she was used to that. She wiggled to the edge and slid off onto the floor.

Jenny watched to see that India was up before going downstairs.

India padded down the hall to the bathroom. She turned the shower on and waited for the hot water to build up a good head of steam. This was the best way, she had discovered, to wake up on slow mornings. Once the water was hot, she climbed in and just stood under the needle spray, letting it wash the sleep out of her system.

Awake at last, India went back to Sandy's bedroom and climbed into the jeans and blouse of the day before. She didn't feel comfortable helping herself to the contents of Jenny's closet, since she wouldn't be coming back.

She hoped she wasn't coming back. She'd enjoyed herself here, but she needed to get back to the Inn. No one was safe until she did. Tommy had been right. There was nothing stopping Bob from finding her. If he knew where she was, he would come get her. It didn't matter that an innocent family was in the way. India had to get out of this house as soon as possible.

She finished putting on her shoes and ran downstairs to find George and Theo already working on heaps of scrambled eggs.

'Grab a plate and help yourself,' said Jenny. She stood at the stove making more of everything. India guessed the kids would be up soon for school.

India sat down at the table with her breakfast, but she didn't eat much.

'You will have to sit tight for a little bit while I arrange for the passes,' George was explaining to Theo. He looked at India. 'Will you be able to handle that? Just sitting, I mean.'

India nodded and cut a sausage into tiny pieces. She didn't do anything more with it, though.

'Jenny and I have some college texts. You can borrow a reader and a card. That will make it look more official. Students never have enough time to study, so it would be natural for you to have brought something along to catch up on. It will also give you something to do to keep you from going crazy with the tension.' George looked askance at her plate. 'It would help if you ate something. Theo tells me you can't really do all those things with your mind if you're hungry or tired.'

India looked up at George and then at Theo.

'How about a vitamin and a glass of juice?' suggested Jenny.

'Okay,' India said, hoping to appease them.

'And maybe just a couple of bites?' asked George.

'I'm still full from dinner last night!' India protested.

Everyone laughed.

'Juice it is, then.' Jenny got up and went to the fridge.

David came into the room.

'Breakfast is on the stove,' Jenny told him as she poured India a glass.

'You're really going away today?' David asked India.

'I hope so,' she said. 'I mean, I like you all a lot, and you've been very kind to me, but I can't stay. It's for you as well as me. Bob won't ever let me go.'

'So we'll never see you again?'

India shrugged. 'It's not likely,' she said. 'I live on Giles Three. That's a long way from here. And I don't even know where the Inn-between-dimensions is.'

'But if you ever did . . .'

'If I ever came back to Earth, I'd see if I could find you all, of course,' said India, smiling at him.

David blushed and turned to the cupboard to get himself a plate.

India noticed he spent a long time filling it up before coming over to sit down with the rest of them. She had also noticed the glances out of the corner of his eye that she wasn't supposed to have seen. She smiled to herself and made an effort to eat enough breakfast to satisfy George and Jenny.

At last George stood up. 'Are we ready?'

India bounced to her feet and ran to put her plate in the sink. Theo shoved a few more mouthfuls down before standing and looking longingly at the remainder of his breakfast.

'I suppose so,' he said regretfully. 'David, come give your Grandpa a hug. Tell your brothers and sister I'll be home for supper. Jenny, my dear, give your old man a kiss.' He kissed her cheek and hugged her, whispering, 'I'll keep an eye out for George for you, so don't you worry.'

'Thanks, Daddy,' Jenny whispered back. She gave him one last squeeze and stepped back, blinking rapidly. 'And you . . .' She turned on India. 'You take care of yourself. David was right. If you ever make it back this way, just remember you're family.'

'Thank you,' said India, extending her hand formally.

'Nonsense,' said Jenny, taking the hand and pulling India forward into a big hug. 'Just watch out for Bob and his friends and you'll be fine.'

India was almost relieved to escape the house. She wasn't used to emotional displays, so they made her feel uncomfortable.

As they climbed into George's huge old electric car, India asked, 'Can we drive into the Old City?'

George shook his head. 'There's a special tube we'll take, but it's on the other side of the valley and I don't like to walk it; takes too long.'

India settled herself in the back seat, feeling a little strange being the only one back there this time. When it was filled with Theo's family it felt much more comfortable. Must be nerves, she told herself as she suppressed a shudder. As they pulled out of the drive, India noticed another car start up and pull into the street behind them, but she was more interested in the view. The sun was coming up through the trees and dew was starting to dry on the grass. A dog barked at them as they drove by. A neighbor out for a walk saw George and waved. 'This would be such a wonderful place to live,' she said softly. 'It's so peaceful.'

Theo nodded his head.

'Old man, when are you going to drop this gruff independent exterior and move out here?' asked George. 'You don't have to live with us. We could help you find a place nearby if you preferred. You need your family and we need you.'

Theo turned and looked at George's profile. 'Son, you and that daughter of mine aren't going to give up until you've worn me down and tired me out, are you?' He winked at India.

India smiled back. She knew how much Theo wanted to live here. Something touched her mind, but she brushed it away.

'No, sir. We aim to leave you a bloody pulp if you don't cry uncle before then,' said George. He also knew Theo wanted to live here.

'Well, hell, son. That would probably upset my grandchildren,' said Theo. 'I'd really hate to disappoint the kids.'

'Shall we vacate the guest room for you?' suggested George.

'I think maybe I'll take you up on the offer to help me find a place. I love you all, but a man needs his privacy, too.'

'Done,' said George, grinning widely. 'We'll begin looking after we settle the matter of our unhappy passenger. What's the matter, India?' he asked, looking at her in the rear-view mirror.

'There's someone following us,' she said.

'There's no one behind us,' George contradicted. 'I'd know if there had been another car. My nerves are jumpy this morning and I've been keeping watch.'

'Just as we were pulling out,' said India. 'Another car pulled out behind us.'

'Yes,' said George. 'I saw that. He turned again a block later. Don't worry. I'm keeping my eye out.'

'That's not good enough,' said India. 'He's following a

block over and a block behind. I felt him in my mind, but I pushed him away before I realized what I was doing. I'm monitoring his progress, just like he's monitoring ours, telepathically. He doesn't need to see us to follow us. I can't shut him out completely, and even if I could, he'd be able to track the blank spot since he knows where it is. If he hadn't found us before I shielded, he wouldn't know where to look and probably wouldn't have been able to locate us. Instead, I'm operating on too much tension, too little sleep, and not enough coffee. I messed up.'

'Do you think he'll try to ambush us at the station?' asked Theo.

'I doubt it,' said India. 'My guess is he wants to know where the door is to the Inn-between-dimensions. I think he'll follow us until we get there. Somehow I've got to find a way to block us before then so he doesn't suspect what I'm doing and can't locate us again.'

'Is there anything we can do to help?' asked Theo.

'It's between him and me,' said India grimly. 'It has been from the start. I have to settle this on my own. Thanks, though. Just keep an eye out. Bob has the perfect disguise: medium height, weight, coloring, looks. Everything completely ordinary to the point where spotting him in a crowd or even remembering his face is almost impossible. Any other description is impossible. He has no outstanding features or mannerisms; someone you would overlook without even realizing that was what you had done.'

George nodded. 'The perfect agent.'

'What?' asked India, startled.

'What we look for in an operative,' said George. 'I'm not allowed to even really explain that, but he's the sort of man we look for if we need to move about unnoticed.'

'Yeah,' said India, nodding. 'That's what I get the impression he does. That, and he's a damned good psi-mechanic. He messed me up pretty well.'

'He sounds like he may have a conscience,' said George.

India snorted. 'Yeah. He'd apologize and then go ahead and screw up my mind anyway!'

'If he was following orders he didn't agree with, that could explain a lot,' said Theo.

'I overheard some conversation when I was in the room in that building just before I escaped,' said India. She frowned in concentration. 'There was a whole group of them who didn't agree with the orders, but they were laughing at Bob for being so soft-hearted. They also said I had to be kept alive, with my mind intact, but they didn't say why.'

'You don't have any idea who these men were?' pressed George. 'It was a government building. What branch would they be likely to be involved with?'

'I have no idea,' said India tiredly. 'What branch kidnaps people and brainwashes them? I've been over and over it in my mind. I just don't know.'

'If Bob is government, he'll have no trouble getting into the Old City,' George pointed out.

'His men had badges that were either real or marvelous forgeries,' said Theo. 'Even if he isn't government, he may have no trouble getting in.'

'I hope our security is able to spot phony credentials,' said George. 'The question should be, how do we prevent him from getting that far to begin with?'

'India, did you get a good look at the car when it pulled out behind us?' asked Theo.

'I guess so, why?' asked India.

'Can you give him a flat tire, or something?'

India grinned. 'I should be able to do better than that. Hang on a second.'

India lowered her conscious level and went to her workplace. On one wall was her VidCon center. She looked at it for a moment and grinned. *This'd better work,* she told herself. *Computer on, please,* she said. She no longer needed the 'please' and 'thank you' commands, but old

286

habits die hard. *Thank you. Please access the onboard computer for the electric car following us.*

Transmit picture, please.

India thought about what the car had looked like and placed her right hand against the screen, sending the image through her palm.

Computer accessed.

Thank you, said India automatically. *Display circuitry for battery to engine connections, and other relevant data, please.*

Displayed.

Thank you. Please find primary connection and block.

Primary connection blocked.

Thank you. Please find secondary connections and block.

Secondary connections blocked.

Thank you. Please disengage from vehicle computer.

Disengaged.

Thank you.

India left her apartment workplace and returned to normal consciousness. Theo was staring at her.

'Well?' he demanded.

'Hang on!' India laughed. 'I haven't checked his real-world progress.' She reached out to reestablish her contact with Bob.

He didn't even notice. His car had stopped dead in the middle of pursuit. He was furious. He was using words India hadn't heard since she was living on the street.

She couldn't resist. She giggled.

He heard her. *You haven't stopped me,* he said. *You're going to be hung up just long enough in getting your passes for me to catch up with you. I won't let you out of my reach.*

Bob, you won't ever catch me again, India told him. *You're out-matched. The reason you're afraid of me is that you know I'm more powerful than you. I'm getting it back.*

*Little by little, but it's coming back. And when I'm whole
again, you're going to wish you'd never even heard of me.*
She terminated contact abruptly and blanked herself and
Theo and George. She knew Bob would be able to trace
the hole they left, but once they were in the tube she could
count on the many other people to help hide them. She
would block them as well. No one would notice what she
was doing.

'Well?' demanded Theo.

'For now, we're all set,' said India. 'I blocked the power
connections in his car. He'll figure out what I've done and
be able to fix it himself, but it will take him a little while.
We can get to the tube without worrying about him, but
he says we'll be held up getting our passes just long enough
for him to catch up.'

'How would he know?' asked George. He was turning
the car into a large parking lot. They had finally reached
the tube station.

India shrugged. 'How has he known anything all along?
Maybe he's clairvoyant on top of everything else? Maybe
he's really with the government and can arrange to have
us delayed. The important thing is that I keep us blocked
so he can't find us telepathically.'

'You'd better do that as soon as possible,' said George,
glancing in the rear-view mirror reflexively.

'I already have,' said India. 'No chances, remember?'

George parked the car and they went into the tube
station. There were several people standing waiting for
the train. India immediately blanked them, increasing their
cover. The train rushed into the station and stopped, opening its doors. Everyone boarded and the doors shut.

'That's weird,' said India, looking around. She blanked
the minds of everyone on the train.

'What?' asked Theo, looking around to see what she was
talking about.

'Everyone got on the train. Usually only a few do. Usually there are people waiting for other trains,' said India.

'There are no other trains,' said George. 'Everyone who rides this train is going to the same place. There are other stops along the way, but no one ever gets off on the way into the Old City. More people will get on, but no one gets off until the last stop. Anyone using this tube for personal transport is severely fined. There are other tubes for getting around. This is for commuters to the Old City only.'

They found seats and settled in for the commute.

Theo and George talked softly about fishing. India closed her eyes, concentrating on maintaining the block on the entire train. As new passengers entered the cars at each stop, they walked into a blanket of nothingness of which they were completely unaware.

After several long minutes of checking each system on his car, Bob finally located the problem.

She's amazing, he thought to himself. He felt a grudging admiration for India, and didn't really blame her for behaving the way she did toward him. He knew he wouldn't like anyone who did to him what he was doing to her. Concentrating briefly, he was able to reestablish contacts and the car engaged again.

Once under way, Bob reached out toward India again. The contact was still there, but she wasn't at the other end of it. There was nothing but a vast emptiness, which he figured probably covered everyone on the train. He chuckled. It would have confused him much more if she had shielded several groups of three, instead of the entire train. He would have to tell her that when he saw her next.

He called, 'VidCon, on.'

The screen brightened immediately.

'Place call to Lieutenant Drucker at Security for Old San Francisco Governmental Installation,' he ordered.

Drucker appeared on the screen. 'Bob! What can I do for you?' he asked.

'I'm coming in, Fred. So are George Bascombe, Theodore Winslow, and India Gilbert. Hang on to them discreetly until I get there, will you? And could you be sure they get their passes?'

'Sure, Bob, anything you say,' said Fred. 'But George works here. He's a friend of mine. What's going on?'

'I can't say much on an unsecured channel,' said Bob. 'Just believe me when I say it's a matter of great importance.'

'Okay, then. I'll see you in a little while.' Drucker broke the contact.

Bob pulled into the tube station parking lot and parked. It wouldn't be long now.

The train reached the Old City at last and the doors opened to let off the passengers. George, Theo and India filed off with everyone else, but instead of pressing thumbs to plates and going through the main door, they went to a small office on the other side of the platform.

'Bascombe, what have you got here?' asked the balding man behind the desk.

'Morning, Fred,' said George, smiling. 'This is Professor Winslow, Modern Governmental Studies, and Miss Gilbert. She's working on her thesis. They need a tour of our facilities here.'

'Well, then they'll be needing visitors' passes,' said Fred. He was positively beaming at Theo and India. 'I'll take care of things.'

'Thank you, Fred,' said George. He led Theo and India to a couple of chairs on the other side of the room. 'I'll be right back,' he told them as they sat down. 'This will take a few minutes, so I'm going to go check my messages. I'll be back shortly.'

'Is that a good idea?' Theo asked him.

'No problem. Drucker's a good man. He'll get you set

up. Don't go anywhere without me. You'll get lost and we need to make this look good to anyone who might be watching.'

As soon as George left, India turned to Theo. 'I don't trust him,' she hissed, nodding at Drucker.

'Why not?' asked Theo. 'He's a friend of George's. He's getting the passes taken care of. He seems like a nice enough man.'

'Too nice,' said India, keeping her voice at a whisper. 'I've tried to probe him, but I can't. Bob said we would be held here just long enough for him to catch up. I believe him. I think Fred here is going to stall us until Bob arrives. We'll be trapped here and have no way of defending ourselves. You may have noticed Fred has a gun under his coat?'

'Uh, no. I hadn't,' said Theo, rather disgruntled. 'Are you sure about this?'

'Theo, remember when you told me my heart makes up my mind, not the other way around?'

Theo nodded.

'Well, I don't trust him, that's all,' said India defensively.

'What are we going to do about it?' asked Theo. 'There's nowhere else for us to go.'

'I guess we just sit tight until George comes back, assuming he does, or wait for Bob and try to play the confrontation by ear. Bob's a good psi-mechanic.

'Why do you think George might not come back?' asked Theo.

'I think he will come back,' said India. 'But I wouldn't be surprised if he didn't. Nothing Bob does surprises me any more.'

'Excuse me,' said Fred.

Theo and India jumped and turned toward him simultaneously.

'I'm sorry, if you'll just come here and sign these

preliminary forms?' He held out several sheets of paper, and smiled apologetically.

'Certainly,' said Theo, standing up. He took the papers and glanced at them. 'You don't mind if we look them over? I don't like to sign anything I haven't read.'

'Of course, of course!' said Fred Drucker. He smiled broadly and gave Theo a pen. 'Take your time.'

'Preliminary?' asked India when Theo came back over to sit down. 'We should have asked George what standard procedure was.'

'We can when he gets back,' said Theo. He was looking intently at the documents, but India was certain he wasn't reading them.

'If he gets back,' said India darkly. She accepted the first sheet when Theo was done with it. 'Why are we looking at papers?' she asked suddenly. 'Even the government is computerized by now. It should be a matter of entering our thumbprints beside a standard declaration kept on file in the mainframe.'

Theo shrugged. 'Maybe they like to have hard copies of this stuff.'

'I don't like it,' said India. 'Besides,' she sighed, 'I'm not sure I remember *how* to write.'

'Tell you what,' said Theo, grinning back at her. 'You sign an "X" and I'll witness it for you.'

'Such a gentleman,' she said, accepting the next sheet. 'I wish George would come back.'

Theo nodded. 'I'd feel better too. In the meantime, we'd better sign the "preliminary round" of paperwork. Maybe this Fred character will speed things up a bit if we play nice.'

'After you,' said India, handing him back the papers.

'No, after you,' said Theo, trying to hand her his.

'But you have the pen,' she protested.

'Chicken. You just don't want to go first,' said Theo, taking the papers from her.

'What are you children squabbling about?' asked George.

'Oh! Thank goodness,' said India. 'We weren't sure you would be coming back.'

'*You* weren't sure,' Theo pointed out. '*I* knew he wouldn't dare leave his father-in-law alone with Mister Happy there, and a dangerous, wanted woman.'

'Are you all set, then?' asked George. 'What are those?'

'These,' said Theo, brandishing the just-signed papers, 'are the preliminary round of paperwork.'

'What are you talking about?' asked George. 'Haven't you thumbed the screen yet?'

'Ah ha!' said India triumphantly.

'You're insufferable when you're right,' said Theo. 'Now shut up for a moment and let the grown-ups talk.' He turned to George and handed him the papers. 'Your friend Fred gave us these to look over and sign. Then he says he can go on to the next step in getting us those passes.'

'That's ridiculous,' said George, looking at the documents. 'Hang on a sec.' He walked over to Fred's desk.

'Sorry, those are my orders on this,' said Fred.

'I'm overriding those orders. Give these people their passes. I don't have all day in which to conduct this tour. I work here, you know,' said George. 'I don't have time for this nonsense.'

'Sir, these are orders you don't have the authority to countermand,' said Fred, adopting a professional, deadpan expression. The VidCon on his desk signaled an incoming call. 'Excuse me.'

George left Fred's desk and sat down beside India.

'Well?' asked Theo.

'Yes, sir. Thank you, sir,' said Fred. He disconnected the call. 'If you two will come over here and thumb the screen, we can get you started on that tour.'

With a frown, India stood up and went over to Drucker's desk to thumb the screen. Theo did the same. They said thank you to Fred, even though they didn't feel like it, and followed George across the platform to thumb the door-plate to get into the Old City. As they walked through the door, a train pulled into the station behind them.

India turned to look at the passengers as they got off, but George steered her through the door before she could really see anyone. With a sigh, she checked to make sure their minds were still blanketed. That made her feel a little safer, but she was certain Bob was getting off that train. They needed to get to the Arboretum before he caught up with them. He knew they were in the Old City. He couldn't possibly know where. India just hoped he wouldn't be able to find the tiny blank spot in the middle of all those people.

India had seen pictures of San Francisco when it had been the financial capital of the North-West. Every schoolchild got that much as part of their history lesson. The War and the earthquake had been milestones in American history. Everything turned on that point. The unification of the Americas, the genesis of world government, and the rebellion of the off-planet colonies. Therefore, every small child had the importance drilled into them, even though it had happened centuries before. Ancient history. Yuk.

But as they walked down what used to be Market Street, India was glad she had been forced to study the pictures. The huge buildings were gone. The street was still in its original place, but instead of being very wide and paved, it was a cobbled path through some of the most beautiful greenery she had ever seen. 'Where did everything go?' she asked at last.

George laughed. 'Underground. In order to be completely earthquake-proof, the builders had to use some really unattractive building materials, so they decided to sink the whole city and grow a forty-nine-square-acre garden. This is proof that the government does occasionally have a good idea.'

'Good?' asked Theo. He too was gaping at the 'park'. 'This is incredible. No wonder they don't want to share this with anyone. If people knew . . .'

'Exactly,' said George. 'The memory of this park is routinely wiped from visitors' minds when they leave. They remember everything else, but they have no memory of the park. That way they can't talk about it. The only buildings left in the entire city that are above ground are in Golden Gate Park. The De Young Museum, the Aquarium, the Japanese Tea Garden, and the Arboretum. Everything else was torn down. They even removed the buffalo. Too dirty and hard to maintain. Besides, there are so many good preserves in the Mid-West now. We really didn't need them. A bunch of bureaucratic suits have no need for wildlife like that. The swans on the ponds are enough for them.'

'What about the horses that used to be down by the race-track?' asked India. 'Is the barn gone too?'

George nodded. 'All of it except those four buildings and the lakes.'

'How are we going to get to the park, then?' asked Theo. He was still craning his neck to see everything at once.

'There's an underground shuttle which will take us there,' said George. 'First, we need to make a pretense of looking at some of the offices and asking some key people questions. I know it'll be boring, but bear with it and we'll get to the park as soon as I think it's safe.'

'How do we get underground?' asked India. She hadn't seen anything man-made except the paths. 'Fall down the rabbit hole?'

'See that clump of bushes over there?' asked George, pointing.

'Mmhmm,' said India.

'That's where we're headed.'

When they got there, India was delighted to find a stairway in the middle of the bushes. It was completely invisible, because a small maze had been set up around it to hide it. 'This is neat!' she said enthusiastically.

'Clever would have been my word choice,' said Theo, 'But she's right, this is neat.'

They went down the flight and wound up in a small room with a light fixture and an elevator door. The door opened as they approached and George walked straight in. India and Theo followed, but India hung back a little.

'There wasn't any button or voice activation,' she said.

'Floor pressure,' said George. 'Just like all the doors at the shopping malls I'm sure you hang out in when you're not being chased across the dimensions.'

'I hate shopping,' said India emphatically. She yawned to ease the pressure building up in her ears. 'How far are we going down?'

'Far enough,' said George.

'I'm not the kind of person who gets claustrophobic about thinking how much dirt there is between me and fresh air, if that's what you're worried about,' said India somewhat disdainfully.

'Maybe not,' said George. 'But I am.'

'You work here!' she objected.

'Only because my clearance is such that I can't do my work at home on a VidCon my bright little children have access to. David learned programming before he could talk and has access to everything in my files, no matter how I safeguard them. The rest of my kids are just as adept.'

India laughed. 'Tough to keep a secret that way.'

'Yup,' said George. 'I don't blame this old man for wanting to live in a place of his own.'

Theo grinned.

The doors slipped open and they stepped out into a brightly lit corridor. India had expected to see people. The hallway was deserted. 'Where do we go first?' she asked.

'To the Boss's office, of course. Ask him as many stupid questions about running a government installation as you can think of. If you appear too bright, it'll raise suspicion.'

'How about if I do a little mental reconnaissance? If I ask questions about his specific interests, he'll be too busy giving me useless detail to wonder just how bright I am.'

George nodded approvingly. 'Just don't let him find out that's what you're doing. The average person kind of resents you people when you do that.'

'How many of me have you met?' asked India, surprised.

'You're the first,' said George. 'But I have to admit, it makes me feel a little strange knowing you could do that to me if you wanted to.'

'Frankly, that's usually more about most people than I want to know,' said India.

'That's reassuring,' said George wryly. He knocked on a door and they waited.

'Come!'

George pushed the door open and stood aside to let Theo and India pass.

'Ladies first,' Theo murmured, giving India a little push.

'Thanks, guys,' she said, regaining her composure and walking forward. She arranged her face in a smile and kept her mouth shut.

'Sir,' said George, closing the door behind them. 'This is Professor Winslow. He teaches Modern Government at Berkeley. This is his student Miss Gilbert. She's studying for her thesis. She'd like to ask you some questions about what we do here. Do you have some time to spare us this morning?'

The Boss leaned back in his chair and looked India over thoroughly. 'I think I could spare a moment or two for the young lady. Ask anything you like, dear. I'll let you know if there's anything I can't talk about.'

'Thank you, sir,' said India, completing her scan. This would be easier than she'd thought. 'I'd like to record this if you don't mind. It makes it easier to get my thoughts together later.' She put a small recorder on the edge of his desk.

'Not at all, dear,' said the Boss.

When she asked her first question, Theo and George both had expressions of approval. It was designed to keep him talking. Every once in a while, India threw in a prompter, but the Boss pretty much entertained himself, which had been the idea.

At last, India shut off the recorder. 'Thank you very much,' she said, putting it into her pocket. 'You've been extremely helpful and I appreciate the time you've given me.'

'I'm glad I could be of help,' said the Boss. He turned to Theo. 'Very promising student.'

'Yes, sir. That's why I came along. I also couldn't resist the chance to see the Old City. I know how it runs, but I've never had the opportunity to come here before. This has been a real treat.'

'Yes, yes, well . . .' The Boss returned to his work, dismissing them. They filed out of his office and into the hall.

'Anyone else we have to talk to?' asked India, hoping there wasn't.

'You did that beautifully,' said George. 'I think we can stop with that.'

'Then we can go to the park?' she asked.

'Right away,' said George. He led them to the underground tube to wait for the next train.

Bob had no trouble locating the blank spot that hid India and her companions once he got off the train. He thumbed the door-plate and stepped out onto Market and followed at a discreet distance, touching the blank spot only enough to keep tabs on their progress. Somewhere in the Old City was the door they were looking for, and Bob wanted to know where it was. Once she was through it, he could follow her and abduct her for the Captain. She wouldn't have the protection of the two men, and those on the other side would be unprepared.

He waited outside the office while she conducted whatever meaningless interview had gotten them into the Old City in the first place. When they finished, Bob slipped into the next office and waited for them to walk past.

'May I help you?' asked the woman behind the desk in an irritated tone of voice.

Bob flashed his ID at her without turning round.

'Yes, sir,' she said, and returned to her screen.

When India was far enough down the hall for him to be sure of where they were going, he slipped out of the office and headed to the underground tube.

'He's behind us,' said India, stopping. She strained her ears, but couldn't hear footsteps behind them. There was no one in the corridor.

'Bob?' asked George. He, too, looked down the hall. 'There's no one there.'

'No,' India agreed. 'He doesn't need to see us to keep track. When I thought I heard him, I relaxed the blanket I've been keeping on us. He was there. Now he knows we know he's there, so he's not coming any closer.'

'Why not?' asked Theo in an angry voice. 'What kind of game is he playing? Wouldn't it be better if he caught you before you went through the door?'

'Maybe not,' said India uneasily. 'Maybe . . . Never mind. Here comes the train. Will we be able to get to the Arboretum before he catches up on the next train?' she asked George.

'I don't think so,' he said. 'But he doesn't seem to be trying to catch up.'

They boarded the train and sat down. India was beginning to feel the pressure to get to the Arboretum before Bob did catch up. She didn't know what game he was playing, but it frightened her. She felt like a mouse being stalked by a cat. He was just playing with them. When he really meant to close in on them, she didn't doubt he could.

The train rushed through the tube. Lights in the tunnel flicked past the windows of the car faster and faster. India wondered idly why there were windows if there was nothing but the lights in the tunnel wall to see. They were mesmerizing, though. She stared without really seeing the long fluorescent tubes, looking into herself instead. Down the long corridor of her mind, seeing the lights flicking past as she went deeper and deeper into her soul.

There stood Ty. Behind him were tens of thousands of people, but they weren't really there.

Why are you here? she asked.

Why are you here? he countered.

I live here, she said defensively. *I didn't invite you in.*

You don't live here. This is a place where no one lives, said Ty. He laughed scornfully. *You don't even know when you've left yourself behind?*

India looked around herself. It was pitch-black. There was nothing behind or beside her. There was only in front of her, and the way was impassable. The corridor down which she had traveled had disappeared. *Let me past,* she demanded.

Say the magic word, said Ty maliciously.

Please?

You weren't very nice to me last time we spoke, he reminded her. *You've been avoiding me since.*

I guess I have, India admitted. *But you haven't been nice to me at all. Even from the very beginning you did things to make me distrust you.*

It took you a pretty long time to figure that out, didn't it? asked Ty. *You should pay more attention to your teachers.*

How would you know about my teachers? asked India, beginning to get scared.

I know about Anara. I know about Theo, he said.

Theo isn't my teacher, said India derisively.

Isn't he? Ty laughed. *You don't pay enough attention to anything, do you? How about the man who is chasing you?*

What about him? India asked suspiciously.

What has he taught you?

To watch my back, said India.

And what has Theo taught you?

The same thing as Anara, she answered slowly.

So you had two people telling you the same thing and you still didn't get it? He laughed again. *You aren't stupid. How can you be so dense?*

What are you doing here? India asked again.

Waiting for you. My friends and I have been waiting for you, he smiled unpleasantly.

Who are your friends? asked India, scanning the vast crowd behind him. There wasn't really anyone there, but she got the impression of a great number of beings.

You've met them already. They have been looking forward to your joining them since you first encountered them. But you ran away the first time. That wasn't very nice, now, was it?

He took a step forward and the crowd surged behind him.

India shrank back. She could hear the susurration of thousands of thoughts, but couldn't make out any words. She bumped into a wall behind her and screamed.

'India?'

Help me!

'India?' The voice penetrated her consciousness. A hand joggled her elbow. 'India, we're at the station. Are you okay?'

She opened her eyes and saw Theo and George staring at her. 'Sorry,' she said, shaking her head and taking a deep breath. She stood up. 'Let's go.'

'Are you okay?' George repeated. He hadn't let go of her arm.

'I'm fine,' she said, trying to smile reassuringly. 'Let's go find a door so I can go home and you can get back to your family.'

'Sounds like a plan,' said Theo.

'You're sure they were going to try to make it to the door today?' Henry asked.

Anara sighed in exasperation and paced the floor a little quicker. Shannon gave Henry her fiercest look, which wasn't really at all threatening. 'Yes, Henry. I'm certain that's what she said. Just like I was certain when she said it and every time you've asked me since. She didn't give me a timetable. I'm sorry now I didn't ask for one.'

'It's just that so many things could go wrong,' said Henry.

'That's been true all along the way,' said Anara. She slowed her pacing to look at the door they stood in front of.

It didn't look like much. They were in a barn. Nothing in a barn ever seems to look like much. The door had holes in it where the knots had been poked out by children over the years. It was really two half-doors, but they had been bolted together. The effect wasn't particularly attractive, but the door worked, so nothing else mattered.

There wasn't anything to see through the knot-holes except darkness. There wouldn't be anything on the other side until the door in the Arboretum was opened. They couldn't even watch to see if India was coming.

Shannon was pacing in the opposite direction from Anara. Henry stood still and kept looking at his watch, as though local time had anything to do with the dimension Old San Francisco was in. 'What if we opened the door?' asked Henry, walking over to it. He laid his hand on the latch.

'It wouldn't do any good,' said Anara sharply. 'Besides, if anyone else is there, we'd be giving ourselves away. What

f the people who are following her have discovered where
he's going and plan to meet her there?'

Henry sighed. Shannon paced faster. Anara resumed her
pacing.

Shannon stopped. 'This is going to drive me mad!' she
exclaimed. She stood rigid in front of the door. 'Open,
damn you!'

Anara laughed. 'Has that ever been known to work?'

'Ooo!' said Shannon. 'Probably not. I just hate standing
here waiting and not knowing what's going on!'

'We all feel the same way,' said Anara. She continued
walking up and down the barn floor.

Shannon started walking again, in the opposite direction.

Henry glared at his watch.

Two men stood on the plane of the Disembodied.

Will it work? asked the older one. He was tall and dark
and fierce.

The younger man was a little afraid of him, but was
trying not to let the tall man know. He stood with his arms
akimbo and his legs straddled, swaggering while standing
still. *It'll work,* he said with more confidence than he felt.

Energy swarmed around them, growing more agitated.
The older man looked around them. He looked at the
younger man, compact and fair, a lock of straight brown
hair falling over his eyes. The body of an athlete, but he
was destroying himself. He was in way over his head and
the older man knew it.

It had better, he said at last. *We can't afford any mistakes. She has to be taken cleanly and re-educated properly.
Bob isn't doing the job we need him to be doing on that.
He'll bring her back, but I'll do the work on her mind
myself.*

Do you think that's wise? asked the younger man. He
couldn't help glancing at the older man's bare feet. He had
the oddest toes: long and slender, almost simian.

Look around you, commanded the older man. The light and energy were growing steadily brighter. The scream came from its heart. *She's coming. We'd better leave. If she ever catches us here, we'll both be dead.*

Or worse, said the younger man, shuddering. *You'll come to us when we have her, then?*

It would probably be safest, the older man agreed. *I can find a pretext for leaving the school.*

We'll be expecting you, then.

The two men left as the energy grew unbearably bright and a huge creature appeared, snapping its claws and roaring with displeasure.

Chapter Thirteen

The park didn't look any different from the rest of the Old City. Oak and Fell Streets still bordered the Panhandle, and Fell still turned into Lincoln if you stayed left instead of going into the park proper, but the streets were now the same cobbled paths that Market and so many others were, and all the traffic was on foot.

The tube had taken them as far as Fell and Kennedy. That was as far in their direction as any of the various lines went. One line continued out into what had been the Sunset district, taking a circular route under Moraga Hill before heading down toward the beach and South San Francisco. The other line went in the opposite direction through the Richmond area. India emerged from the tube station into the bright sunlight and looked around. George and Theo followed her out of the maze of bushes that hid the stairway .

'This used to be a residential area,' said George, making a small effort at being a tour guide. He gestured down the path that was Fell Street.

'I can't believe they tore down all the beautiful old painted ladies,' said Theo mournfully. 'This is beautiful too, but nothing could compare to those old Victorian homes.'

'Did you ever see one?' asked India playfully.

'In a book of historic San Francisco, silly girl,' said Theo, laughing. 'No, I never saw one in person. It just seems a shame to have leveled the most beautiful city in the world.'

'The French would probably disagree with you,' said George.

'Probably. They seem pretty disagreeable to almost everyone,' Theo responded.

They set off in the opposite direction, heading into the park. India kept half an ear focused on Bob, but he was still in the tube. She stared around them as they walked under trees that were huge and ancient, her head swiveling around as she tried not to miss anything. Theo was doing much the same thing, so she didn't feel as silly as she might have. It was obviously lunchtime, and people were scattered across the lawns, singly and in groups, eating, talking, playing games, and staring at the newcomers as they stumbled down the path with their mouths hanging open.

George laughed. 'You two are perfect examples of "Gawker's Walk".'

India and Theo laughed with him. 'There's so much to see!' India exclaimed, stumbling on the cobblestones as her feet tried to keep up with her eyes.

'Golden Gate Park used to be a botanical garden,' said Theo. 'Obviously they've encouraged that since the occupation.'

'Old man, no one lives here,' said George. 'You can't have an occupation if there's no one to occupy.'

'You've taken that criticism before?' Theo winked at India.

'Hey, how do you keep people from approaching the City by boat, or swimming?' India asked, quickly changing the subject. 'And what about down the peninsula?'

'Walls and surveillance,' said George. 'Mostly, no one tries any more, but we still keep an eye out just in case.'

India checked on Bob again, and found that he had left the tube and was following behind at a fairly safe distance.

'How much farther do we have to walk?' asked Theo.

India and George both turned to look at Theo in surprise.

'Are we there yet?' whined George in a wicked imitation of Tommy and Peter on a car trip.

India laughed loudly, and Theo found himself grinning. 'I just meant, will we be able to get there before Bob catches up with us?'

'Where *is* Bob?' George asked India.

She shrugged. 'Behind us,' she said. 'He seems to be following more than trying to catch up.'

Theo frowned. 'That isn't these guys' style. Mutt and Jeff were determined to catch you. They didn't play games.'

'Maybe the game has changed,' suggested George.

'Which is why I was asking how much farther we have to walk, smartass,' said Theo.

'Oh, miles,' said George expansively. 'You'll probably have to be carried the last bit. I understand India does that pretty well.'

India made a face at both of them and levitated herself. Floating just above eye level, she pulled her legs into the lotus position.

'That's a pretty neat trick,' said George admiringly. 'How do you do that?'

India shrugged.

'What does it feel like?' he persisted.

India grinned and said, 'Hang on!'

Both men left the ground and rose to her position.

'Hey!' yelled Theo, flailing his arms and legs, trying to regain control. 'Put me down!'

George just looked bemused. He still stood, but he was several feet off the ground.

India righted Theo and lowered him gently to the ground. 'Okay, Grandpa. If you want to walk, stop complaining about the distance.'

'How do you do this?' asked George again. He was now trying to pull his legs into the lotus in imitation of India, but his muscles objected to the attempt.

'The lotus?' asked India.

'That too, but how do you levitate? What is it you do that's different from what the rest of us do? Can anyone learn this?' He gave up on the lotus and settled for crossing his legs normally. The bottom leg sort of hung down a bit, but he ignored it and looked questioningly at India.

'I don't know,' she said honestly. 'The memory of learning it has been wiped from my mind, but I remember how I do it, and I remember that anyone with the talent can learn how to use it. I don't know how to find out if you have the talent, and I wouldn't know how to teach you if you did.'

'Dad, you ought to give this another try,' George urged.

They were still moving, Theo walking, George and India floating several feet above the ground. More people were staring at them now, and the amused expressions had vanished from most of their faces, replaced by astonishment and disbelief.

Theo held up a hand. 'I'm really glad I was unconscious the night she towed me through the streets of Michigan City. I don't want to be floating around out of control.'

'I have complete control,' said India. 'Watch!' She gestured at a frisbee two men were playing with. It halted in mid-flight and turned on its edge. Then it started rolling across the same arc toward the man who was to catch it. When it got to him, he put his hands behind his back and stepped away from it. India giggled and moved the frisbee around behind him and bumped it against his hands. He bolted forward as if he'd been burned. Instead of dropping it, India flipped it back at the man who had thrown it to begin with. He didn't have to move to catch it. 'See? Complete control. I didn't even waver my grip on George or myself.'

'I don't care what you can do with a frisbee. I don't want to be floating around where *I* don't have control over me. I wouldn't even want to be floating around if I did have control. I don't want to float!' said Theo emphatically.

'Are you afraid of heights?' asked India.

Theo didn't say anything.

'Well, then, we'll walk,' said India. She lowered George to the ground first while untangling her legs, then she joined them on the grass.

That was quite a little show.

India gasped.

'What's the matter?' asked George and Theo simultaneously.

'It's Bob. He's nearby and he managed to breach the barrier I had around us!' India wailed. 'I'm sorry. I don't have the training I should have to be doing this, and I shouldn't have been showing off . . . Why isn't he catching us? He isn't even trying!'

'India, you've got to stop apologizing for things you don't have any control over. Feeling guilty because you don't have enough training isn't going to do any of us any good. You said yourself that he doesn't seem to be trying too hard to catch up. Maybe he's just trying to scare you. Like the way a cat worries a mouse. If we can keep from getting too flustered, we can think our way out of this. The Arboretum is only about a mile away from here. I suggest we hurry up,' said George, putting one hand on India's back and the other on Theo's. 'Maybe we can find the door before he gets there and you'll be through and safe. You can bet they'll close the door behind you and shut it for good.'

'I would hope so,' said India.

They set off across the park, trying to keep a brisk pace. There were so many people out enjoying picnic lunches, and naps in the early afternoon sun, that it took time to thread the most direct course through them. The cobbled paths meandered in a roundabout way, so it was the lesser of two evils to go across the grass.

'Do you ever come here during lunch?' India asked George.

'All the time. It's the best place in the whole city for lunch hour. Sometimes they even pipe a concert out to us if we've been good little girls and boys. Volleyball tournaments are set up between departments and they're great fun to watch while you eat.'

'You don't play?' asked Theo.

'I'm not very good,' George admitted sheepishly. 'I'm not often invited to play. I enjoy it when I get a chance, but these people are highly competitive. The team that gets me usually loses. Too much to compensate for, I guess.' He sighed and looked at the people lounging on the grass. 'What a perfect day.'

'What's that huge glass building?' asked India, pointing.

'The Arboretum,' said George. 'Come on. We're almost there.' He began to jog, an awkward, jolting gait.

India had to run faster in order to keep up. 'What's inside?' she asked incredulously.

'Plants,' panted Theo. He was keeping up, but it was costing him. 'Trees, mostly. What did you think an arboretum was?'

India shrugged. 'I grew up in a fortress and moved off-planet as soon as I could. I've never seen a building made of glass that's just for growing trees. Trees grow outside. I'd never even heard the word before. If I'd been told what to look for, I'd have understood better.'

'Well, now you know,' said George, slowing a little in deference to his father-in-law. 'Where's Bob?'

India was silent for a moment while she reached out with her mind to find him. He wasn't making any real effort to hide from her. It took her almost no time to locate the blank spot that hid him from her. 'He's still behind us by about two minutes. We could probably see him if we took the time to search the crowd for a man who looks totally forgettable.'

'Never mind,' gasped Theo.

Trees stood all around the grounds in front of the immense glass structure. It rose, white and sparkling, in great curves of roof and turret, truly magnificent on the vast green lawn. Between the trees, beside the walk that led to the main entrance, flowers grew in such profusion it was hard to tell what had actually been planted there. Colors vied for attention and scents combined and floated on the breeze, adding to the exotic appearance of the building.

'It's even more magnificent up close,' breathed India. It was difficult to focus on the building; the sun was reflecting off the glass and was almost blinding. 'Come on! I want to see what's inside!' She ran up the path, leaving the two older men to make their way more slowly behind her.

Inside was even more exotic than the outside had promised. Trees and plants from several worlds were thriving in the hothouse environment. It was humid and extremely warm, but the smell of the earth and the vegetation was rich and exciting. India stood in the doorway and stared, head swiveling, eyes not knowing where to look first. This fortunately gave Theo and George time to catch up.

'Oh! There you are. Isn't this incredible? I can't believe this isn't open to the public. It's such a shame to keep this hidden!'

'Lots of people enjoy it,' said George. 'Mostly now it's for genetic experimentation. There are laboratories underneath here where they spend a lot of time monkeying on the cellular level, trying to manipulate the components of the genes.'

'What on earth for?' asked India. 'These plants are perfect the way they are!' She ran over to one. 'Have you ever seen anything so marvelous?'

'Yes,' said George, smiling. 'That's one the scientists are particularly proud of. I can't tell you how many different types and species they took its genetic make-up from, combining them for the most favorable outcome. You should see it when it flowers. And the fruit it produces! Incredible.'

'This isn't a natural plant?' asked India in amazement. 'It looks so real!'

311

George laughed hard. 'Of course it's real. If you don't water it, it'll die. If you pull it up by its roots, it'll go into shock. It just isn't a combination that occurs in nature.'

'They can do that now?' asked Theo. 'They've been talking about it for so many years, I just assumed it was impossible.'

'Impossible just means they haven't found out how to do it yet,' said George. 'They haven't been able to find a way to do it on a large scale yet. Only this one and two other combinations have been successful. They're growing seedlings from the three, though. They want to make sure the splicing breeds true before they go public with any of it. No point getting people's hopes up if it doesn't. Much more spectacular if they can put it out and say from now on this is a new food source, and the florists will have a field day trying to get these blooms featured in arrangements. Now, India. I hate to be a wet blanket, but ogling this plant has probably used up our two-minute lead. What are we supposed to be doing here?'

'Checking doors,' said India, tearing herself away from the amazing plant. She checked on Bob, and found him still two minutes away. With a small frown and shake of her head, she set off in search of other doors in the Arboretum, with George and Theo trailing behind, keeping an eye out for anyone who looked suspicious to them.

They're in the Arboretum, Bob told the Captain.

It had been disturbing to find the Captain had a high psi-rating, but it made communication easier now. Especially since using a portable screen in the middle of Golden Gate Park would look suspicious. No one brought work out in their lunch hour.

When did they enter the building? asked the Captain, sounding more interested in the project than he had in weeks.

About five minutes ago, but they stood in the front door-

way talking for a long time. They've started looking for the door now. Should I go in?

Yes. Keep an eye on them, but don't let them see you. As soon as the girl goes through the door, the men will leave. Go through it as soon as they are far enough away and grab her, instructed the Captain.

Yes, sir, said Bob. He still wasn't happy about this, but he remembered what he'd told Harry and Grindle when this started. He didn't have to like the assignment, but he did like his job. That made everything work out in the end. Lately he was beginning to question that, but when he thought about what he could do about it, he came up with two choices.

Do it, or quit.

He wasn't prepared to quit. What else would he do? He hadn't the training for any other job. He'd never wanted to do anything else. He'd never really been *good* at anything else.

With a sigh, Bob started moving toward the impressive structure of the Arboretum. He'd seen it so many times, he didn't really even notice just how grand it was. Right now it was just a means to an end.

India approached a door, feeling her heart beat in her throat. This could be it, she told herself. She was too excited even to talk out loud, as if somehow that might break the spell, or change her luck. She put her thumb on the plate and the door swung inward. Good, it was keyed for general access. She rushed through and stopped. This wasn't it. Well, of course not, she told herself. If it were that easy, anyone could get through to the Inn, and the door was supposed to be a secret. But this door looked like an air-lock, with a door on one side, a small room with a sink and a recycler. A shelf held a stock of paper gowns and shoe covers. On the other side of that was the other door, leading into the room beyond.

India turned to George. 'They're all like this, aren't they? Every door in here is really two doors?'

George nodded and Theo sighed.

India felt like crying. Every time she opened one of these doors, she had to open the other. Before she could do that, the first door had to be closed so the sterilizer could operate. The second door wouldn't open until the process was complete.

Disappointed, but pragmatic, India went to the next door and thumbed the plate. George and Theo followed her, unsure of what, beyond that, they should be doing.

Doors and doors and doors.

She thumbed plates, feeling a little surge of hope each time. George and Theo followed, unable to assist in any way.

'How many doors are there in this place?' demanded a very frustrated India. 'The Arboretum didn't look this big on the outside!' It stretched back on its vast green lawn much farther than any of them had expected. It was obvious that the original Arboretum, divided into smaller growing areas, was much smaller than the portions that had been added on, even though they were in the same architectural style and the building materials were consistent. George said they had been added on by the Genetic Engineers so that cross-pollination would be made more difficult. The current overall size of the building was deceptive and the number of doors was staggering.

They had wasted two hours on this procedure already.

They were also beginning to attract attention. People worked here. People visited in their lunch hour. Everyone here knew what was in the various rooms. There was no apparent reason for the strange gyrations this little group were going through.

All through this, India was aware of Bob in the periphery of her mind. He was just observing. Waiting. Waiting for me to find The Door. He wants access too, she thought. She would go through The Door and George and Theo would leave. Then he would go through and kidnap her again. She really hoped Anara would be on the other side.

Her conversation with Shannon that morning had been brief and sketchy. She'd only been able to tell Shannon that she was leaving for the Old City in a few moments. There was no guarantee she would even make it that far.

Shannon reminded India of something Anara had said. 'You will recognize the door when you find it.' Well, that would only help when she found it. In the meantime, there were 10,000 doors in this cursed place, and she was going to have to try them all before she found the right one! Always the last place she looked.

She put her thumb on the next plate and the door slid open. Nothing.

Theo sighed and George patted her on the shoulder. 'I guess we get in and wait for the sterilization. Maybe the next one will be it.'

India grimaced. 'You guys are beginning to depress me with your cheerfulness. We aren't going to find it until we've tried every other door in this place. You know that, don't you?'

'Little Miss Optimistic,' said Theo with a small chuckle. 'I've always admired you for that.'

The door slid shut behind them and the tingle of the sterilization field crawled up India's arms and face. It made her want to scratch, which irritated her even more, so she gritted her teeth and refused to. Very adult of her, she knew, but she was frustrated and getting angry. Why couldn't Anara have been more specific about what door she should try first; or at least which area of the Arboretum she was most likely to find it in?

The sterilization field shut off and the other door slid open.

'That's it!' cried India bursting from the lock.

'Where?' asked George and Theo, looking about in puzzlement.

'I don't see anything,' said Theo. 'Are you sure? Where are you looking?'

'Right there,' India insisted, pointing to a blank wall.

'India, there's nothing there,' said George.

'Look closely,' said India. 'Come on!' She ran down the aisle between badly conceived genetic experiments, not even seeing the gross deformities and horrific shapes around her.

Reluctantly, George and Theo started to follow.

'Should we disable the lock on the door?' asked Theo.

'There is no lock to disable. Only the cycle of the sterilization field. It should take too long for this Bob character to be able to catch her,' said George. He looked at the wall India was heading toward. 'Besides, I don't see anything there. Even if there is a door, maybe he won't see it either.'

'They both have the same psi-mechanic abilities,' said Theo. 'You never know.'

George looked at the door again and shrugged. 'I don't know. Let's go see what our girl has discovered. In any case it'll prove entertaining.' They set off down the aisle after India. 'Do you really buy this Inn-between-dimensions?'

'I have no idea,' said Theo. He shook his head. 'What I've seen this girl do, and what we've been through, I doubt it's something she made up for our amusement.'

They looked at India, who was frantically searching the wall she had run to. Whatever she'd seen seemed to have disappeared.

'But the stress could have been too much?' George suggested.

Theo shrugged. 'What's the matter?' he asked as they approached.

'I can't find a way to open the lock,' she complained as she ran her hand over the outline of a door in a wall that appeared to be a plain sheet of glass. It was about eight feet square, clear and clean. There was no door there.

'There's no door there,' said George. 'I know how much you want to find this, but you aren't going to do it here.'

India turned and gave George a blistering look. 'I'm sorry you don't see it,' she said, 'but this is it. You don't think they would use a door everyone else uses, do you? They'd be overrun by people going through it and winding up where they didn't expect to be!'

'Of course,' said Theo smoothly. 'Is there any way we can help?' He looked hard at George. She may have blown a chip, he was trying to say, but he wasn't telepathic, so he tried to make George understand the glare.

'I heard that,' said India. 'Very funny. I'm just fine, thank you. Now help me find the plate, or a knob or latch or something!' She expanded her search to the strips of metal that held the glass in place. 'Maybe one of you could reach the top of the frame?' She looked pointedly at George.

Trying to keep his face impassive, George reached up and ran his hand along the metal frame at the top of the piece of glass.

Theo went to the other side and began to examine it carefully. He felt badly that India had caught him, but he really believed she was deluding herself if she thought she would find a door in the middle of a plain piece of glass.

India dropped to her knees and began checking the floor at the base of the pane.

The air-lock door on the other side of the room began its sterilization cycle, but they didn't really hear it. George and Theo were trying to figure out what India was so adamant about, and India was absorbed in trying to find a locking mechanism for a door no one else could see.

'Ah ha!' she cried. She stood up and stomped with her foot on an ordinary patch of dirt.

'What are you doing?' asked Theo. He and George had both turned away from the glass when India spoke.

India pointed behind them, but they had seen Bob.

'India, we've got to get out of here now,' said George.

'No problem,' she said stepping forward.

They turned to see a barn door in the middle of the glass wall as though it had been there all along. India reached forward and lifted the latch. The door swung outward.

Inside, it was pitch dark.

'It must be nighttime,' said India in a disappointed voice. 'They probably had to sleep and couldn't wait to meet me. It's as dark as a pocket in there.'

'Dark or not, you'd better go in,' said Theo urgently. 'Bob is here.'

India jerked around to face Bob. *You're not taking me back,* she told him.

It's my job, said Bob. His tone was apologetic, but she'd heard it all before. He took a step forward.

India levitated one of the genetic mishaps and threw it at him, but he brushed it aside and kept coming.

There was nothing bigger to throw. She tried to put a barrier between them, but Bob's approach wasn't even slowed. Nothing else to do. India dug deep into her soul and screamed with every ounce of her being. *ANARA!*

I'm right here, said Anara immediately.

Bob is here, India called. *I can't stop him by myself.*

Can you find the door? asked Anara. *You sound so close.*

The door is open, said India. *It's completely pitch-black inside. I assumed it was night and you hadn't been able to wait.*

No, said Anara, sounding puzzled. *We're right here in the barn, Shannon and Henry and I. The door is closed.*

Can you open it from that side? asked India. *I wouldn't even know where in the dark to find it. There are so many air-locks in this place, I wouldn't be surprised if this was another one.*

Daylight streamed in through the door as Anara opened it. The door was in fact another air-lock, but it was still pitch-black just beyond both door-jambs. A small corridor of light joined the doors, but where the other ones in the Arboretum had sinks and disposable clothing, here there was only darkness.

'Anara?' India called through it.

'We're here, come through quickly,' called the familiar voice.

India heard it and almost started crying, but another voice cut across it in her mind.

Captain, we're here. Are you ready? asked Bob.

Ready and waiting, replied another familiar voice. It seemed to be coming from the black nothingness between the door in the Arboretum and the door in the barn.

Ty? asked India, stunned.

Who were you expecting? he asked unpleasantly. *Peter?*

Ty, what are you doing here? she asked. She felt Anara's presence in her mind strengthen. Henry and Shannon were there, too. India took them into herself and breathed deeply, feeling their power increase her own. Feeling their training make up for her deficiencies.

Bob took a step forward.

India reached out and pointed at him. Red light glowed and crackled on her fingertips, gathering strength. Releasing the thought, India blasted him back across the room. He landed in an unconscious heap in the tendrils and vines.

That wasn't very nice, Ty reprimanded. *Anara, have you gotten vengeful in your old age?*

How do you know who she is? demanded India. *Why did Bob call you Captain?*

There are lots of things you don't know about me, said Ty. *Too many things you were stupid enough to overlook that would have been obvious enough if you'd paid attention. That was your biggest mistake. You should also be wondering how I know Bob.*

That was my next question, snapped India.

Bob was stirring on the bed of monstrous greenery. Theo

and George stood by looking helpless and frightened. India clenched and unclenched her fists.

You ask too many rude questions, said Ty.

India squeezed her eyes shut tight and pressed her hands over her ears. *I can't hear you, I can't hear you!* she chanted. Childish, yes, but she was afraid of what might happen if the post-hypnotic suggestion hadn't broken down with the rest of her blocks.

You ask too many rude questions, Ty repeated.

Nothing happened.

You've lost that round, said another voice from the darkness between the doors.

Anara and Shannon gasped. India heard them clearly in her mind. *Who is that?* she asked. *I think I know that voice, too.*

Ashraf, whispered Shannon. *Oh, Ashraf, we need your help!*

That's not why I'm here, he said. *How could you have let this get so out of hand?* His question was obviously directed at Ty.

We don't need to get into that now, said Ty. *We're here; let's solve the problem.*

I'm not a problem! yelled India with as much force as she could muster. *I have a problem. Who are you and what do you want from me?*

That's not something you need to know, said Ashraf. *Just come along quietly and you won't get hurt.*

Or dead? asked India.

Quite possibly, he agreed.

That's not what I heard, she said triumphantly. *I heard you need to keep me alive with my mind intact, or I'm no use to you at all. If you kill me, that won't do either of us any good.*

True enough, Ashraf conceded. *You expect me to try reason?*

It would be a nice change, said India.

Sorry, said Ty. *We don't explain ourselves to anyone.*

You took my life away from me and all you have to say is 'sorry'? India laughed bitterly. *You're such a jerk! I want to know who you are and why you did this to me.*

Captain, World Crime Bureau, said Bob. *And his little dog Spot.*

Police? India gasped. *Real police?*

At your service, ma'am, said Bob.

This time the blast that knocked him across the room came from inside the blackness. No one seemed to be on Bob's side now.

Why on earth . . . she began. Something broke in her mind. *My father!*

Perceptive, said Ty. The Captain. It seemed impossible. (Pay attention, you could get hurt.)

You wanted to get to my father? she asked. She heard the voice, but it was another one she couldn't place. (Hello?) she thought. There was no answer.

That was the idea.

You could have asked, she said. *There was never any love lost.*

Will you please? asked a sarcastic little voice in the back of her mind. Ty was playing another game.

Don't be silly, she said. *You want him, get him yourself. Don't hide behind little girls.*

Ouch. Ty switched from a little voice in the back of her mind back to his own wheedling tone. *There's too much invested in this. You can appreciate that, can't you?*

Across the room, Bob sat up, but made no effort to stand. It didn't seem advisable to become a target again. Instead, he checked himself for injuries as surreptitiously as possible.

George and Theo had backed away from the door, leaving India standing by herself. They couldn't hear a word of the conversation, but seeing Bob take flight again was enough to convince them they didn't want to be nearby when all hell broke loose.

'Do you think we should leave?' whispered George.

'She may need our help,' Theo whispered back.

'How in heaven's name could we help?' George demanded without actually raising his voice. 'You saw what she did to that poor sap over there. She doesn't need any of the help we could provide. I have a family to think about, and that includes a crazy old windmill-tilter.'

'Son, I brought her this far,' said Theo. 'I'm not leaving until I'm certain she's all right.'

George gave up and resigned himself to watching and hoping.

Appreciate this, said India, and, drawing on the power Anara, Henry and Shannon gave her, she blasted the energy into the darkness at the voices hiding within.

All she heard was laughter. *You know why I won't strike back,* said Ty. *Not at you, anyway. The other three are expendable, and nowhere near you. I could kill them and leave you relatively powerless.*

Why don't you, then, taunted India. *Are we afraid we might actually be able to do some damage before they went?*

You're in close contact with them, said Ty. *The abrupt withdrawal from your mind would probably leave you a vegetable. That would make you useless to us, as you observed. Actually, I was referring to the men in the Arboretum with you. But you're right, it wouldn't serve any real purpose.*

Well, are we going to stand here and talk all day instead? asked India. She sent several more bolts of the strange red energy crackling into the void between the doors, shooting at random, since she couldn't see where the men might be standing.

I had rather hoped Bob would be helping us, but he seems to have quit the force. Ty didn't seem upset by this.

So what do you do instead? she demanded, hoping she didn't sound as scared as she felt.

A tendril of energy, so intense it was visible, reached out of the darkness and into the Arboretum. India dodged, but it followed. She tried to deflect it using her mind, but it didn't even react to her efforts. She backed away from it, up the aisle, trying to escape, but it came after her slowly, growing stronger as it focused on her. As if she felt it, India cut to one side, then the other, trying to evade its grasp. It began to move more quickly as it strengthened, seeming to anticipate her movement.

India began throwing plants and trees at it, hoping to put a confusion of movement between it and her, but the tendril continued unwaveringly, growing in size and strength. It pulsed with a rainbow of colors, all of them malevolent.

'Oh, gods! Help me!' she screamed as she ran. She tripped and sprawled flat, lying stunned for a moment, trying to regain her breath.

The tendril reached out and stroked her ankle, beginning to wrap itself around her leg. It started to pull India back toward the door.

With an inhuman scream, India reached out with mind and hand, seized the rope of energy, and wrenched it away from her foot. She rolled to the side and leapt to her feet, running before she was even standing.

The three men on her side of the door stared, paralyzed. They were unable to move at all. The tendril seemed to be sucking their energy out of them, making it impossible to respond to India's cry.

Anara, Henry and Shannon were trapped in India's mind, unable to help her any more, unable to disconnect from her. She was clinging to them tightly; a last line of hope, using their power and knowledge to prevent her capture. Or delay it, she thought to herself as she evaded the grasping cord yet again.

'I can't go back there!' she cried as she felt its grasp. This time, it caught her around the waist and held her securely, lifting her from the ground and beginning to pull her back toward the black void between the doors. She struggled and clawed, writhing, trying to escape, but the energy didn't abate. It held her firmly, oddly gentle. India screamed again.

Above that came another sound, terrible and inescapable. A scream of anger and revenge.

The hair on India's neck stood up and she froze. The tendril had stopped; was frozen as well.

The scream came again, and with it a sound of claws and teeth.

Mama!

India wasn't sure who shouted, but the energy abruptly began snaking back into the darkness, dropping India without letting go, and dragging her across the ground, rough and hurried.

The scream was all around them now. It wasn't a sound any more. It was a feeling of rage that rose up from the depth of the soul and demanded to be satisfied. The claws and teeth snapped and ground as Mama came into view.

They all stood on the plane of the Collective Unconscious now. India looked around and saw Ty and Ashraf standing in front of a field of energy so vast and powerful it was visible only as a blinding light. She knew Anara stood behind her, and Henry and Shannon as well. Ty and Ashraf were only silhouettes, but India knew who they were. She'd seen them like this before.

The fury was all around them now, building and coming closer. Ashraf moved closer to Ty. They both tried to move closer to India, but couldn't.

Out of the light came a dark shape, huge and terrifying. She moved slowly, but her claws snapped at the end of her writhing limbs. Her teeth were sharp and white in the darkness of her maw.

You will not escape me. The voice rumbled out of her, not a sound to be made by such a creature, but belonging to her nonetheless. *You may not use the power of the Disembodied without paying the price.*

She took Ty in one claw and Ashraf fell to his knees. It

was clear he wanted to run away, but he was held fast by unseen bonds.

Mama brandished Ty. He screamed, but she paid no attention. Lifting her other claw up to where she held him, Mama grabbed his arm and pulled, ripping it from the socket. She threw it at Ashraf where he knelt, and reached again for Ty. As the claw came closer, his screams became incoherent, animal-like. He writhed, trying to avoid the inevitable. Mama pulled his other arm from its socket and again threw it at Ashraf's knees. Ashraf babbled, trying to stand up, trying to back away from the horror taking place before him; knowing he was next and unable to stop it.

Blood spurted, stark red against the bright white light of Mama's fury as she continued dismembering Ty, throwing the pieces of his body at Ashraf.

India stared in horror, wishing she could be sick, wishing she could pass out, wishing she could at least close her eyes. She knew she would have nightmares about this for years to come, but like Ashraf, there was nothing she could do to leave the scene. She hated Ty, but she would never have wished such vengeance upon him.

At last, Mama finished with Ty. *That was his price,* she screamed. *He was using me for personal gain.* She looked at Ashraf for a long time, hissing and rattling her bloody claws. *You wanted control over the Disembodied. You wanted control over me. Your price will be much higher.* She reached out with one claw and picked Ashraf up off his knees. *You will continue to live.*

Ashraf had ceased making any sound at all. He hung limply in Mama's claw, too shocked by what he had witnessed even to react to his own fate.

Mama waved her other claw over the mess on the ground and the bloody pieces disappeared. The blood disappeared. The darkness was pushed back by the pristine white light, and there was no trace of the ghastly scene that had just taken place. Only Ty's absence and their memories told

India, Shannon, Anara and Henry that the dismemberment had actually taken place.

You have committed no crime but trespassing, Mama hissed at them. *It was not my intention to punish you while rendering justice to them. Once you pass through the door, you will remember only that there is a very good reason for leaving me alone. You will tell others that attempting to use the power here is fatal. That is all anyone need know.* She shook Ashraf, who flopped limply in her claw like a rag doll. *Leave here at once. Do not return.* She turned away from them and moved off, taking Ashraf with her. The light that surrounded her began to dim as her huge form receded.

Shortly, the four stood in the profound dark once more, alone and shaking.

How long will it be before we get to the door? India wondered out loud, wondering if she would make it that far, hoping that Mama was speaking the truth. She turned to where she sensed Anara's presence in the dark, and reached out her hand.

Anara took it. Shannon took India's other hand, and India knew Henry held Anara's as well. They stood silent for a long moment, each trying to forget what they had seen.

We'd better go, Henry said. *She meant it. She'll be back to check if she senses us still here.*

India turned slowly and looked blankly at Anara and Shannon. *Are you all right?* she asked.

They shook their heads.

Well, now we know, said Shannon.

Know what? asked India.

Who Mama is, said Anara, shuddering. *Remember when you first came to the Inn. You asked me who the horrible creature was.*

Mmhmm, said India. She remembered dimly, as if that had been another life, and she had only been watching someone else live it.

Now we know she's the Guardian of the Disembodied, things make much more sense. Anara seemed to be talking to fill the space between them, the void inside them.

How would you not know something like that? asked India. They were all talking for the same reasons.

They were walking toward the doors to the barn and Arboretum. India knew this, but she couldn't see anything around her. She could only feel the presence of the other three. She could only feel Anara's and Shannon's hands in hers. It was like the No-Place, only dark; no way to measure progress, no sense of departure or destination.

We have so much else to keep track of on our own plane, said Henry, groping for the words to express the reality. Using words to shut out thoughts. *There's so much to learn about where we are and where we're going, we don't have much time to spend on areas we basically want to avoid. The Collective Unconscious is a fascinating place, but the chances of getting lost are great. The Disembodied are very seductive and something to be respected and feared. They have a staggering amount of power, but it can't be tapped or controlled. Obviously Ty and Ashraf were trying to do exactly that. As Mama said, there is a price to pay for everything we do. Hers is more terrible than most.*

Didn't they know that? asked India. She could see the doors up ahead, but the point of light was tiny and far away. Unconsciously, she quickened her pace. So did everyone else. They all wanted to be out of there as soon as possible.

Either they did and they didn't think they would ever be called on to pay, or they didn't and found out the hard way, said Shannon. *Either way, we learned the lesson with them, and can warn others.*

They were now running for the door, which grew larger with every step.

Chapter Fourteen

They burst through the door to the Arboretum rather unceremoniously, panting with fright and their exertions, staring wild-eyed around them as if still seeing danger among the decimated experimental mishaps.

Bob still sat on the floor amidst the deformed greenery where Ty's ministrations had landed him. Theo and George had moved farther away from the door when India had been pulled from the Arboretum. All three had expressions of shock and disbelief on their faces.

When India stepped through the door, Theo whispered, 'Praise the gods.'

George looked at him strangely. 'Since when did you get religious, old man?'

'You get all kinds of things in your dotage, son. Just wait till you get there. I'll be laughing at you from wherever I am,' said Theo.

Bob was standing now, and approached slowly, as if trying to appease terrified animals. George and Theo remained where they stood, trying to make themselves as unobtrusive as possible.

Shannon recovered herself first. *Where are we?* she gasped. She stared at Bob, but she wasn't really seeing him. *What are we doing here?*

Anara shook herself and turned to Henry. *Oh, gods!* she sobbed. *What happened?*

Henry stared at Anara blankly and said nothing.

India saw Theo and forgot everything else. He was safe. He had protected her and cared for her and taken her into his home and heart when she most needed a friend.

'Grandpa!' she cried, and burst into tears. She ran to him and threw her arms around him, burying her head in his chest and holding on as if her life depended on it.

Theo put his arms around her and held her tightly, stroking her ruined hair and murmuring nothing in particular to her as he looked at George over her head. George stared back, wondering much the same thing: what the hell had happened in there?

'Shannon?' asked Bob softly, hoping the sound of his voice would be less frightening and intrusive than a telepathic touch. 'Shannon, it's me, Bob. Are you okay?' He reached out toward her and touched her arm lightly, prepared to snatch his hand away if she showed any signs of feeling threatened by his presence. 'Shannon, are you all right?' He hoped by repeating her name he might bring her back in touch with herself. 'Shannon, can you answer me?'

Shannon shook her head as if to clear it, and focused on Bob's face, searching his features for a clue he didn't seem to possess. 'Umm,' she said at last. She looked down at where his hand touched her arm. 'Bob?' she asked. She looked into his eyes and smiled. *What are you doing here?*

Don't you remember? he asked, keeping his telepathic voice as gentle as his real one.

Shannon shook her head. *It was so dark,* she complained, shuddering. *And there was so much noise. Then we were here.*

Bob drew a deep breath and crossed his fingers. He didn't really believe in crossing fingers, but he figured it couldn't hurt. *I heard Mama,* he said.

Shannon's head snapped back as though she had been struck. She gasped and turned to Anara and Henry, but they were still staring at each other. Slowly, Shannon turned back to Bob. Looking him in the eyes, she nodded. *Mama was there,* she admitted.

India raised her head from Theo's chest and turned to

look at Shannon. *Mama was there,* she repeated.

Mama, agreed Henry and Anara. *She guards the Disembodied.*

Bob gaped at them. *Are you sure?* he asked in disbelief. *Mama was there,* they confirmed.

The spell was broken. *We can't go back there ever again,* said Anara. She reached for Henry's hand, and India, watching, smiled weakly.

So that was your date? she asked. She gave Theo a hug and stepped away from him.

'Could someone around here speak English?' he complained.

Everyone chuckled a little. 'Sorry,' said Bob. 'Among ourselves, we forget.' He studied Theo for a long moment. 'You've got the talent, Winslow. Ever consider the training?'

Theo laughed and shook his head. 'I'm an old man. I've gotten along just fine up to now. Besides, my daughter would have your head for suggesting I stay away any longer than I have already.'

George nodded in agreement. 'She can be pretty determined.'

'I just wanted to make sure India would be okay,' said Theo seriously. He looked at her questioningly.

'Thanks to you,' she said. 'I owe you more than I can ever repay. Your whole family,' she added, looking at George. She approached him and looked up and up into his face. 'You've all been so generous . . .'

George smiled down at her. 'You've provided Tommy with damsel-in-distress stories for years to come,' he said. 'How better can you repay a family debt?'

India smiled. 'But what about the rest of you?'

'Well, let's see,' he began to enumerate. 'Jenny has new "daughter" fantasies, David has romantic fantasies, Sandy has big-sister fantasies, Tommy we've covered, and Peter . . .'

'Peter!' India cried. 'That's the voice I kept hearing!'

'What voice?' asked Anara and Henry simultaneously.

'In the back of my mind,' said India, trying to explain. 'Whenever I was in trouble, there would be this voice. I knew it, but I couldn't figure out who it was. It was Peter!'

'But Peter's only five,' George objected.

India giggled. 'There are a few other Peters in this world,' she said. 'This one is a bit beyond five.'

Anara laughed.

(I'm glad you heard me.)

I'm glad you were there.

(Always, love. Come home soon?)

Soon, she agreed, wondering briefly where home might be.

'Well, regardless of which Peter we're talking about,' said George, bringing India back to the reality of the Arboretum, 'you always have a home with us.' He chuckled. 'And I'm not just saying that because if I don't Jenny will kill me. I really mean it.'

India smiled shyly. 'Thank you, I love you too.'

George caught her in a rough hug, holding her close for a long moment. 'It frightened us so badly when you got dragged out of here. There was nothing we could do to stop that thing from taking you ... We tried, but neither of us could move. We were so scared we would never see you again.'

India pulled away from him a bit and looked up. 'You were afraid to go home and tell Jenny that you'd lost me,' she contradicted, grinning.

George hugged her again. 'Any time you need a home,' he repeated, and released her.

India turned back to Theo. 'You just be sure those little hellions get raised proper,' she warned.

'Thanks for the adventure of a lifetime,' he said. 'And thanks for telling Jenny I was eating Green Things.'

India laughed. 'All I said was they were all over the floor after I stepped in them. I never said you were eating them.' She sobered. 'I owe you a lot of credit, not to mention my life.'

Theo brushed aside the reference to money. 'You just come visit once in a while,' he said, hugging her.

'Often,' she whispered, hugging him back.

'Come on, old man,' said George, slapping Theo on the back. 'It's time to get home and let Jenny know none of us died.'

A shadow crossed the faces of India, Shannon, Anara and Henry, but none of them could remember why that reference disturbed them so. George and Theo threaded their way back through the ruins of the genetic mishaps toward the air-lock, and India watched them go, waiting for the sterilization cycle to end before turning back to the others.

'Well,' she said, and stopped.

Shannon laughed and hugged her. 'How's your head kiddo?' she asked.

India turned and looked at Bob.

'I haven't done anything to you recently,' he protested. 'Harry and Grindle saw to that.'

'How are they?' asked India, feeling a slight twinge of guilt.

'Embarrassed,' said Bob. 'They'll get over it.'

'They won't get fired or anything, will they?' she persisted. 'They just didn't want me to get hurt.'

Everyone turned expectantly toward Bob, who shrugged.

'You're The Man now, aren't you?' asked Henry. 'Mama took Ty and Ashraf. I don't think either of them will be reporting to work on Monday morning. Doesn't that leave you with a hole in the chain of command? Wasn't that the job you should have gotten to begin with?'

Bob nodded slowly. 'I guess that's right,' he said.

'It'll be good to have one of our own in the Big Chair. Maybe we can cooperate with each other a little better now.'

'I expect we can work something out,' said Bob.

'And you can undo whatever it is you did in India's mind?' asked Shannon.

Bob shook his head. He turned to India. 'I'm sorry. It would be better for you if those barriers came down slowly, and of their own accord.'

India grimaced. 'It's just as well,' she said with a trace of hostility. 'I don't want you anywhere near my mind.'

Bob made a gesture of apology.

'Speaking of promotions,' said Henry, rather more loudly. 'There seems to be a position open at the Level One Hostel.'

'Are you coming back?' asked Shannon hopefully.

'Don't be silly,' said Henry. 'I like being a specialist occasionally, but I have a nice little shop and I do good business and I don't have students back-talking me and whining all the time.' He winked at India.

She smiled back at him. 'Who will take Ashraf's job now?' she asked.

'If Henry won't take it.' Shannon looked hopefully at Henry again.

He shook his head.

'Then it belongs to Anara, if she'll come back to us,' Shannon finished.

'Would you do that?' India asked Anara.

Anara thought for a long moment. 'Shannon, how do you feel about making beds, doing laundry, cooking and gardening?'

'Do you mean . . .' Shannon began eagerly.

'You could run the Inn,' said Anara slowly. 'If you really wanted to, that is.'

'Would I?' Shannon skipped forward a step. 'That would be just the greatest!'

'What?' demanded India, genuinely shocked. 'Anara, you told me you'd been sent there as punishment! Why would you offer it to Shannon as if it was a prize?'

Anara and Shannon laughed. 'That's how it started,' Anara explained. 'Ashraf wanted me out of his hair so he could run the hostel any way he wanted. What happened was I took an insolvent service offered to former students and made it into an indispensable part of any psi-job they took in other dimensions. Now it makes money hand over fist, and the revenues help us keep costs down in other areas of the business. It also allows the Innkeeper to coordinate all the projects. Basically, it's a promotion to Manager of the entire psi-network.'

'Isn't that better than Ashraf's job, then?' asked India, confused.

'If the Innkeeper is the Manager, Ashraf's job is President,' Anara explained.

'Besides,' added Shannon, 'we have some revising of the curriculum at Level One to do, and Anara was always the best at course design.'

'Bother, that's right,' Anara shuddered. 'I always get the pleasant tasks, don't I?'

Henry laughed. 'And you love every minute of it, including the complaining.'

'But there's so much to do,' she objected. 'And Shannon has to be trained to take over the Inn before I can go back to Level One and begin the renovation there . . .'

'What about me?' asked India in her smallest, most pitiful voice.

'What about you?' asked Anara. She turned to face India, looking at her as if seeing her for the first time.

'I mean, what about me?' repeated India. 'Where am I supposed to go? What do I do now?'

Anara took India's hand. 'We'd better get back home,' she said, shifting mental gears so fast India couldn't keep up. 'They'll be expecting me to have dinner on the table this evening as always, and I could use a little help if we're going to feed them on time.'

India groaned. 'You just missed your slave,' she laughed. 'Admit it!'

'I admit it. I missed your company,' said Anara. 'Besides, we still have work to do on you.'

'More?' asked India.

'You've got to get your mind back, don't you?' asked Anara.

'Yeah, I guess,' said India. 'But I figured maybe we were done and I'd go home, or somewhere, since it's just a matter of waiting for the rest of the barriers to drop. If that's . . . I mean, what happens to me now?'

'Do you want to go home?' asked Shannon.

India thought about it. 'Could I even if I wanted to?' she asked pragmatically.

'Yes,' said Bob, seriously. The others turned to look at him as if only just noticing him again. 'The Bureau has a cop in your position doing your job while you're on an extended leave of absence. We're also paying your rent. Your life is there if you want it.'

'Really?' India was stunned. 'Why would you do all that?'

'We figured you'd need somewhere to go back to after we'd gotten what we wanted from you,' he explained, rather shamefacedly. 'It was Ty's idea. New at the job. He wanted a major coup to make the Brass sit up and take notice. He wanted the most prestigious bust in the history of the Bureau.'

'What about you?' India asked softly. 'What are you going to do, now that you're in his position?'

Bob shrugged. 'We'll see. You can bet I won't be going after your old man though. Too slippery. He keeps his ass covered too well. I'd have to set him up in order to get him. I probably still couldn't make it stick.'

'I can give you something,' said India. 'Take a long, hard

335

look at the books for the Laughlin building. There are some interesting discrepancies and some interesting tenants.'

Bob frowned at her. 'How would you know?'

'Before I left, I did a little research,' she said simply. 'I thought I needed to know something that would guarantee my safety.'

'Why would you tell me?' he asked.

'Because you genuinely regretted what you had to do to me,' India told him. 'I don't have to like it to understand how difficult it must have been for you. If we're all burying the hatchet here, I can be grown-up enough to do the same. Besides, Father is a sonofabitch and deserves exactly what he'll get.'

Bob nodded. 'Thank you.'

'India, do you want to go back to your old life?' asked Henry.

'I don't know,' she said after a moment. 'I thought I did, when I was sure it wasn't there any more. Now I'm not so sure. Especially since there was no way they could have maintained my friendships for me. After more than a year, I'll have some major explaining to do, and I'm not sure I'm ready to do it in person.'

'You could come back with us and finish getting your head on straight,' he suggested. 'Contact your friends from there and figure out what you can tell them.'

'The Bureau will maintain your apartment and job for you as we have been,' Bob offered. 'You can take as long as you want to decide what you want. It's the least we can do.'

'Thank you,' said India. 'Maybe getting my mind together would be a good idea. I could also use the rest. I've been a little tense recently.'

Everyone laughed.

'Well, I have!' she said. 'Besides, there's this guy . . .'

The laughter subsided as Anara and Henry looked at each other and smiled.

'And maybe once you get your head together, you'd consider training to become a teacher,' said Anara finally.

'A teacher?' India echoed. 'A teacher? Me? Really?'

'Yes, you, really,' laughed Anara. 'You've got potential you don't even know about yet.'

'Maybe,' said India. 'Maybe indeed.'

Bob grinned at her a little lopsidedly. 'Good luck, whatever you decide. Let me know as soon as you decide about your apartment and job.'

'You'll be the first one I call,' she promised. Then she turned to Anara. 'I guess I'm ready to go.'

She stepped through the Arboretum door, crossing the black void as quickly as possible, followed by Anara, Shannon and Henry. Henry pulled it shut behind them and destroyed the latch. 'We won't need this door again.'

When the barn door was shut he started to walk away.

'Don't you want to destroy that, too?' asked India.

'We can always use it for someplace else,' said Shannon. 'You never know when you'll need another escape route.'

'Well,' said Henry, heading for his own barn door, 'I'll see you ladies when you need me next.' He winked at Anara.

'Thank you,' India called after him. He waved a hand at her and disappeared through the door.

'I guess I'll see you when the employment shake-up occurs,' giggled Shannon. She gave India a quick hug and headed to a different door.

'Does that mean you inherit me as slave when Anara takes over for Ashraf?' India asked impudently.

Shannon lifted a shoulder and dropped it again. 'We'll do what's best for you,' she said. 'Even if that means sending you back to Bob for a while.'

'Well, thanks, I love you too!' India objected.

'I know,' said Shannon with a small smile.

'Maybe I'll see you in the No-Place,' suggested India.

'Maybe,' said Shannon. She pulled the door shut behind her.

'That leaves us,' India said to Anara.

'So let's go fix dinner,' said Anara.

India groaned. 'A slave. You needed a slave and that's why I'm here.'

'Yup,' said Anara cheerfully. 'Let's go home.'

Home, thought India. She followed Anara out of the barn and back to the Inn, looking forward to fresh-baked bread and hard work.

And Peter, she thought to herself as she walked through the kitchen door and breathed deeply of the familiar smells. It was good to be home.